PEEP SHOW

Also by Faith Bleasdale

Rubber Gloves or Jimmy Choos?
Pinstripes

To find out more about Faith Bleasdale visit
www.faithbleasdale.com

PEEP SHOW

Faith Bleasdale

Hodder & Stoughton

First published in Great Britain in 2002
by Hodder and Stoughton
A division of Hodder Headline

2 4 6 8 10 9 7 5 3 1

A CIP catalogue record for this title
is available from the British Library

ISBN 0 340 81860 3

Typeset in Centaur by Hewer Text Ltd, Edinburgh
Printed and bound in Great Britain by
Mackays of Chatham, Chatham, Kent

Hodder and Stoughton
A division of Hodder Headline
338 Euston Road
London NW1 3BH

Jonathan.
I love you and that's all there is to it.

ACKNOWLEDGEMENTS

Pre-production

My pre-production thanks go to:

My brother Thom, who has to take credit for concept development and plot development. An invaluable sounding board, I couldn't have got to the production stage without you.

My mother, the strongest person I know and whose strength gives me the feeling that I am invincible.

My sister Mary, and her family. You are all brilliant and you are really loved.

To Jonathan, who patiently listened to every idea without complaint. Thanks for your support, encouragement and presents. Thank you, for being such a wonderful part of my life.

Production

Production thanks go to:

My brother who solved a multitude of dead-ends with his cool ideas. Although of course I wrote the book, you were a wonderful co-pilot.

Jonathan, for telling me to 'get on with it.'

Holly, for always being on hand with support, encouragement and wine.

Jo, who is far away but always, feels near. Vicky, who I've

been through so much with. Tommy, who is lying in the sun full time, but still manages to stay in touch. Tania, the best sounding board ever. And to all my friends who really, really make me feel lucky.

My editor Sara, for telling me to 'get on with it.'

Post-Production

Post-production thanks go to:

My father. Thanks Daddy for all the help. You were wonderful, you are wonderful and I love you very much.

My brother, again.

Simon and Sarah at PFD. The coolest agents in town.

My editor Sara, for brilliant editing.

Jonathan for the celebrations.

Everyone who is going to read the book.

And anybody else who knows me.

Prologue

When you read a story isn't it strange how it sometimes begins with characters who are completely unrelated. That of course isn't curious in itself but as an astute reader you will immediately perceive that each of these groups of people or individuals will be linked in some way.

While you are reading you will perhaps try to imagine or guess how the people who come from a different country or another generation will finally be linked to make the story whole. You imagine lovers or enemies, work colleagues or friends. As you read about such strangers, you know that there will be a link in the end to make the story whole.

As the storyteller there can be no other way. If we wrote about people who start with no obvious connection and end with no connections the reader would be left with a feeling of irrelevance. Or, it would be a collection of stories, not one story. So instead, the reader is forced to imagine how a storyteller can start with diverse characters and end with a complete story which will entertain.

Of course, I have the luxury of knowing the end. No one can suppose that I would be able to tell such a tale without it.

Please don't presume I mock the reader for such ignorance. When I was where you are now I had no idea. Actually, I had less than I can indulge you with. Being determined to give you the full picture, I am giving you things I could not have known or seen. I would love to stop at any point and ask you to guess the outcome. I can say this with confidence that you never will. I can do this with a knowledge that you don't yet possess. But I can't stop and I can't ask.

All I can ask at this point is that when you read my story, and please believe that although it doesn't just belong to me, it is my story too, bear in mind that my ignorance was greater than yours. Until the end and maybe beyond.

If you do guess the twists and turns then you are more perceptive than I am. I lived it. I twisted and turned and I never could have guessed. Lust, friendship, betrayal, love; all in one story. No, all of that in a short time in my life. It is a story within my life.

As with every good story there is an end. An end that also begs a beginning. Because every ending does.

As the reader you have a number of advantages over me. You can read and gain pleasure. You can applaud or boo, you can feel whatever you wish to feel towards the characters and you can enjoy. Surprisingly for me there was no way to do this. Until the end and long after it, I questioned everything in the hope of understanding.

I hope you can understand. Unfortunately, I still do not.

Chapter One

Pre-Pre-Production

Harvey Cannon looked at his feet. He was wearing his lucky shoes. You wouldn't know they were lucky to look at them, they were just plain black loafers, but Harvey knew that they always brought him good fortune. He was holding a telephone handset to his ear and counting to ten. It didn't do to be too eager to pick up the phone. When he got to ten he pressed the 'call receive' button. He knew who the caller was, having already been informed by his assistant's assistant.

'Hi, Steve.'

'Harv, how are you?'

'Great, you?' Harvey rolled his eyes and glanced at his paused computer game. He hated having his name shortened. Unfortunately, everyone in Hollywood did exactly that. Infuriatingly, he could never push the point.

'Fine, fine. The board reviewed your proposal.' Steve Delaney was speaking slowly, a deliberate tease employed when people delivered important news.

'Really and what did the board decide?' Harvey picked up a pen and started clicking the end. He instinctively knew what the outcome would be but he also knew that Steve had to play his game.

'That it's green for go.' Steve's voice betrayed excitement at last.

'Steve, you won't regret this.' Although Harvey had known that it would be an affirmative answer, his heart still started beating fast at the news. He felt shaky as he sat down.

'I hope not. We need to meet to chew over the details, shall I get my assistant to call your assistant?'

'Sure, the sooner the better.'

'OK Harv. I'll see you soon.'

Harvey replaced the handset and smiled. A slow smile that crept over his entire face. Cherry Blythe, his chief assistant, smiled too.

'So we've got it?'

'Yes honey, we certainly have.' He jumped up and hugged her. She hugged him back.

'So what now?' Cherry asked.

'I have no idea.'

'And that's why they call you the Ideas Man,' Cherry teased, as they hugged again.

Harvey was an ideas man in the film industry. The true definition of this was unclear. People approached him to give them ideas for films and he usually delivered. He managed to find concepts, scripts and sometimes even people. Film studios gave him huge amounts of money to do this for them. It was a unique job and not one found advertised in the newspapers. He was a consultant of sorts.

Harvey was tall, slim and good-looking. He was no Brad Pitt, but his dark brown curly hair, brown eyes and straight nose often drew him admiring glances. He knew that it was more his demeanour than his looks that attracted people. He had an in-built confidence which was almost visible, and he traded on that confidence.

He had been doing this 'job' for five years. He was something of a star, a person everyone wanted to know. He had an office, two assistants (who didn't have enough work to do), a nice house, a fast car and a number of adoring women.

He didn't have to work hard. Ideas were ideas and Harvey

4

seemed to have enough of them to keep him in the lifestyle he had grown to love. He sat in his office (which was more for show than necessity) playing video games, watching films and talking to Cherry. Anna, his second assistant, answered calls, opened mail and did anything that needed doing. Cherry was more a companion, someone to lunch with, to talk to and to play computer games with. He also used her as a sounding-board for his ideas.

Harvey had obtained this role by mistake. It was a mistake job gained mainly because he was an excellent networker. He had lived all his life in New York, but by the age of twenty-eight he was in a rut. He worked for a television network selling advertising and had outgrown the challenge it presented. He took the drastic step of leaving everything and moving to Hollywood for no good reason apart from instinct telling him to.

Using all his skills, he managed to meet a number of movie people, charmed them and secured their interest. Knowing nothing about films, he suggested an idea to a director who accepted him as an expert. As he wasn't a scriptwriter, a producer or any of the other traditional film roles, he was hired as a consultant to the director. When he saw his first concept on the big screen he knew he'd found his niche. In Hollywood his first idea was a huge box office success, which made him hot property within the industry. He started to learn and always sold his services in a way that seemed to give him very little work and increasingly big rewards. The challenge that his job provided kept him running on adrenaline. However, now, years later, he was bored again. Bored and rich.

When the bosses of Poplar Films had approached him the previous month with a desperate need for the 'next big thing', Harvey decided he could take this challenge and do something different. Poplar Films were on their knees and Steve Delaney, the studio head, needed to save his bacon. They had suffered from a number of big-budget flops and were fast running out of time in highly competitive Hollywood. They had exhausted every other possibility. Harvey was their only hope. They asked him for a concept, just one. One which would turn their fortunes around. Harvey said he'd think about it.

During this thinking period, Harvey decided that he would move on to a new phase in his life. He offered them a proposal. He would not just give them a concept but he would deliver a finished movie to them within a year. He said he would come up with the idea, find people to work with and direct the film himself. All he needed was their money and their confidence. He told them that he wouldn't discuss the idea with them until the film was finished.

This suggestion was ridiculous even for Harvey. The idea of throwing money at a film that they would know nothing about was totally unacceptable. He was pushing boundaries further than he'd ever pushed them before.

Steve reacted as expected. He said it was a preposterous request. He tried to argue with Harvey, who remained unmoved. Harvey patiently explained that *they* needed *him*, whereas he didn't need them. He held firm and watched Steve beg for mercy. They reached stalemate. Then, as was Harvey's style, he offered them a final concession: if the movie didn't produce the results he promised, he would give back all the money they had invested. A sign of his commitment. He didn't have a clue as to what he was going to do, but he knew that he would have fun doing it. He needed some fun.

After more negotiations, arguments and pleading, they agreed his terms. People trusted Harvey and more importantly they trusted his record of accomplishment. Luckily for Harvey, Poplar Films had very little choice. They had run out of options. It was a last attempt to save themselves and Harvey took full advantage of that fact.

For the first time in his life, Harvey had work to do. He had a film to *make* and yet he'd never actually made one before. Sure, he had been involved in plenty, he had watched people make films, but he had never done it himself. There is a fine line between belief in oneself and arrogance. Harvey appreciated this. He knew he was arrogant. As Harvey felt the surge of excitement rippling through his body, he knew he had made the right decision.

Chapter Two

Leigh Monroe prised her eyes open and sat up slowly. The heaviness in her head almost made her fall down again. She reached one arm behind it and pushed it up with the rest of her upper-body. She was defying gravity. She tried to collect her thoughts on the way up. There weren't many.

She was on the floor. On a mattress on the floor. Her mattress on the floor of Jason Palmer's spare room. She looked at Tanya's bed trying to piece together the shattered memory of the previous night. Then she screamed. Two other people screamed and sat up.

'What?' Tanya shrieked. Leigh couldn't reply. She pointed to the other screaming voice, which now had a head. A male head. Tanya looked at him.

'Oh shit,' Tanya said.

'Morning to you too,' the man replied.

Leigh found it hard to believe that she had shared a room with Tanya and a strange man. She didn't remember meeting him, and she didn't remember Tanya bringing him back. She shuddered at the thought that she had been lying there while they had sex. If they had had sex.

'Who are you?' Leigh asked, trying to save Tanya some embarrassment. She didn't look embarrassed; she was deathly pale with her sun-streaked hair stuck to her face. The man smiled.

'Don't you remember last night?' he asked. Leigh wasn't sure if he was asking her or Tanya. Either way the answer was no. The two girls looked at him at the same time. He was broad with an enormous head and short dark hair.

'I remember a pub,' Tanya offered.

'Me too,' Leigh said, unable to help her best friend any more than that.

'You two were in a pub all right. You were singing.' His voice was ponderous, he was taking his time relaying the details. From his tone, he was obviously enjoying himself.

'We were? I don't remember being at karaoke,' Leigh replied. Tanya looked mortified. She would never dream of going to a karaoke night.

'It wasn't,' the man replied.

'So how come?' Leigh asked, intrigued.

'Well you were standing on a table using beer bottles as microphones and singing *Wham* songs.' He laughed. Tanya and Leigh did not.

'Oh God. How come we didn't get thrown out?' Tanya asked, finding a slightly slurred voice topped up with mortification.

'You were,' he replied.

'So can I just ask how you came to be here?' Leigh decided to cut to the chase.

'I was the bouncer who threw you out,' he said. Tanya groaned.

'If you threw us out, how come you ended up in bed with Tanya?' Leigh asked, suddenly feeling a need for details away from karaoke and eviction from pubs.

'Well, she said that if I came home with her she'd get me on the telly,' he replied, pointing a stubby finger at Tanya. Tanya put her head under the duvet, saw what was under there and took it straight out again.

Whenever Tanya drank too much, she always used that chat-up line. She seemed to believe that because she worked in television she could use it to pull. It nearly always worked,

9

although it should be noted that she hadn't actually put any of her conquests on television to date.

'Right.' Leigh was lost for words. There was just one thing she needed to know. 'So did you two, you know, did you do it?' A groan emerged from Tanya.

'No. She passed out just as we were going to,' he answered. Tanya looked almost relieved. 'I've still got a condom on if you want to see it.' Leigh jumped up from her mattress quicker than she had ever done in her life. Discovering she was still wearing the clothes she had on the previous night, she made a bolt for the door. Tanya was at her heels. They ran into the bathroom and locked the door.

'I can't believe you nearly had sex and I was in the same room,' Leigh accused.

'I can't believe you let me bring him back,' Tanya retorted.

'I don't remember.' Despite the details provided by the bouncer, Leigh's memory was refusing to come flooding back. Or even trickle back.

'Me either.' Tanya shook her head. They sat on the floor of the bathroom.

'We sang . . .' Leigh screwed up her face.

'Yeah and we got thrown out of a pub,' Tanya pointed out.

'You told the bouncer you'd put him on TV,' Leigh giggled.

'Shit, I really should stop using that line.' Tanya laughed. Eventually they decided to go and face the music.

As they walked into the kitchen, they saw that the bouncer was fully clothed and talking to Jason, Tanya's brother.

'Morning girls. Good night I hear.' Jason smiled at them.

'Mmm,' Leigh managed and reached for the kettle.

'Hadn't you better be going?' Tanya said to the bouncer. He smiled again. He was definitely the most cheerful bouncer that Leigh had ever met.

'Sure. Here's my number for the telly thing.' He handed her a piece of paper and she showed him out.

When she returned, Jason said, 'You really have to stop using that line.'

Tanya and Leigh were best friends and had grown up together. They parted when Tanya left school at sixteen and managed to get herself a job in television. After living and working in London for nine years, she was now a producer for a big television production company. Leigh had left Bath and travelled the shorter distance to university in Bristol where she had stayed after graduating and carved out a career in advertising. She had only recently moved to London and been reunited with Tanya courtesy of Jason's floor.

Leigh believed that she had been waiting for years for Tanya's call. When at sixteen, Tanya had bravely announced that she was leaving home and moving to London, Leigh was apprehensive. Not for Tanya, but for herself.

Whereas Tanya had always known what she wanted and had never worried about attaining it, Leigh was unsure. Her whole life she had been uncertain of everything which is why she had leaned on Tanya for her decisions. Tanya had always obliged her by making decisions for both of them. Therefore when Tanya was no longer going to be there Leigh was stumped. She was more than stumped, she was terrified.

She would have followed Tanya to London way back then but there was never any question of that. Her parents wouldn't have allowed it even if Tanya had asked, which she didn't. In fact, when Leigh asked her what she should do, Tanya told her she would be better off staying where she was.

Reluctantly, Leigh accepted this. She took her A levels, went to university and stayed in Bristol and got herself a job. Although she wasn't overjoyed with her life, she wasn't exactly unhappy, but when Tanya called her and suggested it was time for Leigh to move to London, she felt relieved.

The fact that she had managed without Tanya's every-day influence for ten years escaped her notice. Outwardly she had managed to hide her reliance on Tanya; inwardly she had not.

Tanya had moved in recently with Jason as a temporary measure when her relationship with a much older and much richer man ended. She was unhappy with her life and unable to pinpoint what had ended the relationship, (in reality the relationship was past its sell-by-date, but was not the sole cause of her unhappiness).

No one tried to talk her out of it. Including, much to Tanya's disgust, her ex-lover. Her friends didn't approve. Tanya had always been ambitious and ahead of her years in her work and had applied the same principle to men. Everyone thought that he was robbing her of her youth. When she had to move out of his penthouse apartment and in with her brother most of her friends and family breathed a sigh of relief.

Ending the relationship didn't have the desired effect. Instead of finding instant happiness, she was still as miserable. Ignoring her problems again, she decided that she needed her best friend with her. She persuaded Leigh to uproot herself from her job in a small Bristol advertising agency and move to the big city.

Leigh had found a job as an account manager at BBHAT in Soho. Despite her insecurity, she was good at what she did. So far, in the four months she had worked there, she liked it. The company was great, the clients more prestigious than she had experienced before and her boss, Sukie, was a darling. However, her living arrangements were far from ideal.

The original idea was that they would get a flat together. After the previous night, Leigh thought the time had come. Because they were living with Jason, Leigh and Tanya tried consciously not to be under his feet all the time. So they spent most evenings going out and drinking. Leigh wasn't a party girl and she longed for her own room to spend time in. Tanya was used to being a party girl, but only at very exclusive venues. Going to the pub with Leigh wasn't her idea of a social life. They had fallen into a routine of getting drunk to pass the time and they were both fed up with the scrapes they found themselves in. Leigh wanted to meet a nice man and stay in more. Tanya had no idea what she wanted to do; but the pub with Leigh, the bouncer, the hangovers definitely weren't it.

'You girls crack me up, I love having you here,' Jason said.

'It's time to move on.' Leigh couldn't quite look Tanya in the eye as she said this.

'Yeah . . .' Tanya replied, absently.

'So what are you up to today?' Jason asked.

'I'm seeing David,' Leigh replied. 'Do you want to come?' she asked Tanya.

'Yes, just as soon as I get rid of this monster hangover.' Jason handed her a cup of tea. 'Thanks. What are you doing Jas?' Tanya asked.

'I'm going to convince Serena that I'm not a horrible boyfriend despite the fact that I stood her up last night to play poker with the boys.'

'Good luck.' Tanya knew he would need it.

Jason and Serena had been together for five years. Serena was beautiful and uptight. Jason was laid back and fun. Their relationship was a mystery that neither Tanya nor Leigh could fathom, although they both adored Serena. Their screaming matches left Tanya and Leigh cowering underneath their duvets with distant childhood memories of how they'd hidden in their bedrooms when their parents argued. It was another reason Leigh wanted to move out.

They drank their tea in silence, then went to get ready to meet David.

David Monroe was Leigh's cousin and one of Leigh and Tanya's best friends. They had all grown up together. His father was Leigh's father's brother. He had been the first boy to show them his penis – for ten pence – they'd been the first girls to show him their boobs – fifty pence – and that imbalance set the natural of their whole relationship. David was two years older but they bossed him around as if he were younger. They had spent years teasing him, using him and protecting him. David had moved to London after completing a computer degree and Leigh had seen him and Tanya on only occasional weekends. It felt right their all being back together.

They set off from Jason's flat in Primrose Hill to West Kensington where they were meeting David for lunch at The Three Kings. They were silent throughout the tube ride; they were still feeling green. Leigh kept pulling her compact out of her handbag and looking at herself. Tanya ignored her. Leigh was obsessed with her looks especially when she looked so awful. When they arrived, David was already waiting for them.

'Hi, David.' Leigh kissed his cheek. Tanya did the same.

'God you two look rough,' David said, full of concern.

'Hangover,' Tanya explained and went to get two Bloody Marys and a pint.

'Ask her what we got up to last night,' Leigh suggested.

'What did you do last night?' David asked as Tanya returned.

'Nothing much,' Tanya replied defensively and Leigh giggled. David shrugged.

'What about you?' Leigh asked.

'I was working on my website.' David worked for a computer company by day and on his own web empire by night. He built numerous websites, none of which made any money or had even got off the ground.

'So how is it?' Leigh asked although she didn't share his enthusiasm for the computer revolution.

'Not bad. This one might be a winner.' Leigh and Tanya smiled at him indulgently; he said that every time.

'We're going to find a flat,' Leigh announced.

'We are?' Tanya asked.

'Yes, Tanya. I've been on that mattress for four months now. I need my own room. And Jason needs his space back.' This was Leigh's second bold statement that day.

'I suppose.' Tanya's voice lacked enthusiasm.

'So, you two are going to live together?' David asked.

'Of course,' Tanya replied, indignantly.

'Are you sure that's a good idea?' David laughed.

'What do you mean?' Leigh started playing with her blonde curls.

'Well neither of you is very practical and you always end up in trouble.'

'Did you tell him about last night?' Tanya hissed.

'No,' Leigh replied.

David smiled. 'See, I knew it was another disaster story.' He sat back in his chair, crossed his arms and looked smug.

'Well, we'll be fine when we live together and I have my own room,' Leigh said.

'Absolutely,' Tanya agreed.

David was good-looking in a shy way. He had shoulder-length brown hair and brown eyes. He was rarely confident around women, apart from Leigh and Tanya. He described himself as a proper nerd, one who loved his computer and any gadget he could get his hands on. He always said it was because he was trying to secure his future, but Leigh knew that it was because he was terrified of the opposite sex.

'How about me moving in with you?' David suggested casually. He had been thinking about it for a while and he had a plan.

'Really? That would be perfect,' Leigh said.

'I need to get out of the hellhole I'm in now. It's disgusting.' Leigh and Tanya nodded. David was currently sharing a flat with three other guys, none of whom was attractive or particularly nice. David spent most of his time locked in his room while the others ignored him and carried on in their quest to make the place look like the set of *The Young Ones*.

'God, it would be so much fun. The three of us living together,' Tanya said excitedly as her hangover started to lift. 'Where would we live? I mean . . .'

'It wouldn't exactly be the three of us,' David cut in.

'What?' Leigh asked.

'Well, I have this mate, Eric. He's a top bloke and when we were in the pub last night he said he needed to get a new place. His landlord is selling his flat, so I kind of asked if he wanted to move in with me. Then after I thought about it I thought of you two as well.'

'So, you're touting around for flatmates?' Leigh asked feeling a little less excited. She wasn't very good with strangers.

'No, I thought it would be good for all of us to live with more people. Not like the guys I live with now, but you know . . . it might help us all get a much needed social life.'

'I have a social life,' Tanya said.

'Yeah right, remember last night,' Leigh replied.

Tanya ignored her. 'So what's this Eric like?'

'He's great. He's a pharmacist. Very clever man. And he's so much fun, you'll love him.'

'How do you know him?' Tanya asked, acutely aware of David's lack of friends.

'We were at the same university.'

'Is he cute?' Leigh asked.

'I don't know. How am I supposed to know when a man is cute or not?' David got up to go to the bar.

'Well, another man might not be a bad idea. He may turn out to be sexy,' Leigh pointed out.

'Mm,' Tanya answered, absently.

'What?' Leigh asked.

'Well . . . I was just thinking about stuff. Six months ago, I was living in a penthouse overlooking the Thames with a millionaire. Now I'm moving in with you, David and a pharmacist. It feels a bit of a backward step.'

'Thanks.' Leigh knew not to push it. Since Tanya's relationship had become history, Tanya had rewritten that history so that she believed it had been the most wonderful time of her life. Although Leigh had never been allowed to meet this man, neither had David, she could only dream of dumping someone like him. Leigh believed that for Tanya, living on her wages was the worst thing about the break-up.

David returned with more drinks and sat down.

'So what do you say?' he asked.

'Yes,' Leigh answered.

'Great. Tanya?'

'Whatever. I don't care really.' Tanya sighed. David rolled his eyes at Leigh, she stifled a giggle.

'Oh, there's just one more thing,' David added.

'What, don't tell me Eric has a pet snake or something.' Leigh shuddered.

'No, a pet doctor.'

'A what?' Tanya returned to the living world.

'He lives with this friend who's a doctor and he wants him to move in too.'

'No,' Tanya said.

'Why not?' Leigh asked, thinking a doctor meant two men and one of them was bound to be cute.

'Well, we'll be living with three men. Imagine. Porno movies, pizza and dirty underwear strewn everywhere.'

'I suppose.' Leigh's heart sank.

'Darling girls, these guys are professionals and they're really nice. Not at all like that. They're not slobs,' David explained.

'We'd need to meet them first,' Tanya said.

'And what if they don't want to live with us?' Leigh asked.

'Actually I suggested it already.'

'What? You didn't know we were looking.' Leigh narrowed her eyes.

'I did, you haven't talked about anything else but moving out since you came to London. It didn't exactly take a lot of working out,' David said.

'Well what did they say about us?' Leigh asked.

'They thought five would make a good number.'

'Shit, we'll be outnumbered,' Tanya moaned, gulping her drink.

Good, Leigh thought, running to the loo to reapply her lipstick.

'So when shall we meet them?' Leigh asked when she returned.

'I don't know, I'll call when I get home and arrange something. The sooner the better, they only have a month before they're homeless and I've handed in the notice on my flat,' David explained.

'Fast mover,' Tanya said rubbing her head.

'I don't think anyone has ever called me that before. Shall we eat?'

Chapter Three

'Harvey, you're crazy,' Cherry said as she looked over the proposal for the final time.

'Why?' Harvey smiled. He knew she was right.

'Because, you're about to sign this huge contract with Poplar, and the only details we have is that you, me and Bob Rogers are going to London to live for a while.' Bob Rogers was Harvey's favourite technician.

'So?' Harvey smiled again.

'Harvey you're infuriating. You are taking me, a technical expert and yourself to London to make a film about God knows what and we've only got a year.'

'I guess putting it like that does make it sound a little mad,' Harvey chuckled.

'Please don't chuckle Harvey it always makes me think you're drunk. So, I've got to find us an apartment in London, where, by the way, neither of us have ever been, and we and Bob are going to be one happy family as we sit in this apartment and try to work out how to make a film. It's impossible. It's mad and we will end up in deep shit.'

'Honey, when have I ever let you down? We are going to do just as you said and when we come back in a year we will have the "next big thing" with us. I promise. Anyway we might like London.'

'And we might not. Please tell me you have some idea of what we're going to do.'

'I don't.'

'Nothing?'

'Not a thing. But as I said, don't worry, this is going to be a big adventure for all of us.'

'I give up.' Cherry walked out of the office and left Harvey to Lara Croft.

Harvey knew that he was doing the right thing, he just couldn't explain how he knew. He would sign the contract with the studio, he would have an enormous amount of money to play with, and he had chosen London as the location. Why, he didn't know. It was a hunch, and Harvey always trusted his hunches. Always. So far in his life they had never let him down. He knew they wouldn't start now.

They had a month to make arrangements. Cherry was in charge of accommodation, Bob was in charge of being ready for any technical eventuality that might occur, and Harvey was in charge of thinking. He was thinking. He was *always* thinking. It was just that right now his thoughts weren't that relevant.

Just the fact that he was going to live in another country, with only Cherry and Bob as his team, excited him. The fact that he was leaving Anna to run the office was almost like giving her a year's paid leave. He knew that no one else would have the balls to do what he was doing. If anyone else was going to make a film, they'd know what the film was about, they'd have a script, they'd have a huge team. Harvey wasn't anyone else and his perverse need to do things that no one else would even think of ensured that.

Despite her earlier outburst, Cherry also knew he would do it. She was single and devoted to Harvey. She was thirty-four and blessed with all-American good looks. She also possessed an intelligence that complemented Harvey's astute mind. They had met when she was an executive assistant for a big film studio. He saw her and wanted her to work for him. She saw him and fell in love.

She never regretted the move. She loved working with Harvey despite the lack of *actual* work. She earned more money than she ever thought she would and she had a lot of fun. It was a perfect, crazy job and she loved it. She loved Harvey too, but she thought the best thing would be to bide her time on that front. Harvey was far too busy sleeping with glamorous women to be ready to settle down. Cherry would wait until he was, then she knew he'd be hers.

She smiled at Anna and then sat at her desk to make the arrangements. A month was all she had. A month to find somewhere to live, to pack up and to leave LA for a year. Although she still knew it was crazy she had to admit that some of Harvey's enthusiasm had rubbed off on her. Anna interrupted her thoughts.

'Cherry, it's time for you to go to the studio.'

'Oh, of course, thanks honey.' She smiled at Anna. 'Harvey,' she called, 'it's time to go.'

Leaving the office minutes later, Harvey took Cherry and his lucky shoes with him to the offices of Poplar Films. He loved visiting other people's offices because they were real, whereas his wasn't. He loved seeing the bustle that surrounded them: noisy telephones, the vibrant atmosphere. He would have hated to work there, but he liked being a visitor.

After a short time of sitting in the waiting area under the scrutiny of Steve's severe assistant, they were shown into the office. As with most people in Hollywood, Harvey included, the office was large, pompously furnished and smelled of success. It was ironic how Steve maintained that smell when he was dangerously close to falling into the garbage can of Hollywood has-beens.

'Harv,' Steve boomed, as he got up to greet them.

'You remember Cherry, my right-hand woman.' Harvey ushered Cherry forward. Steve shook her hand and prompted them to sit down.

'I've got the agreement drawn up. I know you'll want your lawyers to look over it but we need to get moving. I need it back signed by the next board meeting which is next Tuesday. Is that enough time?' Steve asked.

'Sure,' Harvey answered as Steve passed him the contract. Harvey didn't look at it. He passed it to Cherry.

'There's just one thing,' Steve said, smiling smugly.

'What?' Harvey was under the impression that all the terms had been agreed and he didn't like surprises.

'The board have discussed it and although we know you said you were going to choose your team, we still need the name of the director before we move on. It's in the contract.'

Harvey looked startled. '*I'm* the director.' He felt himself tense.

'No go, Harvey. We can accept you as co-director but you've never even directed a commercial. We'd be crazy not to want a real director involved. I'm sure you can see our position.' Harvey resisted the urge to point out that their position was just one step away from shutdown. He thought about it for a minute. He could object. He could pull out, but he was already too far into the project in his own head.

'OK. I'll call you with the name of a "real" director.' He narrowed his eyes slightly. Then realised that there was a reason why he'd chosen London. Residing in London was a director called Bill Harrison whom he'd helped a few years back. As he thought about it, everything fell into place. This director owed Harvey his success, therefore he could be easily persuaded to pretend to the studio he was involved. When Harvey produced a brilliant film that he, himself had directed, the studio would relent. As always he was one step ahead.

'So, what I need to know at this point is where we go from here?' Steve said, looking slightly nervous.

'Well, as I said, Steve, you need to trust me. I will report back to you on a monthly basis just so you know we haven't run off with the money, but I am not going to disclose any details until we've finished and are ready to actually show you a film. That was what we agreed,' Harvey smiled.

'Sure, but can't you give me an idea? Maybe we could offer some valuable input.'

'I don't think so. Steve, I'll be back within a year with a film that will put your studio back on the map. In the meantime you should stop worrying. I always deliver.'

'I know that Harv, but, well, we are risking a lot on this one.' Steve was getting annoyed.

'We all take risks in this game Steve. And I am risking my reputation. If I don't deliver I'll be finished in this town and you know that. I wouldn't do this if I wasn't one hundred per cent certain.'

For the next few seconds they smiled at each other. But neither budged. Harvey wouldn't. In the end Steve conceded defeat, as Harvey knew he would.

'OK Harv, do your stuff. But you're right. If anything goes wrong you will be finished in this town.' Harvey merely smiled in response. He decided not to point out that Steve would be finished too.

They had clinched it! The contract that would take Harvey to the next stage. The contract which he knew would change his life.

'Honey, get Anna to copy this and dispatch it to the lawyers, then we'll be in business.'

'Fine. But what about this new clause?'

'I've got a plan,' Harvey replied. Cherry shrugged but didn't push for more details. Harvey always had a plan.

Chapter Four

David called Eric to arrange a meeting with Leigh and Tanya. They planned it for early the following week. David loved both Tanya and Leigh, but didn't feel brave enough to live with them on his own. Leigh was insecure about everything. She hated her curly blonde hair, her little nose and her figure. Although David thought she was lovely, Leigh didn't.

Tanya had enough confidence for both of them. David was a little afraid of her. She didn't take no for an answer and David and Leigh rarely said no to her. She was taller than Leigh, with long, straight hair, which was always streaked with highlights of the day. She was slim, wore designer clothes and was gorgeous. She was also incredibly bossy.

He congratulated himself on his great plan. It was a brilliant plan and it was all his.

'What if they don't like us?' Leigh said scrutinising herself in the mirror before they left to meet their potential house-mates.

'What if *we* don't like them?' Tanya replied.

They set off on the tube to West Kensington, to the same pub that they had visited on the previous Saturday. David said that as it was his idea, he was in charge of arrangements. For once the girls didn't argue with him, although they argued with each other on the journey. Their fellow rush-hour passengers gave them funny looks as they bickered.

'Why did you tell me to wear this, I look like a Weeble,' Leigh shouted, looking at her tight black trousers and purple top which seemed to emphasise her chest. It was a chest that needed no emphasis.

'You look great,' Tanya shouted back.

'I do not, I look stupid. This top makes me look like I have nothing but tits.' Commuters giggled.

'Rubbish. Anyway if I had a chest like yours I'd show it off,' Tanya said looking at her own chest which was comparatively flat despite the recent enhancements that her ex-boyfriend had paid for.

'You wouldn't, and you wouldn't listen to me when I said I shouldn't wear purple.'

'There's nothing wrong with purple.'

'I look like a blackberry.'

'Leigh, shut up, you don't. You look great.' Tanya sighed and chewed the end of her hair, a habit she adopted when she was frustrated. She looked at Leigh and had to agree with her. The purple top did make her breasts look massive. Leigh had a very petite frame and an unexplainable chest. She looked as if she would topple forward at any moment.

'I should always wear black,' Leigh announced.

'Good idea,' Tanya agreed, absently.

'Well why didn't you tell me to wear black?'

'I don't know.' They got off the tube and Tanya excused Leigh her obsessiveness yet again.

Tanya was wearing a pair of trendy jeans and a cardigan with velvet along the bottom and sleeves. Her hair looked good because she had sneakily booked into her hairdresser for a wash and blow-dry in her lunch hour. She didn't tell Leigh because that would have started World War Three. Tanya liked to look her best at all times and knew how to achieve it, whereas Leigh was constantly worried that she never looked quite right.

David was sitting at a table as they walked in and they went to join him.

'Where are these men?' Tanya asked.

'Not here yet, don't worry,' David replied.

'I'm not,' Tanya snapped, as she sent David to the bar to get two glasses of wine.

After ten minutes, two men walked into the pub and approached the bar. 'Two pints of Kronenberg please,' said one. 'Do you have any chocolate?' asked the other. Picking up their pints and the Snickers bar, they scanned the room.

David looked over and saw Eric. He waved them across. As they approached, Tanya and Leigh looked up and felt their jaws fall to the ground at the same time. One of the men was tall, and slim with unruly, curly blond hair; the other was a God. He was tall, well-built with short dark hair. His eyes sparkled and he was wearing a blue shirt that matched. He had an incredible smile. As they reached the table, Leigh and Tanya still hadn't quite recovered. David stood up.

'Eric,' he smiled.

'Hi mate,' the untidy one said and sat down. The God followed suit. After waiting a few seconds for Eric to make the introductions, he decided to do them himself.

'I'm Gus Carter.' The God took human form.

'Hi Gus, meet Leigh and Tanya.' The girls still stared.

'Eric Reed,' Eric said, opening his chocolate.

'Hi.' Tanya composed herself and smiled at each of the men in turn. Leigh smiled weakly. 'So, we're proposing a house share.' Tanya took charge as she always did, the earlier lack of composure banished.

'It's a good idea,' Eric said, his mouth full of chocolate.

'Well it is if we all get on,' David pointed out.

'I'm sure we will,' Tanya said quickly. 'Any ideas which area?'

'Isn't that jumping the gun a bit?' Gus asked.

'I know, but there's no point in wasting time. I work in television, although I hope to branch out into films soon. Anyway, I'm a producer, and Leigh here works for BBHAT, the big advertising agency. She's an account manager. I understand you're a doctor.' Tanya flashed Gus her most impressive smile. Leigh wished she could think of something to say.

'Yup. I work at the hospital on Fulham Road. I need to live near my work.'

'I love Fulham,' Tanya gushed. David sat back looking amused. He was enjoying the effect that Gus was having on his two favourite girls.

'I work there too,' Eric added, having finished eating. 'I'm a pharmacist. So Fulham it is then.' He smiled.

'Is it going to be easy to find a house for five?' Leigh asked, toying with her curls nervously.

'Of course it will be.' Tanya gave her a look.

'Anyway, perhaps we should see if we all get on first,' David suggested again.

'Oh I get on with anybody,' Eric said, sipping his pint. 'In fact I think that I'm probably the nicest person in London.' Leigh laughed.

'Right. Well does anyone want another drink?' Gus asked

'Oh, I'd love a glass of dry white wine,' Tanya answered.

'Leigh?' Leigh was staring at a beer mat.

'Same,' Leigh mumbled, unable to look Gus in the eye.

David and Gus went to the bar.

'So, you work in television. Excellent. I always thought I should be on the telly,' Eric said. Leigh shot Tanya a warning look.

'Well you never know, if you live with us, you might get the chance.' Tanya ignored Leigh's look. She was thinking how perfect Gus would be for television.

'Really? How cool. So what programmes do you make? Anything I might have heard of?' Tanya rattled off a number of programmes that everyone had heard of.

'Wow. That's incredible, you've listed my favourite programmes,' Eric enthused. Tanya warmed to him slightly.

'That's a good sign. This is obviously going to be a great household.'

'Yeah, and I can give you loads of ideas. I've got loads you know.' Eric smiled.

'I need the loo,' Leigh announced and went to check her make-up.

'I tried to stop Eric from smoking, but he thought he had another great idea,' Gus said to David at the bar.

'It's fine. I doubt whether the girls will notice, and anyway, he's all right.'

'I know, but if they know about his missions will they want to live with him?' Gus asked.

'Of course they will. They'll find it as entertaining as we do.'

'That's one way of putting it. They seem all right to me.'

'They are. I can't imagine anyone not getting on with them.'

'Well that's perfect. I quite like the idea of a house full of people. It'll be like college.'

'I hope not. When I was at college we lived in a rat-infested hellhole. Actually, thinking about it, I still do.'

'Maybe not that. But it'll be good having the girls there, then women won't feel so intimidated about coming over.' Gus smiled.

'Women? Those two will tear them to shreds.' David laughed.

'What I mean is that if the house has a female touch, it'll be nicer, you know.' A dreamy look appeared on Gus's face.

'Yeah.' Having women to stay was an area of expertise in which David was severely lacking. They returned with the drinks at the same time that Leigh returned from the loo.

'So, Eric tells me you're both single. That's good because so are we and it'll be much easier living together without partners hanging around all the time,' Tanya said.

'So we have to stay single while we live with you?' Gus asked, amused.

'No, but you know, it's good for us to get to know each other first of all without other people.' Leigh couldn't believe how obvious Tanya sounded.

'Right.' Gus was confused.

'I'm always single. I keep losing my girlfriends,' Eric said.

'How?' Leigh asked.

'I don't really know, but I keep forgetting them or something.'

'He forgets their names; where he's supposed to meet them; he even forgets how to use the phone,' Gus explained.

'How come?' Leigh asked again.

'I don't know, I guess I'm just a bit scatty.' Eric laughed at himself.

'What about you, Gus?' Tanya asked.

'Being a doctor isn't that great for relationships. I work crazy hours.'

'Gosh, I don't believe that. Not the hours thing; you obviously haven't met the right girl,' Tanya suggested in a coquettish way.

'Perhaps not,' Gus replied. David shook his head.

'I'm single because I have to concentrate on my career, though I haven't met the right man yet. And Leigh's always single.' Tanya smiled, Leigh blushed.

'Well not always,' she protested.

'Yes you are. When's the last time you had a boyfriend?' Tanya asked.

'Damion,' Leigh replied.

'Shit, that was years ago. Anyway that's what happens if you date men named Damion.' Tanya laughed and Leigh coloured.

'Damion's my middle name,' Eric said.

'Sorry,' Tanya offered, without meaning it.

'It's OK. My mum chose it.' Eric smiled.

'Well I like the name Damion,' Leigh said.

'Oh I just remembered, my middle name is Damon not Damion. But then I wouldn't mind if my name was Damion either. Maybe they just spelt it wrong or something. I must call and ask.'

Gus looked at David and raised an eyebrow, he decided it would be a good idea to change the subject. 'So, Leigh, tell us about advertising.'

'Not much to tell; we go to work late, we sit around discussing stuff for most of the day, we have secretaries who deal with most of the calls and then we have the five o'clock panic.' Leigh smiled, she could hold a conversation with Gus as long as she didn't have look at him too intently.

'What's that?' Eric asked.

'At five we realise that we've done no work, we've been out to lunch for far too long and we start running around like blue-arsed flies trying to get everything done.'

'They don't appreciate time management in advertising. Not like working in television,' Tanya explained.

'What's it like working in television?' Gus asked.

'Oh wonderful. But not at all glamorous. I work on documentaries and it's really hard work. I'm going to move into films as soon as I can,' Tanya replied. Hogging the limelight.

'I'm impressed,' Gus said. Leigh glowered.

'Anyway, tell us about the life of a doctor,' Leigh suggested.

'It's frantic. Stupid hours, stupid coats and patients with ailments you wouldn't believe.'

'What do you actually specialise in?' Tanya asked.

'General medicine, I work in Casualty at the moment.'

'How wonderful,' Leigh said before thinking. Gus looked confused.

'Well, it can be very traumatic.'

'Of course it can, you must be very strong to be able to cope. I know I couldn't,' Tanya smiled and Leigh felt like hitting her again. 'So, what is the verdict on the house?' she asked.

'Well, I'm happy,' Eric said.

'Me too,' Gus agreed.

'Excellent, that's settled, now all we have to do is to find the house.' Tanya looked at Leigh.

'Well, I'm not sure how easy that'll be,' Gus pointed out.

'Oh Gus, don't worry about details. How long before you need to be out of your flat?'

'A month,' Gus said.

'Excellent, well we'll be in our new house within the month.' Tanya beamed.

'We're going to put a notice up at the hospital,' Eric explained.

'I'll post one on this website I found,' David offered.

'Well I guess I can ask around at work,' Leigh added.

'Good,' Tanya said having no intention of getting involved in house-hunting herself.

They drank some more as Eric explained his mission in life: his quest for the perfect joint.

'So you see, I draw up plans, just like an architect, then I work out materials, using weight and balance formulas. It's very scientific. Then I make a prototype and if that works, then I make it. I haven't managed to do it yet, but still, I keep going.'

'How weird. What are you going to do when you find the perfect formula?' Tanya asked.

'Make it and smoke it of course.'

'Is that all?' Leigh said.

'What do you mean is that all? This is a very important project I'm working on, you know. This could change my life.'

'Just yours?' David questioned.

'Well yours too if you want. Anyway that's just one of my hobbies, I won't get into the other one now.'

'Are you sure you still want to live with us now?' Gus asked.

'Yes,' Leigh and Tanya said a bit too quickly and a little too loudly.

'Of course they do. It'll definitely be interesting,' David added.

'I have to go, I have to work tomorrow,' Gus announced. It was only nine o'clock.

'Right.' Tanya looked disappointed. They all said their goodbyes and agreed to keep in touch.

Leigh and Tanya took the tube back to Primrose Hill.

'I can't believe I met the man of my dreams tonight looking like this,' Leigh lamented.

'He's the man of my dreams too,' Tanya said, although he

wasn't. Gorgeous as she found him, he was just too young. She decided his age wouldn't stop her from developing a mild crush on him, because that would add more excitement to moving into the house, but she wouldn't take it any further.

'Well, it doesn't matter because he'd never go for me.'

'He was so lovely. Nice, gorgeous *and* a doctor.'

'Perfect.' Leigh sighed.

'Perfect,' Tanya agreed. They didn't mention Eric once.

Tanya opened the door of Jason's flat. They could hear arguing.

'Hi Jason, hi Serena,' Tanya shouted, ducking out of the way of a flying cup. They made a quick run for the bedroom. Once there, Tanya put a CD on the stereo to drown out the noise.

'So do you think it's really going to happen?' Leigh asked.

'What?' Tanya flinched as something hit the bedroom door.

'The house,' Leigh said, sitting back on Tanya's bed. The spare bedroom was painted white. The double bed now housed Tanya's blue and white checked duvet cover. The only other piece of furniture in the room was a metal clothes rail. Jason didn't have many visitors. Tanya had bought a couple of lamps, some cushions, her stereo and her television, but apart from that the room was plain. With the borrowed single mattress there wasn't much space in the room. As Tanya had an extensive wardrobe which took up all the space on the rail, Leigh's clothes were still in her suitcase.

'Of course it will,' Tanya snapped.

'But what if Gus and Eric decide they don't like us?' Leigh protested.

'What's not to like?' Tanya pulled out her nail polish and started painting her toenails. A new colour: purple with a hint of silver.

'But, well, they just might not.' Leigh couldn't help worrying. She wanted more than anything to live with them. With Gus. She couldn't get his face out of her head.

'Look, you call David tomorrow and find out.' Tanya had already grown bored with the conversation.

'But maybe they were just being polite, they don't really know anything about us,' Leigh continued.

'And we don't know anything about them. We're not marrying them we're moving in with them.' Tanya sighed. She loved Leigh, but she wished she wasn't so infuriating.

'I wish I *was* marrying Gus,' Leigh said.

'Yes you and probably the rest of the women in London. Get real, Leigh. But I thought Eric was a bit strange,' she added as if finally remembering him.

'He was sweet, and I think David's right, he'll be fun.'

'Well so will we. Come on, paint your nails and then we'll have a face-pack.'

'Why?' Leigh asked grabbing the polish.

'So we look stunning for the next time we meet Gus. You can even borrow some of my clothes,' Tanya offered, kindly.

'Tanya, none of your clothes fit me,' Leigh pointed out, wishing it wasn't true. All Tanya's skirts and trousers were too long for Leigh and her tops didn't fit over her bulging breasts.

'Mmm, true. Never mind we'll make sure you look lovely.' Tanya suddenly felt charitable.

'Promise?'

'Promise.'

As the Radiohead CD finished, so did the row. They ventured out and found Jason and Serena on the sofa in each other's arms. They went and sat on the matching sofa opposite them.

'Jason, we're moving out,' Tanya announced.

'When?' Jason asked, stroking Serena's mass of blonde hair and wearing a plaster on his forehead.

'Good shot Serena . . . erm . . . I don't know, but soon, so I'm giving you advance notice.'

'Well, dear sister, I'll miss you, but I'll also be pleased to have the flat back.'

'Will you miss *me*?' Leigh asked.

'Of course, Leigh. Now why don't you go and find something to drink. I could do with a beer,' Jason said.

'Serena?' Tanya asked.

'White wine please darling.' Leigh and Tanya went off. They returned with the drinks and sat down again.

'Serena, if you met this guy who was so gorgeous that he makes you want to faint when you see him, what would you do?' Leigh asked.

'God, I'd go and rip his clothes off,' Serena answered taking a long, slow drag on her menthol cigarette.

'I hope you bloody wouldn't,' Jason said.

'Oh babes, she means if I didn't already have a gorgeous guy. Why? Have you girls met one?'

'Yes, we're going to live with him. He's a doctor and he's such a . . . well he's just wonderful,' Leigh gushed.

'The first bit of advice is don't fight over him. Even if he is the most wonderful man in the world, don't. Also, if you're living with him, be careful. What happens if you split up?' Serena smiled, she loved dishing out motherly advice to Leigh and Tanya.

'I know, I doubt he'd even notice me anyway,' Leigh sighed.

'I'm sure he will notice you, you're both gorgeous,' Serena said kindly. Leigh decided that she loved Serena even if she did spend most of her time being a psychotic bitch.

'But, look at me; my hair, my boobs.'

'Leigh, you have great boobs and great hair,' Jason cut in, having experienced years of Leigh's insecurities.

'Really?' Leigh asked.

'Yes.'

'Where will you be living?' Serena asked after a while.

'Fulham. Gus and Eric both work in a hospital there, so we need to be nearby for them.'

'Fulham? Not a bad place to live,' Serena said.

'I've never been there,' Leigh admitted, 'but it doesn't matter because we'll be living with Gus,' she said dreamily.

'Come on Ser, we need to leave.' Jason stood up.

'Where are you going?' Tanya asked.

'To *my* flat for once,' Serena explained, leaving the sofa.

When Leigh and Tanya went to bed shortly afterwards, Leigh prayed for dreams of Gus.

Chapter Five

Cherry looked up from her desk and smiled at Anna. Ever since the meeting with Steve Delaney, they had been working comparatively hard. She had secured an apartment for them in a serviced building, arranged for all the equipment they needed: computers, mobile phones and other things that Harvey had asked for. She checked that it already had cable television, and had arranged to have an office fitted out in the apartment. She began to enjoy the idea of living in London. Bob was busy preparing himself for whatever Harvey had planned. At this point, a week after getting the contract from Poplar Films, they still didn't have a clue of Harvey's plan for the film, or even if he had one. Anna had booked flights and typed an itinerary, but it was thin. They had less than three weeks left in LA.

Harvey carried on playing computer games. He had paused long enough to read the contract *after* the lawyers had agreed it and he had also managed to sign it. He had called Bill Harrison and while being deliberately vague he had managed to get him to be a 'pretend' director. Bill was naturally reluctant to put his name to anything he knew nothing about, but Harvey wasn't the master of persuasion for nothing and when he pointed out that Bill would get paid for doing nothing, Bill ran out of objections.

He had successfully managed to field any questions about the project that Steve asked him. Steve called daily. Harvey told

Cherry to make sure she didn't give Poplar Films their London number.

He still had no ideas, but he wasn't worried. He told Cherry and convinced himself that as soon as they got settled in London he would be inspired. As he loaded his favourite computer game, he smiled to himself. He could barely believe that his life had come so far.

When he'd lived in New York he'd been a top salesperson, but still in the 'ordinary' league. Now he was a hotshot and he was playing with the big boys. He laughed at the thought, he wasn't the Hollywood type.

Harvey had never believed in the convention of type. He had been a salesperson who didn't behave like most salespeople did, he was just himself. He wasn't scared by the people he dealt with, he wasn't in awe of anybody, which was his recipe for success.

It was the same with women. He could have any woman he wanted, almost. He didn't use the usual Hollywood tricks of promising movie roles, or jobs, or money or anything. All he offered was himself and that seemed to be enough.

He believed in his instinct, he believed in his success, but he didn't understand it any better than anyone else. He craved challenge, he craved something, but again, he didn't know exactly what that was. He had a feeling that London and his latest project would offer it, but that was all he had. A feeling.

He was so far removed from the New York Harvey that sometimes he could barely remember that man. All he knew now was that he was *someone*, and he was someone he really quite liked. He hadn't hurt people to get where he was; he didn't overtly use people, he didn't shout or threaten. He knew he was manipulative but everyone was to an extent. He felt able to justify himself. That was important to him.

As he zapped another alien, he smiled to himself. 'Gotcha!'

Chapter Six

The following week they started house-hunting. Leigh studied *Loot* every day. She said a prayer before she opened the paper. David searched online. Eric composed an ad and Gus pinned it on the hospital noticeboard. Tanya did nothing. She had to come up with new ideas for TV programmes, but she found every new idea she had, had been done before in some form or another. Like David and his websites. It was frustrating but she kept going, jotting down ideas and trying to make them into something she could talk to her boss about.

Leigh was already sunk in her obsession with Gus. Her head was filled with thoughts of him. The way he was interested in what she did, the way he looked cute in his clothes. She could recall every detail about him. The way when he concentrated his eyebrows arched, the way he smiled and how his smile reached her. It spoke to her. She had met him only once.

David decided he would build a flat-seeking website. Then he found there were already hundreds of them and he had no new angles. He felt so depressed he stopped looking.

Eric was busy at work, putting pills together and making up potions. At home he had his mission, so apart from writing the ad his contribution had been minimal.

The ad was successful. A doctor at the hospital saw it as the answer to his prayers. A successful young surgeon, he had bought a dilapidated house and turned it into a dream home, but then he had been given a two-year posting to America. Determined not to sell his house, he realised that the rental income would provide a nice nest egg. If he rented it to someone from the hospital he wouldn't have to worry about engaging an agency to arrange things. Being astute and aware of the demand for houses in London, he had kept it as a four-bedroom house but it also had a room in the basement, which he had intended on making into a study. It would be perfect for them, it would be perfect for him. The convenience of fate struck.

The five of them arranged to view the house together one night after work. Leigh and Tanya took a long time deciding what to wear.

'I'm wearing jeans and a black top,' Leigh said decisively.

'Fine,' Tanya responded.

'Well what are you wearing?' Leigh asked, indignant at Tanya's composure.

'I don't know,' Tanya replied, although she had it all planned.

When Leigh had left the house on the morning of the viewing, she was wearing her chosen outfit. Tanya, who had been at the studio late into the night, was still in bed.

They met in Soho near to where they both worked. Leigh felt her heart sink when she saw Tanya approaching.

'You didn't tell me you were wearing a skirt.' Leigh pouted.

'Well I had a meeting, I had to look good,' Tanya explained, smoothing her designer skirt, and examining her designer shoe-clad feet.

'I hate you sometimes,' Leigh sulked.

'Why? We're only going to look at a house.' The rest of the journey passed in silence.

David met them at the tube station.

'Hi, girls, ready?' he asked excitedly.

' 'Spose so,' Leigh replied and followed him away from the station. Neither of them took up any of David's offers of conversation.

When they reached their destination, ten minutes from the tube, David smiled. It was a tree-lined street filled with houses that were newly painted.

'Apparently most of these houses are flats,' David explained, trying to work out what had caused the hostility. Neither responded.

When they got to number twenty-four Eric and Gus were waiting on the doorstep. They said their hellos and waited anxiously for the owner to answer the doorbell.

The man who answered the door looked young and old at the same time.

'This is Brian.' Gus introduced everyone, as they stepped inside. Tanya looked at him. He was wearing an expensive suit.

'Why haven't you turned the house into flats?' Tanya asked immediately.

'Because I've worked hard to make this my home. I'm off to work in California for two years and I would like to be able to have this to come back to.' He spoke without warmth and Tanya decided that he didn't have a personality.

'Right. And the lease?' Tanya asked.

Brian looked confused. 'I'll get a year's lease drawn up, just a standard lease I guess.'

They followed him round the house. There was a faint smell of paint in every room. Downstairs consisted of a large sitting room with a dining table, a kitchen which had a breakfast bar, and a small loo. There was also a flight of stairs leading to a basement room, which had a door leading to a small patio garden. Upstairs there were three bedrooms and a bathroom and on the top floor just one room a converted attic. Each room was painted in a different pastel shade. Although Brian had made it his home, he had not made a very exciting job of the decor.

'We'll take it,' Tanya announced, apparently the self-appointed spokesperson.

'Don't you want to discuss it with the others?' Brian asked. He was feeling oddly displaced by Tanya. If he had been a more sensitive man he would have decided that he didn't want her in his home. He didn't know why, but he felt that she might *do something* to it.

'No. They all agree.' Everyone looked at her but couldn't argue.

'Fine. I'll get a lease drawn up,' Brian smiled, tightly. 'I'm leaving at the end of the month, in three weeks' time, Gus can bring back the signed lease and the deposit. I'll give him the keys then.'

'Fine. Perfect,' Tanya agreed.

'Thanks Brian,' Gus said.

They went to the pub.

'It's perfect,' Tanya enthused as silence ensued.

'OK. But what about rooms? I am not living in that basement,' Leigh stated, still not having quite shaken off her bad mood.

'I'll take the basement,' David offered, thinking how perfect it would be for his computer.

'Well, I don't mind,' Gus agreed, in conciliatory fashion.

'I think David should have it,' Tanya said.

'Right,' Eric replied.

'Great, so that settles it. I have the top room. You guys take the second floor and David gets the basement.' Everyone looked at Tanya.

'But, *I* might want the top room,' Leigh protested.

'Leigh don't be silly, think of the stairs,' Tanya replied and went to the bar.

'Shit, she can be scary.' Gus stared into his empty pint glass.

'Yes, you better believe it.' Tanya's bossiness might give Leigh a much needed advantage with Gus.

'She's not so bad when you get to know her,' David defended, glaring at Leigh.

'She is,' Leigh laughed.

'I think she's kind of sexy, you know like a dominatrix,' Eric offered. No one knew how they were supposed to react to that.

The rest of the evening passed trying to get to know each other better. Tanya questioned them on their hygiene habits; Leigh tried to flirt with Gus; Eric told jokes; David talked about the Internet.

They discovered that Gus had grown up in South Devon, the only child of parents who were blissfully in love. Gus's pride when he spoke about this and his readiness to extol his own desire to fall in love pushed Leigh even further into her crush.

Eric had lived nearly all his life in London. He lived with just his mother, his father had left them when he was young. When Eric had left home his mother met another man and they were now married.

Tanya filled everyone in on her, Leigh's and David's background, noting that she was the one person there who wasn't an only child. This annoyed her; Tanya hated feeling like the odd one out. They had all grown up in Bath. Leigh's parents were overprotective. Leigh grimaced when Tanya told them this. David's mother had died when he was young, his father had never remarried. David grimaced at her open way of discussing his past, but he was used to Tanya's style. Then she described her mother and father as 'Christmas parents', and told them about her brother Jason.

It was a fact-finding discussion: ages, backgrounds and occupations. The men were all twenty-nine; Leigh and Tanya were both twenty-six. It was the sort of information that new acquaintances swapped; although as such they were about to embark on an adventure that would change their lives forever.

Chapter Seven

Harvey, Cherry and Bob travelled First Class on the BA flight to London. They drank champagne and toasted their new venture. Bob and Cherry couldn't help but be infected by Harvey's enthusiasm. They still had no idea what was going to happen when they reached London, or what kind of movie Harvey thought he was going to make. But for the moment, they relaxed and enjoyed the flight.

The time passed in companionable silence. Cherry was enjoying the new John Travolta movie, Bob seemed to be asleep and Harvey was . . . well Harvey was enjoying his anticipation.

Bob wasn't asleep, he was thinking. For some time now he had proffered his technical expertise when looking at feasibility studies for Harvey's film ideas. Bob was a passive man in his mid-forties with too little hair. He was single. He liked technology more than he liked people and had decided that after sowing his oats in his youth, he had no room in his life for a full-time partner. Cherry always teased him by saying he hadn't met the right girl, but Bob didn't think that such a being existed. Computers and technology were far more reliable.

He was a little concerned by the lack of information on the forthcoming project. Usually Harvey came up trumps, so why should it be any different this time? Sitting on the plane to London he knew better than to question Harvey, and he prayed that this time Harvey's genius hadn't finally turned to madness.

Harvey stretched in his seat and let his happiness wash through him. He knew that anticipation was the best emotion. It invoked in him the greatest of thrills. The anticipation of making love, of moving house, of new beginnings, of new films. Anticipation was far more emotive than the actuality of performing each task. If he could bottle anticipation, he would make a fortune. In his career he had managed to make the most of anticipation, he had built his working life around it. He felt sorry for people who didn't value it as much as he did, because inevitably they didn't get to feel it as much as he did.

As Bob and Harvey wheeled their luggage trolleys through the arrivals hall at Heathrow, the first thing they noticed was the rain. The second was the chill in the air. Pulling her coat tightly around her, Cherry led the others to a taxi rank. Climbing aboard they smiled at each other and hoped that this was not the sort of welcome that London gave to all its visitors.

The apartment they were heading for was a four-bedroomed place in Knightsbridge. Cherry wanted to be near Harrods and Harvey Nichols, two department stores she had heard so much about. Harvey didn't seem to care where they were located, so Cherry arranged everything. One of the rooms was being transformed into an office. As Harvey had negotiated so much money, Cherry thought it would be imprudent not to spend it. As she looked at the glint in Harvey's eyes, once again she knew that everything would work out just fine.

As the cab crept through the London traffic, Harvey couldn't fail to notice how grey everything was. He had never visited the UK before and hadn't thought about how he would find it, but the obvious lack of sunshine was depressing. He made his first decision about the film: he would set it indoors.

Bob clutched his backpack and looked out of the taxi window. He had been to London before and he suddenly remembered how much he'd hated it the last time. The weather had depressed him, the people had depressed him and he had found London's charms rather limited. To be fair he had only stayed a week and perhaps this time, the rain wouldn't be an every day occurrence. He looked over at Cherry and Harvey. Cherry looked horrified by her first glimpses of London, but as always Harvey's emotions were impenetrable.

Cherry shivered for the hundredth time. Harvey had told her to dress warmly, but warmly to Cherry meant her beautiful Prada Mac and a cashmere jumper which barely reached her waist. She was cold. The coldness wasn't merely to do with the temperature. It was due to everything. It was due to the traffic, which sat depressingly in a line. It was the fact that every car seemed to be shielding grey rain. It was the people on the street who clutched umbrellas and seemed to have forgotten how to smile. It was the way the taxi driver looked tired and fed up as he concentrated on his windscreen wipers, it was how the buildings seemed to look unhappy. Or perhaps it was just Cherry that was unhappy. She smiled weakly at Bob, who looked as depressed as she was; she looked at Harvey who looked totally in control.

The taxi pulled up outside a tall building in Knightsbridge. As they got out, Cherry paid the driver while the others unloaded their luggage. They had decided to bring only essentials with them and have anything else shipped over. Thinking about what she'd packed, Cherry realised that she would have to spend her first days in London shopping for jumpers. She couldn't stop shivering.

Harvey turned and kissed her on the cheek as they stood looking at their new home. It looked beautiful despite the weather and Cherry smiled for the first time since getting off the plane. She strode confidently to the door and walked up to the well-dressed man seated at the main desk. It reminded her of a classy hotel reception.

'Hi, we're the Cannon party,' Cherry explained.

'Welcome to London madam. If you could just sign a few forms I'll show you up.'

'Thank you,' Cherry smiled warmly. His was the first London smile she had encountered, she decided to store it in her memory bank. She signed the paperwork and collected three sets of keys.

'Everything is ready for you. The manager will be available later if you want to talk to her about anything.'

'Can I ask your name?' Cherry replied.

'Of course, I'm Simon and I look after the building most days. We have another man here in the evenings, but someone is here at all times. You call me if you need anything.' He smiled. Cherry smiled back. The seriousness with which he addressed them gave her a feeling of security.

They followed Simon to the lift which took them to the fifth floor. Simon unlocked the door and they followed him into an apartment that impressed even Harvey.

The walls were a warm shade of cream. The carpets were deep and sumptuous. The living room was the first room they came to as they stepped through the hallway. Works of modern art hung on the walls and two gigantic beige sofas occupied the middle of the room. They put the luggage down and allowed Simon to show them round the rest of the apartment.

The kitchen was large with a breakfast bar, every modern appliance installed and with cheerful sun-kissed yellow walls. There was even a separate dining area. The bedrooms were identical: king-size beds, closets and televisions. All three had en-suite bathrooms. The fourth room was the fully equipped office. Harvey saw it and decided immediately that he liked it. Cherry had done a brilliant job.

Simon left them to their new home.

'Cherry, you have surpassed yourself. This is fantastic.' Harvey grabbed her in a big bear hug and laughed out loud.

'Harvey, anything to please you,' Cherry teased and hugged him back. 'Bob, what do you think?'

'I think that I could be happy here. Did you know the fridge is already stocked with my favourite beer?' Cherry nodded.

'God, Harvey where did you find such a woman?'

'I don't know, lady luck was smiling on me the day I met Cherry.'

'Perhaps I should spend more time hanging around with you.'

'As long as you don't try to take my favourite lady away.'

'Boys, please . . . I'm now going to unpack and have a long, relaxing bath.'

'I'm having a beer; Harvey?'

'Sure thing. Let's have a beer and check out what television stations my wonderful girl has arranged for us.'

'God, why do I feel like I'm on a boys' holiday rather than a working one?' Cherry asked.

'Probably because you know that for the next few days we are having a holiday, and honey, I'll make sure it's not just fun for the boys.' Harvey pinched Cherry on the bottom and chuckled as he watched her go to her room.

Harvey and Bob settled into the couch with their beers.

'So, do you have any idea what the hell we're doing here?' Bob asked.

'No, but I'll tell you one thing, if it rains like this we are not filming outside.'

'Thank God for that,' Bob laughed.

Chapter Eight

'Why on earth do we need a van?' Leigh asked Tanya as she studied her two suitcases and two boxes.

'Well how did you expect us to move our stuff?'

'Tanya, I have nothing. I could take my stuff on the tube, and since you split up with that old man you don't have much more. We could get a taxi or we could get David to drive us,' Leigh pointed out reasonably.

'Well maybe we could, but a van is so much more "house-moving",' Tanya replied.

'I don't understand and I don't even want to know.' Leigh resumed her packing. When she came from Bristol she had thrown out her old life and brought only essentials with her. She simply had nowhere to put anything and instead of storage, getting rid seemed a better option. All Tanya had was a wardrobe of expensive clothes, but in true dramatic spirit, she had hired a van and a driver to move their pitiful belongings into the new house.

They hadn't seen Gus or Eric since they first saw the house and Leigh was filled with anticipation at having Gus under the same roof. She had put on her best jeans and a soft pale blue jumper, which wasn't the most practical outfit for moving house but it made her look good. She also wore her new high-heeled boots. Tanya had on a tracksuit and scoffed at Leigh's outfit. When Leigh pointed out that she felt comfortable dressed that way, Tanya scoffed again. Unfortunately, because she was scoffing she was unable to go and get changed. For the first time in her life, she looked plain in comparison to Leigh.

'This could be the making of us,' Leigh said; she had been thinking about it for ages.

'What?' Tanya asked.

'It could make us. I mean, I'm not being funny but we are all at a funny stage in life aren't we? We've got careers, we've got each other, but we don't have anything solid. We don't own things, we don't love people. I mean, we do, but we don't love a partner. I think moving into this house is going to consolidate us. The point is that if we believe in fate and things happening because they needed to happen, then this house means something. I *know* it means something. It is either going to be the house that makes us, or the house that doesn't.' In her own confused way, Leigh had hit the nail on the head. It was going to be the house that would both make and break them.

David and his belongings had been packed into his Golf. Although he had spent most of his time worrying about his computer and the risk in moving it he had managed to get everything ready on time. He had also ordered a telephone line to be installed quickly in his basement room so that he wouldn't have to suffer too long without his beloved Internet.

Gus and Eric moved their things on foot. The house was only a ten-minute walk from their old flat and they didn't have too many possessions, which seemed to be a characteristic of the new house. The first observation Tanya made when they started taking things into the house was that it would need a lot of work to make it look lived-in. She had never known in her life five people with fewer possessions.

Everyone went to their pre-allocated rooms. David loved his. It had light from the small garden, a double bed, a wardrobe and a chest of drawers. Although everything was new the furniture was minimal. As he set up his computer desk and equipment, David hoped his room would inspire him.

Leigh's room was next to Gus's. She was pleased about this

because, although Tanya had the bigger room, she would be in closer proximity to the man she craved so much. Only a wall separated them. As she hung her clothes in the wardrobe (which in itself seemed like a luxury after living out of suitcases for months), she smiled to herself. She knew she needed to make the room more homely, but a few pictures, cushions and bits and pieces would make it just that.

Tanya looked out of the window and smiled. Her room was huge. It had two large built-in cupboards, a dressing table, a desk and a comfortable double bed. She arranged her bedding first, her wardrobe second and her jewellery and cosmetics last. She had 'borrowed' some pictures from her brother and set about deciding where to hang them. Finally, when she set up her television and video, her room was ready to be lived in.

Eric rolled a joint to christen his new room. Then he sat on the bed and smoked it. He took in the off-white walls, the pale carpet, the wardrobe and the bedside table and realised he could be happy there. He just had to make it look a bit more colourful. Plainness scared him. He finally unpacked his bedding, his clothes, his smoking equipment, and his posters. He blue-tacked his pictures on the wall, giving his Britney Spears calendar pride of place. He decided that the room looked better already. He rolled another joint.

Gus felt depressed. His room was nice, but nice was boring. Turning a bare room into a romantic room would be no mean feat. He unpacked and tried to think of ways to make the room more inviting and less macho. He decided that the traditional methods were the best and wrote a list. On his list were candles, pictures, cushions and photos. He wanted the girl of his dreams to walk into his room and feel at home. He had to ensure that she, whoever she was, would do so.

Their chores completed they all made it back to the sitting room. Tanya had a bottle of champagne waiting for them.

'Nice one Tanya,' Eric said as he took his position on the couch and started rolling another joint.

'There's more in the fridge, after all this *is* a special occasion.' Tanya opened the bottle and filled five glasses.

'My room is so plain, I need to sort it out,' Leigh said.

'I was thinking the same,' Gus agreed.

'Well, this room could do with some cheering up as well,' David pointed out.

'I've finished my bedroom,' Eric announced.

'Really?' Leigh asked.

'Yup, I've laid out my Star Wars duvet and my Britney calendar and it already feels like home.'

'Eric, how old are you? Christ! Britney!' Tanya giggled.

'So Tanya, have you made up the lists?' Eric asked.

'What lists?' Tanya questioned.

'House rules.'

'No, should I have done?' Tanya coloured slightly.

'No, I just thought you might have,' Eric replied.

'Eric are you trying to say I'm bossy?' Tanya looked agitated.

'No, of course not, just organised. I like that in a woman.'

'Great,' Tanya replied curtly. She wasn't sure she liked the way Eric felt he could tease her.

'Eric shut up. Tanya you'll get used to him, he ribs everyone. Anyway, if it wasn't for your organisational skills we wouldn't be here, let's raise a toast to that. To Tanya!'

'Tanya!' they echoed. Leigh almost cried at the kindness of Gus, but she also felt cheated that she wasn't on the receiving end.

'Smoke anyone?' Eric asked. David was the only one who took him up on his offer.

'So what do you think we should do with this room?' Leigh asked.

'Pictures . . . ? And a big mirror would look good,' Tanya suggested.

'Well I think we need a television, a video, a stereo and a Playstation far more urgently,' Eric pointed out.

On cue the three men got up and disappeared. When they returned they were bearing gifts. David brought a big television that he had initially put in his room, then went back and got the video recorder. Gus carried in a box containing his stereo and Eric produced a Playstation.

'What about us?' Leigh said.

'What about you?' Eric asked.

'Well what should we provide?'

'How about some shiny poles so you can dance for us,' Eric suggested.

'Beer,' David offered.

'How about you two can be in charge of making it look homely,' Gus added sensibly.

'We'll go shopping tomorrow,' Tanya said.

'OK, but I'm not pole dancing,' Leigh giggled.

'Shame,' Eric lamented.

'Well maybe we can be persuaded,' Tanya raised her eyebrows.

'What do I need to do?' Eric asked.

'Behave yourself for one thing.'

'Shit, I think I've met my match,' Eric laughed.

'You better believe it,' Tanya said taking his joint off him. Leigh wished she could be more like her.

'So, here's to the first night in our house,' David said, opening more champagne.

Everyone sipped contentedly, wondering what the new house would have in store.

The five of them were looking for something. In some instances it might have been the same thing. But now that they had moved in, it wasn't just a house any more. They were hoping for something else. If a house does have a personality, then this one had the leftovers from Brian, which didn't amount to much. If the house did have anything in store for them, it might need a bit of help from one or more of its occupants.

Chapter Nine

'Don't you think it feels a bit "studenty", you know, five people living together?' David asked, only to be shot a warning look by Tanya. They were sitting at the breakfast bar, on their first proper day in their new home. Tanya and Leigh had done a bit of shopping and found one or two items to brighten up their surroundings. They had also visited the supermarket. It had been a long and painful trip. Now they were eating sandwiches.

'No, we're all professionals, but we're young. This way we benefit from a nice house, and we get to meet more people,' Tanya responded.

'How?' Eric asked.

'We get to meet each other's friends of course,' Tanya replied. Eric realised that this wasn't the right time to tell her he didn't have any more friends.

'She's right, it'll be more sociable this way,' Gus agreed. He knew that Eric didn't have any friends, apart from David who didn't seem to have any either. Tanya and Leigh were not exactly overwhelmed with friends themselves. Tanya had discarded her 'London companions', when she moved in with Nathan, and the people who had since become her friends had discarded her as soon as the split occurred. Leigh had socialised with people she worked with, but they weren't exactly at the 'come to my place' stage.

'I think it'll be fine, as long as we keep it clean,' Leigh pointed out. Her head was full of parties. Intimate dinners for five, where she would sit opposite Gus. Larger parties where she could invite the cool people she worked with and flirt with Gus. Parties of two, when everyone else was out and she and Gus would have their own private party. In the bath. She shuddered then blushed. Tanya looked at her sharply.

Dinner parties, Tanya thought. She would take charge of catering and guest lists. She would invite people she was intending to meet from the film industry. Gus would play her co-host. She thought that Eric's friends, if they were as mad as him, would add colour to the proceedings. Leigh's advertising friends would be useful too, if she had any. David? Well, David probably wouldn't contribute anybody, unless Internet geeks became fashionable; but Gus would provide intelligent, good-looking doctors.

They were all lost in their own thoughts; ones which bore little resemblance to reality.

The first week in the house passed by quickly. It passed without major incident or much interest. There had been a few minor conflicts. Tanya had unearthed Eric's habit of putting empty milk cartons back in the fridge and had told him sternly to stop. David had left a mess in the bathroom sink after shaving and Tanya ensured that he wouldn't be doing that again. Leigh was accused, by Tanya, of spending too much time in the bathroom and because Tanya had said to her in front of everyone, 'It's not your personal beauty salon', she had been embarrassed and now timed her bathroom visits. Only Gus was innocent of any crime. Eric, who stood up to Tanya, the way no one else did, told her that the things she was picking them up for were insignificant in the whole scheme of things. But, like schoolchildren they all agreed to try harder.

Other than that, they hardly saw each other. Leigh was so happy to have her own room she spent most of her time in it. David spent much of his time on the Internet, which was nothing new. He fell into a routine of coming home from work, eating, spending time on the Internet and emerging late evening to get stoned with Eric. Gus spent most of his time at work. Or on dates that Leigh and Tanya knew nothing about. By the time he arrived home, the only thing he wanted was his bed.

Tanya was disappointed. She didn't know what she had expected, but it was more than she had got. She thought they would spend the first week bonding, talking, laughing and flirting. There was no fun. When Tanya had decided that it was all right for them to move in together, she thought that it would be great. She expected them to behave like the friends in *Friends*. Instead, they were living separate lives. It was not her plan. When she returned from work she would eat with Leigh, David and sometimes Eric, then they would disperse and she would be left alone. Tanya hated being on her own, she wasn't very good at being on her own. Every evening all she had to look forward to was solitary television watching.

By Sunday night, she had had enough. No one had gone out at the weekend. They had spent it in the same way that they had spent the week. David locked to his computer, Leigh shut in her bedroom, Gus working and Eric smoking his new joints. Tanya now decided it was time to talk.

'Guys, we haven't spent any time together this week, I mean, we should at least spend *some* time together,' Tanya whined.

'What?' Eric said.

'What's the point of all living together if we never see each other?' she continued.

'We see each other every day,' Leigh pointed out.

'No. No we don't. We pass each other every day. We should get to know each other, maybe eat together more, spend evenings together, even go out.'

'I've been working,' Gus said.

'I know and that's my first point. Gus, you should put your schedule up on the fridge so we know when you're around.' Leigh had to admit that that was a good idea.

'Why?' Gus asked.

'Because then we know that if you're working nights, we should be quiet in the morning. If we need to discuss things then we know when we can get you.' Tanya smiled.

'Fine,' Gus agreed.

'Eric, you spend hours making joints in your room, if you made them in the living room at least we could share in this pastime of yours. You are highly antisocial,' Tanya stormed. Leigh giggled.

'Leigh don't fucking laugh. All *you* do is read,' Tanya continued.

'That's not fair,' Leigh protested.

'Yeah, come on Tanya, you can't have a go at us for leading normal lives,' David reasoned.

'Normal . . . Normal? You call yourselves normal. David, you spend all your time on that bloody computer and you never ever tell us what you're doing. You are all behaving like a bunch of boring people.' Tanya was shouting. She wasn't quite sure how she had arrived at her anger, but she had.

'Tanya, calm down. If you want us to spend more time together we will, but we've only been here a week.' Leigh tried to pacify Tanya as she always did.

'And Gus isn't boring, he's working,' Eric added.

'And I *have* to spend time on my computer,' David protested.

'Fine. Then you will just have to do it in your own time,' Tanya continued.

'But isn't this our own time?' Eric said, thinking that either he was very stoned or Tanya was off her trolley.

'No, it's *our* time, *all* of us. We are housemates and we need to behave like housemates.' Tanya sat down.

'Right. Well I guess we just endeavour to spend more time together then,' Gus conceded.

'Exactly.' Tanya smiled.

'I still don't quite understand. You want us to hang out more? You want us to bond? You want me to build my joints in here?'

'Yes Eric, I do.'

'I told you, you should have drawn up a list of rules; I guess

I'm just slow on the uptake.' Everyone laughed apart from Tanya.

'Eric, I tell you what. We settle this by playing Tomb Raider and if I win then you spend the next month as I say and if you win you can spend as much time in your room as you like,' Tanya stormed.

'Great idea. God Tanya you are a scary chick.'

'I am not a bloody chick,' she replied and went to the Playstation.

The others looked on, horrified by the scene as the battle commenced. She beat him which he found both surprising and amusing.

'I guess I'm spending more time in here then,' he said.

'Oh yes you are,' Tanya stated.

When Leigh went to bed that night, she thought about what Tanya had said. She loved her with all her heart, but she also knew she was being unreasonable. They were grown ups, they were professionals and Tanya wanted them to behave the way Leigh had when she was at university. After living on the floor at Jason's flat she had relished having her own room and she relished the privacy. The way Leigh saw it was that at their age, sharing a house was just that. She liked the idea of spending more time with Gus, she had to admit, and she loved David and Tanya. She was also fond of Eric, but she liked her own space and she didn't really want Tanya's demands to ruin that.

David walked to his room and passed the computer, feeling his normal compulsion to switch it on. He didn't. He had smoked too much and his head felt giddy. After everyone else had gone to bed he had been smoking and playing racing games with Eric while they tried to dissect Tanya's behaviour. Eric said that at least she let people sleep. David laughed, but he defended her because, although he wasn't sure why, he had always defended her.

David knew Tanya hated being alone. He also knew that her

social life had nose-dived since she had split up with Nathan the ex-lover. When she lived with him, David had only seen Tanya once every three months or so, now she wanted him to spend all his time with her. He understood, but he couldn't help but feel that that wasn't really what being housemates was all about. He was happy with the fact that he had moved out of his old rat hole. He loved his room and he liked the people he lived with. That was all David wanted in life apart from building the website that would make him a millionaire.

David had worked in computers and been there at the beginning of the Internet revolution. He had failed to build a commercially viable site, for reasons he couldn't explain. That was his aim; he needed to keep working at it until he succeeded. So, Tanya saying they had to spend more time together was a hindrance to his plans. He hoped he would be able to find a way to get round her. He doubted whether there was any way round her.

Gus tucked himself into his duvet and wrapped it around himself for comfort. He was more tired than he could remember due to the killer week he'd had. He thought about his first week in the new house and how he hadn't had time for any of his new housemates. This was a temporary blip, he knew that there would be plenty of opportunity to get to know them. Of course, he knew Eric, but that was different. He sighed as he thought of Tanya. He liked her, he really did and he didn't really mind her bossing them around, but he knew that if she really did intend on making them spend loads of time together he wouldn't be able to meet his perfect girl.

Eric looked at the plans laid out on the floor and tried to work out where he'd gone wrong. He had been so sure that the prototype for joint number fifteen would be the perfect one. He numbered each attempt and the reason he was only at fifteen was that he had obliterated his worst ones from the file. He drew up new plans each time. Size, weight, paper, strength, tobacco/ cannabis ratio and roach material were all taken into consideration. However, the perfect formula eluded him still.

He thought of Tanya. She was so bossy and she scared him. He didn't mind spending more time with the others, after all being in his room for hours wasn't healthy, but he couldn't understand why she was so upset. He would have thought that a trendy media type such as herself would have had a million friends and a million places to go. The fact that she wanted to spend time with an Internet nerd, a smoking nerd, a doctor nerd and Leigh puzzled him. The only conclusion he could come to was that Tanya wasn't happy being a media bird and really wanted to be a media nerd. If that were the case then he would be more than happy to hang around with her.

Tanya tidied her room before going to bed. She was glad she had spoken out, but hoped that they didn't think she was a gorgon from hell. She wasn't, she was just assertive. Assertive with her life, her friends and her relationships. After all, she had walked away from Nathan, who was rich and well-connected. She could have stayed, but she didn't. She was assertive with Leigh and she knew she'd done her a favour by persuading her to move to London. She was assertive with David, spending all that time on the computer was unhealthy. No, she knew she'd done the right thing.

She just wished she didn't feel so lonely. Work was a nightmare. Since she had started thinking about films she knew she had come to the end of the road in her current job. She didn't love it any more and she always loved working. She felt hurt that Leigh didn't want to be constantly by her side any more, and, strangely, she missed Nathan.

When they'd lived together, Tanya was never alone. If Nathan wasn't there, someone was. People came to see them all the time; she went out, to parties, clubs and bars. Her life was hectic. She knew that she shouldn't take her loneliness out on her new housemates and she really couldn't make them spend all their time with her. Surely, she wasn't being unreasonable in asking for a bit of it.

Chapter Ten

'Harvey, get up, you've been asleep for ages,' Cherry said, pulling his duvet away.

'I'm jet-lagged,' Harvey replied grumpily, opening his eyes.

'We all are, but we can't spend all our time here asleep; you may have forgotten but we have a movie to make.'

'All in good time Cherry. Now will you make me coffee while I have a shower?'

'OK boss.' Cherry walked into the kitchen.

They had been in London for over a week, although it seemed longer. Bob had got up early and gone to have a look round and Cherry was bored. It was raining again and the outside world looked as uninviting as it could. The lure of the shops didn't get to her. She knew she would ruin her expensive shoes if she stepped out of the door. She wondered how women in London coped.

Cherry made coffee and turned on the television. She was watching shows she'd never heard of that seemed to be aimed at teenagers. At home she wasn't a huge fan of television, in London it seemed to be the only thing she could do to while away the hours.

Bob returned, soaking wet.

'Bob, look at you. Did you have to go out?'

'I was going stir crazy. Anyway, at least now I've been out I know I am never doing it again. Where's Harvey?'

'I finally managed to get him out of bed. He's taking a shower, and you should too, I don't want you getting sick.'

'Yes boss.'

'I'll get you some coffee when you come out.'

'Thanks boss.' Bob gave Cherry an affectionate squeeze and went to his room.

'Something smells good,' Harvey said as he emerged fully-dressed from his room.

'It's me. But there's some coffee too,' Cherry replied.

'You are a goddess. Has anyone told you that?'

'You . . . all the damn time. Harvey have you seen the weather? It's raining real hard and Bob got soaked and he'll probably catch something.'

'Right. Well I'm sure it can't rain every day,' Harvey said reasonably.

'If it does I'm going home. Harvey why didn't you choose Barbados?'

'Because I didn't. Anyway, it's probably the rainy season there.' Harvey drank his coffee and Cherry sat down in front of the television.

'I'll take you shopping,' Harvey offered.

'What about work?'

'Honey, there's plenty of time for work. Anyway, we all need to acclimatise.'

'Harvey, if this weather continues I will never acclimatise.'

'Enough, let's go out,' Harvey said.

'But I can't. I don't have shoes to go out in,' Cherry replied, horrified at the idea.

'Why don't you wear sneakers?' Harvey suggested.

'Harvey, I don't have sneakers, I have Gucci trainers,' Cherry retorted.

'What's the point in that? Trainers are for running, walking and ruining.'

'You're a man. How can I expect you to understand?'

'Good point. Listen how about I go and get you some shoes that you can ruin, and then we'll go out.'

'I don't know.'

'Cherry we've been here for ages and you still refuse to go outside. I said I'd take you shopping and I mean I am taking you shopping. Now, I'll go and buy you some shoes and then when I come back we'll go out. You told me you were desperate to go to Harrods.'

'But, not in the rain.'

'You don't have a choice, it seems to rain all the time here,' Bob piped up.

'Thanks for pointing that out Bob,' Harvey snapped.

'My feet are a size six but I guess the shoes are different here,' Cherry said. She knew that Harvey only used that tone of voice when he meant business.

'Everything is different here. That's why we came.' Harvey was losing patience. 'I'll get you some shoes and when I come back we are going shopping. Oh and that includes you Bob.' Harvey turned and walked out of the door before anyone could protest.

No one was enjoying London. The flat they had admired had become a prison. Bob hated the rain, Cherry hated the rain and Harvey hated the rain. They had taken to snapping at each other and they hadn't done any work. Rain had flooded their brains and Cherry felt cold all the time, even with the heating on full blast. Bob was bored. He didn't come to London to sit in an apartment, and Harvey seemed devoid of ideas.

While he was out an e-mail came from Steve Delaney. He wanted to know how things were going. If only he knew, Cherry said to herself before replying with a positive message which was a blatant lie.

'Bob, why are we doing this?' Cherry asked him as she poured herself some coffee.

'I thought you'd know, you normally know what he's doing,' Bob replied.

'Well I guess we have to humour him, Harvey hates being questioned; it's the one thing he can't cope with. We'll go shopping, get wet and we'll pretend to be happy.' Cherry smiled.

'Sure.' Bob shook his head.

Harvey returned with shopping bags.

'Look guys, look what I've bought you.' He began unpacking with child-like excitement. He pulled out a pair of trainers for Cherry, three beige macs and his most important purchase; three umbrellas.

'Great,' Cherry said putting the trainers on. She hated them.

'Thanks,' Bob said, eyeing the mac suspiciously.

Harvey led them around Knightsbridge like a tour guide. Bob and Cherry followed obediently. It was busy, for a reason they couldn't fathom. The weather had seemed to make everyone in London want to shop. Cherry had no enthusiasm, she would never be able to wear nice clothes in London so saw little point in buying any. Bob wasn't the sort of man who enjoyed shopping anyway.

Eventually Harvey took them to a pub for lunch. Dripping over the stone floor, Cherry didn't think she would be able to survive, especially as they didn't even have any work to keep them focused. Harvey ordered pints of beer for him and Bob, and a double vodka and tonic for the bemused Cherry.

They sat at a wooden table nursing their drinks. Harvey took in the atmosphere but the customers seemed to be mainly other shoppers; he was disappointed not to find any 'eccentric' British characters. Cherry stared into her drink, feeling as if she had a pool of water in her trainers, and Bob drank quickly hoping to warm himself up on the weird concoction he seemed to be drinking.

'So, it's not so bad is it?' Harvey asked.

'No,' Cherry replied, taking a sip of her drink.

'Harvey, can I be honest without risking you ripping out my throat?' Bob requested.

'Sure,' Harvey smiled.

'It's terrible. Not just the weather, but the fact that we aren't getting anywhere. It's been a week, a week of doing nothing, and I for one am going nuts.'

'I know, I agree. But the thing is that we're almost there. I can feel it. We're meeting Bill Harrison, our "director", for dinner tonight. We're going to pick his brains about talent.'

'Well, that sounds like progress,' Bob admitted.

'Sure is. Anyway, we're going to a top restaurant; so we'll do some work and get some decent food.'

'Harvey, can I stay behind, I feel a cold hitting me?'

'Sure honey, you OK? You need anything, a doctor, some medicine, anything?'

'I'll be fine Harvey.' Cherry smiled weakly.

Cherry was fine. Apart from her reluctance to step out in the rain, she had something else she had to do that evening. For a week she had been spending time in her bedroom watching British television. For a week she had become hooked on a number of programmes that they broadcast. These programmes were described as 'reality television' and she hadn't seen anything like it before. She knew they had the same stuff in the States, but she didn't watch them back home. She had three shows she wanted to see that evening.

Cherry hadn't shared any of this with Harvey because she thought he might mock her interest in something so banal.

At the same time she was pleased that Harvey *appeared* to be making some progress. It was about time. As she waved Bob and Harvey off to their dinner she settled in front of the television for her latest instalment of 'Real Urban Housewives'.

Harvey and Bob returned several hour later and found Cherry lying on the sofa watching a TV show about holiday romances.

'What's this?' Harvey asked, giving her an affectionate kiss on the cheek.

'Oh, it's just some dumb show,' Cherry explained.

'So you've become a fan of British television?' Bob asked.

'No, it's just that none of you were here so I had nothing to do,' Cherry protested her innocence.

'How are you feeling?' Harvey asked compassionately.

'Fine honey. How was your dinner?'

'Really great. Bill gave me a list of young talented people who work in film production. He has had them all recommended to him, so I guess we can start by setting up interviews.'

'You mean I have work to do?' Cherry teased, cursing the fact that she would never know if Nigel and Janice ever worked things out.

'Yup, sure do. I want to meet these people as soon as possible. Can you get on to it tomorrow?'

'Sure, but what do I tell them?' Cherry asked.

'Tell them that a Hollywood hotshot wants a meeting. That's all they need to know at this stage.'

'Who's that then?' Bob asked.

'Shit, I knew you shouldn't have had so much brandy,' Harvey responded.

'OK boss, the game's up, I'm hitting the sack.' Bob smiled and went to his room.

'So is British television as dire as ours?' Harvey asked.

'I don't know, I never watch it much at home. But you know what? There seems to be this weird fascination with reality TV,' Cherry replied.

'What, like "The Truman Show"?'

'Not exactly, but if all I've seen is anything to go by, everyone wants to watch real people doing real things. Vets, doctors, holidaymakers, even people in prison, it's all over the place.'

'Any good?' Harvey asked.

'Well, not really. It's dull but compulsive, you know what I mean?'

'Sure, I do. Dull but compulsive. Interesting. What do we have now?'

'Holiday romances. This is a show where they follow young people in a resort somewhere hideous and watch everyone getting off with everyone else.'

'Shit, these girls wear too much make-up and too much Lycra,' Harvey said looking at the screen.

'Tell me about it. The guys aren't much better, they all talk about scoring, as if they're footballers.'

Cherry smiled as Harvey sat down next to her. Having him there made her feel warm inside and safe. She had such love for him, it was growing by the day. She had a feeling that it was only a matter of time. London might not turn out so bad after all.

They watched the end of the show together, had a nightcap at Harvey's insistence, 'to ward off her cold', and they discussed Harvey's evening. Cherry felt as if she had never been closer to him than she was at that moment.

Harvey had trouble sleeping that night. He couldn't figure out what was bothering him but he knew that it meant he was close to an idea. This always happened when he was about to make a discovery. The curse of his insomnia was actually a blessing in disguise.

Chapter Eleven

Cosmetically, the house in Fulham was going through a meta-morphosis. The sitting room had been filled with pictures, candles and cushions to make it look cosy. Eric had added a beanbag, Gus had contributed a painting an ex-girlfriend had given him and David had bought a stacker for their Playstation games and CDs. It was beginning to look lived-in.

Tanya had used Gus's work schedule to organise a house meal once a week. That week, the chosen day was Tuesday. David had offered to make a curry, which Eric helped along by adding a dash of his finest grass to the sauce. Leigh had put on her new denim jeans and snakeskin boots and what seemed to be her entire make-up collection. Tanya chose the wine and all Gus had to do was turn up. He did.

As they sat around their table, adorned with candles, they started eating.

'David, you make the best curries,' Leigh said.

'Thanks.'

'It's really good, what did you use?' Gus asked.

'Trade secret,' David laughed, knowing about Eric's con-tribution.

'So what is everyone doing this weekend?' Tanya asked.

'I'm going to a work dinner on Friday, but I've got no plans for Saturday,' Leigh replied.

'I've got loads of work to do on my Internet site,' David said.

'What site is this?' Tanya asked.

'Well, it's a sort of dating thing,' David mumbled.

'Dating? I'm not being funny but you don't really know much about dating,' Tanya pointed out.

'Tanya, shut up. Aren't there a lot of dating sites out there already?' Leigh asked more kindly. Gus and Eric kept eating.

'Yes, but this will be different.' David looked embarrassed.

'Well, if you think it'll work, then good.' Leigh sensed his obvious discomfort.

'I still think it'll probably have been done before,' Tanya pushed.

'Well maybe it has, but I'll make this better; different,' David answered, defiantly.

'How?' Tanya pushed.

'I haven't worked out all the details yet.' Tanya nodded her head. David never worked out details which is why he'd never been able to set up a site properly.

'We could design a website for my joint mission,' Eric suggested.

'Only if we all want to get arrested,' Gus pointed out.

'Oh yeah. Well, don't worry David, I'm sure between us we can give you some ideas.'

'Thanks.' David smiled. He knew his idea for a dating site was a non-starter. Annoyingly, Tanya was right, nearly everything seemed to have been done before. His room hadn't given him the much hoped for inspiration yet. He was feeling down-hearted, frustrated and restless. He put so much of his energy into his Internet ideas that he had little left.

'Eric?' Tanya said.

'Yes, *sir*.' Eric sat up straight.

'What are you doing this weekend?' she asked trying to ignore the sarcasm.

'I'm working on a new prototype, and Gus has a date on Saturday night,' he added, to ensure any more questions were directed away from him. He was too relaxed to deal with Tanya.

68

FAITH BLEASDALE

Leigh looked at Gus, then she looked at her food. She felt tears welling up.

'Who's the lucky girl?' David asked.

'Oh, just some girl I met at the hospital,' Gus said.

'And does this girl have a name?' Tanya demanded.

'Kate.'

'And she's a trainee doctor and she's on a work placement from university which makes her about, what, nineteen?' Eric teased.

'Twenty-three actually,' Gus said. He looked around the table. Leigh staring at her food, David looking at Leigh and Tanya giving him an evil look. 'It's just a date,' he said, unsure why he had to make excuses.

They lapsed into silence for the rest of the meal, until Leigh went from wanting to suffocate herself in her curry to laughing for no apparent reason.

'Why are you laughing?' Tanya asked.

'Because we all sit here at our house dinner and we all seem to feel really uncomfortable.'

'That's not funny. We are still getting to know each other,' Tanya replied. Then Eric started sniggering.

'Leigh's right. We sit here and we don't seem to have any natural conversation skills. There must be something wrong with us.'

'There is *nothing* wrong with us,' Tanya protested.

'Apart from the fact that we're all really boring,' David said catching the giggles.

'Bloody hell, we *are* all so boring,' Gus agreed, bursting out laughing

'I don't agree,' Tanya said.

'Oh Tanya, don't you see, we're just a bunch of boring, boring people.' Leigh was clutching her sides.

'Not only that but we don't seem to have any sanity,' Eric added.

'Or jokes,' Gus said.

'Or talent,' David finished.

69

'That's because you guys are boring, talentless morons,' Tanya shouted and then *she* started laughing, although she had no idea why.

'I know,' Eric said when the laughing subsided. 'Let's have a football competition on the Playstation.'

They played a mini-tournament and the boys outshone the girls. Tanya couldn't focus and kept thinking she was the other team, Leigh didn't know how the game worked, while Gus, Eric and David seemed to take it too seriously. When Gus was finally declared the winner, they all sat down and had a beer to celebrate.

'I'm hungry,' Tanya announced, surprisingly.

'Me too,' Leigh agreed, 'really hungry.'

'Let's make toast,' Tanya suggested.

'Make some for me will you?' Eric asked.

'I could do with some as well,' Gus added.

'After all the trouble I went to cooking dinner,' David said.

'Sorry, David, I'm not sure why I'm so hungry,' Leigh apologised.

'Well you better get me some then and make sure mine has jam on it.'

While Tanya and Leigh went to the kitchen, the others started laughing.

'You have to stop spiking the food,' Gus said.

'Sorry, but they do smoke sometimes, I wouldn't have done it otherwise,' Eric replied.

'Yeah, but they have no idea why they're giggling like idiots and why they're hungry,' David pointed out.

'I promise I won't do it again. I just thought it might make Tanya easier to handle,' Eric said.

'It'll take more than that,' Gus pointed out.

'You're not wrong there.'

They dug into the toast mountain that Tanya produced. Afterwards she began to feel dizzy.

'I'm going to bed, I feel really drunk,' Tanya announced. Eric and David exchanged glances.

'Me too,' Leigh said, moving reluctantly from beside Gus. She allowed herself one last glance at the object of her desire before leaving the room.

The boys loaded up another game on to the Playstation.

'So where should I take her?' Gus asked.

'Who?' David responded.

'My date . . . Saturday . . . remember.'

'Oh I know, take her to heaven,' Eric suggested, laughing.

'Shut up Eric. I think she might be special,' Gus sighed.

'You always say that,' Eric pointed out.

'I do not. Anyway she's really lovely,' Gus added.

'Yeah and she's blonde, about seven feet tall with a really cute arse,' Eric said.

'How do you do it?' David asked.

'I have no idea. But it's not about looks anyway. I feel a connection with her,' Gus continued.

'You always say that as well,' Eric repeated.

'I do not. Do you think I should talk about poetry?'

'No way mate,' David said quickly.

'Why not?' Gus asked.

'Because it's only a first date. You don't want to scare her with sonnets.'

'But girls like poetry don't they?' Gus pushed.

'Gus, man, you're such a pussy. Take her for dinner, talk about normal stuff and get her into bed. Christ man, it's about time you started behaving like a man,' Eric stated. 'Anyway Melinda the medic will be more interested in anatomy than poetry.'

'She's called Kate and I am a man, I'm just not bothered about sex all the time. I want to get to know her,' Gus persisted.

'Gus, I don't mean to be rude, but, well you don't seem to act like most blokes our age,' David pointed out tactfully.

'Well I'm not most blokes. I want so badly to fall in love. I hate this shallow dating and dumping. It's just not me.'

'Eric's right, you are a pussy,' David laughed.

71

'Thanks, maybe I should ask the girls.' Gus was upset. He was stoned and he always felt oversensitive when he was stoned.

'Not a good idea,' Eric said. He and David exchanged glances.

'Why not?' he asked.

'Well because Tanya will present you with a four-page plan and Leigh will just . . . well I'm not sure Leigh is an expert on dating,' David concluded.

'I wonder why she doesn't have a man,' Gus pondered.

'Maybe she's working on it,' David replied. He exchanged another glance with Eric.

'Who?' Gus asked. They both rolled their eyes. For a man who was so lusted after, Gus was really quite dumb.

'Search me,' Eric answered. They all concentrated on the skateboard game, that was much safer territory.

Chapter Twelve

Cherry worked her way through Bill's list and noticed that the women far outnumbered the men. This annoyed her, although she wasn't sure why. Harvey was purely professional when it came to work, too damn professional Cherry often thought.

She had drawn up a list of twenty people to interview, but for what? Even the interviewer had no idea what he was looking for. When Cherry asked Harvey, he said, 'I'll know when I find them.' The subject was closed.

Cherry's addiction to fly-on-the-wall television had grown. Now Harvey had joined her, they spent their evenings glued to it, and even Bob had become a reluctant convert. He rightly observed that it was as addictive as drugs, and likened its power to that of a religions cult. For these American 'big shots', reality television had become an important part of their lives.

A daily routine had been established. Harvey and Bob would go out during the day, exploring London and getting wet. Cherry would stay at the office, dealing with e-mails, calls from the studio in LA, arranging appointments and anything else she could think of. She would only break away to watch television.

Harvey began to love London. He even liked the rain now that he had a huge umbrella to carry around. They travelled by taxi, and tube, they went all over the city looking for inspiration. By the time the first 'interviews' were due Harvey had had numerous sleepless nights, and knew that he was close to a breakthrough.

Cherry gave Simon on the front desk a list of the people they were expecting. She ordered Bob out of the flat. He wasn't interested in meeting any of these candidates, especially as no one knew what they were candidates for. He took his umbrella – as always – and left for the day.

Cherry made a pot of coffee and ensured that the office was neat and tidy. She was very conscientious and wanted everything to look professional. She even made Harvey wear a suit.

'No one wears suits in our business,' he objected.

'But you look good in a suit, and anyway, British people like suits.' The argument was closed.

The first person arrived. His name was Daniel Fisher and he was wearing what looked like a yellow waterproof outfit.

'Hi, Daniel, I'm Cherry, Harvey Cannon's assistant. Would you come through, please.' Cherry smiled, and thought that maybe Harvey had been right about the suit.

'God, you look bright,' Harvey said when he saw him.

'Hello Mr Cannon,' Daniel stuck out his hand.

'Call me Harvey. So about your outfit?'

'Well, my girlfriend is a fashion designer, she designed this for me,' he explained.

'Take a seat, can I get you coffee?' Cherry interrupted before Harvey could tell him he looked like a banana.

'Yes please, milk no sugar.' Daniel smiled, and tried to look and sound confident. He failed.

'So, tell me, what are you doing at the moment?' Harvey said, already having lost interest. If a guy could dress up like that to please his girlfriend he wasn't what Harvey was looking for.

The meeting lasted twenty minutes. Enough time for Daniel to spill his coffee and for Harvey to ask a few boring questions and not listen to the answers. When he'd gone, Harvey burst out laughing.

'Do you think Bill is playing tricks on me?' he asked.

'Harvey, just because he looked strange doesn't mean he isn't talented,' Cherry protested.

'Well I know, but I couldn't work with him, or his girlfriend. He looked like an egg yolk.'

'Strike one,' Cherry said, and crossed his name from her list.

After Daniel, it wasn't just their dress sense that disappointed. A girl called Miranda had come a close second in the clothes department. She was wearing trousers made out of purple feathers. She looked like a parrot.

Simona talked about arthouse films. Harvey, who had never seen the point in arthouse, found her boring. Danielle flirted with him, which annoyed Cherry. And Louise was too pompous. Harvey knew he wouldn't be seeing any of them again.

'If Bill regards these people as talented, we might as well pack up and go home,' he moaned. Cherry had to agree. Sure, some were confident, knowledgeable and even experienced, but there was nothing there. Harvey was looking for a vital spark. By the end of the day, he was asking people about their personal lives: friends, home; families. Unsure why he was asking these questions, he knew the answers were wrong.

The day was an education for them both.

'I'm calling Bill,' Harvey said.

'There's always tomorrow,' Cherry suggested.

'Fuck tomorrow. If it's anything like today I'll be slitting my wrists.'

'I may join you.'

The second day of interviews proved no more fruitful than the first. Although there were some obviously talented people, Harvey was not impressed.

'Harvey, maybe if we knew what we were looking for it'd be easier,' Cherry suggested.

'I *do* know,' Harvey replied.

'But we don't even know what you need them to do,' she protested.

'I'll know when I find them,' Harvey insisted.

Bill replaced the receiver, sighed and took his feet off the desk. He had sent Harvey every young person he knew who worked in the business. Despite Harvey's objections, he *had* sent him talent.

Bill worked in the newly revived British film industry and had participated in films that had become international hits. Harvey accused him of not knowing what he was talking about, but Bill did know. The reason he tried to pacify Harvey was that he owed him. Harvey had introduced Bill to a film when they were both in LA and he had helped make Bill's career. Due to its success Bill was able to move to England with his British wife. He had a lot to thank Harvey for, although he had forgotten what a pain he could be. Harvey's request had been vague, details about his project had been vague – although Bill wasn't sure how little Harvey actually knew. He wanted to help him, but he was unsure how; his contact list was exhausted.

Just as he was about to admit defeat Bill remembered a party he'd been to the previous week. He'd met a stunning girl called Serena, who let him stare at her cleavage while she questioned him about the film business. He had managed to grasp – despite the fact that the cleavage was magnificent and mesmerising – that her boyfriend's sister was interested in film production. The fact that she hadn't told him that she wanted to be an actress and had only spoken of this other girl had ensured that he remembered. Because he wanted to sleep with her he had suggested they should have lunch to discuss it. If this girl was no good, then he would tell Harvey he was on his own. At least he would get to see Serena again. He picked up the phone.

Chapter Thirteen

The Monday after the first house dinner, everyone was in the sitting room watching television. The phone rang. Tanya looked around but no one moved. She went to answer it.

'Hello,' Tanya said.

'Tanya darling, it's Serena.'

'Hi, Ser, how are you?' Tanya stood staring at her hair in the mirror. The glints from her highlights sparkled.

'I'm fine. Jason and I want to see your house, we can't believe you haven't invited us, but as you haven't then we're inviting ourselves. I really need to talk to you so I thought we'd come on Friday.'

'Oh . . .' Tanya said, with as much enthusiasm as she could muster.

'We can't wait to meet your housemates. We know Leigh of course and we've met David, but we want to meet the new boys.'

'They're probably busy,' Tanya lied, she knew that they would probably be doing exactly what they were doing now, loafing around. That was all anyone seemed to do.

'Nonsense, tell them that it's important. I won't hear any excuses. I need to discuss something really important with you and if I can't meet your housemates then I won't.' The subject was closed. With a sinking heart, Tanya replaced the receiver. She considered this for a moment before walking back to the sitting room. Leigh was sitting on the sofa, staring at Gus. Gus was almost asleep (due not only to work, but also his new girlfriend Kate), Eric was making a joint and David had a notebook on his lap and was staring at a blank page. They were not proving the fun-loving people Tanya wanted to be around, and she wasn't sure she wanted anyone else to know this.

'I'm organising a dinner party for Friday. I expect you're all around, so I guess you have no arguments. I'm inviting my brother and his girlfriend, and if you guys want to invite anyone just let me know,' Tanya announced.

'I don't know anyone,' Leigh said, although she did know Jason and Serena.

'No one I want to have over for dinner anyway, although I have met this girl on the Internet,' David added.

'Well bring your computer to dinner and we'll have a cyber dinner date,' Eric chuckled.

'Eric, shut up. Are you inviting anyone.'

'Only my friend Mr Joint.' Eric smiled at Tanya.

'Christ you sad bunch of losers. Doesn't anyone know anyone apart from us?' Tanya said.

'I'll bring Kate,' Gus offered. He didn't notice Tanya's scowl or Leigh's blush.

'Still seeing her mate?' David asked.

'Well we've had a couple of dates, nothing serious,' Gus said.

'What about the sack?' Eric asked.

'None of your business, but she's really sweet and she asks me questions.'

'Shit, Gus, Tanya asks you questions, you need a girl for . . . sex,' Eric lamented.

'OK, so Gus, you ask whatever her name is, and we'll have dinner at eight. Leigh and I will cook.' Tanya moved the topic quickly away from sex.

'We will?' Leigh squeaked, she was upset.

'Yes; end of story.'

Tanya faced them: arms crossed, lips contorted into a defiant shape, it had become known in the house as 'The Tanya', and, unbeknown to her, Eric had managed to imitate it perfectly.

Leigh was mortified. Gus was bringing a girl – a girl he dated. Part of her wanted to see the competition, another part didn't. She tried to talk to Tanya about it.

'Why did you have to ask him to bring her?' She pouted.

'I didn't, I just asked if anyone wanted to bring anyone. Leigh, he's dating her, we'll have to meet her sooner or later.'

'I know, but well, I just hope she's horrible.' Leigh sulked. Eric walked into the kitchen and put the kettle on.

'What are you two whispering about?'

'How sad you are for not knowing any girls,' Tanya shot.

'Well darling, I hate to point it out, but you two don't seem to know any boys.'

'We do, we just don't want to invite them here,' Tanya spat back.

'Right. So at least I have Mr Joint and David has his cyber babes, you guys are not only not bringing anyone, but you're not bringing *anything*.'

'Eric you're so sad. Your only friend is a joint, and David's only friend is a computer. Leigh and I do know men, we're just fussy. Leigh, you sure you don't know anyone you can bring?' Tanya changed tack.

'I don't know anyone well enough,' Leigh replied.

'What about work?'

'I can't invite someone from work, imagine the gossip,' Leigh was horrified.

'Tanya, how come you aren't asking anyone?' Eric sensed Leigh's discomfort.

'Because I've just come out of a long-term relationship, I'm not ready yet.'

'Sorry, I forgot.' Eric looked at Leigh and winked; Leigh giggled. Tanya scowled as if she was about to tell them off, but then changed her mind and started laughing.

'We're all a bunch of sad fucks,' she finished.

Friday night arrived and Leigh and Tanya were in the kitchen. David and Eric had been banished to the sitting room, and Gus wasn't home.

'Where do you think he is?' Leigh asked.

'Collecting Kate, maybe,' Tanya replied.

'I bet she's a bitch,' Leigh said.

'Of course she will be. Shit, you've got it bad,' Tanya responded.

'I have not. It's just that he deserves someone nice.' Leigh had discovered early on that she was unable to talk to Tanya about her feelings for Gus. Tanya would scoff every time she mentioned him. Now she realised, for the first time, that she couldn't rely on Tanya.

'Someone nice like you?'

'Yes, like me. He's so caring and romantic and she's bound to be a bitch.'

'Of course.' Tanya checked on her lasagna.

Tanya's idea of a dinner party was to keep things simple. Everyone normally drank too much and didn't appreciate the food anyway. So a nice salad with crusty bread to start, then something with pasta was her preferred option. For dessert she had bought a cheesecake. Simple, easy and tasty. The way she liked her food *and* her men.

Leigh had dressed up for the evening. She wore a pair of tight black trousers and her sexy new chiffon top. It made her breasts look appealing, not like footballs. Although she mused that if they did look like footballs Gus might pay her more attention. There was nothing more infuriating than a man you liked not regarding you as a sex object. Gus was gentle, kind and uninterested in her body.

When Jason and Serena arrived, everyone was ready apart from Gus and Kate, who still hadn't turned up. Tanya was getting angry, she didn't tolerate lateness; Eric was stoned and had started playing Tomb Raider with Jason and David. Serena chatted to Leigh while Tanya pretended to be busy in the kitchen. She wasn't busy, she was just consuming copious amounts of red wine. When she heard the key turn in the door, she leapt out ready to levy accusations, but on seeing Gus and his date she stopped in her tracks. Kate was the best looking medical student she'd ever seen, including the TV ones. Tall, blonde, slim, with piercing blue eyes and the longest legs known to man, or to Tanya anyway. She also looked young. Younger than Tanya. She hated Kate on sight.

'Hey, Tanya, sorry we're late,' Gus smiled. 'This is Kate.'

'Pleased to meet you,' Kate said holding out a hand, Tanya shook it and then ushered them into the sitting room. She thought about trying to find a way of breaking the news to Leigh before she saw Kate, softening the blow, but there was no way. When she saw Leigh's face drop as Gus introduced she wanted to hug her. Surprisingly, even Tanya had a heart.

Everyone sat down awkwardly and Tanya began to despair. Before she could do anything about it, Serena grabbed her.

'Can I have a word? In private,' she asked. They both left the room.

'Listen, I didn't want to tell you in front of the others, but I've got some good news for you.'

'Really?' Tanya prayed she wasn't going to become an aunt.

'I met this American guy at a party who is well connected in the film industry, and I gave him my number and told him about you. Well he called me. It turns out that there's this Hollywood guy in London who is looking for young talented people to make some film. Anyway, Bill, that's his name, said that he could arrange a meeting for you. Isn't that great?' Serena's eyes sparkled.

'My god, really? Yes it's great. Who is this guy? What's the movie?'

'I have no idea. All I know is that Bill quite fancies me, and because of that I am able to do you a huge favour. I had to promise to have dinner with him, but that's fine, I'm prepared to deal with that when it happens. I am so excited for you.'

Tanya had a thousand questions. She was elated. She was also apprehensive.

'Bill said he had sent every young person he knew to this guy, and he'd sent them all back. He hasn't found anyone he likes and Bill is running out of ideas. I told him you were brilliant and you are. It's going to be soon doll.'

'How soon?'

'Soon, I think.'

'So how do I prepare? What should I say?' Tanya was a little scared. It was an irrational fear. It was the fear of possible failure. Fear wasn't an emotion that Tanya would allow anyone else to witness in her, but she felt it deep in her bones.

'I don't know. Be yourself, knock his socks off. Oh and speak like the Queen, Americans love that.'

'Thanks, Serena. Oh, and I hope you don't have to spend too much time with this guy because of me.'

'Well, when you're a big Hollywood producer, you can cast me in all your films.'

'Deal.'

'Anyway, we'd better go and get this dinner under way, come on.'

'Don't tell anyone will you? I'd rather not tell anyone until after the interview.'

'That's up to you. Come on.'

As Serena led the way back to the sitting room, Tanya let all the possibilities rush through her mind. Here was the opportunity she had prayed for. The chance for her to leave her rut and do something different? She was grateful to Serena, if not a little put out by how casual she was being.

The scene in the sitting room was one of awkwardness. Kate was perched on the arm of the sofa sipping a gin and tonic; David was next to her with a beer in his hand and a strange expression on his face; Gus was standing up with Eric next to him and they were talking to no one in particular about their work. Jason was looking bemused as he sat in an armchair, staring mainly at Leigh, who was next to David with a look of horror frozen on her face. It was the look that she had adopted as soon as she had met Kate.

Tanya was thinking of her chat with Serena. Everyone noticed the change in her expression, but she offered no explanation and no one dared ask.

As Tanya dished up the starters, everyone at the table sat in silence.

'I guess we should drink a toast to your new house,' Jason said.

'Yes, it's lovely. How are you all settling in?' Serena asked.

'Great,' Leigh replied while still staring at Kate.

'I bet, especially as you have a room of your own now. Did you know she was sleeping on a mattress on the floor of my spare room?' Jason asked. Everyone nodded.

'Jas, how are you? I haven't seen you in ages,' Tanya said with false joviality. She was beginning to regret organising this dinner party and was angry that when she had something to celebrate, however secret, the others were all acting as if they were incapable of having a conversation.

'Not since you moved here. God I thought you guys must be something else to keep my sister from bugging me all the time.' At last everyone laughed.

'It is a lovely house,' Kate said.

'Thanks,' Gus replied, squeezing her hand.

'The food might be a bit plain tonight, they wouldn't let me add any of my special ingredient,' Eric said, suddenly coming to life.

'What ingredient is that?' Serena asked.

'Cannabis.'

'Eric is always stoned,' Tanya explained, shooting him one of her looks.

'Really?' Serena looked at him. 'You look normal to me.'

'Well that is the common misconception. Everyone thinks I'm a freak because I smoke, when in actual fact we all indulge in mind altering things from time to time. Why? Because we actually like to feel a little different to the norm. And is the norm really the norm? I don't think that sober or whatever is our natural state, because we all get so bored with it. It's historical really, people drink or take drugs to feel different and why not? I mean cannabis doesn't kill you and it doesn't make you violent, so I think that perhaps my state is more normal than normal.'

'Right,' Tanya said, 'of course it is Eric.' The housemates

exchanged glances. Eric was off. He was prone to rambling when he smoked. Clearly he was stoned.

'Well, it's just a theory. I mean look at all these people who question whether we really exist and say that we could never know. I mean here we are as dimensions and do we exist or not? I don't really care, but whatever I am or why I am, I like smoking so I will.'

'But it is bad for you,' Kate piped up.

'Is it? How do we know? Drinking is bad, drugs are bad, normality is good. I don't hear too many arguments to support the normal state of mind. Most of the time it's boring. By the end of this dinner most of us will have drunk loads and we'll all be totally different from when we started out. Anyway, I have to stop talking now because I'm hungry.' To emphasise the point Eric ate while everybody else drank.

Tanya couldn't understand what was happening. David hadn't said a word, Leigh was looking heartbroken and Eric was spouting rubbish, although Tanya conceded that that was all Eric did.

Thankfully the conversation returned to the realms of 'normality'. Mainly due to Jason and Serena. David answered Jason's questions about the Internet and what was new in computers. Kate answered Serena's polite questions about how she and Gus met and her course in medicine. Eric spoke whenever he had the chance or the inclination. Only Leigh remained silent.

By the main course, the atmosphere had lightened. The men were discussing football. Serena and Kate were finishing a conversation about the NHS. Leigh remained aloof and uninvolved.

'I think that the only interesting thing about football are the legs,' Kate announced.

'I agree, footballers have such lovely legs,' Serena concurred.

'If we were talking about women's legs like that, then you'd accuse us of being sexist,' Eric said in mock outrage. This comment awakened Tanya who loved nothing more than a battle of the sexes.

'No we wouldn't, as long as you weren't being sleazy, which you probably would be Eric!'

'Fine then. I think you've got great legs Tanya, and Leigh, yours are really sexy,' Eric said. Leigh snapped out of her trancelike state.

'You think I've got nice legs?' she asked.

'Yes I do. Wouldn't mind seeing them run around a field in little shorts.'

'Really Eric,' Tanya chastised, but laughed.

'Well, Serena's got hot legs,' Jason added, smiling.

'Oh Gus has got the best legs in the world,' Kate cooed. Leigh and Tanya stopped smiling immediately. 'They're long, and muscular. Not too hairy but hairy enough – very masculine. I love your legs,' she said in a husky whisper while visibly stroking his legs under the table. Eric stifled his giggles as did David. Serena and Jason exchanged glances. Leigh went back to the verge of tears. Tanya was furious. Even Gus looked uncomfortable.

'I'll help you collect the plates,' Serena announced, jumping up. Tanya looked at her gratefully. They started clearing the table and everyone went back to the safe subject of praising the food.

The party fell apart (not that it had really been together), soon after dessert. Tanya tried to force coffee on people, but Gus complained of tiredness, and Kate made her intentions clear as she dragged him off to bed. Serena and Jason took this as their cue to leave. Eric announced he was going for a smoke as he'd been banned from it all evening.

Leigh ran to her room, followed by David. When Tanya banged on her door a few minutes later, Leigh begged David not to let her in. She couldn't face her. Although Tanya was not to blame for the awfulness of the evening, she hadn't helped and Leigh didn't want Tanya to tell her to pull herself together while she cried. David didn't do that, he just held and soothed her.

Although Leigh had been in love before and David had seen her get hurt, he had never seen her so upset. He knew that it was a crush, but it was a serious crush and he had no idea how to help her get over it. As he rocked her he hoped that Em – a girl he had met in an Internet chat room, would be online later. They had most of their conversations late at night. She knew all about the house and his worries about Leigh, and Em was really understanding. He was looking forward to chatting with her.

Tanya returned to the sitting room and cleaned up. She loaded the dishwasher, emptied the ashtrays, tipped away any leftover wine and put the bottles in a bag for recycling. She was angry. She should have been on top of the world with the news that Serena had delivered that night, but she wasn't. Instead she was on her own, cleaning up after a dinner she cooked with no help from anyone. She couldn't believe that Leigh had behaved so badly. Socially she used to be great fun, it was mean of her not to have made an effort tonight. Tanya went to bed with her bad mood.

Chapter Fourteen

Leigh hadn't been able to sleep. All weekend Kate had been at the house. Or at least slept there. By Sunday night, Leigh was a wreck. She kept thinking about Kate and Gus and what they were doing in his room. It had blanketed her in sadness.

The weekend had been a disaster. On Saturday, Gus and Kate stayed in bed all day. Tanya had a row with Eric about his behaviour at the dinner. She was angry with everyone, but Eric got the brunt. When Gus and Kate finally emerged from his room everyone was sulking. They went out for a bit, came back and went to bed where they stayed for most of Sunday. After a strained dinner on Sunday night, they went back to bed. Tanya and Eric had not said a word to each other. Leigh wasn't talking to anyone and David was lost. He was not the best at dealing with difficult situations and this one was too difficult for him.

On Monday morning, Leigh abandoned her bed at 7 a.m. an hour before her alarm was due to rouse her. As she walked across the cream carpet, the sadness still wrapped itself around her. She showered, dressed and left the house for work still feeling the same. She didn't see anyone else.

She arrived at work before anyone else in the department. Starting at nine thirty was the norm for her, today she was there by eight thirty. She sat at her desk, switched on her computer and tried to obliterate from her mind the way Gus looked at Kate. As the agency slowly filled up, she was still unable to pull herself together. When Sukie, her boss, saw her, tears were streaming down Leigh's cheeks.

'Oh my god, what's wrong?' Sukie asked. Leigh just shook her head.

'Right. We are going out for a breakfast meeting. Kitty, we'll be as long as it takes.' Sukie smiled at her assistant, grabbed Leigh and escorted her outside.

'More like a breakdown meeting,' Kitty said to whoever was in earshot.

They walked to the nearest café. Although café might not have been an apt description. It was too trendy to be a greasy spoon, but it did its best anyway. Sukie sat Leigh at a red and white Formica table and went to the counter. She ordered two coffees and two rounds of toast.

'Leigh tell me what's wrong,' Sukie said as she sat down.

'Gus,' Leigh replied in a small voice.

'Gus? Who's Gus?' Sukie asked, thinking that she liked nothing better than a boyfriend crisis.

'I live with him, and I love him and he's got a girlfriend,' Leigh managed to find a fresh flow of tears. Sukie patiently coaxed the whole story of the crush out of her. She also found out that, apart from outside competition, Leigh's best friend was being very unhelpful. As Sukie ate her toast and Leigh ignored hers, the whole story tumbled out. As it reached its conclusion, Sukie chewed it over with the last of her food.

'Darling you have to win his heart,' Sukie said.

'But how?' Leigh felt as desperate ever.

'Leave it to your Auntie Sukie. I'll have a think. Don't worry petal, I'll help you get this man.'

'Oh Sukie, if only you could. You don't know how much this means to me,' Leigh said as a new torrent of tears cascaded into her uneaten breakfast.

Back at the office, Sukie shut herself away. Sukie had worked at BBHAT for ten years. She had started as a secretary and had, by chance, managed to pacify an angry client on the verge of taking his business elsewhere. She had done this with a combination of charm and her genuine sweet nature. She was rewarded with a promotion and although many people thought she was insane, she had a magic way with clients that had secured her promotion after promotion. She was now one of the most successful account directors at the agency, although no one, not even her bosses knew how. She had a magic way with people, and despite being fluffy and girly, she had an instinct for the business.

After a few hours, she called Leigh in.

'The thing about men is that they really like girly girls,' Sukie explained.

'Really?' Leigh asked. They were sitting in Sukie's office, surrounded by pink desk accessories. Sukie was definitely 'girly'.

'Yes, I know from my own experience. You have to look cute, giggle and blush. Blushing is good.' She smiled.

'I always blush when I'm around him anyway,' Leigh admitted.

'Excellent. Now about your name, perhaps it needs to be more girly, I don't know, something like La La,' Sukie suggested.

'Sukie, I'm not a Tellytubby,' Leigh protested.

'Good point. LeeLee then. That's it, from now on you'll be known as LeeLee.'

'Do you really think it'll work?' Leigh asked.

'LeeLee, trust me, I know all about men. My real name is Susan but I wouldn't dream of using it now.' She called Kitty and asked her to make them some strawberry tea. 'I think that maybe we should work on your laugh,' Sukie suggested, after the tea had been delivered.

'What's wrong with my laugh?' Leigh was perplexed.

'It's not girly enough. You sound a bit like a horse with a cough,' she answered.

Leigh was tempted to ask her boss what a horse with a cough sounded like, but refrained. 'So how do I do that?'

'Listen carefully . . .' Sukie demonstrated her best girly

89

giggle. She sounded so tinkly, if someone could sound tinkly. But she couldn't deny that Sukie sounded definitely girly, and as that was her aim, Leigh leaned in close and started learning how to laugh.

Leigh spent the rest of the day trying to work out how she was going to get everyone at home to call her LeeLee, and practising her laugh. If she asked them, then they would wonder why, and might even guess at her reasons. She couldn't risk that. Then it came to her – David. What was the point of a cousin if he couldn't help her with battles of the heart. She also made a mental note to buy some strawberry tea.

On the journey home she felt relieved. She was panicking about not having Tanya to rely on where Gus was concerned, but she no longer had to panic because now she had Sukie. Although her willingness to become girly, when Sukie suggested it was not the behaviour of an intelligent woman, Leigh was intelligent. The problem was that her common sense was not always in full working order. Especially when it came to her dependence on other people.

She had developed a crush on Gus at such an alarming rate. She believed herself to be in love with him, before she really knew him. This was based more on Leigh's character than Gus's appeal. She needed to need someone, and Gus became another person she was convinced she needed.

That day, Sukie had taken on a similar role in Leigh's life. Ever since she had started working for her, she had wanted to be her. She looked the way Leigh wanted to look, she had the confidence that Leigh wanted, but without any of Tanya's hard edges. Leigh had another crush. A schoolgirl crush: utterly non-sexual but full of adoration.

Leigh's attraction to people stemmed from when she was young and had first met Tanya. Tanya became Leigh's oracle. If Tanya said it was all right to like someone or something then Leigh did, if she didn't approve then neither did Leigh. Although she had known David for longer, he was not strong enough for Leigh. He didn't exploit her insecurities as Tanya did. Other people were not just central to Leigh's life; she had built her life around them.

Cherry was sitting at her office desk when the telephone rang.

'Harvey Cannon's office,' she said.

'Hi, it's Bill here, is Harvey around?'

'Sure Bill, I'll just get him.' She put Bill on hold and told Harvey to pick up.

'Bill, how are you?' he asked.

'I'm fine. Listen I've got one more person for you to see.'

'Who?'

'Her name is Tanya Palmer, she works in TV and she's talented.' Bill crossed his fingers.

'So no experience in films?'

'No, but she has experience in TV, produces documentaries. Very good at it.' He felt tense, Harvey made him feel tense because he was so darn hard to please.

'How do you know her?'

'I just do. Now I am going to give you her number, here it is, ready?'

'Sure.' Bill reeled off a number and Harvey wrote it down, next to it he wrote her name.

'Bill this one better be good,' Harvey said.

'I promise.' He replaced the receiver hoping against hope that this girl whom he'd never met might just save him.

'What was that all about?' Cherry asked when Harvey had finished his conversation.

'He's given me the name of some girl who produces TV documentaries. He has *really* lost it this time.'

'Maybe she knows about the reality TV stuff we watch,' Cherry said, interested only because she was so hooked on the shows. Harvey perked up. 'I think we ought to give her a call then.'

*   *   *

Tanya stared at the details in her diary and smiled. Then she panicked. She had only two days until her meeting with Harvey Cannon. The lack of time was almost more irrelevant than her lack of knowledge about the meeting. When she had spoken to him on the telephone he had evaded all her questions and told her firmly that they would discuss everything at the interview. When the call was over she still had no idea who he was or what he might want from her. She did, however, believe that he was someone who could help her. Serena had said, 'Apparently he's very important', and although she was being infuriatingly vague, Tanya had a feeling that he was. It might have just been hope, but it was there nonetheless. As soon as the call was over, she had told her boss that she had a meeting and had left the office to go home. She was sitting at her desk with emotions wavering between panic and elation.

She looked at the address. It was in Knightsbridge, suitably impressive. She sighed as she looked over the details yet again. Harvey Cannon, the man who could change her life.

She pulled out her collection of work tapes and watched the documentaries she had worked on. It took a while to choose, but she managed to pick out the best to take to the meeting. Not wanting to swamp the man, she decided she would take only three tapes. The first one was a reality television show about a group of young men who worked in traditionally female jobs. The second was an exposé on an employer of illegal immigrants, which had been widely acclaimed. The final show was about young pop acts who had been promised fame by producers and record companies, then dumped just as quickly when they failed to get to number one with any of their first releases. This was Tanya's personal favourite, she had been involved with the kids, who were as young as eighteen, far too innocent to be exploited but they had been.

The chosen tapes displayed different aspects of her talent and creativity. Although she couldn't take all the credit, she could feasibly exaggerate her role in them.

She wrote out some notes about why she wanted to move

from television into films. Deciding not to sound pretentious, or as if she had swallowed a theory book, she decided her 'sell' would come from the heart. Although it was rehearsed, she would make it sound as if it wasn't. After an hour of writing, and a further hour of reciting and remembering, she was almost happy. The only doubt was that she really knew so little about films, only what she watched on TV or during her rare visits to the cinema. She hoped that that wouldn't kick her out of the game.

Having prepared meticulously for the interview, her next decision was what to wear. She could imagine how people when trying to look creative went for the outrageous, or the individual look. Anyone could dress differently; not many people could dress well. Tanya decided that that was what she would do. A pair of black trousers, boots with high stiletto heels. A pink cashmere T-shirt (tight), and a soft black cardigan. She felt confident that the outfit said exactly what she wanted to say about herself. Fashionable, smart, sexy and coordinated.

Smiling again and feeling in control, she ran a bath. She poured her expensive aromatherapy bath oil, stepped in and relaxed totally. In just two days, she would face the opportunity she wanted more than anything else. In just two days, her life could change for ever. As the scent surrounded her she held on to that delicious thought and decided that she was going to make this work.

After her bath she went back to her room and without seeing anyone else she immersed herself in work.

'God it's quiet this evening,' Eric said. Everyone was in the sitting room. David had hired an action video; they had ordered pizza. Gus and Leigh were sprawled on the sofa. Leigh was trying to watch the film, but was too conscious of Gus's proximity to concentrate properly. Eric lay on his beanbag and David sat in the armchair. Everyone was relaxed.

'Of course it's quiet, we're watching a film,' David pointed out.

'No, it's not that. It's quiet because miss bossy boobs is not here,' Eric said.

'Don't be so nasty,' Leigh defended half-heartedly.

'Anyway what's she up to?'

'I have no idea,' Leigh replied. 'When I asked if she wanted pizza she said she was working.'

'Well, I for one am not complaining,' Eric said. Everyone looked at him, but decided not to push the matter further. He was more hurt by the row with Tanya than he would have liked to feel.

Tanya, of course, had already forgotten the exchange, her mind being on far more important things than Eric.

The film ended and Leigh announced she was going to bed. Waving goodnight, the men stayed where they were. She was still waiting for the right moment to get David to start calling her LeeLee.

Eric waited for Leigh to be safely upstairs before he spoke.

'Why did we move in here?' Eric looked sad. David and Gus exchanged glances.

'What do you mean?' David asked.

'Isn't it obvious? You saw the performance that Tanya put on. Why is she so horrible to me? She's such a bitch.'

'Well, she was out of order,' David started.

'Out of order? She made us come to that dinner and then she has a go at all of us for not satisfying her expectations with our behaviour. I ask you.'

'That's just her, don't take any notice,' David said.

'You mean she shouts at everyone like she shouted at me?'

'Well not exactly, but she has been known to have the odd tantrum.'

'That's not really an excuse,' Gus pointed out.

'I know,' David shrugged.

'Well I am not going to stand for it,' Eric announced.

'What are you going to do?' Gus asked.

'Playstation anyone?' Eric grinned and the others relaxed.

'No mate, not in the mood.' David stretched out.

'Me neither. Eric, you haven't smoked much tonight,' Gus said realising that Eric had shown unusual restraint.

'That's because I figure the reason that I haven't built my incredible joint yet is that I am smoking too much. If I don't smoke quite as much as usual, my senses will be sharper. Anyway, I've got a new idea and I started drawing up the plans earlier. It will go into production next week if I can keep a clear head.'

'I guess that could be called logic,' David agreed.

'And when you've made this thing, do you think you may join the real world again?' Gus enquired.

'What do you mean?' Eric replied.

'What I mean mate, is that it's about time you started going out more, maybe even getting laid, you know, normal things,' Gus stated.

'Gus, that's not like you. You say making love not "getting laid". Anyway, when I've built the best joint in the world and succeeded in legalising cannabis for medicinal purposes, then I might just get laid. David?'

'Oh I'm going to wait until I'm an Internet millionaire. When I've cracked the next big thing then I'll maybe go and meet women.'

'You two are ridiculous, you should be out there enjoying yourselves,' Gus argued.

'Anyway, I am far too busy for women. Don't even have time to meet any,' Eric finished.

'Hey, you guys, there are two women living under the same roof,' Gus persisted. David and Eric fell silent. 'Two attractive women,' Gus added.

'Are you suggesting that we date Leigh and Tanya?' Eric asked with little enthusiasm.

'Well maybe you could date Leigh and David could date Tanya,' Gus suggested. Eric laughed and David turned pale.

'I've known Tanya for ever, she's more like a cousin to me

than a girl,' David said, his voice barely audible. Gus had just put the most terrifying thought into his head.

'And I think Leigh's cute, but I know for a fact that I'm not her type,' Eric added.

'You're both hopeless and I'm disappointed. I shall just have to fix you up with women I meet then,' Gus announced. David thought about the gorgeous women that Gus dated. It was enough to part him from his computer.

'Well I wouldn't mind,' he said.

'I bloody would, I told you I am far too busy.' Eric smiled and Gus shook his head. It looked as if his plans of romance for Eric and Leigh or Eric and anyone were not going to come to fruition.

The idea he had had before moving in was someone special for Eric. He had been sure that Leigh and Eric would hit it off. Eric so funny, so caring, so laid back and Leigh so cute, so insecure, so sweet. They would make a perfect couple.

Gus's belief in love meant it was also paramount to him that everyone else found love. He had been planning it since he moved in. A few subtle hints (not so subtle tonight), to Leigh about Eric and vice versa and everyone would be happy. But it wasn't working. Leigh seemed pretty unhappy at the moment and Gus knew that Eric was lonely underneath all of his bravado. He just didn't know how to make them fall in love. Cupid, mate I could do with a hand, he thought as he wished that an arrow was all it took.

Chapter Fifteen

Tanya hadn't slept. Or she felt like she hadn't. She lay awake thinking about the forthcoming meeting, playing the events over in her mind. Best case scenario: Mr Cannon would be so impressed he would offer her a job on the spot. Worst case scenario; she would forget everything she'd rehearsed and he would laugh her out of his office. She thought about questions he might ask, she practised responses, then she worried that he would ask totally different questions and she wouldn't be able to answer them at all. Earlier fears returned. What if she didn't know enough about films? She didn't, she hadn't studied the old great movies, she didn't know much about directors. Most of her knowledge of films was gleaned from Dawson of Dawson's Creek and he was only sixteen!

In fact the more she thought about it the more she wondered what on earth possessed her to think she could work in the film industry. OK, so she knew about television and she was a good producer. However, films were different, weren't they? Then she realised she didn't know the difference between films and television and if he asked her that, which would be a logical question, she had no idea how she would answer. What if there was little difference in fact? Her breathing began to speed up. She took a look at her clock, it was 3 a.m. She pulled her head under her Habitat duvet and took a long deep breath. She was a producer. She produced television documentaries. She could easily produce a film. Couldn't she?

The more she considered it, the more she realised that she had no idea what she was trying to do. Harvey Cannon *would* laugh her out of his office. No he wouldn't, he'd be impressed. She would make him impressed. She wouldn't worry about not knowing anything, she would make him believe in her. After all, she could sell herself. Couldn't she?

By 4 a.m. she was convinced that it would be all right. Fifteen minutes later, she was convinced it would all end in disaster. Her outfit was all wrong. Maybe he wanted an arty-looking type. Maybe he was going to be one of those Hollywood men you read about who would make her sleep with him. She resolved that she wouldn't sleep with him. Then she decided she would. After all it was the twenty-first century and what was a bit of sex compared to a lifelong ambition. Yes she would sleep with him.

She thought through her underwear. He might not expect her to drop her trousers there and then, but what if he did? It would be much better to be prepared. You heard about these things, Hollywood men could be pushy. Just in case, she would wear her best underwear, the expensive stuff that Nathan had been so keen to shower her with. Something lacy, but not too lacy. If he did want to sleep with her there and then, she didn't want him to think that she had been expecting it. Therefore, she would opt for relatively plain but attractive. White or cream rather than black. As she was wearing trousers, stockings were out of the question. Should she wear tights? Socks were so unsexy. There was no way you could maintain a seductive undressing if you were wearing socks. She had learnt that a long time ago.

If he did want to sleep with her, would he provide the condom? On the other hand, would she be expected to have one? Moreover, if she did, how would she explain that she had one with her? It would again look like she was expecting to sleep with him, or perhaps it would look as if she slept with everyone. No, whatever happened she could not produce a condom. How many women carried condoms to job interviews?

Tanya was going mad.

The clock read 5 a.m. She had set her alarm for six. She had to go to work for a few hours before the appointment, which was at eleven. Eleven was a little early in the day for sex wasn't it? Or did these Hollywood bigwigs not consider that? She went through everything one last time. Especially how she would make sure she didn't look like she hadn't slept a wink all night. She spent a while planning her make-up. Just as she started to doze off into a light sleep, her alarm went off.

The house was quiet. No one else would be up for a while apart from Gus who had worked through the night and still had not come home. Tanya wanted to leave without seeing anyone. This was her special day.

She had managed to do some research on Harvey. His name had been connected to a number of successful films although he was a consultant, which confused Tanya. She had no idea that films used consultants. Then there was the film company: Poplar. There was a mountain of information on it. It was one of Hollywood's biggest studios. Everything she had learned screamed big to her and she felt very small.

By the time she left work for her meeting with Harvey, everything had gone to plan. The shadows under her eyes, which had looked huge and unsightly that morning, were well concealed. She looked good and she felt good. Apart from the nerves swimming around inside her.

She arrived at the address just five minutes early as planned; she smiled confidently at the person on the desk who phoned Harvey's office. She held her smile as he directed her to the right floor. She held her smile while she walked to the lift. She even held it in the lift while she inspected her appearance. She held it while she knocked on the door, and she widened it when an attractive woman answered the door. The first thing Tanya noticed was that she was dressed in a similar way to herself.

'You must be Tanya. I'm Cherry, Harvey's assistant. Come in.' Tanya shook the hand that she offered lightly and followed her into what seemed to be a flat. 'This is our base while we're in London. We live and work here,' Cherry explained.

'It's lovely,' Tanya said, still smiling.

'What a lovely accent you've got, you sound so English,' Cherry gushed and took her jacket.

Tanya was ushered to a sofa, given a glass of water, and then Cherry sat down next to her.

'So, Harvey will be with you real soon, he's just on the phone. Anyway, while he's busy, I'll just give you a little bit of background. We have been here for what seems like for ever but it's only just a month. We're working for a big LA studio who need a hit film. Harvey is what most people call a film genius, he comes up with ideas and they always work. That is why they hired him. This situation is very unorthodox, and I can't tell you too much because it's obviously sensitive information at this stage. But we need someone to help produce this movie, working with Harvey, myself, Bob Rogers who looks after the technical side, and a team of people whom we will put together when we're ready to start,' Cherry smiled.

'So you mean I'd be one of the original crew so to speak?' Tanya asked, feeling the opportunity growing by the second.

'Yep. Whatever Harvey has in mind, he has decided to give a pivotal role to a young British talent. But I ought to warn you, he hasn't seen anyone he likes so far.' Cherry smiled warmly.

'Yes, but he hasn't met me yet,' Tanya responded.

As soon as Cherry led Tanya into his office, Harvey knew he'd got his girl. He wasn't sure how he knew, or what he was even going to use her for, but his instinct was strong.

When they started talking about her current work, he knew that fate had intervened. He wanted to do something using a documentary technique. Tanya specialised in documentaries. He asked to hold on to her tapes so he could watch them later. They talked. He liked her confidence. He didn't ask her about her knowledge of films, he didn't need to known. For what he had in mind he needed far more valuable aspects than that.

They talked about London and he asked about her feelings for her capital city. He then asked her about where she lived.

'Fulham, do you know it?' she replied.

'No. Really, I've only been here and into the West End, I suppose I should explore more. So do you live alone?'

Tanya thought this could be the start of the seduction process. 'No, I've got four housemates.'

'Tell me about them,' Harvey asked. Tanya was taken aback. She couldn't understand why he wanted to know. What she didn't realise was that Harvey didn't know why he'd asked the question either.

'There's Leigh, she's my best friend. Met in primary school when we were about six, that sort of thing. She works in advertising, she's quite good. The trouble is she is so neurotic about her looks and just about everything that she can be a bit of a handful. Acts as if she needs Valium constantly. She's attractive and intelligent, but is paranoid about her breasts, they're quite enormous.' Tanya stopped, feeling as though she had just been disloyal. There was no need for her to have mentioned Leigh's chest.

'Please go on,' Harvey coaxed, smiling.

'Well, she has fallen in love with another of our housemates, Gus. He's a doctor and he is rather gorgeous and funnily enough he's really romantic. He's always talking about falling in love and he likes poetry. It's strange because someone as good-looking as him is normally arrogant and always breaking hearts. He does date models mainly, but the poor man only wants to fall in love. Leigh is so besotted, it's quite a scary situation. She is driving herself mad over him. He hasn't shown any interest in her in that way, but she can't think about anything else.

Then there's David, Leigh's cousin and I've known him for ever as well. He's a computer nerd. No, that's mean, he's not a nerd, he's lovely, but he's too obsessed with his computer to have a normal relationship with anyone. He's always talking about setting up his website and becoming an Internet millionaire, but his ideas have either already been done, or they're completely mad. He's so serious about it, he really is. Lastly there's Eric. He is a pharmacist and works at the same hospital as Gus. He is always stoned; well he is when he's at home anyway. He believes in the legalisation of dope for medicinal purposes and is trying to build the "ultimate joint", whatever that is. He even draws plans.' Tanya stopped abruptly, she knew she had gone too far now. She had no idea why she had told a near stranger all that; especially about Eric's questionable activities. But one look at Harvey told her the opposite, he was smiling.

'They sound delightful. A colourful house with colourful people. Anyway Tanya, I have taken up far too much of your time, what I want to do now is to watch your tapes and I'll give you a call as soon as I've seen them.' Tanya looked disappointed.

'But you haven't told me anything about the project,' she protested.

'I can't tell you much yet, but we will talk further,' he stood up and called Cherry in to escort Tanya to the door.

After she had gone, Cherry went to Harvey's office.

'So?' she asked.

'Honey, I think we have our girl,' Harvey beamed in response.

'Tell me,' Cherry urged.

'Let's watch these tapes she left, then I'll tell you everything.'

Harvey put the first tape in the video machine in his office and Cherry sat on the sofa expectantly.

As Tanya walked away, she replayed the meeting in her mind. She had been eloquent when she spoke about her current job. She had been passionate when she explained how she had started out and she knew Harvey had been impressed. But then there was his interest in her personal life. That puzzled her. Unless of course he had more than just professional designs on her.

She didn't mind that. Harvey was impressive. Everything about him had impressed Tanya. He looked like an important person. He was tall, smart, well-presented. She guessed he was in either his late thirties or early forties. He was friendly, but not sleazy, he was confident, in control and he was the sort of person that you could immediately trust. Tanya left the office wanting to work with him even more than she had done at the outset.

He had fielded her questions like an expert. She had blabbed like a baby as soon as he asked a question. But in return he had given away nothing at all. Picturing his smile made her smile. He had a slow, sexy, inviting smile. She was disappointed that he hadn't given her any hint of lustful thoughts. Nevertheless, she couldn't help thinking that his interest in her personal life might be an interest in her. She hoped it was. At that moment, Harvey became the object of her affections.

'He said he'd be in touch,' she said aloud. Then she prayed that it was for the right reasons. A job on an exciting film project and a new man in her life. The idea of floating off into the Hollywood sunset stayed with Tanya for the rest of the day.

Harvey and Cherry watched the tapes with rapt attention. When the last one had finished, Harvey rewound them.

'I need Bob to look at these,' he announced.

'He'll be back soon, he was meeting with a number of people this morning,' Cherry replied.

'Good, because I think I might be ready soon.'

'Ready for what?' Cherry asked.

'Cherry darling, you must be patient. It's like a jigsaw. I brought us here, now I've found Tanya who will be our main girl, believe me. Then I need to find a few more pieces before I can tell you finally. But you will get credit for the idea,' Harvey smiled.

'How can I get credit for an idea when I don't even know what it is?'

'Because you inspired me, and if this Tanya girl lives up to my instinctive feelings she will provide us with a ground-breaking production.'

'You know what honey, you totally confuse me sometimes.' With that Cherry got up to leave the room. As she got to the door she stopped and turned round, 'Harvey, did you find her attractive?'

'What?'

'Tanya, did you find her attractive?' Cherry hoped her voice sounded more level than it felt. Harvey laughed.

'Don't be absurd, I didn't even notice what she looked like,' he winked at Cherry.

Harvey thought about their meeting, then the tapes of Tanya's work. Things were beginning to come together – as he had always known they would. Next thing on the agenda was to go to her house and meet her housemates.

Tanya had taken the rest of the day off work. She took her thoughts shopping to Harrods. She spent two hours in the store without realising it, and left without buying anything. Taking a bus back to Fulham she couldn't get the enigmatic man out of her mind. She watched the grey London streets passing slowly and thought only in colour of Harvey Cannon. He had to call her. Soon.

The first conscious decision Tanya made after the meeting came when she was sitting in the kitchen. She sat at the breakfast bar, sipping tea and trying to stop herself from fantasising about Harvey. From Harrods to home, her thoughts of him had become X-rated. In order to stop them, she decided that she wouldn't tell any of her housemates about the meeting. She had been planning to tell them but now she wanted to keep it to herself. She wouldn't even share it with Leigh. Not until she was ready. For the moment, this was hers alone.

When she finished her tea, she went upstairs and, too exhausted to do anything else, undressed and climbed into bed and returned to her erotic fantasies.

Bob watched Tanya's tapes and declared that the work was 'interesting'. Harvey agreed but didn't say anything else. While Harvey locked himself in his office with his latest computer game, Cherry and Bob tried to speculate on what was going through his mind. They drew a blank.

'I really want to know what's going on,' Cherry said.

'I don't know if I do. Harvey has that crazy look about him again and I'm not sure I've got the energy to deal with it,' Bob replied.

'Bob, honey, there's one thing I'm sure of, you better find that energy because whatever it is that Harvey is planning, it's not going to be easy.'

'I know Cherry, and that's what worries me.'

Harvey joined Cherry and Bob for dinner. They had become like a family, albeit an odd one. They usually ate at least one meal a day together. Cherry and Bob would often join forces to cook, something they both enjoyed. Harvey would emerge from his office like the 'dad' of the house and join them. They would discuss their respective days, which lately had diversified a bit. Bob was meeting technical contacts, putting together a portfolio of people for when they might need them. Because he knew Harvey well, he had every eventuality covered. Cherry was researching casting agencies, extra agencies and running the administrative side of the yet unknown operation. She was also giving the studio in LA false progress reports in order to keep them happy. Harvey was often locked away — with his ideas.

At dinner they would discuss this, although Cherry and Bob knew not to push too much. Even if they did, Harvey would fob them off and leave them feeling frustrated. That night was no exception. They spoke briefly about Tanya, and Harvey revealed plans to meet her again. He mentioned that he would arrange to go to her house. He said he got a better feel about a person in their own environment. But that was all he would say. Bob tried to question him; he couldn't understand why he wanted to go to her house. Cherry was worried that maybe he wanted to go to her house because he found her attractive. She felt depressed.

After dinner, Bob and Cherry cleared the table and loaded the dishwasher. Harvey's one contribution to the chores was to make the coffee. They all retired to the sitting room, to watch television.

By this point, the reality TV addiction had spiralled out of control. It was all they watched. They were lucky that they had so many to choose from. Reality TV had taken over from soap operas in the hearts of the British people. Harvey concluded that the UK was obsessed with 'real people and real lives'. He even understood why. He commented to Bob and Cherry that there would soon be a group for 'Fly-on-the-wall Anonymous', either for people who realised they needed to be cured of the addiction, or when they ran out of subjects to cover. Harvey concluded that, as a trend, it could only go so far because there was only so much of interest in real life.

He had called Anna in LA and asked her to do some research into the American market. He knew that reality TV was a big phenomenon back home and it wasn't a new thing. He knew that a number of films had been based on the idea. What he wanted to ensure was that it was still as popular there as it was in Britain. When Anna reported that the obsession was still strong, Harvey knew he'd hit the jackpot. He loved it when his plans fell into place.

Chapter Sixteen

The following day, Harvey's thoughts returned to Tanya. Should he leave her for a few days, to build up her anticipation? As Harvey loved his own anticipation, he liked to try to bestow the same emotion on others. Then he realised he had spent enough time thinking of the project and it made more sense to actually try to get it under way. After all, there was still a lot of groundwork to cover. He dialled her number at work.

'Tanya Palmer,' she picked up straight away.

'Hi, it's Harvey Cannon.'

Elation filled Tanya and her cheeks coloured slightly, she hadn't expected him to call so quickly. 'Harvey, how are you?' she asked in her sweetest voice.

'Fine, honey. Anyway, we need to meet again. I was thinking that I'd quite like to see your house.' Harvey hoped that didn't sound too weird.

'My house?' Tanya was shocked. Was he going to seduce her? After all, if he was, it made sense to meet at her home. On the other hand, what was wrong with a restaurant? Or was he so important that he skipped the restaurant phase and went straight to the bedroom.

'Yes, that's how I like to do business. I like to meet people in their own environment. Especially if we're going to be making a film together, which means, that I would really like to meet your housemates as well.' Now Harvey knew that his request sounded weird, but he hoped that her ambitious streak would be strong enough not to question his motives.

'My housemates?' Tanya repeated, even more confused. Harvey sighed. British people were so difficult, he decided to stop wasting time and use another approach.

'Well, if it's a problem, then just say. As I said Tanya, I would like to see how you live and who you live with. It's not a test, just an informal meeting for me to decide how we can proceed with the project. If you're not interested then fine, just tell me.'

Tanya coloured even more. 'Of course I'm interested Harvey,' she said, trying to sound confident. She really didn't understand.

'Good. Right then, how about I come for dinner next week? You can arrange for everyone to be there I presume? Anyway, call me back with a date.'

'You want to have dinner with *all* of them?'

Jeez, Harvey thought, why does she have to repeat everything I say? He was impatient. 'Yes honey, all of you. Is that a problem?' He had a sharp edge in his voice, brought on more by impatience than anything else.

Tanya pulled herself together as she saw her hopes slipping away. 'No of course not, it's fine. I'll find out their schedules this evening and call you back tomorrow if that's OK. Harvey, the only thing is I haven't told them anything about you or the project.' Harvey smiled to himself, he had been right about Tanya.

'Honey that's fine, you don't need to. Maybe we could say that I am someone who works with you. Or even better why don't you say I am a new boyfriend?' Tanya had been standing up with one knee on her chair; her other leg collapsed as he said that word: Boyfriend!

'What?' she almost screamed.

'Relax honey, it'll just make things more fun. Come on, what do you say?'

Tanya thought for a second about what he'd said. If they were pretending to be lovers or nearly lovers then they'd have to act like they were. Although she still didn't understand why he wanted to visit her house, she was beginning to find the idea attractive.

'That does sound like fun,' she said.

'Good. I'll wait for your call.'

Tanya was about to say goodbye, but then she realised that he had already hung up. Americans always did that in films or on television. She felt cheated, a telephone conversation didn't seem to end properly unless people said goodbye.

She ignored her workload now and thought about Harvey. As much as she wanted to think just about him, her thoughts were of the dinner he requested. She still couldn't understand why and it was bothering her. Harvey had managed to make her feel good about the plan by mentioning the boyfriend ploy. For a while she had basked in the idea. Then the reality smacked her full on. He wanted to meet her housemates. She thought back to the dinner party they'd had. He was going to meet her housemates. Oh God!

Leigh, lovesick and unable to render a sensible word. David, despondent but still obsessed with the Internet. Eric, constantly stoned, and always going on about the perfect joint and, since their row, her least favourite person. Gus, who although the most normal, had, since he'd split up with Kate (she wasn't the one after all), become even more obsessed with falling in love and had spent a sickening amount of time talking about poetry. These people were going to meet her prospective boss. Could her future depend on them? She wondered if she should slit her wrists now or later.

Someone interrupted her reverie by asking for proposed production costings for her latest project. She waved them away. All of a sudden her office seemed oppressive and her head was pounding. She muttered something about a meeting to anyone who was in earshot, grabbed her coat and fled.

As she made her way home, she tried to calm down and think things through logically. The ideal solution would be to get new housemates but she didn't have time. The only other thing she could do was to ensure that they behaved. She wasn't sure how. The final option was to just hope for the best.

The first part of her plan was to tackle everyone individually. She had checked out Gus's schedule, as he was the only one with a social life and unusual working hours, and decided that the dinner would take place on the following Tuesday evening. Gus wasn't working and *she* would ensure he didn't have a date. Then she planned the menu. She decided that, as Harvey was American, she would produce a traditionally British meal of roast beef. She also decided to serve soup as a starter and finish off the meal with apple crumble. If a way to a man's heart is through his stomach, Tanya planned to make it there. Once the day and the menu were set, she turned her mind to what she would wear. She decided on her new Earl jeans, which were tight enough to show off her slim legs and not make her look too dressed up. Her high stiletto black boots, which she had worn to the first meeting with Harvey, and a tight, black T-shirt. She would look trendy *and* sexy.

Once the food and the wardrobe had been settled, she felt better. Although there were a few days until the dinner, she needed to have as much under control as she could. Then she would have more time to try to do the same with her housemates.

Leigh was the first person she approached. Relations had thawed between them; they were almost back to their pre-dinner-with-Kate level. Leigh, who was awful at holding grudges, especially against Tanya, had forgiven her. She pounced as soon as Leigh walked in the door at half past seven that evening.

'You're late,' Tanya said.

'I had a lot on,' Leigh replied wearily. Her work was taking longer than usual due to her Gus-obsession Also, since she had confided in Sukie, her boss kept dragging her off for tea and regular updates.

'Oh. Well, I'm glad you're here. Cup of tea?' Tanya smiled sweetly.

'Have we got any wine, I could really do with a proper drink.'

'Of course,' Tanya replied, digging out a bottle of red and opening it.

'Where is everyone?' Leigh asked as she watched Tanya pour the wine.

'Eric is in his room, David is in his and Gus isn't back yet.' It was the usual state of affairs.

'Oh.' Leigh looked disappointed.

'But I need to speak to you,' Tanya announced.

'What about?'

'Well . . . I've met someone.'

'Who?' Leigh's voice betrayed little interest.

'A man.'

'A man?'

'Yes. He's an American, he works in the same business as me and he's a little bit older.'

'Oh, not another one. Don't tell me, he's rich, good-looking, an immaculate dresser and he is going to be just like your last older man.' Leigh actually stopped thinking about Gus for a second and began to worry.

'No, nothing like Nathan actually. Harvey is far more laid back, which is why I want you to meet him.' Tanya smiled.

'You want me to meet him?'

'Yes, all of you. I want to invite him to dinner on Tuesday. Please say you'll be there, please.'

'Of course I will.' Leigh was taken aback but she decided not to push. 'Where did you meet him?'

'Oh through work,' Tanya answered, vaguely. She hadn't thought all the details through.

'Really? Well, I'll look forward to it then.' Leigh smiled and Tanya thought that perhaps Leigh would behave herself. After all they had managed an almost normal conversation and Gus's name had barely been mentioned.

Next was David. Tanya went into his basement, a room she rarely visited. As usual, he was tapping away on his computer.

'Hi,' Tanya said, sitting down on his bed.

'Hey,' David said, looking up.

'I need to ask you a favour,' Tanya said in her nicest non-bossy voice.

'Thought you might; I wondered why you'd come to the dungeon,' David replied, good-naturedly. Tanya laughed.

'The thing is I've met someone,' she explained.

'Oh, so you mean someone other than Gus is meeting members of the opposite sex now,' David teased.

'I guess so. But David, I really like him. He's American, granted he's a bit older than me, but not as old as Nathan and he's nothing like Nathan, so don't worry. Anyway, I really like him, and I want you guys to meet him . . . on Tuesday . . . over dinner?'

'Wow, what an honour. We were never allowed to meet the last older man,' David replied.

'I know, and I'm sorry, but that's not important. Will you come to this dinner?' Tanya asked pleadingly.

'Of course, I mean it's not like I've got far to go, just upstairs. So is everyone going to be there?'

'Of course, I want him to meet all my housemates.' Leaving David slightly bemused, she swept out.

She knew that Eric would be the hardest, so she decided to leave him until last. Gus still wasn't back. Leigh had gone to have a bath, so Tanya sat in front of the television. At nine, Gus walked in.

'Gus, how are you?' she asked.

'Hi, I'm knackered. I was supposed to be working all night, but someone else took my shift, which means I have to be in early tomorrow. Shit, being a doctor is hard work.' He looked tired, ruffled and gorgeous. For a minute, Tanya wondered how she could have gone off him.

'You poor thing. Anyway Gus, I need to ask you something, I've met this man and I quite like him and I want him to meet you guys, so I thought I'd ask him round to dinner next Tuesday.'

'Fine,' Gus smiled.

'Great, so you'll make sure you're here, it's really important.'

'Of course. So we're all going to meet him? Is it our approval you're after?'

'Something like that,' Tanya said.

'It'll be fun,' Gus said, thinking that if it was anything like the dinner he had brought Kate to it would be anything but.

'Really?' Tanya knew that wasn't true. 'Is there someone new in *your* life?' Tanya asked, thinking that she really ought to make more of an effort.

'No, I've got a date on Saturday with some girl. The problem is that she's really sweet but I just don't know if I could fall in love with her.'

'Gus, why don't you just worry about having fun.'

'Because, Tanya, I want to fall in love, you know, *really* in love . . .' Gus coloured slightly. He knew he didn't sound exactly masculine but then he was only being himself.

'Mm.' Tanya's mind had already moved on.

'. . . and until I meet that girl I guess I'll just have to keep looking.' Gus sighed and left the room.

And now the hardest part. She climbed the stairs and knocked on Eric's door. She felt nervous, they hadn't spoken since their row.

'Come in,' he said.

'Hi,' Tanya said, walking in. Eric was sitting on the floor with a huge piece of paper in front of him.

'This *is* an honour,' he replied sarcastically.

'Right. How are you?' she asked.

'Fine, what can I do for you?' Eric looked at her suspiciously.

'I thought I should clear the air, I hate the fact that we're not talking,' she started.

'Actually I quite like it. It makes my life much quieter,' Eric replied. Tanya winced, this wasn't going to be easy.

'Eric I am sorry. You do not spout shit all the time, I shouldn't have said that. I don't know what came over me, I know the dinner was awful, but that wasn't your fault. I shouldn't have taken it out on you.'

'No you shouldn't, but as you have apologised, which I thought you would never do, I shall accept your apology,' Eric smiled. He had no idea why he hadn't given her a harder time.

'I was wondering. I've met this new guy and I really like him, and I'd like to invite him here to meet all of you,' Tanya said.

'Aren't you worried about me talking crap?'

'Don't be silly, of course not, I did apologise,' she replied.

'If you really want me there, I will be. But don't you dare tell me how to behave.' Eric scowled. He was angry with himself for being such a walkover.

'I wouldn't dream of it,' said Tanya, wishing that she *could* tell him how to behave.

'Fine, I'll be there. He must be pretty special,' he added.

'He is Eric, you're going to love him.' Tanya's eyes took on a dreamy look as she left the room. Eric made a face at her departing back. He still couldn't understand why he didn't tell her to go to hell, and he wasn't very pleased with himself for it.

Tanya left Eric's room and went into her own, where she remained for the rest of the evening. Everything was organised and she looked forward to speaking to Harvey the following day to tell him so. She traced his phone number with her fingertips. She thought through the menu again, her choice of clothes, and was satisfied that she was on the right track. Then she walked to her lingerie drawer, where, for the second time she picked out her best seductive underwear.

When they were alone, Cherry found the courage to question Harvey's motives for wanting to meet Tanya's friends.

'Why?' she asked.

'Not sure, but trust me,' Harvey replied. 'Oh and before I forget, we decided to pretend I'm her new boyfriend,' he added.

'Why?' Cherry bristled.

'Because that suits me actually and she doesn't want them to know about this new job.'

'Have you offered her a job?' Cherry was still indignant.

'Not yet, but I'm pretty sure I'm going to.'

'And what else are you going to offer her, Harvey?'

'What do you mean?'

'Pretending to be her boyfriend. Are you sure that it's just pretending?'

'Cherry my darling, I am not interested in her if that's what you're implying. This is purely professional, and you know I'm nothing if not professional.' He kissed her on the cheek. Was she jealous?

'Well, I guess it's none of my business anyway,' she said sulkily.

'Honey, if I am going to fall for anyone, it'll be you, you know that.' Harvey knew that would win her round, and it did.

'Sure Harvey,' she said, trying desperately hard to believe that he meant it.

Chapter Seventeen

'I've decided to set up a truth serum site,' David announced.

'A what?' Tanya asked.

'Well, I'll make truth serum and sell it online.'

'But you don't know how to make truth serum?' Tanya asked, her face still in the same, bewildered expression.

'You use herbs or something. Shit, it's a bit flawed, I know, but this could be it.' David looked uncertain. He knew it was a bit of a weird idea, but everything that wasn't strange, and quite a lot that was, had already been done.

'I'm sorry, but it is *seriously* flawed,' Tanya pinched his arm in sympathy.

'I even registered the domain name — *www.truthserum.co.uk* — shit.'

'I think you've been spending too much time with Eric,' Tanya said and left the room to laugh.

Eric and Gus sat in Eric's room.

'So, I've decided, I am going to use a mixture of papers, and make this prototype in three sizes. See,' Eric shoved a piece of paper under Gus's nose. Gus looked at it patiently. As far as he could see Eric's latest joint plan was much the same as all his others, but he knew that if he looked interested he would refrain from hurting Eric's feelings.

'Well mate, I think it looks like a good one,' Gus smiled.

'Shit, I think so too. I'm going to get straight on to making this up.' Eric smiled proudly.

'Let me know how it goes.' Gus smiled again, and got up to leave the room.

'You'll be the first to know.'

Gus bumped into Tanya on the landing.

'How are you?' she asked him.

'OK,' Gus replied.

'You don't look very happy,' Tanya said.

'I'm just a bit depressed about my crap love-life,' Gus explained.

'I'm sorry,' Tanya said, feeling anything but.

'Um, well it seems to be the story of my pitiful life. Anyway, I don't want to burden you with it,' he said.

'Oh, Gus, I don't mind, anytime you want to talk let me know.' She was trying to play the model housemate.

'I think I'll just go and write some poetry, I normally do that when I'm feeling down.' Gus felt embarrassed as he made this admission. It was news to Tanya, and not entirely welcome news. Gus, who was the most normal man in the house, wrote poetry? 'You write poetry?'

'Sometimes, I find it cathartic to write. I never show them to anyone though.' Tanya didn't tell him that she thought it was a good job he didn't.

'Well, I can understand that, it's a personal thing.' She was lost for words.

'Anyway, I better go and get scribing now.' He nodded goodbye and made for his room.

What puzzled Tanya most was that it had taken her so long to discover what an odd house they lived in. It was as if the house had done something to everyone. But houses can't do that – can they? She and Leigh used to have a friendship. They hung out together, they went out together, they giggled, they had fun. Since they'd moved into the house that had stopped. David, although obsessed with the Internet, had some sensible ideas, now he had only crazy ones. Eric, who when they met in the pub was amusing, was now just plain weird. Gus – Gus the gorgeous doctor – was acting like a pathetic lovesick schoolkid. Had the house really done all that? If so, how had Tanya managed to escape unscathed? She hadn't changed — had she? — she wasn't weird, she was just Tanya.

She went to her room in a panic. Pulling out her palm-pilot, she went to the 'To-do' list. She had already done the shopping list. She had also made her outfit list. Next she made her 'How to make housemates presentable' list. She stared at it and felt very callous. She had described the foibles of her housemates to Harvey and he had still suggested visiting them. She was just worried about her chances of employment once he did. She deleted the heading about her friends, and shut her palm-pilot. Sighing she left her room and decided that she needed a drink.

Tanya was sitting at the breakfast bar nursing a glass of wine and thinking dreamily about her future when Leigh walked in.

'You're late,' Tanya said.

'I know, but I've been shopping.' Leigh tried out her new giggle. A look of incomprehension passed over Tanya's face.

'What did you buy?' she asked, and what *was* that noise, she wanted to ask.

'Pink,' Leigh announced, triumphantly.

'What?'

'Well, we decided that pink really is my colour, so I bought loads of pink stuff. Not only does it suit me but it also doesn't make my boobs look too big.' She giggled again, this time it sounded slightly better. Tanya groaned inwardly, just as she thought things couldn't get any worse . . .

'Pink, that's interesting.' The only answer she could muster.

'Well, pink is a romantic, feminine colour. It'll bring out my vulnerable yet desirable nature.' Leigh was quoting directly from Sukie.

'That's great,' Tanya said, thinking the opposite.

'I'm going to try it all on, do you want to come and see?' she asked, still trying out her new giggle.

I would rather slit my wrists, Tanya thought. 'Sure. Maybe

later, I've had a bitch of a day and I really need a couple of drinks.' She smiled, and watched in astonishment as Leigh floated off with her shopping.

It was bad. David and the truth serum, or the manure delivery service, or the dating agency for fat people; Eric and his obsession with building what he claimed would be the best joint in the world; Gus and his poetry; and Leigh doing a wonderful impression of a fairy: this is what would greet Harvey. The man she needed to impress to get her dream job. The man she needed to impress into bed. Putting her head in her hands, she wanted to laugh hysterically. Lunatic asylums had nothing on her housemates. The idea of being in one suddenly became very appealing.

Prayer was her only option.

Chapter Eighteen

Tuesday arrived. Tanya took the afternoon off work to prepare for the dinner. It was lucky that she had not yet been assigned to a new project, which meant that, although she was supposed to be coming up with ideas, all she had to do was attend the odd meeting. If all her housemates had their own strange traits, Tanya's was her belief that, as she was no longer interested in her job, she didn't have to do it. Being sacked didn't occur to her. Armed with a cookbook, half a supermarket and more than half of an off-licence, she began preparing.

Gus emerged from his bed at half past three. He had been on nights.

'Wow, looks like Mrs Beeton's kitchen in here,' Gus said. He was wearing a tracksuit and a sleepy smile. He reached for the kettle.

'If I knew who Mrs Beeton was, I might agree,' Tanya joked. Gus raised an eyebrow, she was in a good mood rather than in the flat panic he expected. She had made such a big deal about this meal, he was surprised at her calm. What he didn't know was that the panic would come later.

'Tea?' he asked.

'Thanks,' she replied. She carried on chopping and smiling. She couldn't help but feel excited about seeing Harvey again. She was the one acting like a lovesick schoolchild now.

'Tan, I'm going to make some toast, then I'll get out of your hair,' Gus smiled.

'No problem, mind you if you stay here any longer than that, I'll probably rope you in.'

'Five minutes then I'm out of here, oh and don't worry, I do intend to have a shower and change before the mystery man turns up.'

'I had no doubt,' Tanya replied and once again Gus marvelled at her composure.

After Gus left, she did a stock check. Vegetables were chopped and ready and waiting in water. The soup (purchased ready-made and in a carton) was sitting in the fridge. The beef had been seasoned and was sitting in tin foil. The batter mix for the Yorkshire puddings was on the counter ready to be mixed. The champagne was chilling, the red wine was sitting on the counter. As Tanya looked around her she realised that everything was as good as ready.

She wandered around to see what else needed to be done. Despite her initial reservations, the house was always kept tidy. Eric was the biggest surprise of all, being the most naturally tidy one amongst them. When they had first moved in, Tanya and Leigh had been so worried about mess that they had washed, Hoovered, and dusted everything in sight, but, as time went on they realised that all the men were houseproud. More so than the girls infact. So their efforts were not noticed. When she discussed this with Leigh, they decided to loosen their grip on the housework but they noticed no difference. They were forced to admit that they lived with twenty-first century men. *Very* twenty-first century men. Tanya had felt almost disappointed when, on the previous night, she was full of nerves, the house was spotless, depriving her of an opportunity to exercise her stress by shouting at anyone. Instead she had shouted at Leigh for her insistence on wearing pink, and that had provoked a lip quivering response that Tanya had never seen before. So she gave up.

For something to do, she Hoovered the sitting room, it

looked no different afterwards. She then pulled out the dining table, put the cloth, the cutlery and the candles on it. Then she took a bath.

Submerged in her 'Relax' bubbles, her mind returned to Leigh and her transformation. First there was the change of name. David had called her LeeLee one night, and although he had done so with a red face, she had smiled and told him she preferred that to plain old Leigh. So everyone now called her LeeLee, with the noticeable absence of Tanya who refused to do so. When she questioned Leigh about the new name, she had simply pointed out that David had called her that and she liked it. She refused to comment further. Apart from the name, there was the funny giggle she had developed and now the pink clothing. It not only baffled Tanya but annoyed her that here was a new and different Leigh. The only thing that she knew for sure was that it was linked to Gus.

Ever since they had first met, Tanya had always known, (and mostly influenced), the way she behaved. Tanya had moved to Leigh's school at the age of seven because her parents had decided they wanted to pay for her education. She was daunted by the 'smartness' of the prep school she'd been sent to, the uniform and the other children. It was the first and last time that Tanya had been daunted by anything. She had been sitting in the playground on the first day and might as well have had a sign saying 'leper' hanging round her neck for all the attention the others were paying her. She fought hard not to cry.

Her breakthrough came at lunchtime. When she was ushered out into the hostile playground once again, she saw a group of girls surrounding another girl. They were shouting at her, 'boy's name, smelly name' and all sorts of other childish taunts. The girl in the middle was crying. Having come from tougher pastures, Tanya forgot how scared she had been that morning, marched up to the group of girls, pushing a couple of them aside and declared, 'Leave her alone you pigs.' At the age of seven it sounded tougher than it did in the re-telling. They started on her, so she simply pulled the hair of the girl with the longest hair and told them that they would all suffer if they didn't apologise. This was enough to scare the other seven-year-olds into submission. From that moment, Tanya was the most scary (and therefore popular) girl in school. She was also Leigh's best friend.

Remembering it now, Tanya knew that the whole 'saving' situation that had arisen when they first met had set the tone for their friendship. It was the toughness of Tanya that made Leigh look to her for advice and, of course, follow it. It was that that saved Leigh from her rut in Bristol and brought her to her new life in London. So where the hell had it gone now? Or more likely, as Tanya knew Leigh so well, who the hell had it at the moment?

Tanya pushed all thoughts of her newly mad friend out of her mind as she towelled herself briskly and returned to the evening ahead. She wanted to see Harvey so much both for personal and professional reasons that the feeling was physical. But she knew which was more important: her dream of working in films. If there ever was a choice to be made between winning Harvey's affections or a job, then the latter was odds-on favourite. She put on a moisturising face mask and sat in her room, combing her long hair. She had thought about a trip to the hairdresser, but decided against it. She didn't want to appear too groomed. She pulled her hair back from the hardening mask. She then went to sit on her bed to relax for the required ten minutes. She concentrated hard on not slipping into another daydream. She had spent too long dwelling on things lately, she needed to focus on the future. Her future.

When Leigh walked in at half past five, the house was unusually calm. The table in the sitting room was fully laid. Tanya had managed to make herself look sexy yet casual. Her tight jeans, high heels and figure hugging T-shirt were a genius outfit. If Leigh wasn't concentrating her efforts on being feminine rather than sexy she would have been jealous.

'Hey,' Leigh said, and gave Tanya a kiss.

'What was that for?' Tanya asked in surprise.

'I know you're nervous, I wanted to show you support.' Leigh smiled.

'Thanks, Leigh.'

'Darling, it's LeeLee,' she replied, skipping out of the room. When she'd gone, Tanya began to take in what Leigh was wearing. A pink Barbie T-shirt, a pink mini-skirt, pink tights and pink trainers. She shook her head and ran upstairs. She couldn't be sure, but she thought that she had also seen pink ankle warmers. She knocked on Leigh's door and walked in. Leigh was sitting at her dressing table, brushing her blonde curls. Tanya looked down and almost groaned as she realised she hadn't imagined the ankle warmers. Leigh looked like a cross between a kid from *Fame* and a doll.

'Hey, Tan,' she said sweetly.

'LeeLee?' Tanya began.

'Mmm,' Leigh replied. Tanya took a deep breath.

'Your outfit,' she managed.

'You like it?' Leigh asked.

'Of course I do. But, well, you don't think it's a bit pink?' Tanya knew she was defeated, even though she was normally good at saying what she thought, Leigh had ensured she didn't even know what she thought.

'I like to be coordinated, I think I look cute,' Leigh said.

'You do look cute,' Tanya replied, thinking that she would look cute if she was five years old, at her age she looked absurd.

'So, what's the problem?' Leigh's lip was quivering again.

'No problem, I was just going to ask where you got the ankle warmers from?' Tanya's voice betrayed no irony as she asked the first question that came into her head.

'They were a present from my boss,' Leigh replied. Tanya realised at that moment whom she'd been usurped by.

'Right, and are you changing for tonight?' She tried to sound as casual as she could.

'No, I thought I'd wear this, but I am going to clip my hair back a bit.' Leigh smiled.

'Good,' Tanya replied with a sunken heart. Not only had she been usurped, but she'd been usurped by a bloody moron.

By half past seven, all thoughts of Leigh's clothing or mad boss had fled, all that was left now was panic.

'Oh God, oh God,' Tanya screamed, as she burned her hand turning the roast potatoes.

'Come here,' David said, and thrust her hand under the cold water tap.

'Shit, it's all going wrong,' Tanya moaned.

'No, it's all fabulous,' David reassured her. He then took control. When Eric, Gus and pink Leigh ventured into the kitchen, calm was restored.

'Shall we have a drink?' Eric asked. Tanya turned to look at him and stopped in her tracks.

'What *are* you wearing?' Eric was wearing a suit.

'My work suit,' he replied, nonplussed.

'Eric, are you taking the piss?' Tanya screeched.

'Why on earth do you think that?' Eric asked. He was, in fact, taking the piss.

'When you come home the first thing you do is change out of your suit and into jeans or something, why are you wearing it?' Her voice was still at screech pitch.

'Because you told us that tonight was important. I'm just making a bloody effort, that's all,' Eric replied.

'Oh shit, no one wears a suit to dinner in their own home,' Tanya pointed out.

'Well it's too late to change now, chill out Tan.' Eric was enjoying himself. 'Who wants a drink?' he said again.

'We'll wait until Harvey's here,' Tanya snapped. Gus tried not to laugh as he made his way into the sitting room with Leigh and Eric on his tail. David remained to help with the cooking.

'He is such a shit,' she said.

'Relax, he is just trying to be helpful,' David lied.

'Well he's not,' she replied. 'Anyway, it doesn't matter does it?'
'Of course not.' He reassured her once again.

The doorbell went just after eight. Everyone knew to let Tanya
answer it. She opened the door to Harvey and her heart flipped.

'Hey,' he said.

'Hello,' Tanya replied and showed him in. She took his coat
as he asked her how she was. She told him she was fine. She then
took a deep breath and led him into the sitting room.

She wanted to cry as she saw them sitting there, eagerly
anticipating their guest. Pink Leigh was sitting on the sofa arm,
Gus was next to her, David was next to Gus in his 'I am a
technoholic' T-shirt (because he'd been so helpful, she hadn't
even noticed it and now she did she was horrified), and Eric in
his suit was on the other arm. They had formed a very obvious
welcoming committee. She took a deep breath.

'This is Harvey. Harvey meet my housemates.' Tanya felt like
a cheap gameshow hostess who was showing the contestant that
he'd won a toaster.

'Hello,' Harvey said studying each of them in turn.

'You can call me LeeLee,' Leigh said, standing up to get a
look at him. She thought that he was handsome, if not a bit old.

'How are you LeeLee,' Harvey obliged, taking her hand
lightly and looking at the amazing pink outfit she was in. Sugar
Plum Fairy sprang to mind.

Behind Leigh in the welcoming committee was Gus. He
shook Harvey's hand and smiled. Harvey looked at him and
could almost understand Leigh's crush. He was a traditionally
good-looking man. And a doctor. He could see the attraction.
Behind Gus was a shaggy – looking man. Harvey knew this was
David. He had committed the details shared with him by Tanya
to memory. He maintained an elephant's recall. As he shook
David's hand, he couldn't fail to be amused by what a visual
stereotype he was. Hair too long to be neat, too short to be
Heavy Metal. His T-shirt was dark blue but had seen better days,

and read 'Technoholic', a joke which had also seen better days. Harvey guessed that it was his favourite T-shirt. His trousers were faded blue jeans, giving just enough of an impression that he wasn't particularly bothered about his looks. Harvey knew that if he had never met a computer geek before, he had met one now. The last hand he shook he knew belonged to Eric. What surprised him was that Eric was wearing a suit and he looked neat and tidy. Not like the 'stonehead' Tanya had described. He smiled pleasantly.

Everyone stood around smiling at him. He decided to take control.

'Tanya honey, what are we eating, I'm starving.' He tried to look adoringly at her, as he squeezed her hand.

'Roast beef, but first, David, can you do drinks?' She was being sweet and everyone looked amused by it.

David and Gus went to get the drinks. Tanya went to supervise them and put the soup on. Harvey sat in an armchair and Eric and Leigh sat back on the sofa.

'So Harvey, you're American?' Leigh said. She immediately wanted to kick herself hard.

'Yep, from sunny LA,' he replied good-naturedly.

'Why are you in England?' Eric asked, as Leigh shot him a look.

'Work,' Harvey responded.

'What do you do?' Leigh asked.

'I work in TV.'

'What do you see in Tanya?' Eric asked. Leigh inadvertently giggled, Harvey looked amused, but before he could answer, Gus, David and Tanya returned with champagne. They handed out glasses, and before Tanya had time to speak, Eric raised his glass, 'A toast to Tanya, for planning a marvellous evening.' Everyone else clinked glasses, but no one missed the horrified look that Tanya gave Eric.

Harvey thought that it was going even better than he could ever have imagined.

Through drinks he talked about his observations on London.

Mainly to make Tanya happy because she clearly was not, but when they sat to dinner, his role changed. He became the observer. Answering questions, asking choice questions and collating all the information he could.

As Tanya dished out the soup, the conversation was stilted. This was made worse by Tanya frowning at anyone who spoke. He decided to find out about David.

'David, you say you work a lot at home on the Internet, so tell me how that works,' he prompted. It was all he needed to ask.

'I have my own set-up downstairs. I really want to develop my own Internet site. I've registered loads, but so far it hasn't really come to much, but I know that I'll get there if I keep going. I once thought about setting up this mail order company for underwear, but seconds you know, slightly imperfect, but the logistics were too much. I registered the name, *www.knickers.directtoyourdoor.co.uk* and loads of perverts tried to visit it. So I scrapped that. I've done loads since then, I could tell you but it would take all night,' he paused to see Tanya looking disapprovingly at him. 'So I won't. Although I thought I'd got this great idea for an Internet dating bureau for fat people. I called it *www.fatpeopleneedlovetoo.co.uk* but, can you believe it, it'd already been done. I'm still trying though.' David paused to eat his soup.

Harvey was amused and also surprisingly touched. David had come to life as soon as he started talking about his sites and his eyes displayed something special. Of course he was totally mad.

'I guess, in order to think up these sites, you need to surf the web a lot,' Harvey said.

'LeeLee says I spend too much time on it, but you get to meet some fascinating people and amazing sites. There are sites where you can put your picture in a gallery and other people vote whether you're sexy or not, and, of course, the chat rooms are cool. I'm speaking to this girl at the moment, she seems great, you know, same interests. The problem is that when you meet them in real life, they often disappoint. It's a shame really.'

'So you date over the Internet?' Harvey asked.

'No of course he doesn't,' Tanya snapped, the evening was proving to be a disaster.

'Well yes, I do actually, I only date online, it's safer than the real world.' Everyone apart from Tanya laughed. 'People don't realise how much of a real love affair you can have online. It mirrors real relationships. You argue, you make up, you have conversations, and of course sex.' Tanya looked ready to explode, Eric noted this and decided to change the subject.

'At least he dates,' Eric pointed out. 'I never date, online or otherwise.'

'Why is that?' Harvey asked. At this point Tanya stood up and picked up the empty soup bowls; in David's case it was a full soup bowl because he'd been talking so much. 'Leigh, can you give me a hand?' she asked. Although her voice was still sweet everyone could detect the tension there.

As soon as they were in the kitchen Tanya screamed.

'What?' Leigh asked, flinching.

'Well, first David talks about home delivery substandard knickers, and now Eric and his theories on dating are going to get an airing. It's a disaster.'

'Tanya you really are too hard on them. Harvey is enjoying himself, you can tell,' Leigh replied.

'Are you sure?'

'Trust me, I'm positive.'

While Leigh and Tanya dished out perfect roast beef and put the potatoes, vegetables and Yorkshire pudding on the table, they only caught snatches of Eric's dating story. Harvey however, got all of it.

'As I was saying, I don't date because I have far more important things to do with my time.'

'Go on,' Harvey requested.

'Well it's cannabis.' Eric had no qualms about talking to strangers about it because although it was illegal, his beliefs meant that he didn't think it wrong. He thought that not talking about it would be hypocritical.

'Cannabis?' Harvey asked.

'Yeah, you know, well it's the wonderful medicinal qualities of it that permeate my time, actually. I'm a pharmacist right, and I know all about drugs and what they do. The thing about cannabis is it's amazing pain-killing qualities. What I believe also, although of course I don't have conclusive evidence, is that the side-effects of it aren't as harmful as many drugs you get on prescription. I know you get a bit stoned, but it's not half the effect of alcohol, and I believe that, for medicinal purposes at least, it should be legalised and available on the NHS. I do a lot of work on this in my spare time.'

Eric finished and looked at his food. 'Great grub, Tan.' She shot him another look. If the dining table could have killed her, it would have done her a favour. She took a look at Harvey who appeared interested. That irritated her.

'So, it's like a crusade, this ambition of yours?' Harvey questioned.

'Yes, that's exactly what it is, a crusade. I believe so strongly in the good it can do, and all the time it's being given this bad press. I don't advocate drugs, I've seen what heroin and stuff can do, but I think that the tenuous link between smoking a bit of hooty and hard drugs is wildly exaggerated. If anything should be banned, I think it should be alcohol, although I like that too.' Eric laughed, and Leigh giggled.

'Tell him about your other mission, Eric,' she said, in her newly acquired girly voice. Tanya now wanted the dining table to kill Leigh. She saw in her mind's eye a shot from a film where everyone at a dinner party lies dead around the table. In her picture it was everyone but her and Harvey, although she was debating letting Gus survive too. She looked at Harvey, who was still focused on Eric.

'Well you see, I do smoke a bit myself as well. Not because I'm ill but I enjoy it, far more than drink. So I've got this mission to build the ultimate in joint technology. The world's best ever. I draw up plans, just like an architect, select materials and then when the plans are ready, I build.' Eric beamed.

'Much success?' Harvey asked.

'No, not yet, it's frustrating, but as soon as I do, I'll let you know.'

'Be sure to.' Harvey laughed. Everyone followed him. Even Tanya, who sounded a little strained. 'This food is delicious Tanya, the best meal I've had since I've been in London.' He smiled at her fondly.

'I'm glad you're enjoying it, I wanted to give you something traditionally British,' she replied, relieved that the conversation had reached a neutral level that she could cope with.

'I thought he'd already had that,' Eric mocked, and sniggers filled the room. Harvey shot a look at Tanya who looked very embarrassed.

'Well anyway, I didn't know you were such a good cook,' he said to diffuse things. Tanya was imagining Eric in tiny pieces. It would be a slow death.

'Actually I quite enjoy cooking, but I don't get much time,' she replied.

'What about you LeeLee, do you cook?' he asked. Tanya couldn't wait to hear how this conversation went.

'Oh I love cooking,' she replied, to the utter amazement of her housemates who had only ever seen her make toast. 'It's one of those wonderful feminine hobbies that I care so much for,' she finished.

'Really?' Harvey asked, 'like what?'

'Oh you know, making things, clothes, make-up that sort of thing.' This was news to her housemates, especially Tanya and David who knew her so well.

'Great,' Harvey said. He was lost for words on this one. The Leigh that Tanya had described was a woman in love, but she hadn't described the mad state that her being in love had driven her to. 'What about your job, advertising isn't it?'

'Oh yes, I work for BBHAT which is one of the biggest London agencies, and my team is all female; it's really wonderful. My boss, Sukie, is one of the best account directors around, she is such an inspiration to work for.' Leigh was gushing and giggling.

'Wow, all women, I never thought of advertising as female dominated,' Harvey said.

'Oh it's not really, but *our* team is. That's why it works so well. We have a feminine understanding that means we can embark on more perceptive advertising solutions.' David chose that moment to choke on a roast potato. Gus managed to distract himself from laughing by patting David on the back. Tanya was strangling Leigh mentally, using her pink ankle warmers.

'Does that mean you're good at advertising Tampax?' Eric asked, and laughter exploded from the others. Not because Eric was funny, but because they needed the release.

'No Eric, it means we are good at advertising everything. It's very serious,' she pouted.

'Sorry,' Eric said, unable to resist Leigh's new girliness. Tanya hated him more for apologising to her.

'Harvey, how do you like London?' Leigh asked, flapping her eyelids madly, in what was supposed to be a flutter.

'I love it. Yeah it's great apart from the rain,' he laughed.

'Oh I know, it makes my hair so frizzy,' Leigh agreed. Tanya wondered why she'd become such a bimbo. 'But of course I have a lovely pink umbrella to stop that now.'

'So what about your love life LeeLee?' Harvey hadn't quite finished with her yet.

'Oh, a girl never tells,' Leigh giggled again. 'But there might be an object of affection out there.' Her eyes rested on Gus, who failed to notice, and Harvey's assumptions were confirmed. It seemed that Leigh was playing girly to get her man, which made the whole picture far more interesting than if she was as morose as Tanya had described her.

'It's time to clear the dinner plates away, Gus can you help me? Does anyone need more drink?' Tanya jumped up and Gus jumped up with her. They picked up plates and took them to the kitchen, just as Leigh was questioning Harvey about the popularity of knitting in LA.

In the kitchen, Tanya kicked the fridge.

'Easy,' Gus said.

'Sorry,' she replied. 'It's just that with David and his Internet schemes, Eric and his drug thing, and now Leigh and her pink act, I don't think that I'll ever see Harvey again.' She sat at the breakfast bar as Gus loaded the dishwasher.

'Don't be so dramatic, he seems to be finding this all amusing. Come on, grab a couple more bottles of red and we'll go and show how normal we are.' Gus touched her arm.

'Thank goodness *you* are,' Tanya said gratefully.

They sat down and refilled the glasses.

'So, how long are you planning on staying in the UK?' Gus asked, smiling reassuringly at Tanya.

'I have no idea. At least a year I guess. It all depends on work.'

'Of course, you work with Tanya, is it the same sort of thing you did in LA?'

'Similar. Nothing like what you do, though. Tanya tells me you save lives.'

'I try. I work in Casualty, a bit like ER. Actually nothing like it, but I wish it was. Far more blood and less glamour, but long hours and loads of stress. I'm worried about losing my hair, I seem to be one of the few remaining doctors who has any,' Gus laughed.

'I bet. So what do you fill your precious spare time with?' Harvey asked.

'Football and poetry,' Gus answered. Tanya felt herself heat up. She had forgotten momentarily about Gus's poetry.

'Would anyone like dessert?' she asked quickly.

'Not yet honey. Tell me about the poetry?'

'Well I write. Always about love. I love love. I mean I want to fall in love so much. The whole caboodle. Knee trembling, loss of appetite, the whole feeling of being engulfed by emotion, that is what I want. But, unfortunately, I haven't found it yet. Well, I did find it and then I lost it. So to fill the void that I have inside me, I write poems.' Tanya was now imagining setting fire to Gus and his poems.

'Do you show anyone these poems?' Harvey asked. He was

thinking that looks could be deceptive. Gus was not how you would imagine him to be at all. Behind the conventional good looks was an oversensitive soul; Harvey had never met a man like him.

'No, no. I'm far too shy. And they're probably rubbish anyway.'

'I don't think so, I bet they're really wonderful, and romantic,' Leigh piped up.

'Thanks LeeLee, you're so sweet,' Gus said, and they shared a moment.

'But it's really great to write your feelings down,' Harvey said. 'In the States you'd be in therapy and paying a fortune just to express how you feel.'

'Have you ever been in therapy Harvey?' Eric asked. Tanya spilled some wine.

'Of course; I'm American!' Harvey laughed. His loudest booming laugh, which infected everyone else, including Tanya. 'I can't believe you guys are all so interesting.'

They're bloody well not, they're insane, Tanya thought. 'Dessert?' she said and before anyone answered she went to heat up the crumble.

Because Harvey had been so interested in everyone, they had all warmed to him. Through dessert, they all tried to tell him more, like children fighting for attention.

David talked about a girl called Sam he had met in person via an introduction on the Internet and who had turned out to be a keen taxidermist: *She was very open about it, told me on our first date; of course I spat my peanuts all over her when she said it.* Eric carried on his theme of legalisation of cannabis for use in medicine: *I keep trying to think of a name for my cause, at the moment I call it: the legalisation of cannabis for medicinal purposes; LCMP for short, but it doesn't quite trip off the tongue does it?* Leigh was talking about things which were totally banal: *There are so many variations of pink lipstick that I could buy one every day for a year and still not have all of them. Of course that's because there are so many different makes and sometimes you can get exactly the same shade by mistake because they have different names. It's a nightmare.* Gus was asking

Harvey his thoughts on love: *Do you think that you fall in love instantly? Like being hit by Cupid's arrow, or does it take a while, because if it takes a while, I worry that I've already dumped it because of my impatience. Could be a poem there . . . cheers.*

Harvey nodded, laughed and smiled in all the right places. By the time that the last drop of wine had been consumed, Tanya was exhausted.

'Does anyone want coffee?' she asked and was relieved to see everyone shake their heads.

'Tanya, why don't you give me a tour of your house?' Harvey asked. Enthusiastically, she led him from the room.

'He wants to see her bedroom,' Eric declared.

They decided that although they were a bit tipsy, they would clear up and give Tanya and Harvey some space.

'Oh, he's a lovely man,' Leigh said, as she scraped the bowls.

'Yeah, top bloke,' David agreed.

'Very intelligent,' Eric slurred.

'And understanding,' Gus added.

They were all correct.

Tanya took Harvey straight to her room and closed the door. Automatically she felt her heart speed up.

'I am so sorry about them, I had no idea they were going to be quite so . . .'

'Interesting? Tanya I've had a fantastic evening. It was great, although *you* have been little quieter than I expected.' He laughed.

'I was mortified,' Tanya protested.

'Well you didn't need to be. It was great fun.'

'So what now?' she asked wanting him to take her in his arms.

'I have to go, if they think that it's weird that I'm not staying, tell them I've got to work early. I'll give you a call tomorrow.' He smiled. 'But I can tell you Tanya, that we will be working together really soon.'

'We will?' Tanya could barely believe her ears.

'Yes, and on a film that is going to be big. But for now, you have to be patient. I have to work out details with my colleagues.

You met Cherry didn't you? Well, Tanya you wanted to work in films, and you shall.' He walked over to her and hugged her. She hugged him with all her strength.

'I don't believe it . . . I'll never be able to sleep again,' she said, laughing.

'Remember Tanya, I don't want you telling your housemates what we are going to be doing. It is going to be secret. Wait until tomorrow when I call and arrange our next meeting at least.'

'I'll do exactly what you say.' Tanya hugged Harvey again. 'I'm going to work in films.'

Tanya saw Harvey out while the others cleaned up discreetly.

'Tan, are you all right?' Leigh asked after he had gone.

'Oh LeeLee, I am more than all right,' she said as she swept off to bed.

Harvey hailed a cab and headed home. He knew that the people he'd just met would give him *the* movie. Although they'd been interesting, they weren't *that* interesting but his instinct told him that they were exactly what he needed.

Chapter Nineteen

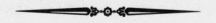

Cherry and Bob had spent the evening in their usual manner, in front of the television. An hour before Harvey reappeared, Bob had retired to bed, moaning about the boredom he was beginning to feel. Cherry placated him, which was one of her best qualities. But when he did disappear off to bed, she decided to wait patiently for Harvey to come home. The time had come for her to find out what was going on. She was still unsure of Harvey's intentions towards Tanya. If he didn't come home then she would fry his balls.

She was lying on the sofa, half watching the news when Harvey walked in. The first thing she noticed was how handsome he was, which was always the first thing she noticed about him, the second was that he was smiling.

'Cherry baby, you waited up,' he teased, squeezing himself into the space on the sofa next to her.

'Well Harvey, I hoped you might be able to tell me something. This thing you're working on is killing me.'

'OK, honey, tonight I met the cast of our film,' he said.

'What?' Cherry sat up straight. 'I didn't know you were auditioning.'

'That's the whole thing, I wasn't. Well, not in the traditional sense. I think it's time that I told you everything. Pour some brandies and I'll begin.'

They sat on the sofa with two brandies. At last Harvey was ready to reveal his plan.

'Should I wake Bob?' Cherry asked.

'No, I'll tell him tomorrow, but just listen and don't ask questions until I've finished.' Harvey sipped his drink. Cherry knew the drill, he hated interruptions when he was outlining his plans.

'It all started with you when we first moved here. Remember how you refused to leave the building, and you started watching all that fly-on-the-wall TV? Well, then we all got hooked on it. So that is what we are going to do.' He paused for dramatic effect. Cherry held her breath. 'We, my darling, are going to make our own fly-on-the-wall movie. Now I know what you're thinking, you're thinking *Truman Show*, *Ed TV*, but you'd be wrong. Those were movies *about* fly-on-the-wall, they had actors and scripts. We are going to make a real fly-on-the-wall movie. No actors, no scripts. Just an unsuspecting group of friends.' Again he paused for dramatic effect. Cherry grabbed the brandy bottle and poured more drinks.

'What I mean is that you, me, Bob, his crew and Tanya are going to make a film. The film has no script. The cast are Tanya's housemates and her, but she will be the only one in the film that knows. You see, she lives with some really crazy people. On the surface they are normal twentysomething's, but they each have this thing about them that makes them a bit insane. Tanya is a total control freak and she's really bossy, I sensed it, although she was obviously on her best behaviour tonight. She's a great girl and she'll be a brilliant producer-cum-puppet master. The other girl she lives with is Leigh. Leigh likes to be called LeeLee and she only wears pink. This is a new development, influenced by the fact she has a massive unrequited crush on Gus, and something to do with her boss, although I couldn't quite figure that part out. She talked about make-up, clothes, even knitting. Can you believe it? But the best thing was the look of utter astonishment on the faces of the others when she was doing this. She isn't normally like that.

'Then there's Gus, the crushee, who, apart from being a very good-looking doctor, is also desperate to fall in love, although not with Leigh I guess, and writes poems about it all the time. Next there's David who is an Internet nerd. He even tried to set up a site for mail-order of substandard knickers. He only dates online as well. Priceless. Next the best of the bunch is Eric, who is trying to get cannabis legalised for medical purposes (he's a pharmacist), and seems to be intent on making it his personal crusade instead of joining an existing group. Oh yeah, and he is also trying to build the ultimate joint, whatever that is. He's very intelligent, well they all are, even Leigh because she's obviously pretending to be dumb.

'They have this great dynamic about them. They seem to find each other slightly absurd although they're friends. For example Tanya and Leigh have been friends for ever but they have nothing in common. So there you have it, that's our cast. The cast who have no idea that they're going to be in a movie. Questions?'

For a minute or two, Cherry tried to digest what she had heard, then she was ready with her questions. She was incredibly calm for someone who had heard the most absurd idea, but that was why Cherry worked with Harvey. In the past he had come out with ideas which were off the scale of strangeness, Cherry was used to this, but remained sceptical.

'Will Tanya agree?'

'Yes, I thought of that. She will because she's desperate to work in movies. We can do that for her. And also, because she's selfish.'

'How do we go about it?'

'Hidden cameras. Tanya will have a control room, Bob will have to sort out logistics.'

'How do you know that it will make good viewing?'

'I just do, have I ever been wrong?' He hadn't.

'How can we release it if they don't know about it?'

'Very good Cherry, you're thinking the right way. That's the hardest part. Once it's finished and edited, we show them. Of course they'll be shocked, maybe angry, but then we have to persuade them to give permission. We'll think of something, but we will get it released. It will happen.'

'So, how do we market it?'

'With an air of subtle mystery. No one will believe it's complete true life, and totally unscripted, so we tell them it is and let the controversy start. A great marketing ploy.'

'Well it's the craziest idea I've ever heard. So crazy it might work, no sorry Harvey, of course it'll work. Have you signed up Tanya yet?'

'No, that's our next step. I'm calling her tomorrow and I want her to meet with all of us next time.'

'Is it legal?'

'I have no idea, but I guess not. There's bound to be invasion of privacy laws. What I want you to do is to ensure that in Tanya's contract she takes the heat for that. It's just insurance. Then, when everyone agrees to its release, we won't have to worry about being sued.'

'Budget. Harvey we took the money to make a movie with a sizeable budget. I know it's not quite on the scale of *Titanic*, but surely this won't cost much.'

'I guess it won't. But how will Poplar figure that? We could fiddle with the numbers. We'll pay Tanya quite a lot if it works — a success fee. We'll have to pay the cast. With Bob and his side, I want the best people. The best editors that Britain has to offer, so they'll cost. Then we have this apartment, and you need an assistant. Any money left over we'll split three ways and hide in the production costs.' He smiled.

'So, you've thought of everything then.'

'No, not quite. I haven't got a title.'

Chapter Twenty

'LeeLee and I are going into a meeting, don't disturb us for anything, especially clients.' Sukie smiled at Kitty, Leigh did the same.

'Fine, Sukie.' Kitty displayed a mouth full of perfect white teeth. Leigh wished she had teeth like her.

Ever since Leigh had confessed to Sukie her love for Gus, the meetings between them had become the focus of her day. Sukie was obsessed with Leigh getting Gus, or being the reason that Leigh got Gus. It was the same approach she took with all her staff. She saw herself as a fairy godmother to them all. As their account director, she had looked after and nurtured numerous assistants, account managers and account executives. Now her team was almost as she wanted it, with the exception of Leigh.

Everyone else in the agency marvelled at the way Sukie controlled the names and personalities of those who worked for her. They also marvelled at the way that, despite the apparent lack of work and the lack of people who seemed capable of doing any work, her team was one of the most successful in the agency.

Leigh closed the door and went to sit opposite Sukie.

'So, progress report,' Sukie requested.

'Oh Sukie, I don't know what to do. They all call me LeeLee now, and I think the giggle is working well. And I wear pink nearly all the time, you know. But he still seems uninterested.' Leigh was tearful.

'Mmm, this one is a tough nut. You know, I was thinking, if changing your name and appearance doesn't work, which it will in the long-term, what you need to do is become his friend.' Sukie looked triumphant.

'I *am* his friend.' Leigh was confused.

'I know honey, but you need to be his *best* friend. Nearly every romance starts out with good friends. Like *When Harry Met Sally*. You need to become his confidante. Then he'll look at you one day and wham! the romance will bloom and it'll be wonderful.' A far-away look passed over Sukie's face. Any sane person would have thought that the foundations for her advice were a little shaky, but Leigh wasn't sane. She was in love, and love and sanity have little in common. Sukie's sanity might be in question but she wasn't in love. Sukie, for all her advice on relationships, was single.

'You think so?' Leigh asked, wide-eyed.

'Oh my dear little LeeLee, I know so. Keep wearing the pink, being LeeLee and giggling, but also be his best friend. Oh, this is so exciting, I can't wait to see how it turns out. Start tonight. Oh, start straight away. Gosh LeeLee, can't you feel that this is going to work?'

'I can, I can,' Leigh replied, eating up Sukie's enthusiasm. If only I were like Sukie, Leigh thought, Gus would want me then.

Gus was having a rare lunch with Eric in the hospital canteen.

'Do you think I should stop dating for a while?' Gus asked.

'Why?' Eric asked. He was used to Gus's obsession and took it, as he took everything else, in his stride.

'Because I just get more and more disappointed with each girl I meet,' Gus explained.

'What brought this on?' Eric asked.

'After Harvey left I was in bed and I was thinking about all the girls I've gone out with.'

'That must have taken most of the night,' Eric joked and Gus smiled.

'Anyway, it all went wrong at one point in my life, I know that now.'

'Natasha,' Eric said, and felt fear run through his veins.

'Natasha.' For once, Eric was lost for a response so he bit into his cheese and pickle sandwich instead.

David had been chatting online to Em for most of the night, so he decided to call in sick to his office. He was sick. Sick with lust and what he thought could only be love. They had spoken so openly to each other and a tenderness had crept in that he had never experienced before. Em was as scared as he was of meeting face to face; she said that she was worried they would lose the magic of their online relationship. David sighed as he lay in bed trying to get some sleep. Their relationship was the most magical thing he had ever encountered and he had never touched her, heard her voice or seen her face.

They discussed exchanging photographs, and both had agreed that they would do that soon. Although David knew that Gus's idea of a love affair and his were totally different, he had empathised with him that morning.

Tanya had gone to work and sat daydreaming through the production meeting. She was waiting for Harvey's call. Then she had had a row with one of her staff because she was so on edge. She had done no work. A file sat on her desk with a proposed new programme, and as she flicked through it half-heartedly she couldn't get Harvey out of her mind. She willed the phone to ring.

Harvey sat in his office with Bob and Cherry. When it was just the three of them it seemed strange to call meetings in the office. However Cherry insisted on it. 'Harvey we live here and we work in there. We need barriers.' The subject was not up for discussion.

'Have you noticed that it's not raining today?' Bob pointed out with a smile.

'Which is appropriate seeing as we are ready for pre-production.' Harvey smiled triumphantly.

'We are?' Bob looked as if an electric shock had hit him as he sat down.

'Yup, now listen to this,' Cherry added as she motioned for Harvey to start. The emotions on Bob's face changed as Harvey unveiled his story. Amused when he described Tanya's household; scared when he explained about the lack of script or actors; horrified when he was told that it would all be done with hidden cameras.

'Harvey, I rarely question your professional decisions, but there's always a first time. I will keep to the technical side of this. Hidden cameras? Bad idea, it gives us so little control over the shots.'

'That is why you will be setting up the most sophisticated editing process. When we get the shots from the house, they'll probably need work to make them cinegraphic, which is where you and your new team come in,' Harvey explained.

'Do I get artistic control?'

'Yes, and Bob, this has never been done before, never. The potential is enormous Do you know how big we can make this?'

'Sure Harvey, but you've got to agree it's crazy. What about this girl, she's never even made a film, how do we know she's up to it?'

'Trust me. Anyway, she has me as the director, she has you as the technical adviser, we'll guide her. I propose we put a control room into the house, in her room so that she can watch footage and keep an eye on what's happening. We then ensure we have the same access at an editing suite, that's your call.'

'What if these people turn out to be boring?' Bob asked, reasonably.

'Then we'll have to ensure that they're not.'

'OK, well I can't talk you out of it, and we need a film. I guess it might just be crazy enough to work. Are you sure this Tanya

will go for it? You are asking her to betray her friends after all.'
Bob shuddered. The idea that someone could do that unnerved
him.

'I would bet Cherry's shoe collection on it.'

'That confident?'

Cherry smiled and went to get more coffee. Next they started
making lists of what needed to be done. Bob was going to find a
top-of-the-range editing suite and some top quality editors. Also,
he was going to employ engineers and lighting specialists for the
house fitting. Cherry was in charge of getting a contract drawn
up for Tanya to sign. She also had to send an estimate of the pre-
production budget to Poplar Films, giving Steve Delaney the
impression of being in control of his money. Even though he
wasn't.

The other issue that they discussed was what would happen
when the film was wrapped and should the cast refuse to allow
its release. It was the only matter that was unresolved in Harvey's
mind, but he knew that he would solve it. Nothing had ever felt
so right in his whole life.

He looked with affection at Cherry and Bob. This was his
baby, and they were its godparents. It was rare in life to develop a
concept which would become the next 'big thing', but that was
what was happening. Here in this London flat with Cherry and
Bob they were about to create something which could not only
change their lives but add a new genre to film history; and the
unsuspecting Tanya was about to be the pawn in his quest to do
this.

Using people was part of life, but using people by giving
them what they wanted expunged blame. Tanya wanted Hollywood and Harvey would give her that. First she would sacrifice
her friends, but that was her decision. If you sell your soul to the
devil you can't blame the devil, and no one could blame Harvey
for what he was doing. Could they?

Chapter Twenty-One

Pre-Production

'Cherry, where's Bob?'

'I don't know, probably in bed or in the shower,' Cherry replied.

'I'll get him, I need a meeting with you both.'

'Fine.' Cherry watched Harvey go off to find Bob and suppressed a stray giggle. At Cherry's behest, the flat was now both an office and a home. Harvey behaved differently whenever he slipped into work mode. He even wore shoes. Cherry, who had taken to wearing nothing on her feet but thick woollen socks found the shoes issue unnerving.

Bob was discovered getting dressed. Harvey gave him ten minutes and then went to organise coffee. He found Cherry already preparing it.

'Amazing. You know you make me feel like J. R. Ewing honey,' he said, taking a cup of coffee from her.

'Harvey, you couldn't be more unlike J. R. if you tried.' The other difference since the plan had been unveiled was that Harvey was more buoyant. He smiled and ushered Cherry into the office. He carried in the coffee tray which he put down on the glass table. As he sat down at his desk he considered Cherry. She made him feel invincible; the only way he could evolve his latest idea was with her. He had decided the first time he met her that one day he could fall in love with her. Perhaps after the movie would be the perfect time.

Bob burst into the room. 'Sorry I'm late, *if* I'm late. Harvey this working at home is weird. Not having a journey to work.'

'Thanks Bob. Let's get on. I'm seeing Tanya this afternoon and I'm ready to offer her the job of producer on our movie. If she agrees we'll need the paperwork to be ready Cherry, and Bob, we'll need to move fast on the technical side.'

'Well, the lawyers are drawing up contracts as requested. They said we could have a draft by tomorrow. If she agrees, then we'll have them ready to sign,' Cherry smiled.

'What about the legal issues?' Bob asked. He was nervous of lawsuits like most Americans.

'In the contract, Tanya takes full responsibility,' Cherry explained.

'In the contract we do ensure she takes full responsibility, but in return we promise to destroy the material if the other participants don't agree in the end.' Harvey stood up and poured more coffee.

'So, she takes any possible trouble, but we ensure that there is no trouble?' Bob asked.

'Exactly. Anyway, let me worry about that side. You worry about the technical side.' Harvey said this knowing full well that Bob would worry.

'Well to be honest, I've been looking at suppliers but I need to see the house and its layout before I know what we need. Staffwise, I am employing three editors to work directly with me and we'll run a crash training course with Tanya when she comes on board. I have also found a lighting contractor who we'll need to get into the house to look at lighting issues. Then I'll need camera experts to design the layout of the hidden cameras, engineers to install them and maybe construction guys. I think that's about it for now. Oh yeah, I also need an assistant in the editing suite,' Bob finished.

'Great Bob, you seem to be on top of everything. You both do.'

'But are we?' Cherry asked.

'What honey?' Harvey replied.

'Are we on top? I know you explained this to us and we have agreed as your faithful servants to go along with it, but you haven't spoken to Tanya yet.' Cherry was concerned.

'Which is why we're here. I want us to have a brainstorm about fly-on-the-wall, docusoaps or whatever we call them. I want us to figure out where we're going with this before I see her next. What is the name we feel most comfortable using for the kind of TV we're basing our film on?' Harvey asked.

'There are so many terms I've learned since I started watching them: "Reality TV", which I hate because it's not real. "Docusoaps", which I don't mind because documentaries follow real things and soaps are drama, so it's a combination of both. "Fly-on-the-wall" is another one to consider. I guess that's it. I think in order to make a difference, our film should be fly-on-the-wall.' Cherry looked at them.

'Even though Tanya will know?' Bob asked.

'Yeah, that's just a technicality isn't it?' Cherry replied.

'Sure. If we call our film fly-on-the-wall, that means that it was made without the knowledge of the cast. Tanya can be overlooked. So, when we say fly-on-the-wall, we mean, un-scripted, no actors and no awareness of being filmed. Excellent. That's how we sell this movie. It's the Jim Carrey part of *The Truman Show*, only it really is! So the next thing is to look at trends. What are the trends, Cherry?'

'Youth. What I noticed with the TV shows is that most of the more popular ones centre around the 18–35 year olds. I see two main categories. First is a show focusing around an airport, a holiday, a desert island, a cruise ship, a corner shop, a lap-dancing club – you know, that kind of thing. Then there's the game shows. But, what I do know is that the younger and the sexier the show, the more popular it is.'

'Fine, so again we've got a selling point. All our characters are under thirty, all nice looking, all professional, all quirky. And as they don't know it's happening and there's no competition we should get a more natural result, shouldn't we?' Harvey said.

'What I think Harvey, is that you know where this conversation is going more than any of us. OK, so we have the youth aspect, we, hopefully, if your deductions are right, have the love aspect. We have strong personalities, and quirky personalities. We have a very sexy cast, and a sexy concept. But let's talk about the reality side of reality TV. How real is it? Forget the fact you know you're being filmed, that's irrelevant in this case. The other aspect is that after these shows finish and the newspapers dissect them, the number of people that complain they were unfairly portrayed is incredible. How can reality TV portray people unfairly, it's like a contradiction in terms. Right? But of course they film people twenty-four hours a day for however long and you get to watch thirty minutes. That takes the reality out of it. Even with the game shows they edit it to only show the best bits. So, in conclusion; is there such a thing as reality TV?'

'Bravo my dear Cherry,' Harvey kissed her on the cheek.

'So, we make a movie that is unscripted and made in ignorance of the majority of the cast, but it still isn't real. That's the point of the exercise?'

'Not exactly. This has never been done before. We are making history.'

Cherry and Bob exchanged glances and smiled. This was the way Harvey operated. No one understood it, but that was just how it was.

'Harvey honey, manipulation, that's what we were talking about, where does that figure in our movie?' Cherry asked.

'I have no idea that it does,' he replied.

'But it could?' Bob pushed.

'Bob, anything is possible. Now we know the history of this kind of show on TV, but we have never seen it done as a movie. All I am saying is that, whatever happens, we start with a blank page and we will be prepared. We are conducting our own reality test. Is there such a thing as reality on the screen be it big or small? That just gives it an edge for me.' Harvey laughed.

'What about the proposition that as a trend it's dying out? People are now sick of it and every idea has been flogged to death?' Cherry asked.

'Irrelevant. When our movie comes out people's voyeuristic natures will get the better of them. Even people who won't believe that we really did fly-on-the-wall will be too curious to stay away. So we are conducting a social experiment as well. To conclude that people are intrinsically nosy.' Harvey smiled triumphantly.

'OK, so finally Harvey, how much of this is Tanya going to be privy to?' Bob asked.

'Only as much as she needs to be of course,' Harvey replied.

The banter continued, but everyone was now full of anticipation for the project. Bob and Cherry were not only behind Harvey, they were also finding themselves increasingly excited at the prospect. They wanted to make history. They believed that they would make history. Although they still held slight reservations about Tanya, they had no reason to suspect that Harvey wouldn't be able to persuade her to go ahead.

Harvey opened the door to Tanya, giving her a peck on the cheek. He smiled and made small talk as he checked her out. She was dressed in a way that Cherry would approve, smart, but fashionable. She was wearing a black straight skirt with a split up one side, a cream jumper and knee-high black boots. Her hair was neat although it was raining outside and her make-up was immaculate. Harvey knew that she would have been his type if they hadn't been going to work together. She was foxy, sassy and more than a bit sexy.

He didn't know that she was doing the same to him. She was taking in every inch of Harvey, from his brown hair, to his black jumper, his black trousers and his black loafers (which she didn't know were his lucky shoes), and she, again, thought what a gorgeous figure he was. She wondered what he thought of her.

It was a shame that people didn't know the good thoughts

other people had about them. If Tanya knew that Harvey *would* have slept with her, then she would have been happier about the fact that he wasn't going to. Although that was more to do with Tanya's perception of life.

'Tanya, come into the office. Coffee?' he asked, leading the way.

'No thanks,' she replied following Harvey into the office. Harvey motioned for her to sit on the sofa. He sat next to her.

'So, I can't wait to hear what you wanted to discuss,' Tanya said, nervously.

'I guess I had better tell you then.' Harvey winked and launched into his idea.

The words seemed to enter Tanya's ears and flow through her body. For the first time in her life, she lost the power of speech. Harvey kept it simple, yet tried to make it sound appealing. After he'd outlined the idea fully, he dangled the golden carrot.

'The offer I am making you is this. You will be a producer on this movie. You will have a control room of your own and you will be in charge in your arena. I will be your boss, but you will also be working with Cherry, Bob and a number of other people. You will have certain responsibilities and rights with your job. I will pay you a salary double what you are making now and if the film is successful you will receive double any money we pay your housemates. This is the job for you, a job in films and the rewards will be your wildest dreams coming true. What I am asking from you is loyalty to me. I am your first priority, not your housemates. It may sound harsh but that's the only way this will work. We'll put it all on paper. Apart from being a way into Hollywood, this could make you a wealthy and famous young woman. Tanya, I want you to do this. Don't ask any questions now, not one. I know you have a million floating around, so go home, think about it, get everything straight, then call me. Any time. Then you can ask me everything you need to and give me your initial reaction. OK?' Harvey looked as deeply as he could into Tanya's eyes. She was in shock, but she managed to nod.

'Why?' she asked in the smallest voice she had ever heard.

'No questions. I explained the appeal of your housemates and the appeal of working with you. Think about it, then ask the questions.' Harvey stood up indicating the end of the meeting. Tanya followed.

As he led her out of the office, through the hallway and into the sitting room the silence filled the entire flat. He led her through the sitting room to the front door, pausing to retrieve her coat from the cupboard. Still they didn't speak. He helped her into her coat, then, as he opened the door, he kissed her cheek. She nodded. Without a word she looked at him, then turned and walked away. And with that Harvey knew he had won. If it was the look in her eyes or the nod, he wasn't sure, but his instincts told him that he'd get what he wanted from her, and he always trusted his instincts.

Tanya found herself at her front door. She couldn't remember the journey at all. As she let herself in she looked at the house and saw it for the first time. It was no longer the house she lived in, it was a proposed film set. Not noticing that it was four in the afternoon, she walked into the kitchen, took a bottle of red wine from the wine rack, a glass from the cupboard and the corkscrew from the drawer. Then she climbed the stairs to her room.

She took her booty to her desk and laid it out. She picked up her handbag and pulled out a pack of cigarettes. Tanya rarely smoked, usually only when she drank. She intended drinking. She opened the pack and to focus read the health warning. *Cigarettes can damage your health*, it screamed. So can life, she screamed back.

Once she had a drink in her glass, a lit cigarette in her hand and her scented candle burning to dispel the smell of smoke, she opened a drawer in the table and pulled out a notebook. It was an A4 red notebook. One she had bought when she first decided that her future lay in films. The idea was that she would write any idea she had in there. So far it was empty, but she had something to write now.

She searched the drawer until she found a pen and she pulled it out. She opened the book, took the cap off the pen, took a gulp of wine and a last drag of her cigarette. Then she began to write.

Today, I was given an opportunity I do not understand. If I ignore my personal feelings for Harvey Cannon, I still feel confused. On the one hand I was offered the job of my dreams, on the other, I was given the price for it. I have to lie to my housemates. I have to spy on them. I don't know if that's even legal and I suspect it is not. So the first thing is betrayal, which I know sounds dramatic, but that's how it feels, dramatic. Also I don't understand why he wants them. Why would he want the people that I live with? Why wasn't I enough?

She put her pen down, refilled her glass and lit another cigarette. The main thing she had to figure out was how she felt. She could see the merits of the idea, Harvey had sold them well. She could see how it would result in a ground-breaking film, whether it was good or terrible. She actually believed in the idea. So what was the problem?

The thing is that, although I see what Harvey means, I don't see why we have to use my household. Not only will I be producing the film and controlling footage from my control room, but also, I will be part of it. I will be the only part of it that knows. Am I worried about how everyone will see me when they finally find out what I've done? Not really because I know how they see me now. I am ambitious, I am selfish and I am bossy. Nothing will change in that. Of course I will have to lie to them, and that isn't something I relish. I would hate to think that I have to ruin their lives in order to get what I want. I hate to think that that is the decision I will have to make. I am afraid that if it came to it, I would do so without a third thought. Why couldn't he have just wanted me?

She slammed her pen down. Anger filled her. How could something that was so good for her make her do something bad to someone else? That wasn't fair. She knew she would need to make a decision quickly. She knew there were other people, other places and she knew that somehow, that night, her pink friend, her dope friend, her computer-geek friend and her doctor had got to this man enough to make him want to use them as part of the 'biggest project of his life', She decided that the most constructive thing she could do was to think about what would happen next.

So, I need to think of questions, but how can I when I want to scream at him? Somehow I feel he gave me gold but charged me platinum. The worst thing is that he knows I'll do it. I felt it from him. He knows how much I want and need this opportunity, he can feel it. And if he'd asked me to strip naked and suck his dick, I would have done so like a whore. But he asked me to sell my friends to him, which I will do, like a pimp. What other option do I have? I could be a drama queen about it, and drag out my decision with indecision, and a guilty conscience, but I know in the end what I'll do. So why delay? Will anyone think any better of me if it takes me longer to make the decision? I don't see how they can, or how it can make me worse than I already am. At least, I am not pretending that I am a great person, if I go through with this I shall be living deceitfully and lying to all my housemates. Even if I use the fact that I barely know Eric and Gus as an excuse, I can't do that with Leigh and David. I could end up hurting them. I could lose them. But sometimes I feel I have already lost them. I've lost Leigh to Gus and her boss. She doesn't need me any more and Leigh had always needed me. Can I use her betrayal of me to justify my betrayal of her?

I would like to say that I believe that this could turn out better for everyone. After all, Harvey did say that they would benefit financially from any project. He also said that without their consent there would be no film release. Although I believe that Harvey could persuade anyone to do anything, he has a confidence that I am finding it hard to hold on to. Even if I can make them agree, even if I can make them rich, I know now that I am also going to hurt them. But what can I do about that? Turning Harvey down is far more scary than any consequences I will face. Would I become a hero if I told my friends what Harvey suggested and how I refused to do it? No, I would be Tanya Palmer, a twenty-six-year-old television producer with an empty life. How could that make me a hero?

For the next hour, Tanya sat drinking in her room. She drank quickly once she abandoned her pen. She smoked quickly. She thought quickly. There wasn't much left to think about. There was, in fact, lots left to think about, but Tanya wasn't a thinker. She didn't believe in dilemmas, she was short on morals. After a bottle of red wine, she was fortified, but not drunk. She decided to phone Harvey. She pulled out her mobile phone, dialled and waited.

'Hello,' Cherry answered.

'Hello, is Harvey there? It's Tanya.'

'Sure he's here.' Cherry handed over the phone.

'Tanya, I didn't think I'd hear from you so soon.' He had, in fact, expected to hear from her that soon.

'I think you know me well enough to know I like to act

quickly. About those questions, I'm ready with them. I am also very hungry. So perhaps you'd like to take me to dinner.' She could almost feel Harvey's smile.

'I can't think of anything I would rather do,' he said.

They met a couple of hours later in The Blue Elephant, on Fulham Road, at Tanya's suggestion. Sitting down opposite her, Harvey took control again. He ordered the wine, asked for the set menu and although he checked with Tanya first, she was under the impression that if she'd said no he would have gone ahead anyway.

'You know, I like your style. I liked it from the first time I met you,' Harvey said, as they settled back with an apéritif.

'Thanks, but that's not all you like.' Harvey looked at her questioningly. She shook her head. 'What I mean is why my housemates?'

'Well, because you're all different, unique, intelligent and fun,' he replied.

'But Harvey, we are not amazing or anything.' Tanya was agitated, but Harvey was smiling.

'I think you are.'

'You could use anyone but you want to use my friends?'

'Think of it as a social experiment. You're not so different, but you are all intelligent, sexy, young and professional. The fact that you have quirks only adds to your appeal. People are going to fall in love with all of you, just as they would any movie star. But you all work as a group in a way that is unique. You have a great dynamic. Everyone will want to live with you, love you, be you. We are going to create five new heart-throbs,' Harvey finished. Although Tanya didn't know it, it was the second time the housemates had been attributed with a 'group dynamic'. One which so far had not lived up to expectations for the first person who coined the phrase, but had more than lived up to it for the second.

'You are? How?'

'Like I said. Hidden cameras.'

'But not in bedrooms, or the bathroom.' This had only just occurred to Tanya and when it did, the idea of spying hit her hard.

'What about if we use bedrooms but promise not to show nudity or sex?'

'No, no way.' Tanya felt stronger for her resolve.

'OK, then communal areas only, except the bathroom. After all it's your interaction we're after.' Harvey smiled. Bedrooms in that house didn't seem to see much action anyway.

'What if it's rubbish?'

'It won't be. There is no way. You've worked on reality TV, or docusoaps or whatever you want to call it. The theory is that life is art itself, and if you film the same spot for long enough something interesting will happen. We are going to put that theory into practice.'

'Without the knowledge of my friends,' Tanya added.

'It wouldn't work otherwise. It has to be unscripted and unacted. If they knew, we might as well kill it off now.'

'What if one of them finds out?'

'It's your job to ensure that that doesn't happen until we're ready.'

'What if it's good enough at the end, but they won't agree to it being released?'

'Then we persuade them,' Harvey said.

'How?'

'Tanya we'll cross that bridge if and when it comes. There are a number of things we can do. Firstly, they will see the film first and hopefully enjoy it so much that we won't need to persuade them. But we can't predict their reaction, because we are at the very beginning, and at this stage we don't know what is going to happen.'

'Why?'

'Why what?'

'Why this? Why this film? What ever possessed you to choose this?'

'Tanya, I have no idea. But I do know something. This is going to be the best film released for a long time and if you want to be linked to that success then you have the opportunity.' Harvey smiled as the starter was delivered.

Tanya questioned Harvey throughout the entire meal. So much so that he barely noticed the food although he noticed his own weariness. He ate, answered a question, took a sip of wine and so on. He answered every question as if he had thought through each issue thoroughly beforehand, even if he hadn't. By the time he ordered a brandy, he was exhausted.

'Tanya, you can have some more time to think about it,' he offered. Tanya looked at him. She saw something in him which told her everything. When she had been preparing to meet him the first time she had worried about him wanting sex. When he had posed as her boyfriend, she had wanted him to want sex. He never did want sex, she wasn't stupid. He wanted something far more complicated than sex. She looked at him to say goodbye. Goodbye to the crush she had on him. She then said hello. Hello to her new boss.

'When do I get the papers?' she asked. Although he had been confident, he still felt relieved.

'A week, tops,' he replied.

'Give them to me and I'll sign. Then I'll resign my job and try to negotiate my notice period. Hopefully I'll be able to start straight away. What do we need to do next?' The thing that Harvey had seen in Tanya, from the first time he met her was her ability to switch herself quickly from one situation to the next. One minute she was asking questions and fretting, the next she was pushing to move forward.

'Well honey, you should meet Cherry and Bob properly. Bob will explain about the technical side to the movie, Cherry deals with everything else. Then I guess we need to bug your house.'

'That makes me feel awful, when you say things like that,' she explained.

'Well stop feeling bad, we are going to spy on your friends because that's how we have to make this film. Any doubts are to be left at this dinner table. Remember Tanya, we are not going to hurt them, we're going to make them stars.'

'Yup. And we're going to make me a star too.'

'Naturally.'

'One more thing, what do I tell them about us?' Tanya asked.

'What about us?'

'We told them we were dating.'

Harvey had already forgotten this. 'Oh, tell them it didn't work out; after all, until the film is finished, they won't see me again.'

'Fine.' Once again she looked at him and saw him as her boss.

Harvey looked at Tanya and finally realised what he had done. Here in front of him was the beginning of his film. He had the idea, he had the location, he had the producer and he had the cast. And as he didn't need a script, he even had his script. All in a matter of weeks.

Normally this work would take months, even years, but here he was. Harvey knew he could be trusted to pull this off, and he knew he would pull it off. This would ensure his immortality, and that was really what he wanted more than anything else.

Chapter Twenty-Two

While Tanya tried not to think about her guilt, Harvey, Bob and Cherry were mobilised into action. As with anything that Harvey did, progress was fast.

Within two weeks, everything was settled.

Cherry produced legal documents for Tanya and the other employees. The new employees were: three highly qualified editors, James Dunn, Amanda Brownlow and John King, whom Bob had employed, an assistant for them, Sally Young and an assistant for Cherry, Millie Harcourt. Bob had hired an editing suite from which his editors would work. Their job was to keep an eye on the whole production, which meant checking out the footage every day. The idea being to discard what they definitely could not use. Even though the plan was thin, at least it was there. Bob had also employed a lighting consultant and two cameramen to plan where the hidden cameras would go. Millie, Cherry's assistant was running around sorting out contracts and retainers for the consultants and the buzz was building.

Everyone had signed the strictest confidentiality agreements.

Tanya met Cherry to collect her contract. They met in a coffee bar in Fulham. It was the first time the two women had met outside the flat, it was the first time that Cherry had been alone with Tanya. Immediately Cherry sensed a hostility from her. Deciding to ignore it, she handed over the contract and explained it clause by clause. When they came to the end, she smiled. 'If you have any problems or questions, please ask.'

Tanya shrugged. 'Why didn't Harvey bring this?' For a moment Cherry was taken aback.

'Tanya, Harvey is the director, I am his assistant. It's my job to deal with this.' She smiled kindly. Cherry was worried about her relationship with Tanya. As Harvey had reminded everyone a million times, Tanya was essential to their project – without her they would all be in trouble.

'Fine. Then I have no more questions. Where do I sign?' As Tanya pulled the cap off her pen, Cherry felt nervous. She had butterflies in her stomach as Tanya signed, although she wasn't sure why.

'Honey, welcome aboard,' Cherry said.

'Thank you . . . thanks Cherry,' Tanya replied. 'Tell me, have I really just done that?'

'You really have.' They laughed. 'Tanya, we are going to have fun doing this and when it works out, you'll be hot property. We all will. So, when are you resigning from your job?'

'Tomorrow. When do I start?'

'The day you finish work. If you can finish sooner rather than later, we can start getting the equipment in place. You'll be working with Bob on that. As soon as that is done, you will meet with Harvey to discuss any ideas and frameworks you both have. If you need anything, and I mean anything, you call me honey and if I'm not around give a message to Millie. As you'll largely be working from home Millie is getting you a laptop, a mobile, which we pay for, and she needs to arrange to have a phone line fitted in your room, for e-mail. What we need is for you to be able to call us anytime and for us to be able to contact you. Is that OK?' Cherry could feel the atmosphere thawing.

'It's all happening so fast. I—' Tanya stopped abruptly.

Cherry moved closer to her. 'Listen honey, you can talk to me, especially if you feel that you need to. This is moving fast, but Harvey made a promise that he would deliver a film within a year. It was a rash promise and something that no one else would do, especially as he had no idea what the film was going to be about. That's why we're moving quickly. That's the way Harvey does things.'

'I just feel that everything's happening too fast. Of course I want it to happen and I am excited, happy, a little nervous and worried. I'm worried it might all go wrong. What if they find out? What if they don't but it turns out to be boring rubbish? What if I'm no good at picking out the best footage?' Tanya stopped again and shook her head. 'I am just experiencing first-night nerves.' She smiled.

'Yes, first-night nerves, that's what we'll put it down to. Listen, we all know this is a crazy plan, but it will work, so relax a little. I know you don't exactly have a job description to follow, but hey you can pick it up, you're smart, which is why Harvey chose you.'

'I can do this. You know, I still feel a little guilty about spying on them,' she added.

'Well, that's understandable, but you know why you're doing it. And hey, we've got a long way to run with this, anything could happen. Anything probably will,' Cherry laughed.

'It's mad isn't it?' Tanya said.

'What is?'

'What he's doing. He is filming five people in their day-to-day lives. Only one knows anything, the others don't have a clue. And he thinks that out of all our lives we'll be able to make a film. That's the mad thing, that any of this will be good enough to make a film out of,' Tanya explained.

'Real life can be boring, huh?' Cherry replied.

'I make documentaries, which are always based on a story, they start with a story. Even the reality TV shows have a framework. And I think that maybe that's what makes it interesting. Did you watch the one that started last week? *Fantasy Holiday*? Well my company produced that although I wasn't involved. They chose people whom they knew would hate each other before they sent them to that house in France. Why they called it fantasy I have no idea, it was more like nightmare holiday. They had twenty thousand people apply, they chose ten to live in this house in the middle of nowhere, knowing that there would be the biggest rows ever.'

'I watched it. You're right, honey. We're proving life is art, or that's what we're trying to prove. We are painting with a blank canvas and you know what, this will make history,' Cherry finished.

'You know what, Cherry, you don't half sound like Harvey.' They both laughed.

Cherry took the signed contract back to the flat with a feeling of satisfaction. She thought she might actually grow to like Tanya.

Tanya returned home, chewed her fingernails and waited. As she waited she pulled out the notebook she had written in the night she had received her offer. She re-read what she'd written, then she turned to the next blank page and pulled out a pen.

Today I signed the contract. Soon I will work for Harvey Cannon, who has such a big reputation. But I still don't know if I trust him. Almost overnight I have become a film producer, and more importantly a film producer who is actually going to produce a film. My boring old job will be behind me. When I thought this through, I had a vision. A self-imposed vision of me living in Hollywood. The sun kept me warm, where my friends might not. I would be in Hollywood, making films, films that people will remember. I will be immortal. So how can I worry about guilt? From now on, I won't worry about guilt.

She put the book back into her drawer, and smiled. She would put guilt behind her, although she had no idea if guilt would accept that. It was time for her to go and see her housemates.

As Tanya walked down the stairs she looked around her and wondered about the cameras. What would they capture? Would having one on the stairs prove interesting? Would it show clandestine meetings? She doubted it. Brushing the thoughts aside she decided instead to concentrate on trying to live life as normally as she could, with the big secret wrapped around her.

When she got downstairs, the first thing she noticed was that Eric and David were cooking.

'Something smells good,' she said walking into the kitchen.

'Didn't know you were in,' Eric replied.

'I came back about an hour ago,' Tanya protested.

'Right, so when you had a go at us for being unsociable, it didn't include not saying hello when you come in?' Eric accused.

'Don't start,' David said. 'Tan, do you want some dinner, it's chilli?'

'And it's hot, hot, hot,' Eric added.

'I would please,' Tanya answered, huffily, feeling as if she'd been left out. Then she felt guilty, because of the secret project that now consumed her.

'Fine, lucky we did enough then,' Eric said. Tanya gave him a dirty look. She left them cooking and walked into the sitting room where she nearly fainted. Leigh and Gus were huddled together on the sofa, watching television and drinking wine. They were giggling like teenagers.

'Have you been smoking Eric's stuff?' she asked.

'No, it's this programme, it is so funny, isn't it Gus?' Leigh replied. Gus smiled.

'It's tops,' he concurred. Tanya, feeling peeved, looked at the television. On screen was the programme that she and Cherry had been discussing, *Fantasy Holiday*.

'My company made that,' she told them.

'It is so funny. Gus and I both think that that big woman and the really tall man are either going to sleep together or kill each other.'

'And LeeLee fancies the muscle-bound hunk with no brain,' Gus added, dissolving into laughter.

'Do not,' Leigh screeched and punched Gus on the arm. Tanya was watching not only intimacy but also physical contact.

She had only been lying low, trying to hide from everyone while she made her decision and signed the contract, and her housemates had become what seemed suspiciously like friends.

Eric carried in a big pot of chilli, while David trailed behind with plates. Leigh jumped up and told Gus to help her get wine. Tanya sat down on the floor and watched as Eric served out the food, David ran to get the bread, which he'd forgotten, Leigh came back in carrying two bottles of red wine and Gus trailed her with glasses. As Eric dished out food, David dished out bread and Leigh dished out wine. It was as if they had set roles and they all fitted them comfortably. Tanya took her food and took her wine, she felt as if she had no role.

For Tanya the evening passed perplexingly. She wondered how she had failed to notice the friendship that had been struck between Gus and Leigh. There was still no romance, but they were acting like best friends. They even appeared to share in-jokes. Eric and David flitted around the edges and Tanya felt frustrated. She couldn't figure out what had happened, but it was as if Leigh and Gus becoming as close as they appeared had rebalanced everything. And they seemed very close. They didn't seem to move apart from one another and although it was Leigh who kept the space between them limited, Gus almost seemed to invite her. Then there was Eric, who teased as usual, but forgot to tease Tanya. David seemed to talk to the others but not address her. All she'd done was hide away for a short while – had they all forgotten her?

Two weeks is a long time in the life of new friends. Leigh had taken Sukie's latest advice and decided to become Gus's best friend. This had proved easier than she thought it would, as Gus was very prone to sweet people and they didn't come any sweeter than Leigh. It had started one evening when Eric and David were on an extremely rare night out with old college friends and Tanya was locked in her room playing her half-hearted moral dilemma game. Gus had come in from work to find Leigh lying on the sofa on her own. This wasn't planned, Leigh had no idea that they would be alone, but the conversation that followed was well rehearsed.

'Hey LeeLee,' Gus said.

'Gus, how are you?' she replied.

'Knackered, you?'

'A bit down actually,' Leigh said.

'Why?' Immediately Gus had been full of concern.

'You know how you said you worry that you'll never fall in love properly. Well I worry that I'll never find anyone to adore me the way I'll adore them. You know like in the poems that you talk about, or in films, it vexes me,' she finished. Gus went to sit next to her and gave her a squeeze. Sukie would have been proud.

'Of course you will. Gosh, it's weird to find someone who feels the way I do. But if we are the last of the romantics, we have to believe that it exists. Come on let's go to the pub, I'll buy you a drink.' Leigh looked up at him, as if she was trying to look through her eyelids, the way Sukie had taught her, she then smiled slowly. 'I'd love to.'

It was all going to plan. Sukie had coached her in the art of being a sympathetic ear, a like-minded individual, a soulmate. Leigh was so glad she had Sukie. She was still wearing mostly pink, although they had reviewed the all pink rule, relaxing it a little. Wearing all pink was proving far too taxing. But Leigh had pink jeans, pink skirts, pink T-shirts, and she managed to convey a vulnerable little girl quality. With that, her new feminine ways and now the friendship she was going to build with Gus, there was no way she could fail.

They walked slowly to the pub. Gus told Leigh about his day and she giggled in the right places. When they got to the pub – more of a bar than a pub – Gus ordered a beer and a glass of wine while Leigh found a table. Then they started talking. They stopped only to replenish their drinks. Neither noticed the bar, which was a pine-hater's nightmare. Neither noticed the two people behind the bar (one male, one female), who both tried hard to flirt with Gus. Neither noticed the looks they were getting from the other occupants.

The observers in the bar thought they were watching two people in love. That was the way they appeared to be. What they were really, was one person in love and one in love with the idea of falling in love, which can appear similar. What they found out that evening was that their connection gave each something to hold on to, and with that they became friends — the best of friends.

Eric and David were quick to notice this development. From that evening, Gus and Leigh took to spending time alone. Sometimes they would go for a walk, or for a drink, or they would sit in Leigh's room talking and watching television. They spent time with the others, but they always spent more time with each other. Eric and David at first thought they had fallen into a romantic relationship, but that was soon cleared up. 'She really understands me,' Gus said about Leigh, 'but we are just good friends.' 'Oh David, of course I still love him, but at least I can have his friendship, which is better than nothing,' Leigh said.

In the house in the tree-lined road in Fulham the housemates had changed. They had become the close knit group that Tanya had longed for from the outset. But as no one saw Tanya and only David ever questioned where she was or what she was doing, no one informed her of this development.

Tanya was puzzled. She hated feeling like an outcast; she wouldn't allow it. 'Doesn't anyone want to know why I haven't seen you in ages?' she demanded. Everyone looked up and seemed to remember for the first time that she was there.

'Oh, sure, why?' David asked.

'Because I've split up with Harvey,' she said, dramatically.

'Oh my god, I am so sorry.' Immediately Leigh left Gus's side and went to Tanya's. 'What happened?'

'Oh, it wouldn't have worked out, he was American after all.' Tanya adopted her most pained look.

'What does that mean?' David asked.

'He was a womanising cad. The day after we, you know, did it for the first time, I found him in the stationery cupboard with his secretary.'

'*Très* tacky,' Leigh said, then realised she shouldn't have.

'Yeah thanks for pointing that out,' Tanya snapped. Once she started with the lie she found that it was taking over. She was enjoying the story, enjoying the looks of sympathy, enjoying the drama and most of all enjoying the attention.

'Sorry,' Leigh said and moved back to Gus. He smiled at her, which made Tanya scowl.

'It's OK,' she replied, sweetly, 'it wouldn't have worked out anyway.'

'Why didn't you tell us, Tan? I can't believe you spent the whole time locked in your room.' David looked extremely guilty.

'David, it only happened recently, I was just busy before then, don't worry, I knew where you guys were if I needed you.' Tanya softened and smiled. She hadn't meant to make them feel guilty. Actually she had, but when she got the desired reaction, she remembered why she really hadn't seen them, and she felt guilty again.

'Well I didn't like him much anyway,' Eric lied.

'Why not?' Tanya snapped.

'Because he wasn't good enough for you.'

'Sorry Eric, you're right, he wasn't.'

The peace in the sitting room had been shattered. Awkwardness that had existed before Tanya's disappearance returned. She felt it, but she wouldn't attribute it to herself. Leigh looked at Gus.

'We should do the dishes,' she said.

'I'll help,' Tanya offered.

'No, you relax Tanya, we'll do them,' Gus answered. As she watched them get up, clear up the plates, joke and laugh before disappearing, Tanya felt a stab of jealousy. Leigh and Gus, Leigh and her boss, Leigh and Eric and David. Tanya felt like she had lost them all and that made her feel lost. She quickly made her excuses and fobbed Eric and David off when they showed concern. She went to her room.

She knew that if the film were to work, one of the strongest storylines was Leigh's crush on Gus. Tanya knew she would have to make this clear, because they were behaving like a couple of lovesick teenagers. She would have to draw Leigh into conversation about it, during the filming. By shutting Tanya out of her life, (even if that was debatable), Leigh had just become the unwitting star of the film. It was a vengeful thought, but Tanya felt lonely again. If her loneliness was her own fault she wouldn't recognise that. Instead it became Leigh's fault.

Chapter Twenty-Three

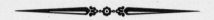

Tanya resigned from her job and was told that she could go after a week of tying up loose ends. Although she had to give a month's notice in her contract, she wasn't going to a competitor. As far as the company were aware she wasn't going anywhere. Tanya was free, and she was about to start working for Harvey.

The first official pre-production meeting involved Harvey, Cherry, Bob and Tanya. Millie Harcourt took notes. The meeting was called in order to work out the logistics: how they were going to get the cameras and the control room into the house.

'What I need to figure out is a practicable timetable,' Bob said.

'I can't guarantee more than a day at a time when they are all out, in fact I can't guarantee more than nine till six and even then I'll have to check Gus isn't working nights,' Tanya replied.

'I need to visit the house first to get an idea of size and rooms we need to work on. Then we'll be able to tell you when we can start work and how long it will take,' Bob explained.

'It sounds a bit complicated,' Tanya replied. Harvey rolled his eyes.

'We are going to have to do some serious work, and it will include construction, I've looked into hiding cameras in clocks, pictures and so on, which we could do, but I'm not sure how safe that is,' Bob continued. Tanya paled at the thought of tearing the house apart. Especially as it was boring Brian's house. She shuddered as she imagined how he would react if he was aware of what was happening.

'Bob, we cannot start knocking walls down,' Harvey told him.

'OK, then we'll have to do it covertly. I've got the best people to work with, but, Tanya, we need things to hide cameras in.' Bob was a little disappointed, he wanted the cameras installed securely.

'Bob, the house is furnished, you know.' Tanya was haughty.

'Sure, if you say so. I'm just worried about security.' Bob was less than pleased.

'Bob, we all are,' Harvey pacified. 'Anyway, let's see what we can use, when the experts go round. Tanya, we might need more than a day, especially to build your control room.'

'Well then they'll have to come back, I can't get my friends out of the house for longer than I said.' Tanya paled again. She began to feel sick with nerves at the thought of it all.

'How about a weekend?' Cherry suggested.

'That's worse! No one goes anywhere at weekends,' Tanya explained.

'Well then, how about a weekend away? Say your very generous boss has a cottage somewhere nice, I have no idea where is nice in England, and he lent it to you for the weekend and you can all go,' Cherry suggested.

'Brilliant idea Cherry,' Harvey said. 'Also it will give you a chance for a bit of pre-filming bonding.'

'It might work, but of course it all depends on Gus, he works weekends you know.'

'Let us know when he's free and we'll arrange it. Oh, and Millie, find a cottage somewhere nice we can send them,' Harvey finished. Millie smiled and made a note.

'So that's what we need to do now, and I do apologise for the chaotic nature of the project, but we are doing something new and as we've never done anything like this before, so I guess it might seem we're less than professional. But we are on top of things, which is important.' Harvey smiled. 'Millie, would you coordinate diaries to arrange for a site visit to Tanya's house?'

Millie smiled. 'Sure, Harvey.'

'Let's have a drink and toast our first planning meeting.' Harvey stood up and Cherry followed him. She retrieved a bottle of champagne from the fridge and poured a glass for everyone.

'A toast, to our movie,' Harvey smiled.

'Our movie,' they all echoed.

'So, Tanya, how do you feel about all this? You OK?' Harvey asked.

'Very excited, but a bit nervous, mainly about logistics. Bob you scared me when you suggested taking walls down.' She laughed.

'Sorry. I guess I'm nervous about how quickly we need to fix the house up, I hear British tradesmen are the worst,' Bob said.

'You better believe it. I had my tiny little flat decorated and it took six months just to paint it,' Millie put in.

'Great, that fills me with confidence,' Bob replied, horrified.

'Hey, relax. We have money, money talks, especially here, if we need to throw more cash at them for a quick job, we will,' Harvey pointed out.

'Yeah, everyone has a price,' Tanya said, thinking of her new huge salary.

'So, relax, OK?' Harvey repeated.

Bob smiled. Tanya smiled. Cherry and Harvey smiled. Even Millie smiled. There was a long way to go but it seemed that another hurdle had just been cleared.

Millie was glad she almost knew what she was doing. When she'd received a call from her employment agency saying a very exciting role had come up, she hadn't expected it to be quite so insane. When she'd started and Cherry, her official boss, had given her a confidentiality contract to sign and hinted that if she so much as breathed a word she would be killed or something like that, Millie had longed for the sanctity of the big investment banks where she normally worked. At only twenty-two she was too young for the pressure.

Millie had been working in various secretarial roles for two years while she tried to decide what she really wanted to do with her life. She had no idea why Cherry had called her employment agency, or why she didn't try to find someone who worked in films. Millie lived in Pimlico with her best friend Harriet, but she was intimidated by what she found at the Americans' flat in Knightsbridge.

Cherry had chosen the agency because she saw the number advertised in an up-market publication. She had no idea about hiring staff in London, therefore had taken a chance. When Millie, with her bobbed blonde hair, smart dark suit and shoes that were far too flat for Cherry's liking had arrived at the flat, and smiled the most sincere smile that Cherry had ever seen, she had immediately known that she wanted Millie to work with her.

Millie soon recovered her confidence and began to like her job. Mainly for the reason that Cherry was lovely, Harvey charming, Bob never there and the work was actually interesting. They had had to explain all about the film idea to her and she was hooked. Keeping quiet was almost killing her as much as spilling the beans would. However she was determined to keep quiet, because she had read about these big Hollywood people who didn't mind killing anyone who got in their way. Life was too precious.

What amused her was that although the meeting they had just had was meant to be the first meeting, they had already had loads of meetings without Tanya. They had discussed the house at an earlier meeting. They'd discussed Tanya. They'd discussed everything, but they hadn't told Tanya this and Millie had managed to conclude, all by herself, that they were playing some kind of double game.

Prior meetings with Millie had been arranged by Harvey to ensure that Bob, Cherry and himself were totally in control of things. Tanya was led to believe she was in the core group, and to an extent she was, but they kept things from her, only because as Harvey pointed out, they needed to. Millie had listened in to every meeting, and nodded when she was told that Tanya didn't need to know. Although she didn't understand, she found it all very exciting, like espionage, and Millie was playing her part admirably.

Harvey didn't want to exclude Tanya deliberately, but his insurance policy was to make her think she was in control. Of course, putting someone who knew little about films in control would be foolish, so he didn't. He, Cherry and Bob had to maintain a little distance from her, but they also had to ensure that she didn't find out.

Preparations moved up a gear and were focused on the house. Bob had contractors and experts on hand to ensure the job was effective and quick. He started by taking himself, his lighting expert, the camera expert and the guy with the equipment round to Tanya's when everyone but her was out. As Tanya made tea and coffee, they looked around. Then they drank and looked around some more.

Four hours later and they were still deep in discussion. Tanya was watching and wondering if she was supposed to find it interesting. She didn't, it was dull. As soon as a place was suggested for a camera, the lighting man would say the lighting was wrong. As soon as the lighting man suggested a place, the camera expert would say the angle was wrong. Bob just looked thoughtful and seemed to agree with everyone.

Tanya was dispatched to make more drinks and was glad of the distraction. She really did not want to have to keep looking interested, it was hurting her face. Martin, the camera expert, drew a sketch of the rooms that they needed to film. Starting with the sitting room, they discussed how they would like cameras filming from a point on each wall. The idea was that Tanya's control room would have a screen per room, and that screen would be split to accommodate each different angle.

Hearing them discuss this made Tanya panic even more, how was she meant to manage that many screens?

After the plans had been drawn up, it was fast approaching six. Tanya noticed the time and again filled herself with panic. 'It's nearly six, Bob, you guys better scoot,' she told them.

'OK, honey, we'll be back tomorrow.' They all left and Tanya breathed a sigh of relief. Could she survive this?

Bob and his team of experts walked to the nearest pub. The nearest pub turned out to be the pine-ridden wine bar that Leigh and Gus had taken a shine to. They bought their drinks, found a table and pulled out the plans as they tried to finalise where they wanted the cameras.

Leigh had left work early after receiving a call from Gus. Gus was upset, he'd received a call from an ex-girlfriend. Although his ex-girlfriends were by no means in short supply, this was Natasha. The same Natasha whose name had provoked fear in Eric. Leigh had arranged to meet Gus in the wine bar.

They arrived five minutes after Bob and his crew. They took their bottle of wine and settled at a corner table; Bob's group occupied the opposite corner. Neither party was aware of the other's existence.

'Why would she do this? When we broke up it was because she slept with someone else, said that she was too young to settle down and it broke my heart. Now she calls and says she has just come back from travelling and she wants to meet me. What should I do LeeLee?' Gus was visibly upset.

'Gus did you love her?' Leigh felt like crying but she had to ask.

'Yes, I did, I loved her, but we were young and she wasn't ready to settle down. What if she's called me now because that's what she wants?' Gus looked at Leigh pleadingly. Leigh felt like pulling her heart out, but she knew being Gus's friend would involve the heartache of knowing about his other women. She took a deep breath. She had become Gus's friend for reasons which were not entirely honourable, but she was now Gus's friend for the right reasons. She loved him, yes, and she cared about him deeply. Enough for her to want his happiness.

'That probably is what she wants. Is she your age? Fast approaching thirty?' Gus nodded. 'Well you know, you should think about seeing her. Take time to think. You need to be clear before you make your next move. And remember Gus, I'm here for you.' She smiled.

'LeeLee, I don't know what I would do without you.' Gus leaned over and kissed her on the cheek.

'So, we put a camera on each wall of the sitting room,' Bob tried to sum up the general consensus.

'Yes, but at different points. That way the cameras give different angles, we don't just want one on each wall staring straight,' Martin the camera expert added.

'Is that OK with lighting?' Bob asked, exhausted.

'Should be, of course we might need to put this into practice then review,' Steve said. He was a top man in his field.

'Sure, of course we might.' Bob felt despondent. Hiding cameras which were supposed to capture every move and every angle of a room was more complicated than filming live.

'I'm putting down five cameras for the living room,' Matt said. He could supply the best film equipment in the business.

'So, she's called Natasha,' Leigh said, breaking the silence.

'Yes,' Gus replied. Leigh thought about the name. It was a name which only stunning girls had. Stunning, bitchy girls.

'Gus, you don't have to see her. I know I told you you should, but you don't have to,' Leigh said, tenderly.

'I know, but now my curiosity is getting at me. What I don't understand is why, when I was well over her, she had to reappear?'

'Exes do that.' Leigh didn't have a clue if that was true. Her last boyfriend had disappeared without trace.

'They shouldn't just be able to drop back into your life and make you feel all confused.' Gus interrupted Leigh's thoughts.

'I know babes, but what we need to do is to face it and decide what you're going to do. In the meantime, why don't you go and get us another bottle of wine?'

While Gus was at the bar, she found it hard to believe that she was being so rational and helpful. Sukie would be proud of her — again!

'I want a camera that can pick up who comes through the door and one to watch people leaving. Is that possible?' Bob asked.

'Sure,' Martin replied, 'but it's a bit dark there.'

'We'll definitely need to light the area, but without it looking obvious. Let me think on that,' Steve offered.

'Then, the rest of the entrance hall, what do you suggest?' Bob asked.

'Well, we need cameras to face the entrance of the sitting room and kitchen as well as one to film anything that goes on there. And there is one bedroom that leads off the hall, so we'll need to incorporate that,' Martin finished.

'What about a shot up the stairs?' Matt suggested.

'Shit, this is complicated.' Steve made notes on the plan of the hallway. 'We need more here than in any one room.'

'What we can do is use specialised cameras to cut down on the numbers,' Matt suggested. 'For example, we can have one covering the hallway, concentrating on who comes in and who goes out; one to cover the kitchen, sitting room and bedroom entrance, plus one more to cover the stairs.'

'Perfect,' Bob said.

'You know LeeLee, you're a great friend. You really understand me, which means so much. Eric is my best mate, but I can't talk to him like I can talk to you, and you've been great about Natasha. I *am* going to see her.' Gus beamed, he was drunk.

'OK, but can I make just one more suggestion?' Leigh asked, slurring slightly in her inebriated state.

'Sure,' Gus replied.

'Don't see her straight away, give yourself some time to get used to the idea of seeing her again and maybe get your feelings a bit straighter.' She smiled.

'You're right. That's what I'll do, and also it won't look to her like I'm falling over myself to see her again. You're such a great friend LeeLee,' Gus said.

'You're my best boyfriend,' Leigh responded, giggling.

'And you're my favourite girl.'

'So that covers everything except bedrooms and bathroom,' Martin said, hoping that the long and painful day might be coming to an end soon.

'No go,' Bob explained.

'So we're done?' Steve asked. He was tired now, Americans knew how to push hard.

'Almost, the editing facility for Tanya's room is still a requirement.'

'I'll order the equipment in line with the cameras we need,' Matt noted.

'What recording system will we be using?' Bob asked.

'The cameras record by remote access straight on to a machine which will be in Tanya's room and your editing suite. This is the technology age Bob,' Matt explained.

'I do know Matt,' Bob said in exasperation. 'Fine then, we need to be back in the house tomorrow. I want plans finalised then, and also I want to know the timescale for getting it done. I reckon you have four days to get everything organised. OK?' Bob asked. The three nodded in unison.

'Great, I'll see you then.' Bob got up and grabbed his coat. The crew followed him out. As Bob hailed a taxi and waved goodbye, the others were still discussing the job.

'I don't think I've done anything this bizarre before,' Matt said.

'I just hope it's legal,' Martin added.

'I've a feeling it isn't,' Steve finished.

'LeeLee, shall we go home?' Gus hiccuped.

'Um, I fink so, yes,' she replied, then giggled. They got on their wobbly legs, left the wine bar, holding on to each other and staggered all the way home.

Chapter Twenty-Four

The second 'official' meeting took place once the detailed plans had been checked, double checked and approved for the camera installation. Tanya was noticeably more nervous at this meeting than at the first. She was excited about starting work, but scared of the implications of having cameras in her house. Bob went through the plans, showed them to Tanya and explained patiently how the work would be carried out.

With the aid of his diagrams Bob explained exactly where the cameras would be. In the sitting room there was a large painting on one wall which would have a camera concealed in its frame. Tanya questioned the logistics of this, but felt embarassed when Bob told her that they'd been through all of that with an espionage expert. Cameras could go anywhere these days, coming in all sizes, and more importantly concealment was perfectly feasible with the right technicians. The curtain rail would house another camera, at an angle to show the sofa and armchair. The third camera would be fixed into the light fitting and would face the entrance to the room. The fourth would be hidden in a clock which was being made especially for the task and Tanya would have to pass off the new timepiece as her latest purchase. The clock camera would cover the dining table. Finally a camera would be fixed to the top of the doorframe providing an overall panoramic perspective of the whole room.

The kitchen was much simpler, as it could be divided into

two parts. One was the cooking area, the other the breakfast bar. Being a square room, the camera which would be hidden in the large kitchen clock would face the breakfast bar and the entrance to the room, the camera concealed in the doorframe would cover the cooking area. The doorframe concealment required construction work but Bob decided that Tanya didn't need to know the extent of that.

In the hallway, cameras were being hidden in a three-pronged light fitting which would cover both people coming in and out of the house. There was a mirror which hung above the phone table which would have a camera in it that would cover the whole hallway and the door that led to David's room. The last camera in the hall was being fitted into the inside front door capturing whoever went up the stairs.

The stairs were restrictive because all they could use were the light fittings. Luckily Brian favoured elaborate ones which would make the cameras more undetectable although Tanya would have to ensure that she changed any dud light bulbs. But they were going to fit long-life bulbs for the whole house as an extra insurance policy. So Tanya could rest easy on that score.

'We need a weekend to do the work. Ideally a bit longer, but if we can have Friday night until Sunday night, we can get it done,' Bob explained.

'So, I've got to organise this weekend away?' Tanya asked, without enthusiasm.

'No, it's been done,' Cherry piped up. 'You said Gus wasn't working, so I've made plans for next weekend. I've booked a cottage for you. It has three bedrooms in a very pretty, quite secluded location. A place called the Lake District?'

'How do we get there?' Tanya's idea of a weekend away would not be in the Lake District. It even sounded wet and cold. She didn't know that Cherry agreed with her wholeheartedly.

'I've got you train tickets, or rather Millie has.' Cherry pulled the cottage information and five train tickets from a folder.

'How on earth am I going to pull this off? "Hey, you guys, I just happen to have a totally free weekend for everyone", they'll never believe it. I thought about the boss story but Leigh knows what a monster my boss is. She'll never buy it,' Tanya protested.

'So, make something up. Tell them that you won a competition for a free weekend and everyone *has* to come. You're sure Gus isn't working?' Harvey asked.

'Positive, unless he changes with someone, but if we go away then he won't be able to. I'll need to tell them soon. Do you really think they'll believe that line about a competition?'

'Why wouldn't they?' Cherry asked.

'I'd believe it,' Millie added. Tanya looked at her, she didn't doubt it for a minute.

The more Tanya thought about it, the more sense it made. Firstly she had been avoiding them. Then when she wanted to be part of the household again, they ignored her. Well they didn't ignore her actually, but she obviously wasn't central to their lives. This way, by giving them a free weekend away they'd be really grateful to her and also she could use the weekend to re-bond with everyone. Maybe even re-establish her relationship with Leigh. After all, they'd be sharing a bedroom.

'OK, maybe I'm just being objectionable. So, I'll give them this story, we go off like the Famous Five into the countryside and when we come back the cameras will be installed, we will obviously have had a great weekend and we'll all be nicely bonded and happy,' Tanya finished, having moved across the scale, from pessimism to fairy-tale optimism.

Harvey smiled. 'Sure, that's why it's such a good idea.'

'I have already agreed to go. Mind you the others are so well bonded at the moment I'm sure they don't need a weekend away.' Everyone detected the bitterness in her voice.

'Oh Tanya, you just need to spend time with them. It's only because you've been working so hard the last few weeks to get this off the ground. A weekend away will put you all back together again,' Millie said. Harvey and Cherry smiled at each other, they were beginning to like working with Millie. She seemed to have a way with people, despite being a bit of a scatter-brain.

'You're right, I must stop being so jealous. After all this is a whole world they know nothing about. But when the film starts we need to make sure I get the time to reassert my role in the house.' Tanya sighed.

'You will. Any editing or watching you want to do is purely weekday, daytime. I will ensure all meetings will be held during the day as well. You won't have to worry until it's finished. Until then you are not only a producer on this movie, but you're one of the cast. And because of the fact that you're a producer and because you're also incredibly special, you are going to be its biggest star. So honey, enjoy yourself because soon you'll be so famous for this. Enjoy the end of your ordinariness.' Harvey beamed. Cherry smiled. Bob attempted not to laugh. Tanya's face muscles visibly relaxed as her mouth curled into a big Cheshire cat grin.

'This weekend is going to be wonderful, I'll make sure of that. Just one more thing. I need a lock on my door and I thought that perhaps the best way to do it would be to have locks fitted on all of the bedroom doors.'

'Fine. When shall we arrange that?' Harvey asked.

'Won't they think it's weird, you putting locks on their doors?' Cherry asked.

'They won't question it. I'll say that I thought privacy and security were important.'

'Maybe we could put a burglar alarm in and you could say that you were working on a programme about how easy it is to break into houses and you got paranoid,' Bob suggested, making a note to put an extra camera in the fake burglar alarm.

'Great idea,' Harvey agreed.

'So can you arrange to have that done for us? Anytime is fine, the sooner the better,' Tanya said. Millie made a note.

'I'll get on to it,' she replied trying to sound efficient.

'Good, and Tanya, I bought you something.' Harvey smiled.

'What?' Harvey got up and walked out of the room. When he

returned he was carrying a box which Cherry had decorated with ribbons.

'My God, this is like a proper present,' Tanya exclaimed, as she clutched it. They watched as she unwrapped and pulled out a small, digital video camera.

'If you're going to work in films, you ought to have one of these,' Bob said, then proceeded to show her how to use it.

'It's fantastic, thank you.'

'Maybe you could use it this weekend,' Harvey suggested, tentatively. Cherry looked at Tanya. She saw her expression of joy at receiving the gift turn to one of suspicion.

'You mean start the film on our weekend away?'

'No, honey, I meant record it for posterity, just like people who take cameras on holiday. I already told you about the artistic power we're giving you. But perhaps having your own camera will make you think about the making of the film. By recording things and playing them back you get to see how it looks afterwards, and it gives you a clearer idea of what works and what doesn't. It'll be fun for you as well as useful.' Harvey looked at Cherry, who gave him a wink. They saw Tanya start to relax.

Although in the past couple of weeks she had swung between behaving like a petulant child to being enthusiastic and full of ideas, they had decided to forgive her. They knew that finding someone else to fill her position was impossible. So they nurtured her, they pacified, they led her to believe that she was far more in control of things than she really was.

Tanya was happy. Or at least happier than most people who were about to betray their friends, lie to everyone they knew and start a new job shrouded in secrecy which came with huge responsibility.

If she didn't know how big Harvey was in the film business and she hadn't seen with her own eyes that the mighty Poplar Films were the backers, she would never have taken it seriously. However she knew that this was bigger than anything she could ever imagine being a part of and if she could pull it off she would be famous. The main problem was that she couldn't help but feel worried about what she was doing and it was worry that caused her to behave badly every so often.

She sat at the table scrutinising her camera and basked in the words that Harvey had bestowed on her. He said that proper filmmakers needed cameras. Casting away any doubts she had as to the validity of the project, Tanya determined there and then that a proper filmmaker was exactly what she was going to be. 'I can't wait to get started.' And she couldn't.

She was excited. She had nothing to start with apart from five people, it was as Cherry had described it, a blank canvas. As she lived in the house there was also the added pressure that if the footage was rubbish it would reflect on her. She also knew that as the only person who knew what was going on, if she 'acted,' it would be obvious. Another concern that ran with the millions already in her mind was that, although she would spend six months knowing she and everyone else was being filmed, she had to pretend that the cameras weren't there.

She was excited, because whatever happened to her, her life was changing, and if she could just pull this off, her life would change beyond her wildest dreams. She had to pull it off. Beginning with the bonding weekend.

Tanya opened the door and the first thing she heard was shrieks of laughter. She threw her keys down and walked into the lounge. The first person she saw was Eric. He was lying on the floor with what looked to be Leigh underneath him. Gus and David were sitting on the sofa doubled up with laughter.

'What *are* you doing?' Tanya said, hoping she didn't sound too much like her mother.

'I am giving a demonstration of a pin,' Eric replied. Leigh giggled from underneath him and Tanya caught a glimpse of pink anklewarmers waggling around.

'What?' she asked trying to sound more fun.

'Wrestling. I was giving a WWF wrestling demonstration, LeeLee kindly volunteered to be my victim,' Eric giggled again.

'I think you won Eric,' Leigh squeaked. Eric stood up and held out his hand to help her up.

'So, what exactly was so funny?' Tanya asked.

'Tan, you really had to be here,' Leigh sniggered.

'LeeLee, I think you should consider a career change, you could be a female wrestler,' Gus said. Immediately Leigh went over to the sofa and sat on him.

'Excellent idea Gus, of course I need to practise on you.'

Tanya watched the scene and wondered where her sense of humour had gone. It hurt to see everyone else have so much fun, especially as they were having fun without her. It was time for her to dangle her carrot.

'I've got a proposition for you,' she said. Everyone looked at her.

'Sounds interesting,' Eric teased.

'A weekend away.'

'A weekend away? What, all of us? Together?' David asked.

'Yup. I won a raffle and the prize was a romantic weekend for two in Paris, but as I am not likely to claim that, I managed to cash in the tickets and book a cottage in the Lake District including five return train tickets.'

'Wow, why didn't you say?' Gus asked.

'I thought it would be a surprise. It's next weekend and the only excuse for not going is . . . well there is no excuse. I think it might do us all good.'

'Brilliant,' Leigh said. 'A weekend in the country would be great. You're tops Tanya.' She went over and kissed her on the cheek. Tanya felt better.

'So no objections then?' Tanya asked. The response was a chorus of 'no.' 'Gus, you're not working then are you?' she asked innocently.

'No, that is a free weekend. I was going to see Natasha, but . . .'

'Oh Gus, it's perfect. Now she'll see that you're independent and she can't walk all over you,' Leigh gushed.

'You're right. Tanya, the timing is perfect.' They all smiled widely.

I love it when a plan comes together, Tanya thought, and with the 'A-Team' fixed in her head, she began to plan some more.

In her room that night, she switched on her laptop and started making another list. The heading was 'Storylines'. She looked around her room. She felt paranoid. Just like she used to feel when at work she would be surfing the Net or playing solitaire. She started to type:

Leigh: *Leigh's main story is her crush on Gus, and her metamorphosis into something out of Cinderella.*
Gus: *His love of poetry. Ex-girlfriend back in life, could be significant. Friendship with Leigh, ignorance of crush.*
Eric: *Cannabis. Plan for the biggest joint. Belief in legalisation. No women, no social life. Might be the comic character.*
David: *His web ideas. Also his Internet dating. Em.*
Tanya: *???*

She looked at the list in despair. Storywise it was a bit thin. But it would work. She would see to it. The worst thing was that everyone had a storyline except her. She was the only one in the house without a mad plan, an addiction or a hopeless crush. She was the only sane person – wasn't she? What would her story be? She refused to be in a film and come across as boring. She sat thinking for a while, until she realised what it was. She went back to the list and deleted the question marks.

Tanya: *The hinge that keeps it all together. The popular character, the good friend, the funny, intelligent one.*

She knew all about the cameras, so her story would not so much be a story, but it would be her, someone that the audience would love.

Although Harvey said that he didn't want any actors or any script in his film, she could break the rules. After all she was the only one that knew them.

Chapter Twenty-Five

On Friday evening they boarded the train destined to take them to the Lake District. When Tanya had actually studied where they were going she had berated Cherry for sending them to the back of beyond. The train journey was set to take most of the night. Cherry said it would be a good opportunity for them to bond. It also ensured that they were out of the house for the maximum time because they wouldn't get in until late on Sunday night.

Planning the weekend had been more difficult than planning a military operation. Gus had nearly cancelled twice due to work. Leigh had announced that she wouldn't go because her pink trainers would get muddy. David had insisted on knowing about phone lines and electric socket availability for his laptop before he would commit. Eric had been suspicious about the whole thing and kept asking weird questions. Tanya had aged about a hundred years. For a person who prided herself so much on her calmness and organisational skills, she had been severely tested.

But at last they were at Euston Station awaiting their train. Tanya laughed inwardly about the way they all looked. Leigh, with her pink rucksack and pink trainers, looked like a teenage runaway. David, with his laptop strapped firmly to his chest, looked like an eccentric going to a business meeting. Eric had appeared to have dressed for a country weekend with what looked suspiciously like a Barbour jacket. Gus was smartly dressed having come straight from the hospital. Once again, Tanya was the only normal member of the group.

When the train pulled in they found their reserved seats and to Tanya's annoyance she found herself sitting on her own. Everyone had scrambled into seats and the four others had automatically sat down together. Eric sensed that Tanya felt uncomfortable so he moved to sit next to her. Tanya was at once both touched and annoyed. Leigh should have moved to be next to her, instead she was sitting as close to Gus as she could get and was feeding him pink biscuits.

'Shall we get some beers?' Eric asked.

'We might as well, it's a long journey,' Tanya replied.

'I'm hungry, I guess it will have to be buffet car sandwiches all round,' Eric said. 'I'll go and get a selection.'

'I'll help,' Tanya said scowling at the others who were still devouring Leigh's pink biscuits.

'God it's ages since I've been in a train buffet queue,' Eric said.

'Mmm,' Tanya replied.

'What's wrong with you? You seem really fed up.'

'Oh, I'm fine, it's just . . .'

'Leigh?' Eric asked.

'Yes, actually. We used to be best friends, but now I don't seem to have the ability to prise her away from Gus's side,' Tanya complained.

'She's got a huge crush on Gus, you know that. You just have to let it run its course,' Eric advised.

'So you don't think it will ever be anything more than a crush?'

'No chance, when Gus falls he falls quickly. If he was going to fall for her, he would have done so already.'

Tanya felt comforted by this thought. 'So she's wasting her time?'

'Not if she wants to be his friend. Gus is an incredibly loyal friend. Try not to be too jealous, remember you'll probably be needed to pick up the pieces at some stage.'

'What can I get you?' the buffet attendant interrupted their conversation.

'Ten cans of lager, five packets of crisps, two plain the rest salt and vinegar, one of each of your fine sandwiches and a packet of peanuts.' The order rolled off Eric's tongue.

'Do we really need all that?' Tanya asked.

'Of course, we're on holiday.'

When the order was complete and they had paid handsomely for it, they made their way back to their seats.

'I have never been able to understand train prices,' Eric said.

'What?' Tanya couldn't think of anything she cared less about.

'Well train tickets are really expensive and you get shit service and the food which is less than gourmet costs a fortune. How do they get away with it?' Tanya shot him a withered look and offered no answer. Eric looked upset.

They sat down and Eric distributed the food and lager.

'Oh, I can't possibly eat crisps, they're so fattening,' Leigh said.

'You love crisps, ever since I've known you you've been addicted to them,' Tanya protested.

'I don't want to be fat so I don't eat crisps any more. Besides who ever heard of an addiction to crisps?' Leigh giggled.

'Stop being so stupid. You're not fat and you never have been and that was with eating crisps. God you are so infuriating.' Tanya's anger was clearly visible.

'Oh my goodness, why are you getting so upset over a bag of crisps?' Leigh asked.

'Tanya, I need some more stuff from the buffet, will you come with me?' Eric stood up, grabbed her hand and led her to the nearest loo.

'Why are you dragging me to the loo?'

'I've got something to calm you down, of course.'

They crammed themselves into the small space. Tanya perched on the counter by the sink and Eric sat on the seat, he had already lit the joint.

'I bet this isn't clean,' Tanya complained.

'Tanya, will you chill out?' He handed the joint to her.

She took a long drag. 'But she's infuriating. You must see that?' She took another drag.

'I think she's sweet,' Eric said.

'Yeah, just as you guys like us to be, sweet and adoring. Not feisty. She used to be fun.' Tanya handed the joint back.

'We don't all like that. I prefer feisty women.'

'Really I'm surprised you know what sort of women you like,' Tanya hit back.

'Oh easy Tanya, you can be really hurtful. You should chill about Leigh, she'll be back to normal at some point, although I haven't noticed that much of a difference, apart from the pink of course.'

'You don't know her as well as I do.'

'No, obviously. But if she is so different, then surely that's not really her.' On that note they both lapsed into silence. Eric made Tanya stay for another joint. When they finally left, Tanya was feeling heavily stoned. Eric was just as normal. As they walked out of the door a guy standing in the corridor gave them a funny look.

'We weren't having sex,' Tanya snapped and Eric dissolved into giggles. By the time they reached their seats Tanya was doubled up with laughter.

'So, you're not so stroppy now then?' Leigh asked.

'Of course not dear LeeLee, who could be angry with you?' Tanya tried to smile but she was laughing too much. An hour later she was sound asleep.

By the time they reached their destination everyone was bored and tired. Tanya was just bored, having slept most of the journey. It was late, it was dark and they seemed to be in the middle of nowhere. Like a knight in shining armour, a man in a people carrier appeared and announced that he was to take them to their destination.

'Tanya you really think of everything,' David said, sleepily. Thank God for Cherry, Tanya thought as she climbed into the front seat.

As they drove it was so dark they were unable to see anything of the surrounding area. After a twenty minute drive, they pulled up outside a cottage which seemed totally isolated. 'Where are the other houses?' Tanya asked.

'Oh, 'bout a mile away,' the driver replied in his Cumbrian accent.

'But how will we get things we need? Where are the shops?'

' 'Bout two miles to the shops, there's a map in the cottage. I know that there're provisions already there for you. The only way to get round is to walk. Two miles ain't far.' Tanya decided not to grace his response with an answer and she also decided to kill Cherry when they got back. She knew the idea had been to go to somewhere remote but this was ridiculous.

'So how do we get back to the station?' Tanya asked.

'I'm coming to pick you up at five on Sunday and run you back to the train.' He smiled.

'That's very kind,' Tanya said.

'Tanya I thought you organised this?' Eric asked, puzzled by all her questions.

'My assistant looked after the little details,' Tanya explained, trying to sound more important than she felt. Not only was she going to kill Cherry but she was going to do it after she'd made her spend a weekend here.

Tanya took the keys from the driver and led the way into the cottage. As soon as she stepped on to the path an outside light came on and she could immediately see that the cottage was beautiful. With ivy trailing the walls and roses hanging over the door it was very 'English country'. Tanya smiled despite herself.

She opened the door and flicked a light switch. Immediately she was in the reception room, which housed a three-piece suite on one side and a dining table on the other. A television was provided. The next doorway leading off the reception room was the kitchen. It was a bit disappointing, almost too modern, although she didn't plan on spending too much time in there. She opened the fridge and found it stocked with all her favourite things. Champagne, white wine, lager, a selection of cheeses, hams and salads filled the shelves. In the freezer there was a selection of desserts. She opened the fridge again and found a large chicken, Sunday roast she guessed. Sitting in a wine rack was red wine. If nothing else they could be drunk all weekend. Exploring some more she found an assortment of snacks and chocolate. Eric would be fine. She worried slightly that the kitchen was too well-stocked, but she tried to shrug it off. The problem with deception was that you were always expecting to get caught. She walked back into the lounge and found everyone slumped on the furniture.

'Don't you want to look round?' she asked.

'I just want my bed,' Leigh replied. Tanya shrugged and led the way upstairs. She immediately picked the nicest bedroom for her and Leigh and no one else argued because it had a double bed in it. Gus, David and Eric played paper, stone, scissors to decide who was sharing a room. Eric won and opted to be alone.

Tanya unpacked her bag and went to the bathroom. Leigh pulled out her pink pyjamas and put them on. She hung up her clothes and waited for Tanya to return. When she did, Leigh went to the bathroom. Later as they lay side by side in bed in the darkness, Tanya spoke.

'LeeLee, I don't feel that we've had a conversation for ages, or had time alone. How are things?'

'Fantastic. I've got my new image, a job I love, a boss I adore and Gus.' Tanya could sense Leigh's smile even though she couldn't see it.

'But, LeeLee, you don't really have Gus do you?'

'He's my friend, we hang out and Sukie says that the way to a man is by being his friend. That's what I'm doing. And I know it'll work.'

'It's not that, it's just that I hate to think of you getting hurt. And we never go out any more. Remember the last time we did, we had fun LeeLee,' Tanya persisted.

'Last time you nearly had sex with a bouncer and neither of us remember any of it,' Leigh argued.

'But we could do that, or not that obviously, but we could go out, have some drinks, chat up men, that sort of thing.'

'Do you think that might make Gus jealous?' Leigh asked.

'How should I know?'

'I'll ask Sukie, and if she thinks it will work then we should do it.'

'So you'll only come out with me to make Gus jealous. You're a great friend LeeLee.'

'How can I expect you to understand. I am in Love. With a capital "L". And I can't think about anything else but Gus, night or day. You have to understand. You should be supporting me, not criticising.' Now Tanya could sense Leigh's lip wobbling.

Tanya tried to sound tender. 'LeeLee, I do support you really, but I also worry about you. And as your oldest friend I think I have a right to worry.'

'I know you do, but you should also be more positive around me. Sukie says that the more positive energy women can conjure up the more attractive they become to men.'

Tanya couldn't reply. She just couldn't. She was far too angry. She would have liked to get her hands on Sukie.

The next morning, Gus knocked loudly on their door. Leigh sat up and smiled, Tanya sat up and groaned.

'What the hell is the time?' she asked.

'About seven,' Gus replied, walking in.

'Seven?' Tanya snapped.

'I'm glad I'm awake, we can explore,' Leigh countered.

'It's so noisy in my room I couldn't sleep,' Gus said and sat down on Leigh's feet. She squealed.

'Is that because of the wonderful sounds of nature?' Leigh asked.

'Not unless you count David's snoring, talking in his sleep and tossing and turning loudly, nature,' Gus replied.

'Oh he's not that bad, I've slept in the same room as him loads of times.' Tanya was still in her early morning bad mood.

'Well then you two can sleep together tonight and I'll sleep with LeeLee,' Gus joked. If it hadn't been for the blush that seemed to creep up Leigh's entire body, Tanya would probably have taken him up on his offer. Instead she got herself out of bed and announced she was taking a shower. She left the room in a decidedly worse mood than she had arrived in.

The shower did little to lessen her anger. She came out and walked towards her room wrapped only in a bath towel. She knew that Leigh would hate her for it, would accuse her of trying to flirt with Gus by appearing provocative. She didn't care. Disappointment hit her as she walked in to find the room empty. Then guilt. She was upset about not having had the opportunity to upset Leigh. That made her a rotten friend. Her only justification was that Leigh was a rather rotten friend to her.

She shivered as she realised suddenly how cold she was. The guest towels were not only small but also flimsy. As she dried herself she noticed that not only had Leigh and Gus disappeared, but the duvet had too. She scowled.

She dressed in jeans, a warm jumper and her Nikes. Then she dried her hair and applied make-up. It was only then that she thought to check the weather. Opening the rosebud curtains she peered out of the small window and disappointment hit again. It was grey, it looked cold, and she would have put money on rain not being far away.

She went downstairs where she found Gus, Leigh and the duvet on the sofa watching television.

'I'm making breakfast,' she announced.

'What, proper breakfast?' Gus asked.

'Absolutely. And perhaps you could round the others up and LeeLee perhaps you could make the drinks, lay the table and do the toast.' She sounded terse.

'Of course,' Leigh replied. She gave Gus a 'what's wrong with her' look and followed Tanya into the kitchen. Leigh filled the kettle while Tanya unburdened the fridge of sausages, bacon, eggs and tomatoes.

'Can you see if you can find the beans?'

'Sure,' Leigh replied and found two cans. They both set to work in near silence. Leigh set the table, prepared tea and coffee and started the toast. Tanya had organised breakfast in her usual way; she only spoke to issue instructions.

When they delivered the hot breakfast, they found Eric, Gus and David sitting at the table in anticipation. Their faces lit up like children as soon as they saw the feast.

'I can't believe I'm the only one who's dressed,' Tanya said as she looked around her. Leigh was in pink pyjamas, Gus was wearing shorts and a T-shirt, Eric was wearing jogging pants and a sweatshirt, too shabby to wear anywhere but in bed, and David had pulled on yesterday's jeans and a jumper.

'What are we going to do today?' Tanya asked.

'It looks horrid outside, perhaps we should stay in,' Leigh suggested.

'No. We didn't come all this way to stay in. We'll go for a walk, maybe to the village that the taxi driver told us about and then we'll find a nice country pub and go for lunch.' Tanya would not entertain resistance.

'But, it's going to rain,' Leigh protested.

'I think it's a good idea,' Eric said, much to everyone else's surprise.

'I didn't have you down as a walker,' Tanya answered.

Eric coloured slightly. 'I just think it's good to go out.'

'Well the idea of a pub lunch is tempting, although I don't know how I can think of food after that breakfast,' Gus added.

'Then it's settled.'

'What am I going to wear?' Leigh asked.

'Something warm,' Eric suggested. Leigh pouted, then stood up. She went to the bathroom to take a shower, and then she went to get changed.

Tanya was impatient. She hated waiting more than anything. The breakfast dishes had been cleared away, she was watching irritating television and no one had appeared. Leigh had had the first shower but still hadn't emerged from their room. Tanya had been tempted to go and hurry her up, but she could see in her head the scene she would find. Leigh would be going through all the clothes she had brought with her, putting them on, pulling them off, seeing if Tanya had anything, going through her clothes again. Tanya could not face it.

She was exactly right. Leigh was on her fifth change of clothes. She had tried every outfit on twice. Finally more out of frustration than satisfaction, she settled on a pink roll-neck jumper, her dark blue jeans (she decided against the pink ones) and her pink trainers. She looked a little more subdued than normal.

Gus and David had both showered and dressed and were chatting. They were wearing a similar uniform of jeans, fleeces and trainers, although Gus somehow managed to pull it off a bit more slickly than David. They hadn't gone downstairs because they were waiting for Eric. They all arrived in the sitting room within seconds of each other, which made Tanya feel paranoid that they were having a party without her. 'About time,' she snapped, and handed out coats. At the last minute she remembered to get the video camera. Then they left.

The rain chose to arrive just as they set off. Tanya walked while looking at the map which was in danger of becoming soggy. Eric walked beside her and tried to crack her bad mood.

'Country air, isn't it wonderful?' he said.

'It smells of shit.'

Gus, Leigh and David were behind them. Leigh was in the middle with her arms linked through theirs.

'It was your idea to come out,' David said, reasonably. Tanya turned round and gave him her 'look'.

'You know what, we're just like the Famous Five,' Eric said.

'A bit older,' Tanya replied and giggled. She had said the same thing to Harvey.

'But we didn't bring lashings of ginger beer and sandwiches,' Gus pointed out.

'Oh, I brought some crisps though,' Eric said, pulling a bag out of his pocket. 'But I can't eat them, they'll get soggy.'

They walked on the country lanes, refusing to go into fields while the ground was so muddy. Leigh thought they would all sink, Tanya didn't want her expensive trainers ruined, and the guys were happy enough on the tarmac. Eventually, after what seemed more like two-hundred miles than two, they arrived at a very small village.

'So this is what they call a village,' Eric said, looking around. There were a handful of houses, a post office-cum-general store, and a pub.

'It's very, erm, small,' Leigh offered.

'Oh LeeLee, this isn't small, you should have seen some of the villages in Devon where I grew up, they make this look enormous,' Gus told her. Leigh was thinking that she would very much like to have seen them, she held on to him a little bit tighter.

'Maybe next time we can go to your home for a weekend,' she suggested.

'That would be really good,' Gus said. He smiled broadly.

'Shall we go to the pub?' Tanya suggested, having no idea what else to do. They were cold, wet and tired.

'Brilliant,' Eric replied and led the way.

It was a pretty pub — floral and chintzy. Just as everyone imagined a country pub to be. Enhanced by the weather outside it was warm and inviting. They walked, almost in formation, up to the bar. Once there they all turned and looked at the barmaid, drawn immediately to her ageing cleavage. The barmaid watched them as they discussed what they were going to drink. It was early, the pub was empty, she was bored and the five young people ('the likes of who you don't normally see round here,' she would tell her husband later) were a welcome distraction.

'What can I get you?' she asked, tired by the procrastination. Eric thought they should have bitter, Tanya thought it was a little early for them to be drinking. Eric said that as it was cold and wet outside, they had little else to do. Eventually Eric won. He sent Tanya and Leigh to choose a table while he ordered.

'We'll have three pints of bitter and two vodka tonics,

doubles.' When he collected the drinks he took them to the table leaving Gus to pay.

Tanya had selected the table nearest the fire and she and Leigh were busy warming themselves up. When they all had their drinks in front of them, Tanya pulled out the video recorder.

'Wow, that's really neat,' Eric exclaimed, peering into the lens.

'I borrowed it from work. I thought it might be nice to film the weekend.'

'Don't film me, my hair must be a mess,' Leigh screeched. Tanya ignored her and turned the camera on her. She screamed. The camera proved a point of interest for the whole of the first round of drinks. David was particularly keen and they all took turns with it. By the time David went to the bar for the next round, everyone had relaxed.

'How many drinks have I had?' Leigh asked a while later.

'About four,' David answered.

'Why do I feel giddy then?' she asked.

'I don't know but I feel a bit tipsy,' Tanya added. Eric, Gus and David grinned.

'They obviously serve stronger vodka here,' Eric said.

'Or bigger measures,' David added.

'Or less mixers,' Gus finished.

'You got us doubles,' Tanya groaned.

'You said you were cold, we were only trying to warm you up,' Eric protested. Leigh hiccuped then giggled.

'Come on, let's walk back, that will sober us up.' Eric stood up, helped Tanya to her feet and led her outside.

'I know, I know,' Tanya said.

'What?' Eric asked.

'We'll walk back through the fields, like proper country walkers.'

'But it's really muddy,' Leigh objected.

'LeeLee, it'll be fun, we might see cows,' Tanya pushed.

'Aren't cows scary?' Leigh asked.

'No, they're lovely and fluffy, come on.' Tanya grabbed Leigh

by the hand and they ran into the nearest field. The men looked
at each other and laughed.

'We better go after them, God knows what'll happen
otherwise.'

They sprinted after the girls who were in the middle of a
field, running around in circles and shouting about how wonderful the country was. Tanya was filming Leigh but she couldn't
hold the camera still.

'David, why don't you film us?' Tanya suggested. David took
the camera and tried to hold it steady as he followed Tanya and
Leigh who were shrieking and running. Eric and Gus were on
their heels. The rain was now a drizzle.

'Are we going the right way?' David asked.

'Of course we are,' Tanya said.

'Actually we need to go left,' Gus pointed out.

'Are you sure?' Tanya asked.

'Oh I'm sure he's sure,' Leigh slurred.

'Then what are we waiting for?' Tanya led the way once
more. She and Leigh climbed over a stile into a neighbouring
field and headed left.

'This field is slippier than the last,' Leigh shouted. Just then
Tanya fell on her bottom. Seeing the usually composed girl lying
in a heap in a muddy field was too much for everyone. As Leigh
tentatively went to her and tried to help her up she was laughing
so much that she almost fell over. Eric and Gus were doubled up
and the camera was shaking with David's laughter. Tanya was
laughing more than anyone.

'Eric help me up,' she begged, when she caught her voice. Eric
went over to her and offered his hand. She grabbed it and pulled
him over.

'Bitch,' he hissed, through his laughter, as they lay in the mud.

'You look like you've both been mud wrestling.' Gus started
walking off in the direction of home.

They continued their journey. Leigh was dripping wet and
her clothes were clinging to her and her hair was frizz. Gus
looked similar, his hair was stuck to his face. David had managed

to keep marginally drier due to the huge coat he was wearing, and Eric and Tanya looked like mud monsters.

'Nearly there.' Gus pointed at a gate which would bring them out near the cottage. 'Careful, this is really muddy,' he added as he stepped slowly towards the gate.

'My shoe,' Leigh screamed as she tried to balance.

'What?' Gus ran to her.

'My shoe's in the mud,' she giggled. She wagged her socked foot around and pointed at her trainer.

'How are we going to get it?' David asked still filming.

'A stick.' Gus got Tanya and Eric to hold on to Leigh while he went off in search of one. When he came back, he hooked the shoe with the stick and held it out triumphantly. Everyone cheered. He waved it in front of Leigh.

'I can't wear it.' Leigh was horrified.

'OK, Eric, take the stick and carry the shoe home and I will carry Leigh.' Leigh looked like she had just become a millionaire as Gus scooped her up and took her in his arms.

When they reached home, Eric and Tanya mock fought to be the first into the bathroom. Tanya won and then banished Eric to the garden. He sat on the steps in the small cottage garden smoking a soggy joint and moaning, while Leigh sat beside him watching Gus gallantly hosing her trainers. David filmed it all from the kitchen door.

'I'm going to light a real fire tonight and we'll stuff some newspaper into your trainers and dry them off by the fire.' Gus smiled.

'You are my hero Gus,' Leigh responded. She hopped over to him and kissed his cheek. She hopped inside and poked her head round the door, 'Eric, I'm going for the next bath,' she said, sweetly, then ran up the stairs.

'I'll catch bloody pneumonia before I'm allowed to clean up,' he moaned.

'There's always the hosepipe,' Gus suggested.

*　　*　　*

It was dusk before they were all cleaned and recovered from the drink and the day behind them. Gus had lit a roaring fire; Eric had eventually got an opportunity to bathe. David had become addicted to using the camera and was following everyone everywhere. Tanya and Leigh were almost sober again.

'Let's cook dinner,' Tanya suggested.

'What shall we have?' Eric asked.

'Pasta of course,' she replied.

'It's all she cooks,' Leigh added.

'No, she cooked breakfast this morning,' Eric answered.

'Yeah, but past breakfast and pasta I am a bit limited. Which means I'll cook tonight but someone else will have to do the roast tomorrow.' Tanya was not only sober but she was far more relaxed.

'Well luckily for you I'm here,' Gus said. 'Eric, how fabulous are my roasts?'

'I have to admit you do a mean roast.' Eric reached over and punched Gus on the arm.

'I didn't even know you could cook,' Leigh said.

'He's like Tanya, he only cooks one thing,' Eric explained. 'I'll make the salad and be your assistant, tonight,' he offered. Tanya looked at him with surprise but didn't argue.

'Which means I'll be your assistant tomorrow,' Leigh offered.

'What about me?' David asked.

'Washing up!' they all said in unison.

It was as Tanya had imagined it would be before they had all moved in together. They were seated around the table, eating huge plates of food; picking at bread so warm that the butter melted into its creases, munching on salad with home-made dressing, drinking full-bodied red wine, chatting easily, laughing. Looking around at the animated scene, she saw bright eyes, wide smiles, happiness, and Tanya suddenly realised what had happened. *They had become friends.* The awkwardness of the house had lifted. They gelled. They were comfortable with each other. More than that, they enjoyed each other.

It hit Tanya right at that moment. It hit her so hard that she had to grab the table to steady herself. She looked around and felt tears threaten. For someone who never cried, it was an extreme feeling of loss of control. She jumped up and ran outside banging the door shut behind her.

Tanya's thoughts were in turmoil. The realisation that she was about to deceive her friends hit her hard. She would hurt them, she knew she would, but sometimes that wasn't enough reason not to do something. Neither was it enough to make her look for justification. As quickly as she had fallen apart, she pulled herself together and went back to join the others. Her eyes glistened in the aftermath of tears. Apart from that, composure had returned. 'Sorry,' she said as she sat down. No one mentioned her outburst, although they were all confused by it.

When they got into bed, Leigh snuggled up to Tanya in a way they had done when they were younger. Leigh's vivid memories of sleepovers were of tangled legs and arms. She had always loved the closeness of being with Tanya and Tanya felt the same. It was the non-sexual intimacy of friends who knew each other so well they were comfortable. Growing up put an end to this. For some reason they felt they needed to pull back as they got older, and when they did share a bed they would keep a slight distance. Leigh snuggled up to Tanya who kissed her head in a moment of rare affection.

'Are you going to tell me why you were upset tonight?' Leigh asked.

'I would love nothing more than to tell you Lee Lee, but I can't.'

'You can't or you won't?'

'Can't. I don't understand why myself.' It was a lie, but not wholly.

'Tanya, I know things have been a bit weird between us, but you are my oldest friend and if you ever need me, then just ask. I know I've been neglecting you over Gus, and I'm sorry, but I can't help it.' Leigh sounded so sincere, it took every shred of strength Tanya had to ensure her heart didn't break. She lay back and enjoyed the warmth of having Leigh so close. She tried to pinpoint where it had all gone wrong, but couldn't find the answer. All she knew was that friendships were easier when you were younger. They had struggled so hard to remain friends but why did they? They would always help each other out in times of crisis, but when there wasn't a crisis what was left? They had little in common, they annoyed each other. Leigh was in love with Gus. Tanya was embarking on her own project. They were wrapped up in themselves, their dreams, other people. Leigh was breathing gently in sleep as Tanya tried to figure out what had happened to the girl who once had been the most important person in her life. How had they got to where they were?

On Sunday morning everyone was a little subdued. Hungover would be a more accurate description. They had only toast for breakfast in anticipation of the roast that Gus would cook. They planned to eat at two which would given them some time to relax before they left for home. Leigh made Tanya a cup of coffee and kissed her cheek as she handed it to her. Tanya looked at her and felt the tears threaten again. Leigh had on a pink jumper, pink jeans and pink socks. Her blonde curls were pinned back with a couple of clips. Suddenly Tanya grabbed her and hugged her. She had to pull herself together. She told herself that she was doing this for Leigh, for the others as well as for herself. Harvey said they would all be stars and they would all be rich. They would also thank her in the end.

'I want to go for a walk,' Tanya announced. 'Any takers?'

'No, we have to make lunch,' Leigh said, relishing the time she would get to spend alone with Gus.

'I'll come,' Eric offered.

'David?' Tanya asked.

'All right.' They gathered their coats and were about to set off when Tanya had an idea.

'I know, why don't I leave my camera running in the kitchen and then when we get back we can see what Leigh and Gus got up to,' she said with enthusiasm.

'They're going to cook, that's all, what's worth filming?' Eric asked.

'It might be fun,' Tanya said, unsure why she was suggesting it.

'No,' David replied.

'What?'

'Tanya no. It would be like spying. You don't spy on friends.'

They walked through lanes, chatting easily, laughing, arguing occasionally. Tanya had brought the camera with her and was doing an impression of a professional filmmaker walking backwards recording the other two. Eric teased her mercilessly, David was the referee.

Leigh was relishing her time alone with Gus.

'It's been a great weekend,' Gus announced.

'It really has. You know lately, we've become quite close,' Leigh said.

'What us, or all of us?'

'Both. At first I wasn't sure the house would work out, but now it really seems to have.' Leigh smiled. Gus walked over to her and planted a kiss on her head.

'I think you're great LeeLee.' Leigh flushed with pleasure.

Later as they sat round the table, the scene was almost a repeat of the night before. They laughed, joked, teased and argued. But, mainly they ate and drank.

'Although we're not there at the moment, I would like to propose a toast to our house,' Leigh said suddenly. 'The house that has brought me so much happiness lately, and I hope all of us. It's a wonderful, wonderful place to live.' Her eyes filled, due to too much drink and too much sentimentality. 'And I love living with you all.'

The mood as they alighted from the train in London was sombre. Leigh had been asleep for most of the journey having drunk too much at lunch. Tanya and Eric had spent the entire journey reading magazines and making bitchy comments. Gus was reading a book of poetry and David had brought his laptop out.

Tanya led them to the taxi rank and eventually they found themselves at the front of the queue. When they pulled up outside their house they all felt relieved and very tired. The weekend was over.

Tanya sat in her room and watched the video of the weekend. When she remembered what had happened in their absence, relief was the first emotion she felt. She hadn't noticed anything different; the house looked exactly as they'd left it. She thanked Bob, silently, for his efficiency. Then she panicked. What if they hadn't noticed because they were so tired? Perhaps they would all descend the stairs tomorrow morning and find that their house had been pulled apart. She calmed herself down and turned to her own secret cupboard: the control room. The cupboard had been disguised by using a wall hanging, which looked whole but split in the middle. It was attached to two panels of wood. The wall hanging was striped in vibrant primary colours. Tanya shuddered. She was being paid a great deal but that was not going to be easy to live with. She would ask Bob why he couldn't have chosen something more tasteful. Then she decided she wouldn't. After all he was a technician and therefore couldn't be expected to share her good taste.

She shook her head. Her thoughts were shooting off in a million different directions. She tried to pull them into line. She opened the drawer of her desk and found a note. The big spidery scrawl belonged to Bob. It explained that the work had been completed although they'd been there all weekend without a break, and he was exhausted. He explained about the camera positions again, and attached a map of the layout. He then went on to explain the control room. The wall hanging was African, apparently. Tanya stifled a yawn, she didn't care where it came from, it was horrid. It had taken a dedicated team the whole weekend to arrange the covering and build the cupboard, and at one point they thought they might have brought down a wall. But they hadn't, and the cupboard had been built. The problem was that they had run out of time and had been unable to fit the equipment. That would need to be done when everyone was out of the house again, but would take only a day. Tanya groaned. This was becoming irritating – the note as well as the process. He went on to tell her that her remote control to open the cupboard was in the drawer.

She pulled it out. It looked just like any television remote control. It even had television channel buttons on it. She pressed the standby button that Bob's note said opened the cupboard. As if by magic the wall hanging parted and revealed her control room. The way it worked was enough to make even the most tired of people feel exuberant. How could you not? It was like a secret door. She pressed the standby button again and the wall hanging shut. She could barely make out the middle split. It was a wonderful job.

Tanya might have been given a role in the production of the film, but she was left ignorant of many things. Budget being one of them. If she had known how much her cupboard had cost she would have been horrified. To Harvey it was just small change.

She opened and closed it again and again, noting how it made hardly any sound. When she had tired of the novelty, she actually studied her control room closely. It was well lit, it had a desktop and a chair, devoid of equipment, but obviously not for long. She could sit inside it and close the door behind her, which, she discovered, made her feel claustrophobic, so she kept the door open. She tried to imagine how it would be when it was fully functional. Then she smiled. This was more exciting than she had ever imagined.

After leaving her room she took a tour around the house. Thankfully the others had gone to bed. She carried the layout plans with her so that she could see exactly where the cameras were. She looked as closely as she could but couldn't notice even the slightest difference. Relief returned. They had achieved exactly what they said they would and when she had her equipment, they could test it. Every negative emotion left her and she experienced a shudder of anticipation. Harvey was right, this was better than sex. Better than the best sex ever.

After she completed the tour, Tanya went to bed. She needed to sleep. She was tired after the weekend, but thrilled with excitement for the future and she would see Harvey the following morning. Despite having abandoned her crush on him, she needed to look her best.

Chapter Twenty-Six

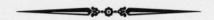

From her bed, Tanya listened to her housemates leaving. She had spent considerable time, since leaving her job, learning their daily routines. What amused her was the regular daily pattern. It was the commuter hell they were all a part of. You would get up, shower, dress and leave the house for work at the same time every day. After a while you would do it on automatic pilot. Gus was the only exception.

Eric, amazingly, was always the first to leave unless Gus was on a day shift. David would follow about half an hour later. Leigh would normally leave at a quarter to nine. In the old days Tanya had left at nine. She could almost set her watch by her housemates' movements.

The first person left the house at seven, so she knew that Gus was working days. Eric left at his usual time. After she heard Leigh leave, bouncing down the stairs in her pink trainers, Tanya jumped out of bed.

She hadn't told anyone that she had left her job. She said that she worked at home sometimes and had the laptop to prove it. So, she would wait until everyone had gone before emerging. This morning she walked downstairs with the mobile phone Harvey had given her and, while she waited for the kettle to boil, she called him.

'Harvey Cannon's office.' Cherry answered the phone.

'Cherry, hi it's Tanya.'

'Hello honey. How was the weekend?' Tanya thought about how it was and decided on the truth.

'Actually it was lovely despite the rain. We all had a really nice time.'

Cherry smiled. 'That's great. So you're back and everything is OK?'

'It looks fine but Bob needs to finish off. The coast is clear today. The earliest anyone will be back is about half five.'

'Hang on. I'll just go see what the boys are doing.'

Tanya laughed at her calling Harvey and Bob 'boys'. After a few minutes, Cherry's voice came back.

'Hey, guess what, we're all coming over.'

'You are?' Tanya was surprised.

'Sure, as well as Bob's engineers, who are on standby to do your control room, Harvey, Bob, myself and Millie are coming round. Tanya, we are so excited to see the movie set.'

'Gosh, I hadn't thought of it like that,' Tanya replied. It hit her, she was no longer standing in her home, she was on a film set.

'We'll be over in about half an hour.' Cherry replaced the receiver.

Tanya sprang into action. She ran upstairs, took a shower, dressed in plain black trousers and a red shirt. The cameras would be running soon. She would need to look good. But it would look odd if she was always fully dressed and made up in her own house, she resolved to buy a robe to wear in the morning. Cashmere. She would look lovely in a cashmere robe. The rest of the time she would look as she always did. Smart, expensive and fashionable. It was an important detail that she kicked herself for almost overlooking.

By the time she had put on her make-up and dried her hair, the doorbell rang. Perfect timing. She ran downstairs and opened it to find them all crammed on the doorstep like excited children. She stood aside and let them in.

'I'll give you a grand tour,' Bob announced, 'and by the time we finish the engineers better be here.' He led the way. Tanya followed behind with the distinct feeling that this was no longer her home.

As Bob pointed out where the cameras were hidden, everyone else became animated. They finished up in Tanya's bedroom where the magic control room proved the most exciting thing of all. After everyone was allowed to open and close it the doorbell went. Tanya made to go downstairs, but was brushed aside by Bob. 'I'll get it,' he announced.

They all followed him back downstairs where Millie proceeded to make coffee while Bob disappeared with the engineers. Tanya was redundant.

'I can't believe what a great job they've done,' Cherry said.

'I told you, Bob's the best and when he organises something it always works out perfectly,' Harvey replied.

'How was the weekend Tanya?' Millie asked, handing her a coffee.

'Great, it rained, we got drunk, muddy and wet in that order.' She laughed at the memory.

'Did you get good footage on your camera?' Harvey asked.

'Of course,' Tanya replied. 'I need to do some editing and then I'll show you.' She smiled.

'I'll look forward to it.' Harvey smiled back, then his face became grave. 'Tanya, honey, we start filming tomorrow. You know that don't you? Tuesday, the twenty-fourth is the most important date for all of us and will only be surpassed by the date we finish filming.' Harvey's tones were gentle, but the effect of his words produced nerves. 'Next Monday we will have our first editing meeting. You will spend the day with Bob and the others in the editing suite, pulling apart the footage from the first week. Then on Tuesday afternoon we will all meet in my office to discuss that footage. Those will be weekly meetings. Every month you spend a further amount of time cutting down the monthly footage. Are you happy, because honey, if you have any questions at this point we really need to iron them out. After tomorrow this movie is in production and we really need to be on top of it.'

'It's fine,' Tanya whispered, the effects of the words were about to eat her alive. In twenty-four hours she would be making a film.

Everyone but Bob left a short time later. Bob and his engineers were working as quickly as they could on the control room to have it fully functional by the end of the day. There could be no question of it not being. Tanya decided to leave them to it and go shopping.

As she walked down the King's Road she thought more about the film they were about to make. She then tried not to. As she bought herself nightwear in the shape of a matching T-shirt and shorts, and an extravagant cashmere robe, she tried to quash her nervous excitement.

This was her first foray into filmmaking and they were producing a ground-breaking film. What more could she ask for? Nothing, she decided. She had everything she wanted, therefore it had to be a success.

With a positive spring in her step, Tanya returned home to be given a lesson by Bob on how to work the control room. He then left her to it, marking the end of an incredibly swift pre-production.

Chapter Twenty-Seven

Production

At six on Tuesday morning, Tanya got up to switch the cameras on. Her hands shook as she did so. The moment had arrived. Immediately the four screens buzzed into life. She could see the kitchen, the sitting room, the hallway and the stairwell. She could see various angles of each. It looked complicated. She knew that everything was being recorded and she didn't have to worry. She knew that in Bob's editing suite he would be seeing what she saw. She guessed they did that in order to ensure she didn't try to wipe off what she didn't like. Their insurance policy. Instead of objecting, it made her feel better. Tanya didn't want too much technical responsibility. She wanted only the glory. As it was, she seemed to have little to do apart from watch.

While she waited for activity in the rest of the house, she began editing the footage of the weekend. As she took out some parts that she didn't want Harvey to see, she realised that she would have to be careful from now on; she couldn't hide her behaviour from Harvey. He was like 'Big Brother'; someone who would see everything she did, or everything she did in certain parts of the house.

She put on her new robe. She felt good about things as she settled once more in front of the screens to watch the morning activity.

At half-past-six Gus emerged from his room looking sleepy and incredibly sexy, and went to the bathroom. When he came out again he went back to his room where Tanya could hear the faint sound of the radio spilling out under the door. Ten minutes later the door opened and he came out wearing a shirt and tie and a pair of trousers. He still looked sexy. He practically ran down the stairs, ignored the kitchen and went to the cupboard where they kept their coats. He pulled out his black jacket, put it on and without a glance anywhere but straight ahead he left the house.

At just after seven, Eric emerged on to the landing and went into the bathroom. A short time later he came out wearing a towel over his lower body and walked back to his room. Tanya noted his surprisingly athletic body.

The next person to emerge was David, who came up the stairs in a dark blue tatty towelling bathrobe and walked into the bathroom. Half an hour later he came out and went back downstairs.

At eight, Eric bounded down the stairs wearing his suit and carrying a small rucksack. She laughed as she saw him stop and look in the hall mirror, as he tried to flatten his unruly hair. Then, to her delight, he smiled at his reflection before bounding towards the front door and leaving the house. David appeared again, still in his bathrobe. He walked into the kitchen, filled the kettle up, put it on, and put two slices of bread into the toaster. Tanya couldn't believe how good it was. Not what was actually happening — David in a bathrobe, Eric in a towel, not exactly earth shattering stuff — but the screens. She could see them from the front, back, all sorts of different angles. She began to see it from an artistic point of view as well as a technical one.

She missed seeing Leigh walk into the bathroom, but when she came out, wrapped in a pink towel, her bust looked even bigger on screen than it did in real life. If she wasn't careful Leigh would be inundated with glamour model offers when the film was released. She walked back to her room. What seemed like an eternity later she emerged wearing her pink mini-skirt, pale tights, a white T-shirt and cardigan and of course her pink trainers. Her pink handbag hung from her shoulders. She went into the kitchen just as David was leaving for work. Tanya realised that she had to develop the talent of watching more than one screen at a time because she had missed David's breakfast and him going downstairs.

'Hey LeeLee,' David said as he hugged her.

'Have a good day,' Leigh giggled and hugged him back. David left. Leigh opened the fridge and pulled out a carton of orange juice and a pink grapefruit. That was her breakfast. She sat at the breakfast bar, sipping her drink, scooping her grapefruit and humming intermittently to herself.

After she finished breakfast she washed her dishes and went to the hall mirror to apply her pink lipstick. She blew herself a kiss as she grabbed her pink denim jacket and left the house.

Tanya laughed to herself. She was getting to see things she never knew about her housemates and it was only day one.

She left her room now that the house was empty. She went to the kitchen and made herself a cup of coffee. The new luxury of not having to go out to work included her being able to have breakfast before she had to hit the shower. It was something she enjoyed. She took her coffee into the sitting room and flicked on the television. As she watched the breakfast show come to an end, so did her coffee. She took a shower, got dressed and put on her make-up. She went then to check her e-mails. Millie had sent a good luck message. She smiled.

She finished editing the rest of the weekend footage, then lay down on her bed and wondered just what the hell she was supposed to do for the rest of the day. The film was in production and she still had nothing to do.

She was woken from her unintentional nap by the shrill of her mobile phone. She grabbed at it.

'Tanya, it's Cherry.' Tanya tried to remember where she was and what she was doing.

'Hi,' she mumbled. She sat up and pushed her hair out of her eyes. She wondered how long she'd been asleep.

'Just calling to see how you are. Do you want to go to lunch?'
Harvey had warned her that the first few days would be boring
for Tanya. He had then suggested the lunch outing. Cherry had
obliged. She was quite fond of Tanya in her own way.

'I'd love that. Where shall I meet you?' Tanya felt oddly
elated by the invitation; she was relieved that she now had
something to do.

'Meet me in the fifth floor bar at Harvey Nichols. We can
shop afterwards,' Cherry suggested.

'What time?' Tanya glanced at her watch and noticed that it
was half past eleven.

'Half past twelve?' Cherry suggested.

'I'll be there, bye.'

Cherry was already seated at a table when Tanya arrived. She was
sipping mineral water. They air kissed.

'Honey, what can I get you?'

'I'll have a glass of red wine,' Tanya said, boldly. From what
she had heard about LA, she didn't think its inhabitants were
keen on big drinkers, or not public drinking anyway. Tanya,
however, was English so she decided to do as she wanted. Cherry
ordered the wine and looked over the menu. Tanya did the same.
They both ordered salads, but Tanya ordered fries on the side.
Cherry looked at her.

'It must be wonderful to eat what you like and stay so slim,'
she sighed, enviously.

'I do have to exercise,' Tanya replied. She never did.

'Well, so do I, although since I've been here I haven't really
bothered. There's a gym in our building which I visit sometimes,
but you know, the lack of sunshine seems to put me off. So
instead I give up fattening food.' She smiled.

'You look great,' Tanya said truthfully. Cherry was about
five-foot-eight, slim with straight, long blonde hair. To Tanya
she looked like a slightly older cheerleader, but she also had
something in her face which stopped the assumption of 'dumb

blonde'. Tanya couldn't identify it, but she had an intelligence, a composure about her. She was classy. Her outfits always looked expensive and smart. She managed to make herself sexy but not tarty, attractive rather than pretty. However she managed it, she was a package. Tanya liked her because she admired her. She wanted to be like her.

Her thoughts were interrupted by the waiter. Cherry ordered for both of them, then smiled. 'So, how did it go this morning?'

'The only footage is of everyone leaving the house, and then me getting my coffee. It wasn't exciting, but there was a bit where Eric of all people looked at himself in the mirror and tried to sort out his hair, then he smiled at his reflection, and Leigh, for some reason, blew a kiss into the same mirror. Gosh can you imagine how they'd feel if they knew I'd seen that?'

'Tanya, stop worrying about that. You mustn't worry about that. Now, I was thinking, you have everyone leaving the house but you. Maybe you should leave too.'

'I don't understand. I left to come here, that will be on tape.'

'Of course. So we can do a sequence where you all leave the house, and include you in that. It won't look normal if you stay at home all day while everyone else is out.'

'I guess, but we might not use that footage,' Tanya pointed out.

'No, but think of it, we speed it up a bit, have the bathroom bit then you all leaving . . . a bit of music . . . it could be fun.' Cherry smiled and took another sip of water.

'Oh yes, I see. Christ I have to start thinking like a film-maker.'

'Don't worry, honey, you will soon. It's early days. As soon as you start editing with Harvey and Bob, things will fall into place.'

'Sure. Of course they will.' Tanya was reassured.

The waiter brought their food and they started eating. Tanya could have kicked herself for sounding so unprofessional. She should be coming up with ideas. She determined to be more on top of things from now on. Cherry smiled kindly. She knew Tanya would do fine, although she would probably need a bit of pushing in the right direction. That was the trouble with Harvey. He chose people he could control to an extent. It wasn't malicious, but Cherry knew that when he chose her he knew that he could control her. She was under no illusion about that.

'Tanya, you know it will take time to see things coming together on this. The footage needs to be collected first, so be relaxed about it. In two months if we still have nothing of interest, then we'll worry.'

'OK. I'll try to relax.'

Cherry steered the conversation on to more neutral territory for the rest of lunch. She didn't want Tanya panicking about the film, or even thinking about it. Harvey knew what he was doing. That was enough. Instead she talked about fashion trends and how she found London and its people. Cherry knew her stuff when it came to designers, she pointed out what every woman was wearing; although Tanya didn't know if she was right, she believed her. 'That's Prada, last season in the States, although I guess maybe you guys are behind.' She seemed to be able to identify not only the garment but also the season it came from. It was safe ground, like a lunch between two new friends. Tanya began to think of Cherry as just that.

Harvey was playing a computer game in his office when Cherry returned.

'So?' he asked.

'She was fine. Just as we predicted. She's just panicking a bit, but I managed to reassure her.'

'You're an angel. So what about the footage so far?'

'Harvey all we have is the "in and out" of the bathroom, making breakfast and going to work. Oh, and Tanya having coffee.'

'Which is all I was expecting.'

'On Monday when you go to the editing suite, then you'll get an idea as to what it is we're getting, or going to get.'

'Expectations are high.'

'Honey, real life has its dramas, more than movies and books sometimes.'

'Maybe, but we have only six months, and if nothing happens to these guys in six months then we're stuffed.'

'Cherry where did you pick up such a charming expression? Now please stop worrying, it'll all be fine. We are going to produce the movie of the year and we'll all get loads of credit for it.'

'Sure Harvey, I just get a bit nervous, you know?'

'I know honey, but we have to keep ourselves on top of this one. Jesus, I sent you out to check that Tanya was OK and you come back in a worse state.' Harvey laughed.

Cherry laughed. 'Sorry, Just first night nerves.'

'Look we're all bound to worry about this, after all we've never done anything like it before. But let's leave the panic until a couple of months, I guess that's what you told Tanya, right?'

'Sure Harvey that's what I told her.'

'That's my girl.' Harvey kissed her on the cheek.

Back on location, Tanya was watching television and waiting for her housemates to come home so that there would be something on film. She kept changing positions on the sofa because she was unsure how she would look to the cameras. She was about to go upstairs to her control room to have a look, but then she heard the door. Her first 'star' had returned.

The star turned out to be David.

'David, in here,' Tanya shouted. He walked into the sitting room. Tanya jumped up and hugged him.

'Wow, I don't normally get such a welcome,' he said, with a look of bemusement on his face. Tanya cursed silently, she was hoping that on film it would look like they were always that friendly. This wasn't as easy as she had first thought. She stepped back and looked at David. He was wearing his favourite jeans, a pair of Converse boots and a sweatshirt. He looked a bit boring, but then David was not exactly a dynamic dresser. There would be no expensive wardrobe department in this film.

'Didn't you go to work today?' he asked.

'This morning, but I brought work home.'

'Do you want tea?' David was looking at Tanya, she was acting strangely.

'No, I'd like some wine. Why don't we open a bottle?'

'Sure.' Tanya heard David go into the kitchen. He came back carrying a bottle of red wine and two glasses. He sat on the sofa next to Tanya and opened it. He handed her a glass and she kissed him on the cheek. Again, he looked at her somewhat bemused. The thought that she might have been smoking Eric's grass flitted across his mind.

'Cheers babes,' Tanya said. As David was about to reply he stopped and looked on with amazement as Tanya drank the glass of wine in one go and poured herself another.

'Tanya are you all right?' he asked.

'Never better babes,' she winked at him. What David didn't know, what he couldn't know was that Tanya had decided that the filming should begin with a bit of a helping hand. Her idea that afternoon, post-lunch, was that if they all had a few drinks then someone was bound to do or say something funny. The other part that David didn't, couldn't know, was that Tanya was intent on being the funny one. In his ignorance, he wished that Eric, Leigh or Gus would come home. He wasn't sure he felt comfortable with the person masquerading as Tanya. He wished even harder as he saw her finish her second glass of wine, when he was still on his first. He flicked on the television and lit a cigarette. Tanya grabbed the remote control and flicked it off.

'Why did you do that?' he asked.

'Because I thought it was time we chatted instead of watching television. All we do is watch television.' Tanya started on her third glass of wine, David puffed hard on his cigarette and wished he had worked late.

Just as the bottle of wine was emptied, Eric came in.

'You're late,' Tanya said, accusingly.

'What for?' Eric asked.

'Just generally,' Tanya replied. 'Why don't you get another bottle of wine from the kitchen and have a drink?'

'Let me get out of my suit first.' He went upstairs shooting David a quizzical look. While Eric was getting changed Leigh appeared.

'LeeLee,' Tanya said, jumping up to hug her.

'Are you drunk?' Leigh asked. Tanya immediately bristled. She was trying to work hard to get them all to look like a group of friends for the camera and as usual her housemates were being highly uncooperative.

'No, just pleased to see you.' Tanya smiled.

'That's sweet.' Leigh went to get the wine that Eric was supposed to get. Eric met her in the kitchen, he was dressed in his tracksuit bottoms and a T-shirt.

'Hi.'

'Hi, Eric. Do you know what's going on?'

'What?'

'Tanya, she hugged me, she never hugs me these days,' Leigh explained.

'I know, it's really disconcerting, she told me I was late.'

'Is she drunk?' Leigh asked.

'I'd say by the look of her she's well on the way. It won't be long.'

'How strange.'

Eric shrugged. 'Oh well, we better take her some more wine before she starts screaming.'

'Why were you late home?' David asked Leigh, sounding too much like Tanya for his liking.

'I went for a drink with Zsa Zsa,' Leigh replied.

'Zsa Zsa? What kind of name is that for a normal person?' Tanya asked, before taking a large mouthful of wine.

'She's really called Alexandra, but Zsa Zsa is a much better name,' Leigh explained.

'Like LeeLee. I guess this was another of Sukie's ideas,' Tanya said, unkindly.

'Why aren't we watching telly?' Leigh refused to rise to Tanya's bait. She knew that for some reason Tanya was jealous of her boss.

'Because we *always* watch TV. Tonight we are going to have a conversation,' Tanya explained.

Eric lit a joint. 'What about food? I am going to be really hungry in approximately twenty minutes.'

'I'd really like Thai,' David said. 'In fact I've been craving it all day.'

'OK, Thai it is,' Eric replied, jumping up to find menus.

'What if I don't want Thai?' Tanya asked.

'Well do you?' Eric's voice lacked patience.

'Yes as a matter of fact I would like Thai, but it's nice to be asked.'

'You are such a pain in the arse,' Eric said, before leaving the room. Tanya looked for a minute like she was going to explode. As David and Leigh watched her closely, they saw the pulse throbbing in her temple. Just as they expected her to launch an attack on Eric, she seemed to have a change of heart. She laughed. 'Eric, give me the menus, I'll be in charge of the ordering.' As everyone had expected a row they all started laughing with relief. As they were choosing, Leigh's mobile rang.

'Hello Gus,' she said, as her phone announced Gus on its display.

'Hey, LeeLee. Listen, I'm being roped in to do an extra shift tonight, I won't be back until about midnight. I just didn't want you to worry.'

'Are you OK?' Leigh's voice was filled with love and concern.

'Sort of. I spoke to Natasha today, she called me again you know. But I'll tell you all about it tomorrow. Can we go out for a drink or something?' he asked. Leigh's heart felt as if it had been hit, not because of Natasha but because Gus sounded so miserable.

'Of course. Call me tomorrow at work and let me know where and when. Bye darling.'

'Bye LeeLee and thanks.' As Leigh ended the call she smiled into the phone.

'That was Gus?' Tanya asked.

'Yes, he's working late, so when we order dinner we can exclude him,' Leigh explained.

'Why did he call your mobile, what's wrong with the home phone?' Tanya demanded.

'He needed to talk to me about something.' Leigh was running his voice through her head.

'What is it with you two?' Tanya asked.

'What?' Leigh replied.

'Secrets. Since when did you decide that you two were the only two who live here? You're like a married couple. Minus the sex of course,' Tanya sneered.

'I don't know what you mean, we're not like that at all. We're just friends. Like *we're* friends.' Leigh was obviously distressed. Tanya was obviously drunk. David and Eric exchanged terrified looks.

'Oh right, so that means you're dying to jump *my* bones then,' Tanya said.

'Tanya . . .' Eric started.

'You shut up,' Tanya shouted at him. Eric looked as if he'd been struck.

'Why are you being so horrid?' Leigh asked.

'You think I'm being horrid do you? Let me tell you something little Miss Pink Pain in the Arse, I am not the horrid one around here. Since we moved in all you care about is Gus. Not only have you changed your whole personality and looks for him, you are now his best friend and you've stopped caring about your other friends, namely me. You don't give a toss about me any more. That is why I am being horrid. We have just returned from a marvellous weekend away and I thought that you were going to try not to ignore all your other friends, I thought you might make an effort with me. But no, you don't care about anyone else.' Tanya stormed out and returned seconds later with another bottle of wine.

'Don't you think you've had enough?' David asked.

'Piss off.' David and Eric looked at Tanya then they looked at Leigh. She was close to tears.

'I do care about you Tanya,' Leigh said, in a quiet voice.

'Yeah? You've got a funny way of showing it,' Tanya spat back.

'Maybe. At the moment there are things going on in my life which make it hard for me,' Leigh answered.

'Oh yeah, like turning into a freak because you want Gus. For fuck's sake how sad you are. Gus doesn't fancy you. If he was going to he would by now, why don't you stop being a sad fuck and get on with your life?'

'Tanya shut it!' David said. It was the first time Eric had seen David get angry.

'We're just friends. I know that and I accept it. At least he doesn't talk to me the way you do,' Leigh said. Eric felt a great deal of respect for her, she hadn't shed a tear yet.

'I only shout at you because you fucking well deserve it. Leigh – sorry, *LeeLee* – it's about time you took a long hard look at yourself, because the way you're behaving Gus isn't the only man who doesn't want you. No one would.' Tanya was met by silence. David looked as if he would hit her. Eric stared at the carpet. He had even forgotten about the aborted Thai meal. Leigh looked at David. She immediately burst into tears and fled the room.

'I'll go,' David said shooting a furious look at Tanya before following Leigh out.

She was sitting on the stairs outside her room, where she had collapsed. She might have made it all the way to her room had she known that the cameras were there. David kneeled in front of her and pulled her to him.

'LeeLee, she was wrong. You're lovely as you are, please don't let her make you think anything different.'

'She's right though, Gus doesn't want me,' Leigh sobbed.

'Maybe not, but that's not something we should dwell on. You're his friend as you said and you are very important to him.

Remember that. Tanya is jealous. You know what she's like. She hated you having other friends the whole time you were growing up. I was the only one she accepted. She might act all tough but we both know she's not. She's lonely. She would never admit it but she is. And she got drunk. Leigh, you know what'll happen, she'll be all hungover and full of remorse tomorrow and you'll forgive her.' David attempted a reassuring smile.

'I know you're right. I will forgive her. God knows why but I will. She is such a bitch and she knows where my weak points are. But I'll forgive her. David, sometimes I don't know why we are friends,' Leigh said, her tears now dried on to her cheeks.

'Because you are,' David replied, which was the truth.

'Soppy cow,' Tanya stormed.

'Tanya, I am not sure why I am still sitting here with you, but don't you think that even for you that was completely out of order?' Eric said. He wished he'd run after David and Leigh, that would have been the safer option.

'I spoke the truth,' Tanya replied, her voice slightly slurred.

'Which bits were the truth?' Eric asked.

'She is obsessed with Gus. And she has this psycho boss who tells her to act girly to get him. She has hardly spent any time with me since we moved in. It's all true.'

'Shame you couldn't have put it like that to her and left out the "sad fuck" bits,' Eric pointed out.

'I was angry,' Tanya replied, but had the grace to blush.

'Tanya she's in love. Or she thinks she is and it's shitty because Gus is not only good-looking but a great guy. She is going to have to get over him herself, because I agree that I don't think he will fall for her.'

While Eric was talking Tanya began to feel guilty. 'I hate to say it but you're right. I'll have to apologise.' Eric nodded. Tanya then proceeded to empty her wine glass as well as Leigh's and David's abandoned ones. Eric watched as she drank another half bottle of red wine in record time.

Tanya stood up, stumbled, then giggled. 'My legs have turned to jelly.'

'Maybe you should apologise tomorrow,' Eric suggested.

'I feel sick.'

Shit, why do I get the crap jobs, Eric thought to himself, as he picked up Tanya and took her upstairs. When Eric put her in front of the loo, moaning that she was heavy for such a skinny bird, Tanya decided that she didn't feel sick after all. Eric sighed, picked her up again and half carried, half dragged her to her bedroom. He turned the handle of her door and found it didn't open.

'Shit Tanya, you're the only one of us who uses those blasted locks you had fitted.' Eric was losing any patience he may have had.

'The key is in my knickers.' Tanya giggled.

'Well I am bloody well not rooting around in there.'

'No, in my bra.' Tanya fell about laughing again. Eric shook his head. She had turned from being a monster to behaving like a pissed tart.

Just as Eric was contemplating throwing her down the stairs, David emerged from Leigh's room and hearing the commotion made his way upstairs to where Eric and Tanya were.

'I'm sorry Davey,' Tanya said, looking contrite.

'It's not me you have to tell. I expect you to grovel tomorrow,' David replied.

'Ohhh I will . . . I promise. Come on, babes . . . I need to get into my room.' Tanya giggled again.

'She's locked her door,' Eric explained.

'Why the hell does she do that?' David asked.

'To stop the baddies.' Tanya burst out laughing.

'Tanya, give me the key,' David ordered.

'No. I need water.' With that she leaped up and half ran half stumbled down the stairs.

'Christ, I can't cope,' David lamented.

'Come on, let's leave her to it and go and have a smoke.'

'Sitting room?'

'No way am I risking having to deal with her again. We'll go to my room, and maybe I *will* start to use the bloody lock.'

Tanya grabbed a bottle of water and managed to find her way back to her room. It took her a while because the stairs kept moving. She pulled her key out of her bra – she did keep it there – and opened the door, just making it to her bed before passing out with the abandoned water beside her. The first day of filming ended at nine o'clock.

Bob watched the footage and took a copy home for Harvey and Cherry. When he arrived there he found them drinking champagne

'Wow, what is this?'

'We are celebrating,' Cherry explained.

'Wait until you see what I've got, it's hilarious.' He put the tape into the VCR. He hadn't edited anything, apart from the fact that he had combined the simultaneous conversations of Leigh and David on the stairs, and Tanya and Eric in the sitting room. It was a rough cut. He had ideas about how to cut from Leigh and David to Eric and Tanya, but he'd do that later.

Cherry and Harvey watched in silence as they saw the whole exchange.

'My God,' Harvey said, when it finished. 'I didn't expect Tanya to make a complete fool of herself on the first day.'

'I like Tanya a lot, but she was way out of line there,' Cherry said. 'Poor Leigh.' She shook her head. Harvey burst out laughing.

'You see, we've been filming for one night and already Cherry is hooked. I knew this would work.'

'I don't think Tanya will be too chuffed when she watches it,' Bob pointed out.

'Well no, she'll be real embarrassed,' Cherry added.

'Oh, stop worrying, Tanya will probably watch it back and think that she didn't do anything wrong. That girl is able to justify almost everything. Bob, call her first thing tomorrow morning and tell her it was very clever of her to invoke a bit of drama into the first night of filming. Tell her we all appreciate the fact that she did it for the film. Tell her to apologise to Leigh on film which will then redeem her in the eyes of the viewers. Make her think that instead of being a bitch she's a fucking genius.' Harvey smiled. Bob nodded.

'Harvey, you really are playing with the poor girl. I'm not sure I approve,' Cherry chastised.

'You saw the way she abused Leigh. I'm not sure she deserves any sympathy. Anyway we're making a movie. We need to ensure that it'll be a great movie.' Tanya was not the only person who could justify everything.

'OK boss.' Cherry smiled. When it came down to it, Cherry would support Harvey, even if it meant humiliating Tanya.

Chapter Twenty-Eight

Tanya woke up on top of her duvet. She was fully clothed. Her head hurt. She looked at the clock, it was 5 a.m. She let out a long, painful groan. She needed water badly; her mouth felt as if it was filled with gravel. She could barely swallow. She saw the bottle of mineral water lying on the floor and thanked God she was so sensible. As she took long gulps she tried to remember how she had got so drunk. Then she remembered the first night of filming. She jumped out of bed and stumbled to her control cupboard.

Her hand shook as she pressed the remote control. Her head pounded. She sat down and looked at the screens — nothing. Then she flicked the computer on and keyed in the time that she wanted to watch. For once she was unimpressed by the technology. She sat still as she watched the events of last night unfold on her small screen. She watched her drunkenness, her row, her falling over. It was a major humiliation. She was furious with the things the others had said about her. OK she was drunk, and she was a bit out of order. She knew that she would have to apologise to Leigh, she didn't relish that. Damn Gus. Unwittingly it was all his fault. She had to admit as she rubbed her head that they all looked quite good on the screen. At least she managed to find one positive aspect.

She got up and grabbed her water. Then she thought about deleting the footage, but what was the point, she knew that Bob would have already seen it. The only thing she could do was to fight for it to be cut. She was the producer after all.

She shut the cupboard and went back to bed. The only way she could cope with her hangover was sleep.

Tanya was woken abruptly by her mobile ringing. She answered it to Bob. He did exactly what Harvey had told him too. He marvelled at how Harvey seemed to be able to gauge people accurately, as Tanya proceeded to pretend that she had planned the whole thing for entertainment value. She even claimed that she was feigning to be drunk. She fell for the flattery, as Harvey had predicted. She almost believed it all herself. When she came off the phone, she felt she could justify her behaviour. After all she was starring in a film wasn't she?

Bob and the editors – James, Amanda and John – made notes for each frame of film, in order to generate ideas for putting things together. It seemed excessive to have four people working full time on this, but Bob had insisted that there would be a huge amount of work to do and everyone had to be there from the start, otherwise they wouldn't have the feel for it. Amanda had already suggested the first morning routine, as a great opening credit sequence. It was the sort of thing that had been used to open a film before, but, of course, it had never been real before. They had someone watching the footage most of the time. They stopped when everyone had gone to bed. They knew that on the previous night, after doors had closed, Gus had come home late, had a drink of water, taken a shower and then gone to bed. They knew that David had emerged stoned from Eric's room at about two in the morning and had held on to the banisters for dear life as he made his way downstairs to his room. They had to keep a close eye on things, it couldn't be left to chance. Or to Tanya.

Tanya spent the rest of the day nursing her hangover. She realised that, at this early stage, the job of producer wasn't exactly going to run her into the ground. She was bored. So she went out and bought comfort food and magazines which both filled her and her afternoon. At five-thirty she was sitting on the sofa watching television, eating chocolate and waiting for Leigh to come home. After all she had an apology to make.

David arrived, he looked into the sitting room and said a cold hello. Tanya smiled and told him she was waiting for Leigh because she wanted to apologise. David softened as he always did.

'She won't be home for ages though,' he said.

'How come?' Tanya asked.

'She and Gus have gone for dinner.'

'Why? They're not dating. Why are they acting like they're dating?' Tanya was agitated again.

'Don't start. Just leave them alone. I really don't understand why this bothers you so much.'

'Sorry. I just feel awful about last night. I shouldn't have got so drunk and I shouldn't have been such a complete cow to Leigh. She didn't deserve it. David, I feel like she's ousted me. She has Gus and she has her boss and she never has time for me any more.'

'Tanya, this is kid's stuff. Leigh is in the middle of a monster crush. We all know the wisdom of it can be questioned, but we love her, and while she feels she needs to spend all her time with Gus we have to accept it. Tanya you have your work colleagues, you have me and Eric, and although we might not be much, we are you friends.' David's voice was comforting.

'I'm lonely,' Tanya said, simply. 'Bloody lonely.' She had forgotten about the cameras.

'Come on, why don't we go to the pub, just the two of us,' David suggested, giving her a squeeze.

'I'd like that,' Tanya answered, and smiled.

They left to go to the Bierodrome on Fulham Road. Tanya had begged David to go there, although at a fifteen minute walk he said it was a bit far. Apart from the nearest pub, everything was too far according to him, but, as he was trying to make Tanya feel better, he conceded.

Eric didn't get home until seven. He had been for a quick, unexciting drink with a work colleague. Something that happened only rarely. He walked into the house and welcomed the silence. After the scene the previous night he was grateful.

As was his normal routine, he went upstairs to change. Then he pulled out a shoebox and his notebook and took them back to the sitting room. He left everything on the table while he went to the kitchen to get himself a beer and a cheese sandwich. He was smiling broadly for the camera as he carried them into the sitting room.

He ate his sandwich and picked up his shoebox.

'Joint time,' he said aloud, as he started rolling one. He was half watching television, half looking at his blossoming joint. When he finished, he alternated between drinking and smoking. He also kept smiling.

Being alone had become a novelty. When he had lived with Gus, he was alone quite a lot of the time. Now there was usually someone around. Not that he was complaining, but a few minutes on his own was nice. He was going to make the most of it.

He picked up his notebook and started writing. At the same time he began talking to himself. No one would have known that this was something he did often. He liked to talk to himself and he didn't buy into the whole 'first sign of madness' school of thought.

'Now, if I just think about it, there must be something that I can do. How about expanding my range of roach material to include household packaging that I haven't considered before. Let me see . . . cereal boxes would do I guess . . .'

Bob was sitting with Amanda, watching the evening's events.

'Oh my God,' Amanda said, giggling. They had just seen Eric

stand up and do a kung fu kick and say, 'I'm gonna kick arse with my new joint.' It was lucky for the film that Eric did talk to himself. As he had got more stoned, he had become increasingly entertaining. First he had gone to the kitchen to make more sandwiches – with salad cream. Then he had brought back four bottles of beer and worked his way through the food and the drink. He had smoked countless joints and added to his roach material list. When he was finally satisfied, he had started having a conversation with the television. He turned the volume down and put his own dialogue into the characters on screen. At the same time as doing this he kept bursting into laughter at his own humour. Bob could safely say he had never seen anything like it. It seemed to go on for ever. Bob was thinking about cutting it down, using only the funniest lines.

All of a sudden Eric stopped. He turned the volume back up on the TV and sat quietly, concentrating.

Bob and Amanda looked at each other.

'He's crazy,' Bob said.

'But good footage there if we cut the rubbish out.' Amanda smiled.

'What next?' Bob said, more to himself than to her.

'It's nearly eleven. They should be back soon from the pub or wherever they've gone. I wonder if we get to see the big Tanya apology tonight.' Amanda smiled, she had developed rather a soft spot for Bob. Bob shrugged. He returned his full attention to the screen.

David and Tanya were the first to return.

'Hi Eric, what's up?' David asked, sitting down on the sofa next to him.

'Chilling out. Just had a very quiet evening in.' Tanya looked at the beer bottles littering the table.

'Looks like it,' she said, but she smiled.

'I've been watching TV, that's all,' Eric protested.

'I know,' Tanya replied, she wasn't in the mood for a row of any sort. Not with the apology due. 'No sign of Princess and Prince Charming then?'

'Tanya,' David warned.

'It was a joke. I'm nervous. I'm going to grovel, don't worry.' Eric and David shot her a warning look. 'Relax,' she continued. 'I really am sorry you know, I've been feeling guilty all day.'

'Good,' David said, retracting his eyes in suspicion. They sat together, watching television in silence until Gus and Leigh came home.

'Hi,' Gus said. Leigh stood half behind him in the doorway as soon as she saw Tanya. David nudged Tanya in the ribs. She looked at him.

'LeeLee, can we talk?' she asked.

'I think you said enough last night,' Gus replied, his usual friendly manner noticeably absent.

'Gus, please, give me a chance. LeeLee, I was drunk last night. I was jealous of the friendship you have with Gus. Please can you let me explain?' Tanya wanted to tell Gus to fuck off and mind his own business, but she didn't. Leigh emerged from behind Gus.

'Fine, we can talk,' she sighed.

'Can we go into the kitchen?' Tanya asked. Eric looked disappointed. He had been waiting all night to witness the apology.

Leigh shrugged in response and walked into the kitchen. Gus shot Tanya a warning look as she followed Leigh.

'So, where did you go?' Eric asked.

'Just to the wine bar. Will they be all right? I couldn't believe it when Leigh told me about last night. I can't believe what a bitch she was. LeeLee made me promise not to have a go at her, but I hate seeing her unhappy.' David and Eric knew that Leigh would have given Gus a heavily edited version.

'She's promised to apologise and I think she is sorry. I know Tanya's been way out of order but she's jealous of your friendship. She's really insecure,' David explained.

'She is mate. I mean bull in a china shop and insecure don't exactly seem to go together but she is. She's terrified of being alone.' Eric backed up David.

'I don't know. I guess it makes sense. If she's insecure you'd think she'd try to be a bit nicer to people,' Gus reasoned.

'I can't argue with that.' Eric laughed.

'So, what did you decide about Natasha?' David asked.

'Well I talked it over with LeeLee and I'm going to see her on Friday.'

'You sure that's a good idea?' Eric asked, shuddering.

'Yes. Since she called I can't get her out of my mind, I think about her night and day. It's mad. Until I see her there's no way I can move on. All those shitty emotions I felt when she left me the last time have come back. It doesn't help that I haven't met anyone else that I care about like I cared about her.' Gus looked sad.

'Be careful,' Eric almost whispered, David looked at him.

'I'm going to my room. Tell LeeLee she can come up if she needs to talk.' Gus left the room.

Leigh sat at the breakfast bar. Tanya stood with her back against the closed kitchen door. She took a deep breath.

'I am so sorry,' she said, wishing it was that easy.

'Really are you? You seem to be saying that a lot to me lately.' Leigh had perfected her best 'put out' look.

'I know. I don't know what's wrong with me. Correction, I do. Since we moved in here, I thought that it would be a chance for me to get close to you again and also get close to David and the others. But it's almost like at school, where everyone breaks off into cliques. There's the Gus and LeeLee clique, there's the Eric and David clique, then there's me.'

'That's ridiculous. When you were seeing Harvey we didn't see you for ages. In fact, we didn't really see you until last weekend. So of course we got used to our own company, and I have wanted to talk to you loads of times, but I guess I just got used to you not being here.' Leigh was not going to back down as easily as she normally did. She knew Tanya well enough to know that her apology was always defensive and usually resulted in the person she was apologising to apologising as well. She wasn't about to let that happen.

'You're right. I know you're right. Christ, I am a bitch. You know how much I hate being alone, you know that. Which is why I behaved so badly. Shit, I really am sorry.' Tanya moved a little closer but instead of sitting down she leant her arms on the breakfast bar.

'Tanya it's OK. We've known each other for twenty years, I'm always going to forgive you, you know that. But it's been hard for me too since we moved in here. God, I've never wanted anyone as much as I want Gus. He occupies my every thought, whether I'm awake or asleep. I can't get him out of my mind, I really can't. But, being his confidant is almost killing me. Tonight we talked about how much he had loved his ex-girlfriend, Natasha. How he would have married her had she not run off and left him. How he had never met anyone to compare to her, how she was his only love. And I sat opposite him, not only hearing the words but really feeling them, piercing my heart and I wanted to kill her, although I've never met her, and I wanted to cry and scream and tell him that I deserve his love more than her. But I didn't. Instead I told him to see her. It's killing me Tanya, eating me from the inside. That's what my friendship with Gus is like.'

'I had no idea it was so bad. Why the hell are you his confidant then? If this is killing you, and I don't care if your boss told you to do it, you have to stop.'

'Oh Tanya, I can see why you'd think that. I know that Sukie suggested the friendship angle, but you don't pretend to be someone's friend when you care about that person as much as I do. I *really* am his friend, I really do care about him, and I hate to see him sad. If it takes Natasha to make him happy then I'll accept it because all I want is for him to be happy. I know I want him to be happy with me, but if that isn't going to happen, then I just want his happiness.' The tears streamed down her pale face.

'You are so special LeeLee, you really are. And you know

what? Gus might have you to talk to about all his love problems, but you can't talk to him about yours, because *he* is the problem. You can talk to me though. I know I haven't been the best friend to you and I am jealous, and I'm a bitch. But I'm also your oldest friend and I really do care about you. Promise me you'll talk to me about stuff if you need to.' Tanya had never been so sincere in her life.

'Promise,' Leigh replied and lunged off her stool to hug Tanya.

They stood there hugging for a long time.

'Come on, let's go and tell the others we didn't kill each other.' Tanya got a piece of kitchen roll and handed it to Leigh. She could still feel the damp tears on her shoulder.

They walked back into the sitting room.

'I've grovelled really hard,' Tanya said, trying to lighten up the atmosphere.

'She did. She could win a prize for her grovelling.' Leigh managed a giggle.

'Gus has gone to his room to ruminate. He said to tell you if you needed him to go up,' Eric explained, glad that the rowing had been resolved. Eric didn't like conflict of any kind.

'I'm going to bed anyway,' Leigh replied. 'So I'll just pop in and say goodnight.' She kissed Eric, Tanya and David and made her way upstairs.

'So everything is back to normal?' Eric asked.

'Whatever that is,' Tanya replied. 'Anyway you up for a challenge on the Playstation?'

'Always, Tanya, always.' Eric went to set it up. David declared it was time for him to go to bed too. The events of the last couple of days had got to him.

'Are you all right?' Eric asked.

'What you mean is have I got my megalomaniac bitchy side under control?' she replied.

'Something like that.' Eric laughed. When Tanya wasn't being a total nightmare she was actually nice.

'Well I think I have, although I just do what I do, and I never mean to hurt people, but I guess I don't always think. Feet first you know – I really am sorry.'

They smiled at each other and concentrated on the F1 Grand Prix race they were playing.

Leigh lay in bed replaying her conversation with Tanya. She had long ago given up analysing their friendship. Despite everything she still believed she needed her. She sighed as she wondered why it was all getting so complicated.

The cameras got to watch Tanya and Eric for another hour. In that hour they didn't have another conversation as such. Instead they raced their cars and restricted their comments to the game. When Eric finally received the chequered flag and Tanya conceded defeat they decided to call it a night and both climbed the stairs. The cameras watched them go separately to the bathroom before catching the last glimpse of them as they went to their rooms. Tanya hadn't thought once about the cameras that evening, and ignoring her control room, she went straight to bed.

On day two of the filming the producer had found something more important to fill her thoughts than the film.

Bob took the footage home for Harvey and Cherry. They watched it the following morning and decided that with the row and the making up, and also with Gus's bit about this Natasha girl, they had some good material. It was the age old love triangle. Old as the hills, but usually a winner. Especially as this was a *real* love triangle. Harvey thought that this might give him the backbone to his story.

Although they didn't have much footage, what they had looked promising.

'See, I told you Tanya was a nice person,' Cherry said, after she had seen her apology.

'Yeah, but she loses it really quickly,' Bob added.

'I'm not sure I would want her to be my friend,' Millie put in. Everyone looked at her.

'Y'know, the thing is that, already, you guys are talking about the characters, it's wonderful. People will be getting into the characters as much as they get into the plot. I bet you guys want Leigh to get Gus, and for something good to happen to Eric and David already,' Harvey said.

'You're right Harvey, I do,' Millie stated.

'Millie, Harvey is always right,' Cherry pointed out.

'But the point is that *it is* working, I know it's early days, but we were right. This idea is a killer, my unsuspecting cast is turning out to be just as I expected, and my producer is an asset. In six months or so we'll have enough footage and then we'll be the next big thing!'

Chapter Twenty-Nine

Leigh sat on the sofa expectantly. She knew he would be beside her soon. She knew how he would smell, how he would sound, how he would feel. She also knew that he would be telling her all about his evening.

The others had given up at eleven. After a night of sitting on the sofa, watching television and struggling for conversation, Tanya, Eric and David had abandoned Leigh and gone to bed. They had tried to stay with her because they knew that Gus was on his first date with Natasha, or 'meeting' as Leigh insisted on calling it. They had tried to cheer her up but Leigh refused to be cheered up. She was glad because she wanted to be alone and anyway she was bored with their false joviality.

Midnight. The key turned in the door. Leigh held her breath. Was he going to walk in with Natasha on his arm? Would he have fallen under her spell again so quickly? She stared straight ahead at the television.

'Hi.' His voice sent shivers down her spine. She held her breath as she turned around slowly. Immense relief flooded her as she saw he was alone.

'Hi Gus, how was it?' she asked. She felt more in control. At least he was alone. Gus sat down next to her and smiled sadly.

'All my feelings for her came flooding straight back LeeLee. I didn't want them to, I wanted to feel nothing, but I felt so much.' He didn't notice that Leigh's cheeks had begun to turn pink. He continued. 'She apologised to me, said that when we split up she was young and scared and wanted to see the world, and that's what she did, well she went to Australia and Asia anyway. She's only just got back and she said that when she knew she was coming back she couldn't stop thinking about me and she knew that she wanted to see me as soon as she got back. LeeLee, she says she wanted us to get back together again.' His face was flushed, his eyes glistening. All Leigh wanted to do was cry.

'What did you say?' she asked, smiling at him.

'You would have been proud of me. I told her how much it had hurt last time and how I wasn't sure if I could go through that again. She told me that she would never put me through that again and I believed her, she was so sincere. So I told her that I needed time to think, and that I'd call her tomorrow. LeeLee, I'm going to invite her over tomorrow night. I need you to meet her, I need you to like her, and everyone else of course, but especially you. I think I am going to make a go of it. But LeeLee, you were right, by leaving it open-ended tonight and saying I'd call her at least she won't think I am a pushover. But the thing is, as far as she's concerned, I am.' Gus leaned over and kissed Leigh on the cheek. Leigh mustered all her remaining strength.

'So we get to meet her, that's something to look forward to.' Already she was wondering how she would be able to handle it.

'You're going to love her, you really will. Right, I need my beauty sleep, are you going to bed?' Gus stood up.

'In a mo. I'll just clean up down here.' She gestured to the coffee table with its two empty wine glasses and two empty beer bottles.

'OK, goodnight.' Gus kissed her again.

'Goodnight,' she replied as she watched him walk out of the room.

If it hadn't been for his 'glow', his voice would have betrayed how happy he was; if it wasn't for his voice, the way he 'floated' out of the room was the give away. Love is wonderful, thought Leigh, but so, so painful. For Gus it was the tops, for Leigh the absolute pits.

She picked up the two empty wine glasses and clutching them tightly to her chest walked into the kitchen with tears streaming down her cheeks. She walked over to the counter, gently set the glasses down, put her head in her arms and wept. She didn't know how long she stood there crying, but by the time she felt strong enough to stop the tears she was exhausted. Unlike Gus's euphoric exit, Leigh dragged herself upstairs and crawled into bed.

Bob and Amanda watched.

'Poor Leigh,' Amanda said, when the house was still.

'I know, she's a real cutie,' Bob added. He had found himself to be more voyeuristic than he ever thought possible, as he eagerly watched the dramatic events.

'And we've got a possible new character,' Amanda pointed out.

'Oh yeah, the girlfriend, or potential girlfriend. Well I'm not being critical but I think we could do with a few more characters,' Bob replied.

'You're right. I know it's early days but I get the impression that if we only have the five of them, it might get a bit repetitious. I wonder what Natasha will be like.'

'Well Amanda, meet me here tomorrow night and we might just find out.' Bob laughed.

'It's a date,' Amanda answered, wishing it was.

Harvey and Cherry watched the Leigh–Gus exchange.

'I love Leigh, she's so sensitive,' Cherry said, moved by her predicament.

'Poor kid, she really is besotted,' Harvey replied. Cherry shot him a look, she wondered if he felt the same way for her.

'What about this Natasha?' she asked.

'Could make it really interesting. But we need to wait and see what happens with this girl before we make any decisions. Then of course we need to get her to agree to the film. The problem with adding to the cast is that maybe this means we add to our problems.'

'Harvey, what problems? I guess we deal with it when we need to.'

'Right. Anyway we need to wait until the next instalment before we make any decisions.' He smiled at Cherry. They were both hooked on the lives of the unsuspecting housemates. They hadn't even been filming for a week yet.

Chapter Thirty

Gus was home early. He had managed to persuade someone else to finish off his shift, so he would be able to have a bath and get changed in plenty of time for Natasha. When he walked through the door he saw Tanya standing at the bottom of the stairs making faces at the mirror. When she saw him she coloured embarrassingly. Gus had walked in on Tanya's new game. When she was alone she would communicate to whoever was on duty at the editing suite by talking via one of the hidden cameras. Of course they couldn't talk back to her but she liked doing it to stave off her feeling of isolation.

It was day four of filming; Tanya numbered every day instead of naming them. Day Four would bring her closer to the first editing meeting, which was what she focused on now. She had made notes about how each scene they had so far should be used, but, as she believed that almost every scene worth showing should be shown intact (after all that was the idea, it was supposed to be real) her notes didn't fill her days. So she ran around the house making faces. Immature, perhaps, but a necessary distraction.

'What *are* you doing?' Gus asked, with a bemused look on his face.

'Facial toning exercises,' Tanya retorted. Luckily, Gus was too happy to be bothered by Tanya's antics.

'Love to stay and talk, but I need to go get changed.'

'Do you want a cup of tea? I'll make you one if you like,' Tanya offered. She had watched the footage from the previous night and learned two things. Gus was the happiest person she had ever seen — Leigh the most miserable. But she also was at a loss about what to do about it. Tea was a start.

'Can you shout when it's ready and I'll drink it in the bath?' Gus replied.

'What utter decadence,' Tanya teased.

'It's nothing like LeeLee. Every time she has a bath she drinks about half a bottle of wine.'

'Well I guess you could have a beer,' Tanya suggested, wondering why she didn't know that Leigh always drank wine in the bath, or why her not knowing should bother her.

'No, I need to keep a clear head, Tanya. Tonight is really important to me, you see Natasha is coming over.' Gus smiled, Tanya smiled. It was characteristic of Gus that everybody in the house knew the whole Natasha history. He wasn't a man who believed in hiding his feelings.

'I can't wait to meet her,' Tanya said. Actually she *was* looking forward to meeting Natasha, anything to relieve her weariness.

'She is really looking forward to meeting all of you,' Gus replied as he ran upstairs.

That evening, Leigh was sitting on the sofa, sharing a glass of wine with Tanya and chatting amiably to Gus and Eric while they waited for David and Natasha. David was in his basement with urgent 'chat room business' to attend to. Natasha was late. They were discussing the fact that they didn't have any food in the house, and, as usual, Eric had gone to get the take-away menus.

'What is David doing in there?' Tanya asked, feeling agitated without knowing why.

'I'll give him a shout.' Leigh was doing well. She looked gorgeous in a black leather skirt, pink low-cut ballet top and, of course, her pink trainers. She had spent time doing her hair and make-up and Tanya had commented that she looked like she had spent the day in a beauty salon. The main ingredient to Leigh's attractiveness that evening was that she felt confident. Positive. Thanks to Sukie who had convinced her that the way to Gus's heart was to prove herself more charming than Natasha. 'Play the opposition at their own game, but play to win,' that was Sukie's strategy for Leigh.

David emerged with a beer in his hand.

'So where is she then?' he asked, grumpily, having been dragged away from surfing the Net.

'She's a bit late that's all,' Gus almost snapped. He was apprehensive.

'Sure.' Eric folded his arms.

The doorbell rang. It was the sound they were all waiting for, yet it still startled them. Gus looked relieved as he got up and went to open the door. Everyone tensed visibly.

'This is Natasha,' Gus announced in an unnaturally loud voice, guiding her to the centre of the sitting room. They gasped. Natasha was gorgeous. Breathtakingly gorgeous. She had long, straight chestnut hair, her eyes were big and a deep brown. Her whole face was perfect, as was her skin. She was tall with long legs and of course she was slim. She had walked straight out of the pages of *Vogue*.

'Hi,' said the beautiful cut-crystal accent. Gus introduced her to everyone.

Leigh noticed how Gus didn't take his eyes off her, which meant that Leigh didn't either. Eric looked slightly pale and was wondering how on earth a man would ever get over losing a girl like that. David was in lust. Tanya was jealous. Natasha was a goddess.

As she settled down in an armchair, Gus went to get her a glass of wine. 'So you glad to be back home, Natasha?' David asked. Gus returned and handed her the wine.

'Absolutely, but it's very hard to adjust to being back in cold, old England after Australia, but I missed the place so much. I love it here, I really do. I will never go away again. Travelling is great but I've come back and all my old friends have careers and stuff, and here I am almost middle-aged with nothing but a bit of travelling and a bit of waitressing under my belt.' She smiled, displaying the most beautiful white teeth. It was a shame that her voice was a bit too loud.

'What did you do before you left?' David asked with an urgency in his voice, he really wanted to know.

'I was a model. But now I want to be a writer. I hope that I might get a bit of modelling work while I work on a book; I'm going to write about my travel experiences, but of course I need to live and I have no idea how long it will take me to finish it. It will also give me a chance to see if I like writing. Of course I might find it really dull.' Natasha reached over and squeezed Gus's thigh. Leigh wondered at her confidence. Not only did she sound as if she believed that she could do anything she wanted, everyone else believed it too.

Natasha was beautiful, confident and she had Gus. Leigh immediately wanted to be her. As did Tanya, but she would never admit it.

'So, Tanya, tell me about television, while modelling I fancied switching to acting,' Natasha said.

'Well, I work mainly in documentaries, but I love it, well I like it. What I really want to do is get into film production.' The conversation seemed false and stilted. It was as if they were being asked questions by the Queen.

'Oh, that sounds like fun. I hope you manage to do it.' She smiled that smile again.

'What about food?' Eric said. He was not happy about this girl and to top it all he was hungry.

'I quite fancy a curry,' David said.

'Oh, I love Chinese, oh please can we have Chinese?' Natasha begged.

'Of course,' everyone agreed.

Eric shuddered. Clearly Natasha was dangerous.

They ate their takeaway when it eventually came, they drank, they chatted. Leigh had managed to get Natasha into a conversation which lasted for ages, while Gus looked on fondly. Tanya was watching Eric quite closely. She was amazed at how well Leigh was holding it together and how Eric wasn't. She stood up and ushered him into the kitchen on the pretence of getting some more wine.

'What is wrong with you, you look like you might cry,' Tanya said.

'I might. Look Tanya, I met Gus when that girl first broke his heart. Now it looks like it'll happen all over again.'

'But she seems all right,' Tanya protested. Actually Tanya didn't think she was all right; she thought she was a self-absorbed, overconfident bitch, but that was because she was jealous.

'Yeah, exactly. The sort of girl who has everyone fooled. Even Leigh's being nice to her and Leigh must hate her more than I do.' Eric was perplexed.

'Eric, Leigh is probably playing the same game with Natasha as she is with Gus. She's being nice to her because she figures that that will mean that Gus will like her more. And I bet Leigh thinks that they'll split up at some point because otherwise her head would be in the oven by now.'

'I guess,' Eric said. 'I know whose head I'd like to see in the oven.'

'Oh Eric, look, we have to support Gus now, and that means keeping quiet about our true feelings. When it goes wrong we'll help him, but while he's happy we can't spoil it. We can't.' Tanya had probably just uttered the truest words she'd ever spoken.

'You are right Tanya, which is unlike you. What's wrong . . . ?' Eric laughed then ducked as Tanya took a swing at his head. He grabbed a bottle of wine and fled to the sitting room.

'My God, she is stunning,' Bob said, leaning into the screen for a closer look.

'She is,' Amanda agreed, hating her on sight. They watched and listened.

'She seems really nice too. That Gus is one hell of a lucky guy. She is an absolute knockout,' Bob enthused.

'Actually I think she's a fake,' Amanda replied haughtily, as she watched Tanya drag Eric out to the kitchen.

While Bob was immobilised watching the scene in the sitting room, or rather devouring Natasha, Amanda switched to Eric and Tanya.

'Tanya has gone up one thousand per cent in my estimation,' she said.

'Really? Well I think Natasha has lovely tits,' Bob replied.

'Bob!' Amanda was more annoyed than shocked.

'Shit, I'm sorry Amanda, I didn't mean to say that aloud.' He smiled at her then went back to watching the screen. Amanda felt a stab of jealousy. Had he ever noticed *her* tits?

Natasha held court for the rest of the evening. She discussed beauty tips with Leigh, television programmes with Tanya, the Internet with David, and cannabis with Eric. She didn't discuss anything with Gus, she just touched him occasionally. Natasha managed to speak with authority on all the chosen subjects covered. Or with an assumed authority, because she was talking rubbish most of the time.

'You know she's really a bit of a pain,' Bob concluded, but that was when Gus and Natasha headed for the bedroom. It seemed that he wasn't the only one who thought that.

'Shit, that girl don't half talk a lot,' Eric said, yawning.

'And she has funny ideas. I mean the way she was talking about the Internet was totally wrong, but she didn't want to listen when I tried to put her right,' David added.

'She knows fuck all about television but she talks as if she is a fucking expert,' Tanya stormed.

'Well I am really pleased. When I saw her and saw how gorgeous she was I thought I would never be able to compete. But she's stupid, she loves the sound of her own voice and obviously Gus is blinded only by her looks, because as soon as he realises just how dumb she is, he's bound to fall straight out of love with her.' Leigh was almost singing.

'I hope so,' Eric said.

'Me too. She is gorgeous to look at but give me my e-mail woman any time,' David agreed.

'Don't worry guys. Gus is a bit soppy and romantic but he's not a total moron. He'll soon realise what a mistake he's making and we can all go back to normal.' Tanya announced this with a confidence that would have put Natasha to shame.

'Wow!' Harvey said.

'She is a beauty,' Cherry agreed.

'I am so glad she is going to be in this movie, even if she ends up as only a small cameo,' Harvey added.

'I guess she adds glamour.'

'My God, *does she*. Where does Gus find them?'

'Well he's not exactly lacking on the looks side,' Cherry pointed out.

'But did you hear her talk? She was dull. It's a shame really that someone that good-looking turns out to be such a disappointment.'

'I'm glad you thought so Harvey, I thought for a minute you couldn't see past the beauty.'

'Honey I can always see past physical beauty.' Harvey chuckled. 'What we need to do Bob, is to edit this bit, we need to keep it short. What about making it a monologue and then cut to Eric yawning or something?' Harvey suggested.

'That would work,' Bob replied.

'I thought the idea was to keep everything natural,' Cherry said.

'It is, but we have to be aware of time. Conversations and so on. Don't worry about it Cherry, it's just technical direction.' They turned back to the footage.

✳ ✳ ✳

When Leigh finally got up the following day, she went down-stairs to make tea and bumped into a bathrobe-clad Natasha. As she had had to endure a night of hearing Natasha's loud voice through the wall that separated Leigh's and Gus's rooms, she wasn't in the sweetest of moods.

'Good morning LeeLee,' Natasha boomed.

'Hi,' Leigh replied.

'Tea?' Natasha asked. Leigh bristled. It was her kitchen and her tea. She should be the one to ask.

'Thanks,' she replied and sat at the breakfast bar while she watched Natasha switch on the kettle.

'You seem to be making yourself at home,' Leigh said, without thinking. But Natasha was thick-skinned.

'Well I hope I shall be here rather a lot. Gus and I are getting on superbly. I trust that we can all be great friends.' She smiled. Leigh noticed that she had full make-up on.

'Sure,' Leigh replied and waited for her tea.

'Have you thought about rearranging things in here?' Natasha asked.

'No, why should we?' Leigh replied.

As Natasha poured out the tea, Gus walked in. 'Hey, my two favourite ladies.'

'Gus darling, tea?' Natasha was already making him a cup.

'It's funny, you don't look like the tea-making sort,' Leigh said, as Natasha passed her the cup. Again she realised she should keep more thoughts in her head. 'I mean, you are so glamorous,' she added quickly.

'Thank you, LeeLee, you are a sweetie.' With Gus and Natasha both giving her chewing gum smiles, Leigh took her tea upstairs.

She went straight to Tanya's room and knocked on the door. Tanya had just finished watching the previous night's footage. She was pleased with it, and she was pleased about the way she had come across.

'Hold on,' she shouted, as she closed the cupboard and the

wall hanging and hid the remote control in her desk drawer. She had a final check before she went to open the door.

'Hi, can I come in?' Leigh asked.

'Of course you can LeeLee, did you bring me tea?'

'Oh shit no, I didn't think. Anyway that bitch Natasha made it so you can have mine.' She thrust the cup into Tanya's hands and crawled into her bed. 'What is that?' Leigh asked, pointing at the wall hanging. Tanya groaned inwardly. She had forgotten that no one had been to her room since it had been pulled apart.

'Hideous isn't it? Serena gave it to me. Bad night?' Tanya asked, desperate to change the subject.

'You could say that. Do you know, I have no idea if the two of them had sex because if they did, she didn't stop talking the whole way through. She wasn't saying anything that sounded sexy, but I couldn't be sure because her voice never changes pitch. They bloody well kept me awake all night, but not for the reasons I thought they would. Thank goodness.'

Tanya laughed. 'Oh my God, you mean she booms her sweet nothings as well?'

'Yup.'

'So the lady is still here?'

'She's in our kitchen offering to make tea for all and sundry. How sweet is that? And she told me she is planning on spending loads of time here, which is really good news.'

'So here is our mission if we wish to accept it. Our mission is to get rid of the nauseating Natasha.' Tanya giggled.

'I'll drink to that. Or I would if I had any tea.' Leigh grabbed the cup off Tanya and took a sip.

'Leigh, let's find out what Tweedledum and Tweedledee are doing tonight, then we can decide what we're going to do. I don't intend on sitting in my room all night, and if they are going out then we can stay in and get drunk, but if they're staying in we can go out and get drunk.'

'Good thinking. Actually I wouldn't mind going out anyway.'

They went downstairs like a united front. Natasha and Gus informed them that they were staying in.

'Oh, we're going out,' Tanya said quickly on hearing the news.'

'Where to?' Gus asked.

'Just for a few drinks with my brother and Serena,' Tanya lied. At the same time she made a mental note to call Jason. She'd avoided them both ever since she had started working on the film, unsure of their reaction to her. She fielded all their questions by telling them she was swamped with work, but she couldn't avoid them forever. She decided she'd call the following week.

'Are the boys going too?' Natasha asked.

'I think so,' Tanya said quickly. As they walked out of the room she turned to Leigh. 'You tell David and I'll tell Eric.'

By eight, the four of them were dressed to go on their outing. David had taken no persuading, he had actually adopted cabin fever for the first time in his life and Eric was stoned enough to think that going out was a good idea. It turned out to be a *very* good idea.

They went out to a bar in Fulham and proceeded to do what they said and got drunk. Eric pleaded just before kicking out time that he really needed to go home, via the kebab shop.

The four of them, clutching kebabs, argued over who would be the best person to open the door – Leigh finally won and led the way inside. Tanya turned the light on. Leigh froze. Eric choked. David screamed.

'Oh my God!' Tanya exclaimed. Four pairs of eyes observed two naked bodies prostrate on the stairs.

'I'm s-sorry,' Gus gasped before grabbing his T-shirt and fleeing upstairs.

Natasha stood up. 'Well I'm not,' she said, proudly displaying her magnificent body for all to see. Slowly she made her exit as if she was still parading the catwalk.

'I'm not sure I want my kebab now,' Leigh said, wanting to cry with jealousy but being too drunk to even find any tears.

'Me either, do you think it looks a bit like Gus's penis?' Tanya asked, before dissolving into laughter.

'No,' Leigh said, 'but it reminds me of Natasha's cellulite.' (Which everyone knew full well Natasha didn't have). Leigh started laughing. Then she started crying.

'Why her? Why does he want her? And on our stairs. Shit. I feel sick. Oh my God I'm going to throw up.' Leigh ran to the kitchen where she was sick in the sink.

'Yuk.' David went to Leigh and started the clean-up operation. Tanya joined him, got Leigh some water from the fridge and then took her upstairs to get her teeth cleaned and put her to bed. When David had cleaned up he joined Eric who was busy munching his kebab.

'I can't believe you can eat after what you just saw,' David said.

'I always eat when I'm upset,' Eric replied.

'Why are you upset?' David asked.

'It's something to do with hearts. You see, Leigh has a broken heart, and Gus will soon have one too. She's so miserable and he will be soon.'

'You seem quite sure that she is going to hurt him,' David said.

'I'd bet a whole year's pizza on it.'

Tanya knew that she had drunk too much, but she couldn't wait to watch the footage of what Gus and Natasha had got up to while they were out. If she couldn't remember it in the morning she would rerun it. As she started at the point when they had gone out, she settled back in her chair. First was more snogging and chatting. Then they ate. Natasha cooked some Mexican chicken thing. Tanya scowled at the screen. They drank rather a lot – Gus had gone out and bought expensive white wine. Then Natasha had just stripped off.

The next scene sobered her up and made her realise that what she was doing could land her in jail.

When Natasha had peeled off all her clothes she had then performed an erotic dance for Gus. Then she had stripped him bare and kissed him all over – well nearly all over. Although Tanya didn't want to watch what she knew was coming up, she just had to. She saw them having sex on the sofa. It was normal sex although Leigh had been right – Natasha talked all the way through, and not dirty talk either. Tanya had the grace to look away when they climaxed and she made a mental note to clean the sofa. Then they had had another glass of wine. Still naked.

Perhaps it is appropriate to describe Gus's body. His chest was as broad as it needed to be, and fairly hair free. His legs had muscles obtained from football and again had just enough hair to be masculine. His shoulders were sexy, if shoulders could be. Tanya almost decided to have another crush on him herself.

It was a while later when Natasha suggested they 'do it on the stairs', and it was just as they were about to do so that they had been so rudely interrupted.

Tanya laughed as she watched the kebab scene and she knew that there was no way they could show the sex or the nudity, but they had to show the kebab bit.

Bob and Amanda had also watched the sex. They didn't turn away for the climax.

'Editing will have to be heavy here,' Amanda said, flushed but determined to be businesslike.

'Shame,' Bob replied. He was feeling slightly turned on and was unable to look Amanda in the eye.

'Unless the girl agrees to nudity, then at least you pervs could have her body but the sex is going too far.'

'What about Gus? The girls might want to see him.' Bob snapped out of his lascivious thoughts. When he looked at Amanda, he noticed for the first time that she was attractive. He shook his head slightly, it was just the sex scene having a porno-like effect on him.

'Yeah, but his chest will be enough for us, which means we

could show the scene of the others coming in. After all, it's her boobs and bum we see, he covers his bits,' Amanda pointed out.

'So, if she agrees, we get to show her body, but we shouldn't ask him?' Bob was confused.

'I just know that she'll say yes, and he won't,' Amanda finished.

Chapter Thirty-One

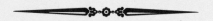

It was the first editing meeting and was being held in the hired editing suite in Chelsea. Tanya was excited. She had seen all the up-to-date footage, she knew which parts she would use and which parts she would cut. She knew how she would put it together were it a television programme, but as a movie, with a long way to run, and not much footage she was unsure. She wanted to hear what Bob and the others suggested.

She needed to be in Chelsea for half past eleven. She had showered and dressed after the others had left for work. She then made toast and coffee and sat in the quiet kitchen of the quiet house. When she had finished breakfast she went upstairs and phoned Millie to confirm that the taxi was picking her up at eleven fifteen.

It was still only ten thirty. She opened her control room and flicked through the silent screens. She nearly jumped from her seat when she saw someone walking down the stairs. Then as her heartbeat slowed down, she realised it was Natasha wearing Gus's bathrobe. Tanya had assumed that although she had stayed the previous night, she would have gone with the others. She remembered that Natasha didn't have a job. Tanya watched, intrigued, as Natasha walked into the kitchen and made herself a drink. She was infuriatingly at home. She picked up the cup, walked into the hall where she picked up the phone. Incredibly, infuriatingly at home, Tanya thought, and she almost marched downstairs to say so. But she didn't. Instead she watched as a true voyeur should. She also turned up the sound. What she heard was one half of a phone conversation, but even half was too much.

'Lise, it's Tash. I'm at Gus's, in Fulham, I wondered if you could make it for lunch.'

Pause.

'Oh God I didn't think about work. But I can meet you tonight, for a quick drink. I can't be too long because Gus and I are going out for dinner.'

Pause.

'Yes . . . Gus. You remember Gus, surely.'

Pause.

'Well I know I said he was boring, and darling he still is, but I don't have much choice. The poor boy's besotted with me. He's got a good job as a doctor and a nice house in Fulham, although some of his housemates are a bit weird. Actually they're all a bit weird. They walked in on us the other night having sex on the stairs. It was so funny. I know I said he was crap in bed, but actually he seems to have got a bit better. I mean he's really quite good now.'

Pause.

'Lise, stop it. Look, of course I don't love him, I never did. He was just good arm candy. Anyway I don't have any choice. It's either Gus and his bed or a cardboard box.'

Pause.

'I am not being dramatic. My father went mad when he found out how much of his money I spent in Oz. My mother refuses to give me any at all, and my darling sister informed me that she wants me out of her flat so she can carry on some sordid affair she's having. I have nowhere to go and no money to go there.'

Pause.

'No, I am going to get a job, really I am, it's just that I don't want to have to do some shitty secretarial job for crap money if I don't have to. I'm going to stay here and sponge off Gus until I have enough money to leave. I'm going to have to sign up with my old modelling agency I suppose.'

Pause.

'Of course he doesn't know, anyway he's mad about me. He knows I'm utterly skint from travelling and has lent me some spending money, or he's going to when I see him tonight.'

Pause.

'Of course I'm going to dump him. I don't want to be with a dull doctor for the rest of my life. As soon as I'm sorted I am going to do some serious social climbing. Until then I'm going to be here. What . . . ? Of course Gus doesn't exactly know I've moved in. I told him I'm staying with my sister, but he won't want me to leave him. Look, I'll meet you at your office at half-five. Give me the address. Bye darling, see you later.'

Tanya stared at the screen in total disbelief. She knew she didn't like Natasha but she couldn't believe how callously she was using Gus. If only Leigh knew but Tanya couldn't tell Leigh. She didn't know what to do. Then she heard the doorbell and saw Natasha open the front door. Tanya took a deep breath, grabbed her handbag, and, ensuring that her bedroom door was locked, made her way down the stairs. Natasha seemed to be having a conversation with the cab driver.

'Oh Tanya, there you are,' Natasha said.

'Yes, and I'm late for a meeting, so excuse me.' Giving Natasha one of her best killer looks she walked out of the door and slammed it behind her with as much force as she could muster.

'Come on, I said I was late,' Tanya snapped at the cab driver.

She fumed silently for the entire cab journey and tried to work out what she could do about Natasha. How could she convince Gus that the girl he thought he loved was a Class A bitch?

She walked into the editing suite and was met by a girl who introduced herself as Sally Young, one of the team. Sally immediately reminded Tanya of herself during those early years when she first started working in television. She was young but confident. She looked the part, and she was friendly. Tanya immediately warmed to her. She was led to a meeting room, where Harvey, Bob, and Cherry were sitting around the table with three other people. Tanya was introduced to James Dunn, (not much hair but still quite attractive), Amanda Brownlow, (tall, thin, and with a face which was a bit sharp), and John King, (short and overweight), the editing team.

'Right, guys, let's get on. First I would like to congratulate Tanya on the great footage we have already. It's a bit too early to talk about how we are going to put it together, but we can decide what we keep and what goes. So has everyone here seen all the footage now?' Harvey asked – everyone nodded. He smiled, then continued, 'Great. So what stays and what goes? Tanya, give us your thoughts.' Tanya pulled out her notebook. She cleared her throat.

'The first thing is the row and the making up. I know I made myself look bad, but I think I made up for it when I apologised.' Tanya laughed, as did the others. 'So, we have a row between friends, we have the apology, and of course the confession of Leigh's crush. We have the closeness of Leigh and Gus, and the sadness of Leigh. We have that great scene where Eric shows us what he is about, but we don't have much with David so far, apart from this e-mail relationship he's having. Then of course there's Natasha.' Tanya shuddered.

'I agree with Tanya, Bob, can we get all this stuff sectioned? I want it done by date and label it, like "Row", "Apology", et cetera. Then the dialogue that doesn't fit anywhere but could be used, put it all on one section for us to use later. What do you think?'

'I'm there. We've already started doing it. James is building up a catalogue of scenes so we can decide later what fits where,' Bob replied.

'What do you mean?' Tanya asked.

'Well we're going to put it together to make the best film, so for example just because the row was the first night doesn't mean it will be at the beginning of the film,' Amanda explained.

'But I thought this was meant to be real,' Tanya protested. She could feel her petulant child mode arriving.

'It *is* real,' Harvey said.

'But distorted,' Tanya finished.

'Only to make it better,' Harvey added. Tanya looked around the table and made a decision. These people were already talking about manipulating the sequence of events, they were keeping dialogue ready to put in places where it didn't happen. This wasn't as real as real, but then Tanya knew that when she worked in TV, nothing was real as real.

'Fine, agreed. Can I bring up something?' Tanya asked.

'Sure,' Harvey replied.

'It's about Natasha.'

'Nice bod,' Bob said, Cherry shot him a warning look.

Tanya ignored him. 'No one has mentioned the sex scene yet. I watched them having sex, although I did fast forward through most of it, and I know we can't show that on film because this isn't a porno film. What I mean is that we all know that at the end of the project we'll have the issue of getting the others to sign the release papers, but what about Natasha? We'll need her permission won't we?'

'Yes we will, but we can do that at the end,' Cherry said.

'What about getting it before the end?' Tanya suggested.

'Why?' Harvey asked.

'To make it better,' Tanya said.

'I'm confused.' Cherry turned to look at Tanya.

'Has anyone seen her telephone conversation?' Tanya asked. Everyone shook their heads.

'We haven't seen any of today's footage, we were preparing for the meeting,' Bob explained.

'Bob can we play the tape for the hall at about half ten?' Tanya asked. Harvey looked at her questioningly. Bob shrugged and set up the computer, then they all crowded around the screen and viewed Natasha's phone call scene.

'Wow!' Harvey exclaimed.

'Well, as you know from the previous footage, she isn't exactly winning any popularity contests in our house, but the problem is that it didn't matter so much that we didn't like her because Gus did. Now however, she is using him, and I want rid of her.' Tanya was frustrated. Here they were all watching the film of her life, her housemates' lives and they were talking about it as if it was a soap opera. To her it wasn't.

'How do you propose to do that?' Amanda asked, thinking things were getting interesting.

'I don't know. I was going to say I overheard her conversation but Gus is so smitten, I doubt he'd believe me. And she would scheme her way out of it. Then I thought maybe we could set a trap so Gus finds out what she's really like.' Tanya folded her arms.

'Wait a minute,' Harvey said. 'We have good footage with her. Not only the naked bit, but then the phone call which gives us the movie's first villain. If we expose her and she goes we might have to sacrifice the lot.'

'To be honest Harvey, at the moment I am more worried about getting her out of Gus's life,' Tanya snapped.

'I know, honey and we will. But how about we get her out of his life, and get to keep her in the film both at the same time?' Harvey suggested.

'How?' Bob asked.

'By paying her,' Harvey said.

'What?' Tanya was outraged. Not only was she a stinking bitch whore but she was going to get paid for it.

'Just listen a minute. We offer Natasha a cash sum. She needs the money. In exchange for that money she signs a release to allow us to use her in the film and we get a heartbreaking scene with her and Gus, where she confesses to using him and not being in love with him.'

'Hang on, that's not on,' Tanya stormed.

'Why not? She is going to dump him at some point, we all heard her say it. This way we won't allow her to drag it out, which will make it easier for Gus in the long run, so everyone gets what they want. You get her out of your life. Gus has his heart broken but not as badly as it could have been. Natasha gets her money so she can social climb, and we get some great viewing.' Harvey smiled.

'Harvey's so right,' Cherry said.

'Maybe he is, but *she* should pay for what she's doing.' Tanya's face was red with anger.

'Hey, Tanya, when she goes on screen, everyone will see what a bitch she is. That will be her punishment.' Harvey smiled. Tanya thought for a moment, it only took a moment for her to change her point of view.

She smiled. 'She will won't she? Especially as we will offer her the money, then tell her how she has to dump him. Can we make her say that I overheard a conversation, confronted her and made her tell him the truth?'

'That's what we'll do,' Harvey agreed.

'Fine. When shall we set it up?'

'Why don't we arrange for a meeting? The first thing we'll do is get her to sign the confidentiality agreement. Cherry you need to get a contract drawn up. I want it watertight. Tanya, arrange for us to meet her during the day at my office.'

'I'll do that and call you,' Tanya agreed.

'Oh, and Tanya, say that I'm a literary agent. That should lure her.' Harvey smiled. 'Leave it to me honey. This girl is history.'

Chapter Thirty-Two

That evening, Tanya decided to celebrate by cooking her famous lasagna. She was the only one who knew they were celebrating. Gus and Natasha had gone out.

As they ate, the conversation turned inevitably to Natasha.

'I can't believe he's seeing her again,' Leigh said. 'I called him today, because I haven't spoken to him all weekend and he said that he was going to take her for dinner tonight. Then he said that, although she keeps talking about going home, he is happy with her staying here. She's practically moved in and he's so happy,' Leigh whined. She was feeling lost without him.

'Oh shit. It's bad enough that we don't like her, but it must be awful for you LeeLee,' Eric said, giving her a sad smile.

'Well, I still think that he is going to wake up and realise what a pain she is,' David said, loyally.

'I agree with David. Let's let this little romance run its course, it won't take long, I just know it won't,' Tanya finished.

'I'm a bit bored with all this Natasha speak. Fancy coming for a drink?' Bob asked. Amanda was startled, they hadn't been away from the screens all week. She didn't realise that Bob was as surprised by the suggestion as she was. That week her feelings for Bob had developed. Amanda loved her job, she lived for it and not only had she grown to admire Bob professionally she admired him personally too. It wasn't that she had fainted with lust the first time she'd seen him. He was tall, he was slim, he was good-looking in a 'technical person' way. His eyes were grey, his hair thinning, his nose pointed, but he was a package, and Amanda only ever fell for packages.

'I'd love a drink,' she replied. As they left, Amanda was delighted by the fact that this was the first time he had spent any time with her socially. He waited while she got her coat and bag. Bob was uptight.

'Harvey, don't you think we're treading on dangerous ground the way this new direction could take us?' Cherry asked when they were having dinner at the flat. She harboured the same worries as Tanya; it could all go wrong.

'We need to take risks. This whole project is like one giant risk, and this storyline is gripping. If she agrees to be a part of it, then we have a stronger film. It's not so bad is it?'

'No, no it isn't. It's just that I think we need to be careful. If Natasha spills the beans or anything . . .'

'Cherry, she won't. We offer her money, she takes it, she signs a confidentiality agreement, then she signs a watertight contract before she gets the money. She won't talk, because if she does she loses the money. Actually we should make the payment in instalments to coincide with the release of the film.'

'Fine,' Cherry agreed. 'I don't know what's wrong with me, but I seem to worry so much about this film now.'

'That's because we love it and we want it to work.'

'Yeah, and I guess sometimes we need to give it a helping hand.'

'That's exactly what we're doing, honey, just a helping hand.'

Tanya had to wait until Thursday when she was told by Harvey it was time to put 'Operation Get Rid Of Natasha' into action. It couldn't come soon enough. They had spent an awkward couple of evenings trying to be pleasant as they watched her maul Gus, and in the end it had got too much for Leigh who was now fraying at the edges. Her eyes had lost their sparkle, even her hair seemed to have wilted.

Taking on the role of superhero, Tanya prepared her tactics. As she sat at the breakfast bar in the kitchen waiting for Natasha to emerge, she felt a mixture of emotions.

Natasha was fully dressed when she walked into the kitchen – that was the first shock. Instead of being in Gus's blue bathrobe she was wearing white jeans, a gold belt, a black top and high-heeled boots. She had full make-up on and was so stunning it was almost painful to look.

'You look nice,' Tanya said, wishing she looked better. She needed the upper hand.

'Thanks, I have a lunch date today,' Natasha replied.

'A date?'

'Well hardly a date. I'm meeting my father for lunch because he demanded it. He's that type of father.'

'Nice. You know I'm glad we're alone, I wanted to have a chat with you.' Tanya kept her voice friendly and even toned.

'Really, what about?' Natasha shot back.

'Writing. You said you wanted to be a writer, and I have this wonderful friend who is an American literary agent. I told him a bit about your travels, and *you* of course, and he'd like to meet you.' Tanya smiled. It was a victorious smile because she could see that Natasha had snapped the bait.

'Really? Tanya you are a darling. When can I meet him?'

'I was going to suggest tomorrow. Maybe the three of us could have lunch at his office. in Knightsbridge?'

'Mmm, I'd like that. Why did you do that for me?' she asked with a hint of suspicion.

'Because it seemed a logical move. You want to write: he's an agent. That's all there is to it.'

Tanya told her she would arrange it, and added that it was best not to tell the others, even Gus.

'Why ever not?' Natasha asked.

'I'm superstitious. It jinxes things if you tell before they happen.'

'Fine. I look forward to it.' Natasha flashed her smile, and left for her lunch date.

Tanya phoned Harvey and told him to expect them the next day. Everything would be arranged: the contract, the confidentiality agreement and, of course, the footage of Natasha's phone call would be on stand-by ready to roll.

'You bring them into the office when they get here. You usher them to the sofa then you stay by the door. I tell her we have something really exciting to discuss but it has to be confidential. She signs the agreement, then we play the tape.' Harvey outlined the plan for the thousandth time.

'Fine,' Cherry said.

'Harvey we know all this,' Bob pointed out. Millie smiled, but kept quiet. She hadn't been given a role in the proceedings, she was going to have to stay in the kitchen until it was over. She'd tried to protest to Cherry, but to no avail. She was upset that she was going to miss the unfolding drama.

'OK, OK. Let's have some coffee too, we don't have any coffee in the plan yet.' Harvey was pumped up. He was enjoying this so much and was looking forward to getting a foxy bitch chick in his movie.

Tanya had asked Millie to arrange a cab for them. She had no intention of being with Natasha any longer than she had to. A short cab ride to Knightsbridge was quite enough. When Natasha walked downstairs, she was wearing the same outfit as she had the previous day, except she had switched the black top for a white one, and the gold belt had been replaced by a black one.

'Ready?' Tanya asked tersely. She had had enough of the chums act.

'Yes.' They looked at each other before they walked out of the house and got into the cab.

'Do you get cabs everywhere?' Natasha asked, with a hint of envy in her voice.

'Mostly.' Tanya shrugged and sat back in the seat. No further conversation was exchanged. They arrived at their destination and got out of the cab. Tanya led the way into Harvey's building. Natasha was visibly impressed so much so that she had made up her mind to seduce Tanya's agent friend. She decided it would be much easier than writing a book.

They took the lift to Harvey's floor, and Tanya cringed as Natasha tousled her hair in the mirror. They waited at the door until Cherry opened it.

'Hi Tanya.' Cherry grabbed Tanya and kissed her cheek.

'This is Natasha, Natasha this is Cherry.' Tanya made the introductions.

'I thought you said the agent was a he,' Natasha said, a little too sulkily.

'He is, but I am his assistant.' Cherry gave Natasha a look of disdain and led them into the office.

Harvey was sitting behind his desk, Bob on a chair facing him. They stood up when Cherry led Tanya and Natasha into the office. Tanya threw her arms around them air kissing as she went. Harvey shook Natasha's hand, and gestured for Bob to do the same. When the introductions were over, Harvey began.

'Please take a seat. Can I get you coffee?'

'Thanks,' Natasha replied. She sat on the sofa and Tanya sat next to her. Cherry left the room and came back with a tray of coffee that Millie – from her hiding place in the kitchen – had made. No one spoke until Cherry returned.

'Natasha, there is something I need to ask you,' Harvey started.

'Fire away.'

'I have a project which is top secret and the only people who know about it are the people who are part of it, and most of them are in this room. This could involve you and in a very lucrative way. But before we go ahead we need you to sign a confidentiality agreement which is for your protection as much as ours.' Harvey stood up and walked over to Natasha.

Natasha looked up at him. 'It all sounds a bit heavy.' She was thinking that there was little possibility of seducing the man in front of her while he was being so scary.

'Heavy? Well, yeah. It *is* serious. But it is also worth money . . . To you.' Harvey waved the piece of paper in front of Natasha's face, she grabbed it. Cherry handed her a pen. For a minute she tried to read it, but because it was full of legal jargon she didn't get very far.

'This doesn't commit me to anything weird or illegal does it? I mean it's just an agreement to make me keep quiet?'

'Exactly,' Harvey said and watched as she scrawled her name across the bottom. Bob witnessed the agreement and Harvey took it back to his desk. 'Now, I would like to show you something.'

Bob got up and switched on the television and video recorder.

Natasha looked at the screen. Harvey looked at Natasha. She was transfixed. He was amused.

'Oh shit,' she groaned, as Bob flicked the off button.

'Yes, it really is shit what you're doing to Gus,' Tanya replied.

'How on earth did you film that?' Natasha asked, trying desperately to regain her composure.

'That's the secret that has to stay a secret. We are filming in Tanya's house.' Harvey went on to briefly explain.

'So Gus doesn't know any of this . . . ? He'll go mad. It's crazy. You can't do this, you just can't. Shit.'

'If anyone finds out, Natasha, I'll go mad and believe me that's not a pretty sight. I would also like to remind you of this' – he dangled the signed agreement in front of her – 'I'm American and I just love lawsuits.'

'So what are you saying?' Natasha asked. She looked scared.

'Here's the story. You are going to finish with Gus. You'll tell him the truth, or our version of it. You'll say that Tanya overheard you on the phone to a friend. You'll admit that you've been using him because your father has cut you off and although you don't love him he's preferable to a job. You'll tell him that

Tanya confronted you and threatened to tell everyone everything and tell him that you are truly sorry, but you didn't know what else to do. He's a great guy who deserves better than you – and isn't that the truth . . . tell him that as well. Then you leave the house and never go back. For this I will pay you a sum of money and you will sign a contract agreeing to end your relationship with Gus in the manner we choose, and also giving us exclusive control over the footage we have of you.'

'So, why are you filming them in the house?' she asked.

'Like I said it's a top secret project, a major investment. Whatever happens this is going to be big, and you can be part of it *if* you decide to cooperate.'

'How much money?' Natasha asked quickly, she couldn't believe what she was hearing, and she was scared. The man she had been told was a literary agent was the most frightening person she had ever come across. Tanya was obviously involved in something that no one else knew about. Although she had never found Tanya scary before, she did now. It was all too much for her to make sense of, her brain was in turmoil. She could only focus on the money.

'Well it depends. You get ten thousand pounds if you agree to my terms. You get fifteen thou if you agree to let us use the nudity as well.'

'Nudity?'

'Remember, we have footage of you in your birthday suit. A few nude shots of you would make things more interesting.'

'It's not much is it?' Natasha asked.

'No, but then you didn't really do a lot, did you? If you think about it in terms of time, then you're being paid very well.'

'What if I refuse?'

'If you refuse we cut you out of the film and threaten you. You signed the confidentiality so you can't tell anyone, and if you do, I'll expose you in the worst way. You'd be better off agreeing. After all there's enough there to rent a nice flat for a while before you find your next victim. And when the footage is released, you might look like a bitch but everyone will see how gorgeous you are. You'll be famous. Your name will be on the credits, you'll have a media presence. To be honest with you, *darling*, you'll probably end up doing quite well out of this.'

'I'm not sure,' Natasha was trying to decide how she should play it. She knew she'd take the money. Any money to get her away from boring old Gus. But she had to try for more. After all money was her middle name.

'You better get sure. If you don't agree, or if you say a word to anyone you'll pay.' Harvey's tone was threatening.

'How?' Natasha whispered.

'With your life. I guess you're the type to read Jackie Collins' novels. If you do then you know that people from LA don't take any crap.'

'You'd really kill me?' Natasha asked, her eyes widening.

'You better believe I would,' Harvey replied, bluffing like a master poker player.

'Twenty grand,' Natasha announced. 'I'll do it all for twenty grand.'

'Fine,' Harvey replied. 'You've got a deal.'

Tanya was a silent witness to the entire proceedings and watched as Natasha signed the contract.

By the time Natasha received her instructions as to how to end her sham of a relationship with Gus, she was already showing a new excitement about the fact that she would be a star.

Tanya left with Natasha, because she didn't want to let her go on her own. She still didn't trust her. Natasha refused to speak to Tanya on the way home, but changed her mind when they got into the house. As Tanya made coffee, Natasha sat at the breakfast bar.

'I underestimated you. Here I was thinking that everyone that Gus lived with was as dull as him. But not you, you are deceiving everyone. Wow Tanya, the fact that you're a bitch makes you more interesting than I ever thought you were.'

'Thanks.' Tanya refused to rise to the bait.

'Pleasure. You know, you might try to justify what you've done as being for Gus, but guess what? I get to be in a movie and

I get money so I won't need a job for a while. All Gus gets is a broken heart.'

'Whatever.' Tanya took her coffee up to her room. Her cheeks were so red that she could barely stand to walk past Natasha. Natasha didn't miss it either and she smirked as she watched Tanya leave. In the privacy of her own room Tanya's tears came, and, as tears of guilt often do, they ran and ran for hours.

Chapter Thirty-Three

Natasha had been told that she was to end things with Gus that evening. Tanya, David and Eric were playing on the Playstation, while they waited for Leigh and Gus to return from work. Natasha was out of sight. Leigh came in and sat on the sofa.

'I need a beer, anyone else?' Leigh said. Three people said yes. She returned with the beers just as the game finished and they all sat down in various parts of the sitting room to drink their beers. Leigh lit a cigarette.

'You haven't smoked for two years,' David cried.

'I know but I need this. I'm tired.' Tanya looked at David and shrugged. Leigh's behaviour was beyond unpredictable these days.

Gus walked in as Leigh was on her second cigarette. He didn't seem to notice as he kissed her on the cheek. That was why she had taken up smoking. Not only was he not in love with her, but now he had stopped noticing her. She puffed harder on her cigarette.

Natasha appeared in the doorway. Everyone looked at her.

'I was just wondering where you were,' Gus said as he jumped up and kissed her. Tanya felt sick. She had never seen anyone as full as affection as Gus was. He didn't deserve to be hurt the way he was going to be.

'Would you all mind if Gus and I could have some privacy?' Natasha asked.

'What's wrong with his room?' Eric replied.

'Please, Eric,' she begged.

'Come on, we'll take our beers to the kitchen,' Tanya said and as she stood up everyone followed.

They sat round the breakfast bar, beer in hand.

'What's going on?' David asked. Tanya took a deep breath and she told them about the telephone conversation.

'My God.' Eric paled. Leigh lost the power of speech.

'So you made her tell him?' David asked.

'I guess that's what she's doing right now,' Tanya explained.

'But, why didn't you tell us before?' Eric stammered.

'Because I thought that it was really unfair for us all to know before Gus knew. I'm only telling you now because he will need a huge amount of support from us.' Everyone nodded.

They felt uneasy and restless so sat in silence. It was an hour before they heard the sitting room door open, and then the front-door slam shut. It was another ten minutes before anyone would venture out. But Gus wasn't there. He had fled to his room and used his lock for the first time ever.

He lay on the bed, staring at the ceiling. He couldn't believe she had done it to him *again*. The only girl he'd ever loved. He still loved her, although he hated her. He hated her for coming back into his life but now she had gone forever. She wasn't meant for him, obviously. She was so wrong for him. It was hard to understand why he loved her when she didn't love him back. Life can be a bucket of shit.

He decided to sleep.

The others decided to give him his own space and time. They knew Gus well enough to know he would seek them out if he wanted them. Leigh put a note under his door, saying: 'I care, I will always care. LeeLee xx.' It was all she needed to say, and although she didn't see Gus read it, he did read it and he smiled. Because love was one thing and friendship quite another. Friendship didn't normally threaten as much pain.

When everyone went to bed, Tanya went to her control room to watch the tapes. As she rewound to the part where

Natasha finished with Gus she took a deep breath. This would be even harder to watch than them having sex.

Clearly Natasha was acting. She tried to look sincere but her facial expressions were as genuine as she was. However Gus looked so vulnerable that it was heartbreaking. You could feel Gus's physical pain just by watching. He tried to talk her out of it, in a quiet reasonable way. Again he told her he loved her. Natasha walked away. She had to – that's what she had been paid to do.

Tanya's tears coursed down her cheeks. She also had Natasha's words ringing in her ears: 'You've got a wonderful friend in Tanya, Gus.' Tanya would be the only person who would hear the sarcasm in her voice.

She immediately called Jason and although it was late, she ordered a cab to take her to his flat.

Jason and Serena were having a discussion as they waited for her.

'I have no idea what's going on, she didn't say, but she sounded so distraught,' Jason explained.

'I hope it's nothing to do with that film guy. If it is then I will feel personally responsible.'

'Ser, all you did was help her, I'm sure it's not that.'

'But think about it. It was about the time that I arranged that meeting that she stopped seeing us. God, I hope he hasn't got her into some weird cult or something.'

'Don't let your imagination run wild. Tanya's smart and she's tough. Let's just wait and see.' It seemed an eternity later when the buzzer went. As Jason held the door open and waited for his sister to climb the stairs he tried to stop his imagination running wild.

Tanya flung herself up the last few stairs and into his arms. He led her to the sofa, where Serena took her in her arms. 'Tanya, what's happened?' Tanya merely sobbed.

After a while she felt strong enough to speak.

'You know I cry all the time now,' she said, 'and I always hated crying.' Jason and Serena looked at each other. The story tumbled out of her. Having stopped crying she couldn't stop talking.

'Hang on,' Jason said when she'd finished. 'This film guy, Harvey, wanted to make a film about your flat?' He had never heard a crazier story. Serena shook her head.

'I don't understand.'

'Neither do I. Look at what happened with Gus and Natasha. What am I going to do?'

'Why didn't you tell us?' Serena asked.

'Because you'd have told me not to do it.'

'Too damn right we would. Tanya you've known Leigh and David nearly your whole life. How can you contemplate doing this to them?' Jason wasn't pleased with his little sister. Tanya shook her head.

'You know we love you,' Serena started. Tanya nodded. 'Look darling, I am so sorry that you're upset, but you are doing this for selfish reasons. Now you have to live with those reasons or pull out.'

'I know what I'd like you to do,' Jason added.

'Do you hate me?' she asked.

'No, I'll never hate you. I love you, but I don't think it'd be fair for me to say I approve or give you justification. I just can't.' It was the best he could do.

They talked some more. Tanya was looking for reassurance. Once she realised she wouldn't get their approval, she needed to know they would never disown her. She promised she would let them know what she decided and she left them feeling more confused than ever.

Chapter Thirty-Four

In the morning, as soon as everyone had left Tanya ran from the house, hailed a black cab and directed it to Harvey's flat. She didn't really know what she was doing, yesterday had been rehearsed, today wasn't. She just knew she had to do something. It was the guilt. She was being eaten up by it. She couldn't push it back any more.

Bob opened the door.

'Hey Tanya, come in. I was just leaving for the editing suite. Last night we had a bit of a tear jerker. Although Natasha was on the phone straight away asking when she'd get her money. That girl has a heart of stone.'

'Right,' Tanya said and walked into the flat. 'Where's Harvey?'

'In the office, just go through.' Bob walked out of the door leaving Tanya standing alone in the sitting room. She walked shakily through to the office, and knocked on the open door before walking in. Cherry and Harvey were sitting behind their desks.

Harvey grinned. 'Hey Tanya, how are you?'

'Not good Harvey.'

'I'll make some coffee shall I?' Cherry said – as she always did – and Harvey nodded. Tanya sat down on the sofa.

'We have a problem right?' Harvey asked.

'It broke my heart. I cried myself to sleep. Not only because

of Gus and his pain but for what I was doing. I engineered the
split with Natasha, then I watched it. I mean how bad a person
can you be? I can't live with myself.' Tanya was sobbing. Cherry
came back in with the coffee. She poured them both a cup as
Harvey came over and sat next to Tanya.

'Tanya, you are being perfectly reasonable. We've been
filming for such a short time and already it's been very emotional. We didn't expect that. You didn't expect that, and I'm
sorry, because I've made you unhappy and I feel responsible,'
Harvey soothed.

'Really?' Tanya asked.

'Yes. I am sorry. But on the other hand, and you knew there
had to be another hand, I feel that we have gone too far now. I
know it's only been a short time, but all the equipment, all the
staff we've hired, the editing suite, apart from anything else it has
cost us a lot of money. You know how much getting rid of
Natasha alone cost. Also, we don't have time to start again. I'm
sorry but we don't. I have two choices. If you want me to pull the
plug on this I will, but that means we abandon the whole project
and all go back to LA and carry on with our lives as best we can
with egg on our faces. And I probably get sued for every buck
I've got. Or . . . we carry on.' He smiled kindly. He had known
she would do this at some point but he hadn't expected it to be
so soon. He wasn't worried. He knew she would let him
continue. It was all working out so perfectly for him. What
was a little tantrum every now and again?

'But I don't think I can do it?' Tanya's little voice said.

'Fine. We rip up the contracts and we start to plan our
moving out. What the hell! It's gone wrong but that's OK.'
Harvey shrugged.

'What about me?' Tanya said.

'I guess you go back to what you were doing before,' Cherry
intervened.

'Tanya, please stop this. Look, you knew what you were
getting into. We all did, and as it didn't work we'll chalk it up to
experience and start packing.' Harvey's tone was getting sharper.

He and Cherry had discussed doing a 'good cop – bad cop' routine if this showdown with Tanya happened.

'Harvey don't upset her,' Cherry chastised.

'Cherry we are all having to go home, lose huge amounts of money and any respect we had. We'll probably never work in the movie business again. I *am* upset.'

'So if I do pull out it's all over?' Tanya asked.

'Yup,' Harvey answered.

'Oh shit, shit, shit,' Tanya said as she found a fresh batch of tears.

Then she began to think it through. The thing about this film, the *special* thing, was that anything could happen and even Tanya, its producer and Harvey, its director didn't know what was round the next corner. The whole thing was based on the unpredictable. That was its uniqueness and recipe for its success.

She took a deep breath, pulled the tears back and prepared herself. 'I'm sorry,' she said, simply.

'Sorry that you're pulling out?' Harvey asked.

'I'm not pulling out, I'm just sorry that I was so confused. Of course I'm not pulling out. This is the most exciting thing that will ever happen to me and it's working. That's the amazing thing, it's working. It's just that I wish sometimes we were filming strangers or actors. I'm just having a hard time dealing with my guilt.' She smiled through her tears.

'I understand how you feel Tanya, but you're doing a great job. I have great things planned for you when this is over. Honey you're going places.' Harvey smiled and gave Tanya a hug.

'We're like a family Tanya, and we support each other. Especially when it is something as difficult as this. You're special and your housemates are special. Difficult as it might be, please remember that.' Cherry smiled.

Tanya left and went straight to Jason's office. She felt a little silly about her outburst both that day and the previous night, but she had promised to let Jason know her decision. She waited nervously in reception until he appeared, then she told him about her meeting with Harvey.

'You were always ambitious. Almost from the day you were born,' he said tenderly.

'I hate myself but I can't not do it. I tried but I can't. Listen, I'll call Serena when I get home and explain to her. I love you but I am going to carry on.'

'Promise you'll call if anything goes wrong?' Jason couldn't believe Tanya's transformation. Last night she was crumbling but today she was completely composed.

'I'll call you and I'll see you when it's over.'

'When will that be?'

'I don't know.' All she knew was that it would be over and for the first time she looked forward to that day.

Chapter Thirty-Five

Tanya felt in control again. At times she forgot the uneasy position she had put her housemates in. She developed an unbelievable ability to forget about the cameras when she was in front of them, and remember them only when she was viewing the footage. She often said things she regretted saying, did things she regretted doing because of this.

Bob and his team worked slavishly and, because Harvey asked him to, he worked closely with Tanya teaching her new skills. Tanya was willing to learn, because the more she learned the more she was able to justify what she was doing. No one else was any the wiser.

Production was well underway.

'OK, so far we've broken it down into two sections. We've got story and we've got inserts.' Bob was meeting with his team of editors. 'Story covers the main scenes we can use. Inserts are pieces of conversation that we like and want to use, but need to find frameworks to put them in. Amanda, can you run through the stories we have so far?' Bob took charge of his team in a similar way to Harvey. He commanded the respect of a leader, and the adoration of a dictator. Amanda demonstrated this last point by giving him her most alluring smile.

'So far the storylines we have are fitting together perfectly.

We have the friendship of Leigh and Tanya, the row, the making up, Leigh's feelings about Gus and vice versa, and Tanya's jealousy. Then there's Gus's romanticism. Then we have the love story. The Gus and Natasha love story. We have humour (kebabs), and then deceit (Natasha), the dumping, her leaving and everyone comforting him. Which brings us full circle back to him and Leigh.' Amanda finished talking and smiled directly at Bob.

'I think it's great,' James said. 'I had bloody big doubts at the beginning, but so far, so good.' He smiled at Bob.

'I agree, and we are going to have more and more work to do as we progress. The only way this film is going to be good, due to lack of direction and everything else that movies traditionally require, is if we edit it brilliantly. This is the biggest challenge we will ever face in an editing suite. Now, John, why don't you outline what we've got so far with inserts.' Bob returned everyone's smile. In the castle that was his editing suite, he was king.

'We all know we have these conversations, sometimes even just a couple of words that we kept in case we can slip them in somewhere. What we should do is get them all cut and put on tapes. I've made a list of those I think we should keep.' John smiled.

'Why don't we go through your list, then we'll compile the tapes. That way we can be extra sure about what we want to keep,' Bob suggested.

'Fine. First we have my favourite, the Boob Conversation. Then we have James's favourite, the Grape Conversation. Followed by the Love Conversation and the Best Spliff in the World Conversation.'

'What about one liners?' Bob asked.

'I've made a separate tape of those and I got Sally to type the lines up.'

'I am so glad we're on top of everything. Let's take a look at them.' Bob stood up and went to the video player. He put the first tape in: the 'Boob Conversation.'

The Setting:

Eric, David, Gus and Leigh sitting in their usual places in the sitting room. The strange thing, Bob observed, was the way that when they walked into the room they immediately took their places, as though they were being stage managed. Eric was in his red beanbag, normally smoking a joint. Gus and Leigh were sitting next to each other on the sofa. David was in what he thought of as 'his armchair'. The coffee table was littered with various drinks and magazines, and the television was on. They were discussing plastic surgery when Tanya walked in.

The Conversation:

'I think that the addiction isn't about looks, I think it's about power,' Eric said.

'What do you mean?' David asked.

'Well once you change one thing, you realise you've got this power over how you look so you use that power because you get addicted to it,' Eric explained.

'What on earth are you talking about?' Tanya asked walking into the room and sitting down on the sofa next to Leigh.

'Plastic surgery,' Leigh said.

'Why?' Tanya asked.

'Because a woman who had had nearly everything done to her plastic surgerywise came into Casualty today and she still wasn't happy with her nose so she actually tried to cut it off with a knife,' Gus explained.

'Ugh. Shit, that's horrible,' Tanya replied, wide-eyed.

'And I think that plastic surgery becomes an addiction because of power. See, that woman thought that she could change herself, she believed in her power to do that, but she couldn't. What happened anyway?' Eric asked.

'It's sick, I don't think I want to know,' David shuddered.

'Well we stitched her, so she'll be all right, but she looked weird, you know, not like a proper person. You remember when you were little and there was that game where you had different faces and you could move them around so that you had the wrong eyes with the wrong nose and so on and the idea of the game was to put them back in the right order? Well she reminded me of that.'

'Yuk,' Leigh said.

'And then we wondered why women always seemed to start with their boobs,' David stated.

'Do they?' Tanya asked.

'Apparently, it was on this Internet survey I read. Women want to change their boobs more than anything else, not sure why,' David expanded.

'Imagine if LeeLee had a breast enlargement. You'd be, well you'd be like someone with incredibly big tits.' Eric laughed.

'You may not have noticed, but I already have incredibly big boobs,' Leigh answered.

'Of course I've noticed, I'm not blind,' Eric replied.

'I think you've got great boobs,' Gus said, smiling.

'Do you?' she asked, colouring. Gus nodded.

'Can we not talk about my cousin's boobs, it's not a subject I am comfortable with,' David protested, and everyone laughed at him.

'Talk about Tanya's boobs, then,' Leigh suggested.

'Let's not,' Tanya answered, quickly.

'Why not?' Eric asked.

'Because they're not . . .' Leigh started and Tanya jumped on her and held her hands over her mouth. 'Muumphhh.'

'Tanya, are your tits fake?' Eric asked.

'No,' Tanya replied.

'They are aren't they?' Eric screamed. Tanya let go of Leigh and lurched toward Eric. Instead of attacking him, she lifted her blouse to reveal her bra-clad bust.

'Yes I had an enlargement and you know what? I like them now, I think they're great but I am not on a power trip to change anything else about me and I'm not addicted to plastic surgery.' Everyone was silent.

'Why did you have it done?' David asked.

'Because I fancied bigger ones and Nathan paid for it. I was always wearing Wonderbras and I was so jealous of Leigh's cleavage, that's all.' Tanya shrugged.

'But you might do it again, you don't know. You might keep going back for more and get bigger and bigger and you'll have bigger tits than Leigh and bigger tits than anyone.' Eric was warming to his theme.

'Right and I'll die young because me and my enormous tits will board a plane one day and I'll by flying over the ocean and they'll explode and kill me,' Tanya mocked.

'Not only you but they'll also kill two hundred innocent passengers and the crew,' David said.

'Well then that settles it, I can't get any more boob jobs. Think of the innocent lives at stake,' Tanya finished.

They worked their way through the rest of the tapes. Taking notes, sharing opinions, collating new ideas.

When they had finished watching, they had a pile of tapes ready for cataloguing. Bob knew that it wasn't much but it was the start he wanted. Bob looked at his team proudly. They were shaping up well.

They had gathered for a meeting but without Tanya.

'Bob, this is great, but I have one concern. Nearly all the footage we've got is from the first week and a half. The rest of the month we've got bits and pieces but no whole scenes. We are going to have to edit this more thoroughly than we thought,' Harvey said.

'Which means that we're messing with a fly-on-the-wall. Harvey the idea was to film six months in the life of this house and make those six months into a film. Now what you're doing is making a film not *of* the six months but *out* of the six months. Which isn't fly-on-the-wall,' Cherry protested. She knew right from the beginning that that would happen and she suspected that Harvey did too.

'OK, but at least everything we show did happen, so it's still real,' Harvey replied.

'Even if it happened in a different way or a different order?' Cherry asked.

'Yes,' Harvey smiled. 'That's the nature of movies – that's how they're made.'

'I agree,' Bob said. 'But what I need is scenes. We have only a handful of real scenes. Storylines are proving a little thin. David and Eric are great but neither of them have done much. Also, as Leigh has a crush on Gus we know why she's not dating anyone else, but we don't know why Tanya doesn't date. Now I'm not saying she never will but for a month of filming we have very little footage and we only have another five months left. Leaving it to chance might be too much.' Evidently Bob was worried.

'Let's wait until the two-month mark is up. If we have nothing then we'll kick in with Plan B,' Harvey replied.

'What's Plan B?' Cherry asked.

'It's the one we're about to come up with.' Harvey smiled supremely.

Tanya had no knowledge of this conversation, although Millie did. She didn't minute the unofficial meetings but she paid attention and remembered them. She felt that Tanya looked down on her a bit and she was pleased at the little extra knowledge she had. Not that she would ever tell her, that would be stupid, but she liked it. It made her feel important and she had never felt important before.

They all sat around the same table, but this time Tanya was included. Bob was in the chair. 'I want us all to watch the footage I recommend we use and see where it's going. I know we've seen it before, but I've made some refinements. So here goes.'

'What about popcorn?' Millie joked. Tanya shot her a withering look.

They watched the tapes in silence. As they had seen most of the footage before, there were no surprises. Tanya tried to watch it with a certain amount of detachment, but she wasn't able to. It all seemed much shorter than she thought it would be. How could so much of their lives take up so little time on screen? It was confusing.

She felt there was a lot of humiliating footage, and she felt her face redden as she watched. She was trying desperately hard to laugh along with the others in the room, but she couldn't. She knew that she didn't come across on the screen the way she wanted to, but she was also aware that there was nothing she could do about it.

She decided to be more aware of her behaviour in future. She would try her best to ensure that she remembered to do so.

When the tapes finished, Bob spoke again. 'OK. That's it so far, we're happy with what we have, but it's a rough framework. The conversations will have to be inserted at the end.' He smiled. But when Bob smiled, he looked in pain. His face reflected his uptight nature. A nature that he believed was down to the uptight nature of technology.

'Excellent,' Harvey said. The meeting reminded Tanya of school projects. When you had to work in teams and the enthusiasm or excitement at doing something new took you over. They were not acting like Hollywood big shots who made movies all the time. Of course, what Tanya didn't know was that these people didn't actually make films anyway. Not really.

'I have one more suggestion,' Bob continued. 'The tape of the weekend in the Lake District is really good Tanya, and I'd like to use it in some way, or use parts of it.'

'But that wasn't the intention . . .' Tanya protested.

'I know, but we can use it somehow, you did a good job filming that,' Bob countered.

'Let's decide later, shall we?' Tanya said.

'Sure. We'll do that,' Harvey agreed.

If everyone knew how much money was available for what they were doing, they perhaps would not have been so relaxed. It was proper money, as Harvey said often to Cherry. The money for the budget that Poplar Films had agreed would have intimidated anyone. Because as Tanya rightly thought, it was just like a project. And although they all took it seriously, no one took it *that* seriously. If Steve Delaney had been there, he would have wanted to kill them all.

It was part of Harvey's direction that allowed it to appear to be as unprofessional as it was. He believed that if they thought it was an experiment, or a project, as Tanya thought, rather than a big deal movie, they wouldn't be consumed with worry.

Tanya stayed with the editing team all day. It was part of her learning curve: an education she didn't know the value of, but welcomed anyway. She also welcomed being out of the house and having something to do. She was taking it seriously, perhaps more so than anyone else on the project and it showed. When Tanya returned home that night no one was around. She looked straight at one of the cameras in the sitting room, gazed at her forlorn expression and said; 'This is a movie of my life and, as you can see, it's a bit empty.'

Chapter Thirty-Six

When Harvey's two-month deadline was up, they held an emergency meeting. Bob, who was not the calmest man when it came to work, was panicking more than usual; Harvey who was usually calmer than anyone else, was beginning to lose it. Even Cherry was worried. The meeting was held in the sitting room of the apartment at eleven o'clock one evening when Bob returned from the editing suite, walked in the door and declared: 'We need an emergency meeting.'

Harvey wasn't surprised by this request. Things had been not going well.

The first editing meeting had resulted in a huge feeling of celebration. The cast looked even better on screen than in real life. Leigh had a china-doll prettiness, Tanya was attractive, Gus was handsome, David had sex appeal, Eric was cute, Natasha was stunning. For a month everything had been perfect.

Then it started to go wrong. All the drama had hit them full force in the early days, then it petered off. Leigh and Gus spent nearly all their time either locked in his room, or out at their favourite bar. Eric and David were still spending time in the sitting room, but as David's on-line affair with Em had become more passionate (which they had footage of him explaining), he spent more and more time talking about her or to her. Eric, left with the choice between the sitting room with Tanya or his room, often went to his room. Tanya sat alone.

She was furious. She had noticed a disappointing lack of footage. Everyone had become too self-absorbed to be fun, sociable or even remotely interesting to the hidden cameras. Almost the only footage they had was of Tanya talking to herself. She didn't talk to herself, she talked to the cameras. She told the cameras how she felt.

'*I am all alone because my housemates are a bunch of morons.*' Tanya was drunk when she started the conversation with the sitting room curtain rail. '*I hate being on my own.*' Whenever she was alone she would talk to the camera, sometimes addressing it as 'Bob'. Tanya had become fond of them; they made her feel less lonely.

But even if they used some of Tanya's lonely footage, it didn't give them much. Tanya was despairing. She felt alone in her despair. Whenever she spoke to Harvey he didn't mention that there was nothing interesting happening, and if he didn't mention it, then she wouldn't. She wanted the film to work more than anything.

What Tanya was ignorant of was that Harvey did mention it, just not to her. This was, of course, a calculated move on his part. He knew that they would have to discuss it, but it was going to be up to him when. Harvey began the emergency meeting.

'I don't think that there is anything wrong with the funda-mental idea, the problem that I didn't take into account is time. I take full responsibility. We have, in total, used up three months of our time. Bob, how much time do we need for editing and putting it together?'

'I want three months. You have to direct the footage, then we have to edit it, then we might want to play with lighting, colour etc. And that's not taking things like soundtrack into account.' Bob was panicking badly, sweat was building up on his forehead.

'Bob, Bob, relax. The soundtrack is way down the line.' Harvey patted his shoulder.

'We need longer,' Bob said.

'We don't have longer,' Harvey replied.

'So what are we going to do?' Bob had lost his cool so far back that he had no idea where it was.

'Bob, try to keep calm, so far we are doing OK.' Cherry shot a look at Harvey who said: 'Right then, listen carefully because this is going to change everything for us. What I want are some stronger individual storylines. I want something to happen to David and Eric (because nothing has), I want to give Gus a storyline which doesn't involve love, I want Leigh to have a storyline, although I would like hers to somehow involve love, and Tanya, Tanya needs a storyline because at the moment all she does is be stroppy and talk to herself. I want stories. They have the personalities but if we give them the framework we can make it better.'

'I'm not sure I like the sound of this,' Cherry said.

'Relax. You knew when we started that we might have to do something like this.'

'But . . .'

'We have no choice.' Harvey sat back triumphantly.

'It's against the whole idea of the movie,' Cherry pointed out.

'Fly-on-the-wall, that's what we decided on. Not reality,' Harvey argued.

'It doesn't matter. This was meant to be unscripted. You said that Harvey,' Bob retaliated.

'I know, but we now need a bit of a script, not much but a bit. I am not arguing about this. Cherry, find me a writer, I want the hottest young writer in Britain. Bob, I want you to put all the footage together on one tape, in order as much as possible, so we can show it to this writer. I want them to get a feel for the characters they'll be creating for. Then I want Tanya and the writer to work together to get us some results fast. I will have to persuade Tanya that this is the best way, but as she is lonely and bored at the moment I'm not too worried. Is that all clear?'

'Yes,' Cherry and Bob said.

Tanya held an emergency meeting with herself. She watched the footage over and over and picked out anything she could use. She even picked out parts of her talking to herself; she was going mad after all, there seemed no point in hiding it. She tried to understand why it had gone wrong. Then she realised that it had gone wrong because it had never been right. She began to believe that this was her punishment. She would be punished by not only ending up alone, but by the whole project falling apart and leaving her with nothing.

From the whole month she was left with a couple of conversations, no story, unless you counted the ongoing one of Gus's heartbreak, which was getting tedious to live with and therefore would be tedious to watch. She stared at the notes she had made and went through the footage again.

She was so frustrated. It wasn't working out the way she hoped. She had no idea what to do.

Harvey's emergency meeting was effectively over, but they were still all in the same places. Cherry was worried, really worried for the first time. She thought that Harvey might push Tanya and her ignorant cast over the edge. Bob was worried because he always was and even Harvey was a little worried (not that he would admit it). He was worried that he might actually have been wrong.

'When are you going to talk to Tanya?' Bob asked.

'No time to waste, I'll call her first thing tomorrow morning.'

'I'll start looking for a writer. You know what, if we got a girl around Tanya's age and they became friends it might make it easier for her,' Cherry said.

'Good point. When you find someone, tell them that they need to make friends with Tanya, which, seeing as she seems a little short on friends at the moment, shouldn't be too hard.'

'On that note I'm going to turn in,' Bob said.

Chapter Thirty-Seven

Tanya had just dressed. She had no reason to get out of bed lately and that was depressing her. She wondered if she were nearing a breakdown. She had to force herself to get up. Her mobile rang, which was a welcome distraction from her current state.

'Hello.'

'Tanya, it's Harvey, I thought we might have lunch.'

'I'd love to, where?'

'L'Escargot.'

'Harvey you are an angel, what time?'

'I'll meet you there at one.'

'Great, I'll see you there.'

Tanya put down her phone and went to her wardrobe. She had dressed as if she was staying at home on her own all day; she needed to change.

As soon as Millie arrived at work that morning, Cherry pounced.

'We have a very urgent task. We need to find a young writer,' Cherry informed her.

'What sort of writer?' Millie asked.

'Either a fiction writer or a scriptwriter. Not a journalist, no way do we want a journalist.'

'Any other specifications?' Millie adopted her most professional look.

'Well it would help if she were female. She has to work closely with Tanya.'

'Poor thing,' Millie said, without thinking. She still didn't like Tanya.

'What?' Cherry asked.

'Nothing, I was thinking of how hard Tanya must be working on this.'

'Right. So you can start looking into it.'

'I'll get straight on to it.' Cherry smiled at Millie, she was turning out to be an excellent secretary.

Bob explained to his editors what was going to be happening.

'I think it's good,' James said.

'It'll make things more interesting,' John agreed.

'Which ultimately will make our jobs much easier right?' Amanda asked, nervously. Her feelings for Bob were growing by the day.

'How is this writer going to get them to perform a script when they don't know they're being filmed?' Sally asked, innocently.

'We're not getting a script honey, we're going to get her to come up with story ideas and then she and Tanya will develop them. They have to be ideas that we ensure happen. That's the main thing. So we'll be getting extras in, which will give us more variety,' Bob explained. He had decided, in bed last night, that this was the best way they could go. After all, their reputations were on the line.

'But how are we going to market it then, now it has a writer?' Amanda asked.

'No one but us knows that. Nothing has changed, it is still the first fly-on-the-wall movie, it won't be totally scripted, the cast will still have no idea what is happening, so please, don't push the point.' Harvey would have been proud.

* * *

'Tanya you look great,' Harvey said as he walked to join her at their table. He noticed that she looked anything but great. She looked tired, worried and as if she had lost weight.

'Thanks,' Tanya replied offering him her cheek.

'Have you ordered drinks?' Harvey asked.

'I ordered a spritzer,' she replied.

'I think I'll join you.' Harvey didn't believe in not drinking at lunchtime, unlike so many of his compatriots in LA. He had seen too many people taking to drinking in secret, then destroying themselves. His only rule with drinking was that it should be totally out in the open.

He waited until they'd ordered and they had their drinks in front of them before he launched into what he needed to say.

'It's not going so well,' he started.

'I know,' Tanya squeaked. She hadn't expected him to say it, but when he did she felt a weird sense of relief.

'How do you feel about it?' he asked. Tanya looked at Harvey. He had been so good to her, so right, so perceptive. She decided to be honest with him.

'You know what's funny? I'm angry with them. I'm angry with all of them. I'm angry that they're boring, I'm angry that they're not with me. Yet they don't know about the cameras and I'm even angry at them for that.' She smiled, sadly.

'I do kind of understand,' Harvey said. 'And I am sorry. It's my fault too. You see if we had all the time in the world to film we could just let things happen, and eventually we'd have our movie. The thing is that we're on limited time, and the first month was great, really great, but this month has been too quiet. We don't have time to take any more risks with this.' For once Harvey questioned his decision. He didn't like the way Tanya looked; she looked as if she was one step away from being ill. It was the same with Bob. He sighed as he realised the responsibility that came with his crazy ideas. He had to remember to take more care of those who worked with him.

'I know,' Tanya said, quietly, 'but what are we going to do?' She wanted to cry. She wouldn't let herself. What if Harvey said they would pack up and go? He had a commitment to her and she wouldn't allow him to go. She would do anything to keep him and the film.

'Look honey, we'll fix it. I promise you that I am not going to abandon you, I'm not giving up on you. You have become important to me, important to all of us, and so has this movie.' He paused and watched the relief flow through Tanya. He could see her whole body relaxing. 'I know what we need, we need stories, we need action, we need things to happen.' Harvey reached over and took Tanya's hand. He gave it a squeeze. He felt for her, he genuinely did. Harvey wasn't a bad person himself. He merely liked to get what he wanted. Manipulation was necessary.

'I know,' Tanya concurred. She looked at him expectantly. He said he would fix it and she needed him to fix her. The waiters bought their starters over and Tanya stared intently at her cutlery as if trying to remember what they were used for. Then she looked at Harvey.

'Perhaps we could introduce a new character, I don't know . . . maybe a boyfriend for you who could be an actor. But I know you'll never agree to that because that would mean we are controlling the film, which is against the initial idea. Maybe I should just admit I was wrong . . .' Harvey smiled, sadly.

'That's a great idea! It could be just the thing to revitalise the film,' Tanya said, with enthusiasm.

'Really, you think so? We could hire a writer to make up the character. They could work with you, then we can cast someone, but we have to move fast.'

'I know. Harvey, me having a boyfriend might give us another storyline, but it's not going to make a whole film,' she said.

'I know, but it's a start and I guess we could do other things too.'

'Like what?'

'I don't know, harmless storylines involving the others. We could get a writer to work on some ideas with you, what do you say?'

'Well . . . yeah it could work.'

'We might not do anything, it's your call, Tanya. But if you met with this writer and worked out your own boyfriend storyline, then other ideas might come up. I don't know, but it's worth a shot. I would hate to admit failure on this project.' Harvey smiled again.

'I won't let that happen. But how can we bring in actors anonymously? Most actors wouldn't want to be in a film where they got no credit.' A fresh wave of panic hit. But Harvey had already thought of that.

'What we do is we find an unknown actor who is desperate for money, believe me there's a lot of them around. Then they keep their own names, and they say in the film that they are an actor, so they come across as playing themselves – up to a point.'

'Of course.' Tanya was animated, she was excited. She needed more stimulation, and here it was, being offered to her on a plate. As the boyfriend ploy revolved around *her* no one would be hurt by it, it was perfect. It was exciting. It would make life, as well as the film more interesting.

Harvey smiled at Tanya; he knew she was going to save the film.

When Harvey returned home, Cherry pounced straight away.

'I think we found the perfect writer. It's amazing that we got her so quickly, but that's thanks to Millie.' Cherry's eyes were shining.

'Cherry, easy, give it to me from the top.'

'OK. Well, Millie has a cousin who works for a big publisher, she called her, and after some time she came back and suggested Lucy Havers. She's twenty-eight, has released two books, both bestsellers, and she's writing her third. I already called her and she sounded intrigued, although I couldn't tell her much. She said that she had some time on her hands, and she needed the money or something, so she is coming here this evening.'

'Cherry, you angel, you fast worker, you are amazing.'

'It was Millie who found her,' Cherry pointed out.

'And she's an angel too.'

'Anyway, how did it go with Tanya?'

'Perfect. Just listen.' Harvey talked Cherry through his lunch with Tanya as she made him coffee. Because Millie had been the heroine of the day, she had been allowed to go home early.

'You are unbelievable,' she said when he finished.

'It's a load off my mind.'

'Harvey, she has agreed to work with a writer, she's agreed to give herself a storyline, but she hasn't exactly agreed to manipulate the others,' Cherry pointed out.

'I know, but it's a start. As soon as Tanya realises she has power, she'll do anything.'

'I hope you're right.' Cherry smiled.

'But I am worried about her. Personally more than professionally. She's lonely and she's bored. We need to take better care of her. We should have given her more support in the last month.'

'So my plan to get Lucy to be her friend goes into action.'

'Let's meet this Lucy first,' Harvey replied.

At five on the dot, the doorbell rang and Cherry answered it. Lucy Havers stood at the door. Cherry's first thought was that she didn't look like an author. She was medium height, slim, with black leather trousers and a fawn jumper. On her feet were snakeskin high heels, her handbag matched. Her dark blonde hair was highlighted; she also didn't look like she needed the money.

'I'm Cherry, you must be Lucy.'

'Yes. Nice to meet you.' Lucy stuck out a hand for Cherry to shake and Cherry thought she sounded even more like the Queen than Tanya.

Cherry took her to the office where Harvey was at his desk. She showed her to the sofa and indicated for her to sit down. Then she made all the introductions, and went to make coffee.

'I know this might sound odd, but before I tell you anything I need you to sign a confidentiality document,' Harvey said, taking one over to her.

'Sure,' Lucy said. She had heard of Harvey Cannon through her American agent. When she called him, he told her to get her arse over to Cannon's office because this could make her career. He also warned her that Harvey was perhaps a little less than orthodox. She handed back the signed agreement.

'First, I'd like to tell you the background of what we are doing.' Harvey began to tell the story. He explained the concept, Tanya's household, what had happened so far, what the problem was. He then put the tape in the machine and played the footage. He ended up by explaining what happened at his lunch with Tanya. He explained that Tanya had to be made to feel in control. He told her about the boyfriend idea, he told her that she would be working with Tanya but working for him. Lucy listened to every word in wonderment.

'So you want me to come up with ideas to make it more interesting? I don't need to *write* anything?' she asked.

'Basically, yes. Your ideas have to take into account the people who are in the house, and fit the storylines around them. Also you can't script it, we need to rely on Tanya for that.'

'What credit would *I* get, you said that the movie is unscripted, and if you hire me how will my part in it be recognised?'

'I will make you an executive producer,' Harvey offered, after all it was only a title.

'Really?' Lucy asked.

'Yes and you will get one hundred thousand pounds for your efforts,' he added.

'Fine, I accept.' Lucy thought about trying to get more money, but decided against it. After all the work didn't sound too taxing and her agent had said that Harvey wasn't a man to argue with.

'Cherry will get contracts drawn up for you to sign, I need you to start straight away. Can you go to Tanya's house tomorrow? You'll be visiting the set, and you'll meet her and get an idea of what's what. We will have the contract by tomorrow night for you to pick up on your way back from Tanya's. Is that OK?' Harvey was buoyant again.

'That sounds great. I can start right now if you want. Give me the details.'

Harvey welcomed on board another member to the team.

Cherry e-mailed their lawyers with the terms of the agreement. Then she called Tanya and told her she would be meeting the new writer the following day. Lucy took the tape home with her so that she could watch it again. When Bob returned from his editing suite that evening, he found progress had been made. This made him feel better and calmer. Everything was back on track.

Tanya was pleased that something was being done. She was looking forward to meeting Lucy Havers, whose books she hadn't read. Tanya wasn't much of a reader.

Tanya spent most of the next day thinking about what Lucy would be like and wondering if they'd get on. Lucy spent time being prepared by Harvey and told that part of her job was to 'take care' of Tanya. By the time she arrived at Tanya's front door she was well prepared.

'Hi,' Tanya said, opening the door. 'Come in.' She was glad that Lucy wasn't how she imagined a writer to be. Tanya's idea of writers was kaftans and sandals, but Lucy wore leather trousers, a red top and had beautifully highlighted hair. Tanya was someone who always judged on appearance. Lucy's appearance passed the test.

'Thanks. I'm Lucy.'

'Would you like a coffee or something? Or shall we do the grand tour first?'

'I'd like a look around if that's OK?' Lucy said.

After she showed Lucy around the communal areas, she took her to her bedroom and of course the control room. Lucy was impressed. 'So, you ready for that drink now?'

'Not really, thanks. Anyway, let's go through things in here, after all it isn't wired. Harvey doesn't need to watch our meeting does he?' Lucy had been told to do this by Harvey.

'You're right. I didn't think of that. Let's start.' Tanya smiled at Lucy, she thought she might have found a new friend.

'Harvey mentioned that the storyline would involve a boyfriend for you.' Lucy pulled out a pad and a pen.

'Yes, I thought maybe we could have an intense relationship, then split up,' Tanya suggested.

'Great idea. I like it. I can see that I am not going to have too much to do here. I think an interesting way for you to split up would be to make him gay. So this guy, this actor, we need to make sure he knows exactly what he needs to do.'

'And how we met,' Tanya added.

'Yes, because we need some impact here. OK. You and whoever met when you were filming a television show; Harvey told me everyone thinks you work in TV. He is early twenties and he wants to be an actor.' Lucy was scribbling furiously.

'But I never go out with younger men, can't he be in his thirties?'

'No. A man in his thirties should know his sexuality and if he doesn't then it would be weird. If we keep the gay storyline, which I think will work, then we should make it realistic. A young wannabe actor who has been battling with his sexuality, makes a last ditch attempt to convince himself he's straight with an attractive woman who is a few years older than him. He falls into a passionate affair, but, unfortunately, he is so attracted to one of her male housemates that he has to tell her and confront his true feelings,' Lucy finished.

'Will it look real?' Tanya asked. She wondered if Lucy was getting carried away.

'You bet. This happens all the time in real life. So, which one of your housemates you want him to fall for?'

'Eric,' Tanya replied immediately. Lucy giggled.

'Why Eric?'

'Because he hasn't had a storyline yet. And out of everyone, we bicker the most, so it would seem fitting for my boyfriend to fancy him.'

'And Eric isn't gay?'

'No, I don't think Eric is gay or straight. He's kind of asexual.'

'Right. Well, we've got our first story.'

'And he definitely has to be a younger man?'

'I'm sorry, but yes. Why don't we call Cherry and get casting? Gosh what I wouldn't give to have a young sex bomb falling for me.'

'Yes, but it's not for real though,' Tanya pointed out.

'It is, we've got to ensure that everyone who watches it thinks it's real. So as far as *we* are concerned it is.'

'You're right. I hope I don't turn out to be a crap actress.'

'Tanya you won't, you'll be fabulous.'

'What I want you to do,' Harvey said to Lucy, when she dropped by to pick up her contract, 'is to develop stories for each one of them.'

'What if Tanya won't allow it?' Lucy asked.

'I've already hinted at it and as long as we don't hurt people she seemed to accept the idea. What we need to do is to make her think it was her idea. Tanya would do anything if it were her idea.'

'Good. I have some ideas already, do you want to go through them now?'

'Sure, fire away.'

Lucy detailed her ideas for the four remaining housemates. Harvey was impressed. 'But what about Tanya?'

'What about her?'

'Well did you two get on?'

'Yes. I liked her, although how she can do what she's doing to her friends is beyond me. Don't worry I didn't talk to her about that. Apart from that I think we have a lot in common.'

'That's exactly what I wanted to hear.'

Harvey believed in fate as much as he believed in instinct. It was his belief in such things that made him so open and available to them. Despite the anxiety of the last few days, his belief in fate had allowed him to turn everything around so quickly. The less people worried, the quicker people resolved things. That was Harvey's religion. The religion that had brought him Lucy.

When he showed Lucy out he thought about her ideas. She was brilliant and her ideas were easily executable.

Tanya had nipped to the shops to buy cigarettes. Her nerves were in shreds and smoking was her answer. At least she hadn't turned to drink, or not all the time anyway. She walked into the house expecting to find it as quiet as it had been when she left, but instead she heard noise. It was coming from the sitting room. For the first time in ages, everyone was there.

'Hi,' they chorused. The irony wasn't lost on Tanya. Just as they had decided that they needed to vamp up the film, the others decided to act like housemates again. They passed a pleasant evening together. Although the footage wasn't interesting, the evening had been. It had been fun for them, it had brought them closer and everyone had enjoyed it. An audience wouldn't. That struck Tanya when she was in bed later. An audience wouldn't enjoy the aspects of their lives that they enjoyed. So what was the point? Her friends' lives had become out-takes. Their lives had become too uninteresting. The reality wasn't good enough; is reality ever good enough?

Chapter Thirty-Eight

Another meeting. Today they were auditioning for an actor to play the boyfriend. Cherry and Millie had gone through piles of casting books, before they picked out ten possibilities. It had been the most fun job Millie had had. They were both giggling when they presented Harvey with their list. Harvey had crossed off five straight away for various reasons, and they had arranged to see the other five.

Tanya had made an effort to meet her prospective boyfriend. She wore a short skirt, high heels and a white jumper. Lucy was wearing leather trousers (which seemed to be all she ever wore), and she sat in between Cherry and Tanya, chain smoking and scribbling in her little notebook. She had greeted Tanya as if they were old friends. Bob's assistant, Sally, made everyone a drink but Bob refused to attend, he said he had no interest in auditions, he just set up the camera to record the auditions.

The first candidate was Robert. He was gorgeous. Unfortunately he was the hammiest actor ever, and it turned out that he had a bit part on *Casualty*. Cherry was annoyed, she had asked for people who had never worked on television.

'That's no good,' Tanya said when he'd gone, 'Leigh is addicted to *Casualty*, she'll recognise him straight away.'

Second was Lee who was sexy and could act, but he dribbled a bit when he spoke and Tanya declared there was no way she could kiss him. Then they met Howard Wade. Howard was perfect. No one could find fault in him. He was twenty-two, tall, dark and incredibly cute in a rumpled way, he was also the tiniest bit camp, but not too much, and he seemed to be able to act. Tanya could imagine kissing him and she wanted to do so. When it was Gary's turn, Tanya was uninterested and Ewan didn't stand a chance.

'I want Howard,' Tanya declared.

'Shit, so do I,' Lucy replied, laughing.

'So, Howard it is?' Cherry asked Harvey.

'Let's check the tape out and if he comes across as good on camera as he did in here, then we'll hire him.' As it happened he looked even better on screen than he did in real life, so Howard was duly hired.

He was invited back to the flat in Knightsbridge to sign the contract. At this stage he had little idea what he had auditioned for. As with everyone, Harvey had kept the information flow to a minimum. This hadn't worried Howard; he'd never had an acting job and he would have done anything to get one. Which was just what Harvey wanted.

He stood at the door wearing a crumpled sweatshirt, an old pair of jeans and baseball boots when Millie answered the door to him.

'Hi,' she said, thinking that he was perfect.

'Hi,' he replied, flashing a beautiful smile. She led him into the office where Harvey, Cherry and Lucy were waiting for him. The first thing he had to do was to sign the confidentiality clause. When he had done Harvey explained the idea to him. He didn't even flicker.

'There is one thing,' Harvey said.

'What?' Howard asked.

'This movie is going to be released as real. Which is why you keep your real name and your real occupation. But no one can know you were paid as an actor to appear in it.'

'But I have to. How can I use this as experience if no one knows I acted?'

'You will have exposure, fame and you can trade off that.

Your screen presence will probably be enough to land you loads of offers and I will personally help you if you want to keep working in movies.'

'You will?' Howard asked.

'In return for your silence about this film, I will ensure that you get plenty of great jobs in the future.' It was an offer Harvey was in a position to make, and Howard was not in a position to refuse.

'I'll do it then,' Howard said, smiling. Howard Wade became the first prop in the film that was supposed to be real. Harvey decided that this wasn't the moment to tell him that as well as playing himself, he had to play himself as gay.

Lucy left shortly after Howard to meet Tanya.

'Everything go OK?' Tanya asked.

'Like a dream. Don't forget you've only just got together so you're going to be all over each other. You are actually going to be all over him. *You* make the moves, you know,' Lucy responded.

'Yeah, I'm like this woman possessed and I can't keep my hands off him.'

'Tanya that's perfect. You're going to be really vampy. Wow, this'll be brilliant. We are going to have such a good time.'

'How long before he realises he's gay?'

'Two weeks. You don't have to see him every day, but you need to see him quite a lot. Then, and this is the brilliant bit, you are going to throw a dinner for him and the rest of your housemates. At the dinner you keep touching him and he pushes you away. When you can't stand it any more and you ask him what's going on, he tells you he is gay and he really fancies Eric. Now that should cause a wonderful scene.' Lucy and Tanya laughed.

Tanya spent the following day working with Howard and Lucy. Lucy instructed them on what to do, how to act and because Howard didn't have a script, she taught him what sort of person to be. Lucy worked with Howard, while Tanya watched. She was enjoying herself. Tanya and Howard practised kissing. Tanya couldn't remember the last time she had kissed a man, but she presumed that it was the bouncer. That was months ago. Kissing Howard was a revelation. He had obviously been trained in 'film kissing', or whatever it was called, and he was good. He told Tanya that he'd had a lot of practice and with his looks she didn't doubt it. He also told her that *she* was a good kisser to which Tanya actually blushed. Lucy enjoyed that exchange.

Lucy went over and over his character to ensure that he got it right.

'You are young, you have just met Tanya, who scares you a bit because she's sexy and she's older than you. She also scares you for reasons you are not sure of, reasons buried so deep inside you. You're gay. Not only are you gay but you are terrified of being gay which is why you are attracted to Tanya. She is a nymphomaniac where you are concerned. Other than that, be yourself. If anyone finds out you're acting we'll probably have to kill you.' Lucy smiled. Tanya smiled. Howard looked terrified.

'Can we go back a step from the killing thing? Why do I have to be gay?'

'We told you yesterday that that would happen, that's the whole point of the story.' Lucy had been surprised that he hadn't objected to being gay, after all he would need to convince the public afterwards that he wasn't, which he assured them was the case. She realised now that he was suffering delayed reaction.

'I just remembered that I am going to be known as me in this film. Not an actor. Shit, my mum will see it.'

'Then tell your mum you made it up to get rid of Tanya because she scared you so much.' Lucy had a way about her similar to Harvey.

'Right.' He seemed unsure.

'Howard, you better not mess up.' She sliced her hand across her throat.

'I promise I won't mess up,' he said.

The three of them went to dinner, they had a few drinks and

they made sure that Howard was ready. When Lucy was satisfied, she waved them off and wished them luck.

'Tanya, call me tomorrow and let me know how it goes.' She kissed them both and left.

As Howard and Tanya sat side by side in a taxi, they were both quiet, deep in their own thoughts. Howard was a little nervous and he was trying to remember everything that Lucy had told him. Tanya was full of expectation and anticipation. The movie was about to be transformed.

Chapter Thirty-Nine

It was just past nine when the taxi pulled up outside Tanya's house. The time was important. Obviously, as a date it was early, but Lucy said it was enough time for Tanya to be so fired up that all she wanted to do was to get Howard into bed.

Tanya would later think back on this and the whole project and wonder why she didn't take up acting. Not only was she good at it, but also she enjoyed it immensely.

Eric was in the kitchen pulling open a pizza box when Tanya walked in with Howard in tow.

'Hi Eric,' she said coyly.

'Hey.' He didn't look up.

'Eric, I'd like you to meet Howard, Howard that's Eric.' Eric finally looked up and at Howard. He looked puzzled.

'I didn't know you knew a Howard,' he said.

'Well since you've been spending most of your time locked in your room, I'm not surprised you didn't know. Mind you, nor does anyone. Where are the others?' She tried to sound casual. Howard still hadn't spoken. Unbeknown to Eric, who was now looking at the young man with amusement, Howard had stage fright.

'David and Leigh are in the sitting room. Gus is working,' Eric explained. 'Nice to meet you Howard,' he added, reaching out a hand. Tanya was not impressed by the performance so far, she nudged Howard who blinked, looked at Eric as if he'd never seen him, then looked at the outstretched hand. Somehow he managed to get his hand to connect to Eric's.

'Right. Well, I better get this pizza in the sitting room before the others start eating each other.' He laughed and walked out.

As soon as he was out of earshot, Tanya closed the kitchen door.

'Howard, you froze.'

'Sorry, sorry Tanya. It's just that I stood here and it hit me that I was making my first movie. It's a bit overwhelming.'

Tanya walked over to him. 'Now I am going to take you into the sitting room. I will sit you down in a chair and then I'll sit on your lap. I expect you to attempt some conversation. But if you can't, then tell me now because we can't risk exposure.'

'Darling, I'm going to be fine. Did I tell you how sexy you look tonight?' Howard slipped into character.

Leigh stared open-mouthed at the man in front of her. He was gorgeous. Absolutely drop-dead gorgeous. Nearly as gorgeous as Gus. David smiled at him and Eric behaved as if he was old news. He concentrated on his pizza.

'Where did you meet?' David asked, once Tanya had done as she had said she would. She had her arms around his neck, practically constricting him.

'I'm an actor. I was working on something for Tanya's company and we met,' he said, now having fully recovered, and playing his part admirably. Tanya (who was playing her part more than admirably) leaned over and kissed him.

'Why didn't you tell us?' Leigh asked, clearly feeling a bit miffed.

'When? I haven't seen you guys for ages,' Tanya responded, calmly.

'I guess we've all been busy,' David said.

'Yeah,' Eric finished.

It wasn't the fact that Tanya was sitting on a man that made them gape. It was the way that she alternated between stroking his hair and kissing him and the way that her hand had moved under his shirt. It was a little unnerving to be watching TV and eating pizza with that happening in your sitting room.

'How old are you?' Eric asked, with his mouth full.

'Twenty-two,' Howard replied. David choked on his beer.

'Shit, I thought you only went out with old men,' Eric said.

'Eric, age is irrelevant, it's attraction that counts,' Tanya answered.

'I think it's great. Tanya and I just clicked,' Howard said.

'And obviously we can't keep our hands off each other. Speaking of which Howard, let's go to bed.' Leaving three red-faced individuals who had suddenly lost their appetites, Tanya and Howard made off upstairs.

'Christ,' David said.

'I know,' Eric agreed.

'How on earth can she give us a hard time about not being around when she is living a double life?' Leigh pointed out.

'I hardly think that Howard is a double life,' David replied. 'But she's right, we haven't seen much of each other lately.'

'He's only twenty-two?' Eric asked.

'Tanya never goes out with younger men, especially that much younger,' Leigh protested.

'You're right there. But we should just be pleased that she's got someone.' David smiled.

'Not if we have to watch those public displays of affection while we're eating.' Eric looked worried.

'He looks like he should be in a boyband.' Leigh *was* worried.

'He said he was an actor, oh God, you don't think Tanya used her line do you?' David asked.

'What line?' Eric questioned.

'She went through a phase of chatting up men by saying that she would put them on TV,' Leigh explained.

'So Howard is using her for his career?' Eric looked even more worried.

'It makes sense,' Leigh agreed. 'After all he's young and he is trying to be an actor, she's older and she's a producer. Oh no, poor Tanya.'

'What should we do?' Eric asked.

'There's nothing we can do, you know Tanya never listens to anyone,' Leigh lamented.

'We'll just have to be there for her and pick up the pieces if it all goes wrong,' David stated.

'I didn't like the look of him, he looks the type that uses people,' Eric finished, and the others nodded in agreement.

Tanya showed Howard the control room.

'Wow,' he said as they watched the conversation in the sitting room. 'I can't believe they think I'm using you.'

'At least they care.' Momentarily Tanya felt guilty. They were worried about her, she was deceiving them more and more.

'Do you think I was all right?' he asked, with the insecurity of a struggling actor. 'I mean I thought I was, but I need to know what you thought?'

'I thought you were great.' Tanya had been told by Lucy how to bolster a fragile ego. She had been told to pander to him for as long as he was working with her. She wasn't sure how easy that would be.

'So what now?' He left the control cupboard and sat on the bed.

'What do you mean?'

'What do we do now? I have to stay here and I guess I have to stay in your room otherwise we might have a problem. But what do we do? Do we go to sleep, do I sleep in your bed?'

'Yes, you can sleep in my bed. I don't want the others to suspect anything. But now we shall watch TV.' Tanya reached for the remote control.

At eleven, Howard yawned. 'It's been an exciting day, but I'm tired.' Tanya looked at him.

'Well you can go to sleep now if you like,' she offered.

'I'll just go to the bathroom,' he replied. Tanya gave him the toothbrush that they'd got for him. 'You can use anything you need,' she told him.

'Thanks.'

Howard cleaned his teeth. Then he washed his face. He had to use Tanya's moisturiser because there didn't seem to be any male toiletries. He looked around a bit and then decided that he quite fancied Tanya. She was incredibly sexy, and he wasn't that tired. When he was finished he walked back to her room.

Tanya was wearing a T-shirt and her knickers and was sitting on the bed.

'Hi,' he said.

'Hi yourself,' she replied. He walked over to her and kissed her. She kissed him back.

'So, you want to really pretend I'm your boyfriend?' he asked raising an eyebrow.

'Oh yes,' Tanya cooed as she slipped his jumper over his head. It had been so long since she'd made love to anyone and a good-looking, young actor was nothing to complain about. Even if he was being paid.

Bob took the footage home to Harvey and Cherry and they laughed. (They had no idea about the bedroom scene of course.)

'I can't believe they think he's using her. He looked terrified to me.' Cherry laughed.

'You see sometimes it takes a bit of a nudge to get things moving,' Harvey pointed out. He had a good feeling about what would happen next.

Tanya fell asleep in Howard's arms. She woke up still in his arms and with a broad smile on her face.

'Eric *is* good looking,' Howard said. It was the first thing he said.

'What?'

'I'm practising. Do you think I'm convincing? Would *you* believe I was gay?'

'Not with that huge erection I can feel against my leg,'

Tanya replied. 'Now, how about we forget Eric for now and not waste it?'

Gus's first encounter with Howard was in the afternoon. Howard and Tanya were in the sitting room eating sandwiches and Gus had emerged from sleeping off the night shift. Although he had received a garbled message on his mobile from Leigh, warning him about a 'despicable cad', he wasn't entirely sure what was going on.

'What are you doing here?' he asked Tanya.

'Playing hookey. I told them I was working from home, but I have far more fun things to do. Gus, meet Howard. Everyone else has. Howard this is Gus.'

'Nice to meet you,' Gus said, smiling. His first thought was that the guy in front of him looked a bit too young to be any sort of cad.

'Hi,' Howard replied, sweetly.

'Can I make you some sandwiches Gus?' Tanya asked, much to Gus's surprise.

'Sure.'

'Ham, cheese and mustard OK?'

'Lovely.' He watched amused, as Tanya leapt up and appeared to bounce out of the room. He had never seen her like that.

'So, have you two been together long?' Gus asked when he and Howard were alone.

'No, only a couple of days really, isn't she lovely?' Howard smiled. Gus grinned. He would never think of lovely as a word to attribute to Tanya.

'She is,' Gus lied.

'She's a bit scary,' Howard laughed, in a nervous way, 'but I really like her,' he added quickly.

'I'm sure,' he said.

'What about you? Have you got a girlfriend?' Howard asked.

'No. Me and women are a bit of a sore subject at the moment. A month ago I split up with someone. Anyway it's a long and complicated story so I won't bore you with it. I'm happy for you and Tanya. Great.' At that point Tanya returned with Gus's food.

'Thanks.'

'You're welcome.' Tanya smiled.

They chatted easily while Gus ate his sandwich. He was a little put off by Tanya's continual groping of Howard. In her message, Leigh had made it sound as if Tanya was in imminent danger from this man. By the look of it, Howard was the one they should have been worrying about.

Once he'd finished eating, he went upstairs to get ready for work.

'If I was going to fancy one of the men in this house, wouldn't it be Gus?' Howard asked when they were once again in Tanya's room.

'Probably, but he's not your type. Too obvious. You're going to fancy Eric and that's that.'

'This could ruin my life.'

'How?'

'I have to pretend that this is me.'

'I know that.'

'Well, if this is on the big screen and people seeing me declare my preference for men, and Eric in particular, then how on earth am I going to live that down?'

'We discussed this already,' Tanya was uninterested.

'Yes, I could say that I'm not gay after all I was going through a phase or something. Or that I did it because I was so scared of you. I guess it would make a good press story to promote the film.'

'You must be really desperate to have agreed to do this. I mean you get no acting credit, you will have to persuade people you are really straight and no-one can ever know the truth, apart from us.' Tanya suddenly felt sorry for him.

'I was desperate. I graduated from drama college last year

and I haven't had one job. And I have auditioned. Shit, have I auditioned. Harvey offered me a lot of money for this. I mean a lot. He offered me enough to pay my rent for ages and for me to concentrate on auditions. And he said he'd help me get on. That's why I agreed to it all, including the gay thing. I mean, for the money I'm getting I would consider becoming gay.'

'You know Howard, you're quite funny. Do you think you might like to come back to bed?'

'OK.' He grinned and Tanya kissed him.

'So how are things going?' Lucy asked into her mobile.

'Great,' Tanya said. She felt as if she were twenty-two again.

'Good, I spoke to Harvey and he says the footage is great. We're all happy. Now is there anything you need?'

'Well, when Howard moved in, we didn't think about how he'd need a change of clothes. I was thinking that perhaps he should stay here for the whole two weeks. That way, when he leaves there will be a bigger impact.' Tanya was actually thinking that two weeks' worth of Howard *and* sex would be good for her, this was nothing to do with the film.

'Good idea,' Lucy replied.

'About his clothes?'

'Why don't you go shopping with him? He'd like that and it will give you a chance to get to know each other even more. And think what a nice touch it will be when Howard explains to your housemates that you took him shopping and bought him loads of new clothes. It'll be hilarious.'

'What a good idea. But it's already half past three.'

'Then get going. I'll call you tomorrow. Bye, babe.'

'Bye.'

Tanya found, as she shopped with Howard, that, although he was young, he was vain, and he was a bit of a princess when it came to clothes; still she was enjoying his company. She turned to look at him, he was laden down with shopping bags. He looked so adorable. It was a shame that he was too young, too stupid and too vain for her. Otherwise he would have been perfect.

Lucy would be delighted. When they walked through the front door with all the shopping, the others were in the kitchen cooking.

'My God, what *have* you bought?' Leigh asked.

'Tanya bought me loads of really cool clothes,' Howard answered. He was genuinely excited because he had never before been able to spend so much money on clothes. It was endearing.

'That is kind of her,' Eric said, but he wasn't smiling. David squirmed.

'Why don't we take these to my room and you can try them on?' Tanya suggested, suggestively, as she pinched his bottom.

'Now he wants her money,' Leigh shrieked.

'Why can't she see how much he's using her?' David said.

'Maybe I should have a word,' Eric suggested.

'Tanya would just go mad,' Leigh told him.

'You're right. Do you think it's our fault? I mean we've all been a bit wrapped up in our own lives lately, do you think that that might be why she's turned to him? Because she's lonely?' David quizzed.

'Probably. More likely my fault though, I'm a rotten friend.' Leigh went over to David and hugged him.

'Don't worry, he'll slip up soon enough and then we will give Tanya all the support she needs,' Eric finished. He couldn't understand why, but he was feeling more upset about the whole situation than he ever thought he could. It wasn't as if he was Tanya's biggest fan, but he disliked Howard, and he rarely disliked anyone.

Tanya and Howard were watching in the control room, and laughing.

'The worst thing is that I'm harmless,' Howard said.

'And certainly not a match for me,' Tanya pointed out. 'My God, when did they get so stupid?' They fell on to the bed laughing.

'While we're here, it would be a shame not to . . .' Tanya unbuckled Howard's jeans. She was supposed to be portraying the part of a nymphomaniac, but instead she was becoming one. Fast.

'The reaction of the housemates is priceless. You couldn't have scripted this,' Amanda said to Bob.

'I know, they're all quite mad. Imagine anyone thinking Howard could get one over on Tanya. He's stupid. She's scary.'

'I know. But I love it anyway.'

'The main thing is that Harvey will be pleased.'

'Yeah, at last we seem to be making a movie.' Bob and Amanda smiled at each other.

The original idea had been to give the housemates only glimpses of Howard. In order to make everyone think they were having an intense affair they were supposed to stay in Tanya's room for most of the time. Then everyone would think they were having sex. Actually they stayed in Tanya's room for the whole evening and they *were* having sex. Most nights, they didn't leave the room until midnight when the household was asleep, and then they only left to eat. They fell asleep every night in each other's arms.

The time passed quickly for them because they were lovers. Tanya found that Howard gave her something she needed, although she wasn't sure exactly what that something was. She knew it wasn't just the sex, although that was welcome, but it was also the companionship. Howard might never win *Mastermind*, but he was pleasant company and he made her laugh. She realised that she wanted a relationship, needed a relationship. She was more relaxed with him around, she felt less insecure, she didn't feel lonely. But she knew it wasn't him. Or

not enough of him to make her want to keep seeing him, even if
that were possible.

Wednesday morning of the second week saw Howard up early.
This was his own improvisation and Tanya slept through it. He
decided to be standing in the kitchen, in a bath towel having
breakfast. He had a good body and he wanted some of it on film.
Eric saw him first.

' 'Morning,' he said.

'Hi,' Howard replied. 'You look nice today.'

'What?'

'You look nice, your tie, it matches your eyes.'

'Right. I'm going to be late. Goodbye.' What a weirdo, Eric
thought as he walked out of the house.

Next to see him was David. 'Hi, you're up early,' David said,
although he had no idea what time he normally got up.

'I know, well it seems a shame to waste the day.'

'But Tanya doesn't normally get up for another hour,' David
protested.

'I left her sleeping. I wanted something to eat.'

'Right. Well I'll be off then,' David said. Howard thought
David was strange.

Leigh walked into the kitchen to get some cereal. 'Good
morning,' she said.

'I like your outfit,' Howard replied. Tanya had told him
about Leigh's thing for pink. Today she had pink jeans, pink
trainers, a pink belt and a pink T-shirt.

'Thanks,' Leigh replied, smiling tightly.

'So what are you doing today?' Howard asked.

'Working for a living. You should try it.' Howard gave her
his best crestfallen look.

Later, Tanya had to attend a progress meeting. Unsure of what
to do with Howard, she had left him at the house with strict

instructions to be quiet and not wake or upset Gus. Howard
obliged. He spent the day on the phone to his friends telling
them about Tanya, the big house in Fulham (he exaggerated a
bit), and his new clothes. When he had suitably impressed
everyone he knew, he tried on his new clothes. He couldn't
believe his luck. The other thing he was happy about was Tanya;
he was really enjoying himself. He went downstairs, creeping
quietly past Gus's room. In the sitting room he placed himself in
front of the Playstation where he stayed for the rest of the
afternoon.

'I'm really pleased with the progress now that we've got Howard,'
Harvey said. Millie took notes. This was what was known as the
first official editorial meeting. Millie knew that it wasn't the first
because there had been a couple of unofficial meetings already. At
the unofficial meetings, Harvey, Lucy and Cherry had discussed
other ideas for storylines. Again, Millie had been sworn to secrecy,
because Tanya was only aware of official meetings.

'Me too, I'm really pleased,' Tanya replied. Millie hid a
smirk, she wondered how long Tanya would remain happy.

'So, we've got this great storyline, but it'll be over on Friday.
We still have a lot more filming to do before we have a wrap.
Any ideas?' Harvey finished.

'I was thinking,' Lucy started, 'I was thinking that perhaps we
could expand the idea.'

'What do you mean?' Tanya asked.

'OK, now this is up to you Tanya, totally up to you. But I was
thinking that maybe *everyone* would benefit from a storyline.'
Lucy smiled, no one had any idea how Tanya would react. After
all, they had already discussed this, unknown to Tanya.

'What do you mean?' Tanya asked.

'Well I was thinking about things we could set up but they'd
still be ignorant that it is a storyline.'

'Oh I see. For example we could get a girl to chat up Gus, but
we would have arranged it,' Tanya said.

'Exactly.'

'No.'

'No?'

'Look, I think you might be on the right track. The film of my house isn't the most exciting viewing ever. So yeah, of course we need to give everyone else a storyline. But I am not letting them meet people then get hurt,' Tanya finished. Lucy and Harvey looked relieved.

'That's my girl,' Harvey said. Cherry shot him a look.

'I just want to say that this is against the initial idea. I said at the beginning that it wouldn't be interesting enough, if you remember, Harvey, but you stuck to your guns because you wanted to make a real film. But it's not real any more.' Tanya paused. 'I am having a pretend relationship with a guy who is so skint that he's going to pretend he's gay. He is also going to be acting in a film, which is his ambition but he won't be able to tell anyone he's acting. How real is all of this now? Not very.'

'OK Tanya, we know. I hold my hands up, I was wrong. I had a great idea and to an extent I was able to carry it through, but not to a big enough extent. Now I am admitting I was wrong and trying to save all our arses by rectifying the situation,' Harvey finished.

'I don't think we can blame Harvey. This was an experiment, for all of us and I think we'll not only come out of it with a hit film, because whatever stunts we pull, everyone will think it's real. Not only that but we'll also have discovered the secret of reality shows,' Cherry added. She didn't like to hear Harvey criticised.

'I'm sorry Harvey, you're both right. Now the thing is that if we do arrange some stuff, I want the final say over what we do,' Tanya said. Harvey nodded. 'Right, if we do arrange things, then when we reveal that everyone has been filmed, we have to make them think that everything that has happened to them would have happened anyway.'

'Will they believe *that*?' Lucy asked.

'Does it matter? If we stick to our stories that it is real, then they won't ever know for sure. After all Harvey, you said that that would be your marketing strategy.' Tanya made her point.

'Sure,' Harvey agreed. He couldn't believe it.

Tanya felt the guilt sitting on her shoulders. It had been there since the project started, but it became lighter and heavier. Now it sat heavily. Guilt permeated every area. She felt guilty for everything. For her housemates, for Harvey, for the film.

The reason she had agreed so quickly was that she wanted to be in control. The less they had to persuade her, the more in control she was. When it all came out into the open, when the final explosion came she wanted to know that she would walk out of it with a winner's job and a winner's new life to go to. She didn't want to be left amongst the debris.

'Shall we come up with a list of suggestions?' Lucy asked.

'I think so, I think that some storylines should be longer than others and I think that they should be staggered, I don't want a load of weirdness happening all at one time. I want the story development to be something that I do with Lucy and something we go through with you two. Is that agreed?' Tanya asked.

'Yes, Tanya, it is all agreed.'

'Thank you Harvey for putting your trust in me.'

'I always knew you'd be great and I've never been wrong about someone yet.'

Chapter Forty

'I don't want to have dinner with them,' Eric sulked, when Leigh told him of Tanya's request for a house meal on Friday.

'And I have plans,' Gus protested.

'I'll have to restrain myself from hitting him. Every time I see him I want to hit him,' David added. Even though his grounds for wanting to hit Howard were imaginary.

'Listen, we have to be here. Tanya is smitten by Howard and even if he is making a complete fool out of her then it is our job to help her. We can't try and tell her about him because she won't believe us. She'll think we're jealous and we'll end up hurting her. If he hurts her then we have to be around to pick up the pieces. That's what friends do,' Leigh said.

'LeeLee, that's really sweet of you, although I doubt that Tanya would stand by and keep her mouth shut,' Gus responded.

'That doesn't matter. Please do this. If you don't do it for Tanya, then do it for me, please.' Leigh had become such an expert at being sweet under Sukie's expert tuition.

'Of course, if you think it's best I'll cancel my plans,' Gus conceded and gave Leigh a hug.

'I'll be there, but I'm warning you, I might not be able to stop myself from hitting him,' David repeated. Eric and Gus laughed. The idea of David hitting anyone was absurd.

'I'll be right behind you. The bastard will not get away with it,' Eric concurred.

'Shall we calm down? After all, he hasn't actually done anything yet,' Gus pointed out.

'He has. He let her buy him all those clothes.' David was agitated.

'Let's just have this dinner and try to be nice around him. I find it really hard to believe that Tanya is being so gullible,' Gus finished.

'Most women are gullible when it comes to men,' Leigh said with a sigh.

'This is great, it's unbelievable.' Tanya laughed as she watched her housemates' discussion on screen.

'Don't you feel bad?' Howard asked.

'Bad about what?'

'Well, them. I mean you said they were all weird and boring and they didn't care about you, But they obviously do. Ever since I came on the scene they've been worried about you.'

'Oh don't be taken in by that. They're just like a bunch of old women and that's why they're making a drama out of us. Before you came here, they all ignored me. Do you know I spent a month of evenings alone in the sitting room or alone here, they didn't make any effort with me? And this display of loyalty to me is all a load of old bollocks.' Tanya's face was red and her voice raised.

'All right, sorry. It's just that I thought . . .'

'You're not paid to think,' Tanya snapped, then immediately regretted it.

'Tanya I'm glad it's all over tomorrow night. I've enjoyed myself, I've enjoyed your company and I've enjoyed the sex. But even though I'm young and not that intelligent, I don't enjoy being treated like a male prostitute, because that isn't why I slept with you and if you only slept with me because you paid for me, then that makes me sad.'

'Oh shit, I'm so sorry Howard, I didn't mean it. You're right, you're right about everything. I do feel bad, and I'm angry with them and I'm confused. Now Harvey wants me to make storylines up for them and I agreed.' Tanya stood up and started pacing. 'When Harvey came into my life, I couldn't believe it. It was a dream come true; it was like a miracle. Then he told me what he wanted to do and I said yes almost straight away. I tried to think about it, but I couldn't, because I knew that if I thought too much then I would be forced by my conscience to say no. So I said yes before my conscience could kick in, and then I felt guilty but I pushed it aside.' She stopped pacing and looked at Howard. All he could do was nod. 'I became good at justifying things. This was my big chance. If I didn't do it then I knew I'd never get into films. Because Harvey wanted my housemates, I got my dream.' She sat down on the bed again. 'Ambition. That's what it's all about. My ambition. Really it's bigger than every-thing. It's the biggest thing.' Tears were pouring down Tanya's face; Howard was listening to the confession with his mouth wide open. 'Then there was all that business with Natasha. I told them I had second thoughts and they said fine but that would be the end of my working with them. I know that this makes me a terrible person and I don't understand, I don't.' She brushed a tear from her cheek. 'But I am going to do it and I am going to manipulate. I'm nearly twenty-seven and I need more from my life, I need to be a success.'

Howard leaned in and put his arms around Tanya. She gave in to his warm embrace. For the moment Howard was there to keep her propped up. He was doing far more than he had ever been paid for.

Tanya was back to her usual self by Friday. Howard packed his new clothes into bags, ready for his dramatic departure later on. He had made love to Tanya for the last time. The sex was great. Neither of them wanted a relationship, but they did acknowledge a bond.

'Are you ready?' she asked Howard.

'As I'll ever be.'

'Break a leg,' she teased. They gave each other a last hug before they went downstairs.

Tanya had asked everyone to be in the sitting room by seven that evening. With the exception of Gus, who was running late and was in the shower, everyone was there when Tanya and Howard walked in. Their first job was to set the scene. So far their public appearances had consisted of them being as physically close as was possible. On this occasion, Howard had to start by putting some distance between them. Tanya sat down on the sofa next to Leigh and patted the space beside her while looking at Howard. Howard ignored her and sat on the floor so he was facing Eric on the beanbag. Tanya scowled, eyebrows were raised. Howard looked at Eric then at the floor. He repeated this several times.

'The reason I said seven was that I wanted to order the curry now,' Tanya said.

'I know what Gus wants, so we can,' Leigh replied. They then spent the next ten minutes arguing about which curry house they would use. Once that was settled (Tanya overruled Eric), Leigh took out a pad and pen and wrote down everyone's orders. The whole process was long and painful.

'Howard, help me set the table.' Tanya jumped up.

Howard shot her an obvious dirty look before getting up slowly and following her from the room.

'This was a bad idea,' David said.

'Shush,' Leigh chastised.

'He is making me feel uncomfortable,' Eric sulked.

'What?'

'Well he keeps looking at me,' Eric explained.

'I hadn't noticed,' Leigh said.

'Me either.'

'Well watch him when he comes back, he keeps looking at me.' Eric folded his arms defiantly.

'They don't seem to be very together,' David said.

'And if it weren't for the fact he keeps looking at me, I'd say that was a good thing,' Eric sulked.

When they returned, Leigh and David noticed that Howard did spend a lot of time looking at Eric. By the time Gus joined them, they were all feeling a little unsettled. It was like waiting for things to happen, but having no idea what you were waiting for.

'Give me a beer, I've had such a shitty day,' Gus said when he sat down next to Leigh. He took her hand. 'Did you order my food baby?'

'Of course I did.' Leigh blushed and giggled.

'Well I hope the food hurries up, I'm starving,' Eric said.

'Poor thing,' Howard said. Everyone looked at him. 'Eric, would you like me to call them and ask when they'll be here?' he offered.

'No thanks,' Eric replied.

'If you're sure.' Howard winked at Eric. A wink that was not missed by anyone. Eric bristled.

Tanya and Howard had rehearsed the scene for most of the day.

Eric looked at David, who shrugged. The delivery boy ringing the doorbell saved them. Eric jumped up to open it, unfortunately so did Howard. Eric shot him a dirty look as he opened the door, but Howard just smiled and stood as close to Eric as he could. Eric grabbed the six brown paper bags from the startled delivery boy and sprinted back into the sitting room. Tanya paid for the food.

Everyone sat at the table; Tanya took charge of unpacking the food. She looked at Howard; it was his cue.

'Eric, tell me about your job?'

'What?' Eric had started eating and had a mouth full of food.

'Tell us about acting,' Leigh interjected, suddenly pleased she had thought of a distraction.

'All my life I've wanted to act, but it's so hard. I've auditioned for everything from bit parts in telly programmes to awful commercials. Sometimes I think I'll never get any work and it breaks my heart.' Howard was pleased for the chance to gain public sympathy.

Tanya got up from the table and walked to Howard's seat. She leaned down to kiss him but he pulled away. 'You'll make it,' she said.

'What do *you* know?' Howard replied, angrily. 'You've got a successful career. I've got nothing. It's people like you that make my life so fucking difficult.' Tanya physically recoiled from his words and went to sit down in front of her full plate.

'That's not fair,' Tanya said.

'Isn't it? At least Eric does some good in his work.'

'What's the fascination with Eric?' Tanya shouted. Eric stared at his empty plate willing it to fill up again and offer him a distraction. He had no idea why he was in the middle of all this.

It was time for the dramatic announcement. As rehearsed, Howard would admit to everyone his confusion over his sexuality and his attraction to Eric. Silence ensued around the table. Tanya was preparing herself to react to Howard's news. Everyone else looked at their plates and concentrated on their food. No one had any idea what was going on, but whatever it was, they were not comfortable with it.

Howard knew that the time had arrived. All he had to do was to say he was gay, say he fancied Eric and then his part would be over. Just a few minutes more.

'I . . .' he faltered. He looked at Tanya who was trying to maintain her hurt look but appeared to be growing impatient. He looked around the table at everyone who seemed to be staring straight at him. He thought about the film, its release, him being known. Finally. All he had to do was say three words and his performance would be over. 'I . . .' He faltered again. He couldn't do it. He wasn't playing a part; he was himself. He would have to live with the consequences. He would have to deal with the fallout. In that instant, he knew that there was no way he could go through with it.

Tanya was impatient. She had directed the scene perfectly up until now. Then it had slipped away. Howard had slipped away. She needed to bring him back into line.

'Howard, what exactly is it you're trying to say?' she demanded.

'I . . . well, I . . . It's hard.' Howard was genuinely crestfallen. He didn't know how to get out of the situation; he decided to improvise.

'It has something to do with Eric?' Tanya prompted.

'What?' Eric asked.

'No. Nothing to do with Eric.' Howard looked at his feet.

Tanya felt herself turn hot, then cold. What was going on?

'But you haven't stopped talking about Eric all night,' she pushed.

'Really?' Howard said. He was desperately trying to buy some time. Eric began to feel slightly better. Whatever was going on he now knew was not about him.

'Yes fucking really,' Tanya replied.

'This has nothing to do with Eric,' Howard almost whispered. Tanya turned red.

'What?' she asked.

'Tanya, this is between the two of us. There isn't anyone else involved. Why can't you accept that?'

'Because . . . I don't understand.' Tanya really didn't understand but she wanted to kill Howard. How dare he mess around with her film?

'Look Tanya, I didn't want this to be a public thing, but you haven't given me any choice. I can't be with you anymore. You scare me, you boss me around, you don't listen to my feelings, and you don't want to discuss things. You just want me for sex.' His improvisation was going well.

'And you don't like having sex with me because you don't like girls?' Tanya was desperately grasping at straws. Everyone let out an audible gasp.

'You mean you're gay?' Eric practically screamed.

'No I am not.'

'Yes you are,' Tanya said, then cringed inwardly. It was all going horribly wrong.

'I am not gay. I think I'd know if I was gay or not wouldn't I?'

'So, what is it?' Tanya was panicking. How could she regain control of the scene? She had no idea.

'I told you. You scare me . . .' Howard stopped. He hadn't thought about the trouble he might be in. Harvey wouldn't be happy about his diversion from the script. He couldn't afford to alienate him. He couldn't pretend to be gay, not under the circumstances, but he could give them some drama. If he gave them good drama, then maybe Harvey wouldn't ruin his career.

'No, it's not that. You are scary, but it's just that I can't do this anymore. Tanya, I don't fancy you, I never did. I met you and you said you might be able to help with my career, I wanted that more than anything so I let you seduce me. I let you bring me here because it's far nicer than my bedsit and I let you spend money on me. Don't you see I was using you? Using you for all I could get. So, I'm a bastard but you offered it on a plate and I wasn't in a position to refuse. The thing is that I've had enough. Christ, Tanya, don't you see, I don't fucking well want you.'

Everyone was stunned. No-one more than Tanya.

'Because you like men?' she reiterated. If he was not going to say it himself, she would have to make him say it.

'No, I don't. Christ you are so vain. You think just because I don't want you, that means I'm gay. Well I'm not. I'm straight and I love women, I adore women. Just not you.'

'You tosser. You bastard tosser. How could you? How dare you? Only the worst kind of man could use someone like that. I really liked you, I can't believe that you did that to me.' With that Tanya returned to the script, grabbed her full plate of chicken Korma (ordered specially for the event), and jumped up from the table to empty it over Howard's head.

'You tosser,' she screamed one last time, before Howard left the room, dripping in Korma.

Tanya burst into tears. She eased herself into her seat and wept, really wept. Her whole body shook. She was crying because the scene had gone wrong and she thought Harvey would be furious. She cried because she felt bad for Howard. She cried because she was on her own again. Everyone just watched, unsure what to do.

David was the first person to mobilise. As they heard Howard coming back down the stairs, he jumped up, ran out of the room and marched up to Howard, now minus the Korma.

'You shit. You fucking little shit. She didn't deserve to be used by you, and I will not stand by while you hurt her.' David was standing only inches from Howard. He pulled his arm back and then whacked his fist as hard as he could into Howard's face. Howard reeled under the blow before finally regaining his balance.

Leigh gasped. Gus rushed forward to see if Howard was all right (it was the doctor in him); Tanya looked horrified. Eric was still in his seat, staring at his food.

Howard managed to shake Gus off, picked up his bags and left the house. David had whacked his eye, which would be swollen and black in a few hours, but luckily there was no blood. As he walked unsteadily out of the door, everyone looked at David.

'My hero,' Leigh said as she hugged him, noting that David looked considerably more shaken than anyone else – bar Eric.

'That was some punch,' Gus said. Gus was torn between wanting to go after Howard and staying loyal to his housemates.

'Right,' David replied and he went back to the dining table where he sat down again.

Tanya rushed over to him, threw her arms around him and kissed his cheek. 'David, that's the nicest thing anyone has ever done for me,' she said.

'I wish I'd punched the bastard,' Eric said.

'He'll be fine. He was a wanker after all,' Leigh reassured.

Why was she crying so hard? Leigh pulled her chair close to Tanya and put her arms around her. She held her; she hugged her.

Not knowing what else to do, they persuaded Tanya to get

some sleep. They all followed shortly afterwards having tried, but failed, to make sense of the evening.

Bob and Amanda stared open-mouthed at the screen.

'I better call Harvey.' Bob went to the phone.

'Make sure he gets Howard to a doctor. He could have concussion or anything,' Amanda pointed out.

'After the way Howard screwed with the scene, I'm not sure Harvey will care.'

'I can't blame him for changing his mind,' Amanda said.

'To be honest, neither can I. And I guess it was quite dramatic.'

'If not a bit confusing. First of all he flirts with Eric, then completely changes tack. We'll need to edit it.'

'That is what we're here for.'

Harvey took the news with his usual calm.

'That's what happens when you make this type of movie.'

'Sure, but we didn't get the gay boyfriend.'

'But you say it was dramatic and David hit him, so it can't be all bad.'

'No, and it's funny how Tanya keeps going on about him being gay.'

'Bring the footage home. In the meantime I'll arrange for the car to take Howard to casualty and I'll get Lucy to meet him there.'

Later, Harvey and Cherry watched the footage together.

'Shit,' Harvey said once the tape had finished.

'It didn't go according to plan,' Cherry pointed out.

'Some things never do, especially with this movie.'

'You think it's OK?'

'I think it's great. I love the way Tanya tried to persuade him he was gay. I loved that David hit him. I loved Tanya's tears, geez, I've never seen tears like that. Cherry honey, I think it's fine.'

'But what about Tanya? Her tears looked real to me. What if she's not OK?'

'Call her in the morning and check she's fine. Tell her we love the footage, she might be worried about that. But tonight has proved me right. It's brilliant. I can't have her screwing up now.'

Chapter Forty-One

When Tanya woke up she didn't need a mirror to tell her that her eyes were swollen and red. Her head was filled with spikes. She got up and went to the bathroom. The house was silent. Doors were closed.

Tanya showered, dressed, drank a litre of water and went back to her room. She knew she had to watch the footage. As she saw the events unfold, she realised the way her memory had recorded events and the way that they had actually happened were quite different. Suddenly, everything clicked into place. This stuff was great; this was the kind of dramatic footage she craved. And it had its moments of comedy. Even though it wasn't what they'd planned.

Her mobile rang. 'Hello.'

'Tanya, it's Cherry. You OK?'

'Never been better,' Tanya replied. Cherry thought that she sounded unnaturally cheerful.

'But last night . . .'

'Is Harvey angry?'

'No, honey he's really pleased, but we were worried about you. You seemed a little upset.' Cherry was the master of understatement.

'Oh the tears. I suppose there were a lot of them. But tell Harvey not to worry, tell him my catharsis was long overdue. Can you arrange a meeting today? I want to meet with you all.'

'Right. I'll set it up' Cherry said.

'Harvey, I've spoken to Tanya.'
   'What did she say?'
   'She asked if you were angry. I told her you weren't great she said she had freed herself from guilt or something and she would ensure that this film is the best thing ever.'
   'No kidding?' Harvey smiled.
   'She wants a meeting today. Shall I set it up?'
   'Go ahead.'

The meeting was arranged quickly. They were waiting for Lucy.
   'Why did it take you so long to get here?' Tanya asked, when Lucy, who looked a little worse for wear, turned up.
   'I was in bed when I got the call. Tanya, this part you don't know, after the fight, Harvey called me and as everyone seems to have decided that I am responsible for storylines I had to go and meet Howard in casualty. So I spent half the night there while he told me everything that happened and how wonderful his improvisation was. Then I had to take him home, because he didn't want to be alone, where we proceeded to drink an entire bottle of rather good brandy while he told me the whole story again.' Lucy was in a foul mood.
   'Sorry,' Tanya said.
   'So what's the urgency? Why the meeting?'
   'Right. Well I think that last night was brilliant. It was wonderful. It couldn't have been better. So I thought that, as we have so little time left we better get the rest organised,' Tanya suggested.
   'I think you're right. Last night's footage was great. So now we need the others to have their own storylines, then that will give the film enough structure. That's all we need.' Harvey smiled. 'But, whatever we do has to be in the realms of plausibility.'
   'Sure, that won't be a problem.' Lucy was scribbling furiously.

'OK. So we want four storylines for four disparate characters – get on it right away, Lucy.'

'Can we get back to the point at hand,' Tanya asked.

'I have a few ideas,' Lucy started. 'How about I run them past you and we'll see what develops?' Everyone nodded. 'First we have David. He is obsessed with this girl he's never met, so his storyline should naturally revolve around that. Gus is totally focused on falling in love so I think he needs to be put off romance a bit, I thought maybe a stalker or something, after all as a good-looking doctor he's the perfect candidate to be stalked. Eric is our comedy element, so his story should make use of that fact. Finally Leigh. Leigh needs a big kick up the arse to get her over Gus, but she also needs an ego boost. So she should get some male attention, an admirer or something.' Lucy stopped abruptly, slightly breathless in her excitement.

'I am not letting you hire someone to pretend to fall in love with Leigh,' Tanya stormed.

'That isn't necessarily what I meant. As I said, these are just outlines, I haven't worked out the details yet.' Lucy laughed.

'In that case, I think you and Tanya should sit down after this meeting and do a full synopsis of each idea. That can include who we need to hire and anything else we need to do, so that we can get going on Monday,' Harvey ordered.

Tanya and Lucy spent the rest of the day planning. When Tanya returned home she was so fired up about the future production that she had almost forgotten the past. When she walked into the sitting room and saw everyone there she smiled broadly.

'Tanya,' Leigh shouted jumping up. 'We've been worried sick about you.'

'Why?' Tanya asked.

'Howard of course,' Leigh continued. Tanya looked stricken. She was stricken. How could she have been so stupid?

'I don't want to talk about it,' she snapped.

'But . . .' Leigh started.

'LeeLee, please. I've been through enough humiliation to last me a lifetime. I don't need to spell it out.'

'We were just worried about you,' Eric said.

'I know. I want to thank you guys for the support. David, you were great, and I'm just sorry that you had to hit him. I'm sorry to all of you, but please, I really need to put it all behind me now.' She smiled, a little tragically.

'Where were you today?' Leigh asked.

'I spent the day with a friend.' Tanya sat down.

Lucy spent Saturday night with her computer. She was a little annoyed by the fact that her latest job seemed to be taking over her life. First she had to baby-sit Howard, then spend Saturday working. Although for the money she was being paid she ought not complain. She found to her surprise that she really did like Tanya. She enjoyed her company, she found her enthusiasm and energy inspiring, especially now.

Lucy spent the evening typing up the ideas ready to e-mail to Harvey. Tanya and Lucy had decided in the end that in the manner of the project, in *honour* of the project, they would push start each story, but allow it to build up momentum on its own.

The theory of this was best explained with the example of David. They were going to find out who or *what* Em was. How many females on the Internet were actually guys? They decided that by taking this simple step there would be a whole sequence of events that would follow. Whatever happened, there was a story there. A true story, that needed only the minimum manipulation. That was what they wanted. Lucy liked to believe in fate, she believed that some things were going to happen regardless of people's actions. Tanya *didn't* believe in fate. Things happened because you made them happen. They were now setting things in motion, but also leaving fate or whatever it was called to do some work as well.

When Lucy finished writing the ideas, she e-mailed them straight to Harvey and copied Tanya.

Chapter Forty-Two

Harvey, Cherry and Bob read through the proposal and agreed it. The first task they had was to find an Internet expert, so that they could set David's contribution in motion.

The storylines weren't overly dramatic, and there was scope for improvisation. Moreover, as Lucy perceived correctly, the cast were the sort of people that liked to over-dramatise everything; which the Howard situation proved.

Tanya was doing everyone a favour. The storylines that Lucy and she had created proved that. David needed a push or he needed to end his fictional romance, because that is what she thought it was: fictional. Leigh needed an ego boost which is what the pretend secret admirer would provide. Gus needed a stalker, although the justification for that was a bit woolly, Tanya believed that it might push him into Leigh's waiting arms. And Eric needed prizes. He would love his prizes. Not only was she making a film which would be wonderful, but she was making her friends' lives better. She was trying desperately to believe that this was true.

Tanya watched David go into the shower on Sunday morning and sneaked into his room. His computer gleamed at her as soon as she entered. She sat down at his desk and looked at the screen. Looking back at her was a grinning Britney Spears. She nudged the mouse and Britney the screensaver disappeared. She clicked on e-mail inbox icon and up it popped.

It only took a matter of seconds for her to find Em's e-mail address; she scribbled it down quickly and left the room silently.

When she was back in the safety of her room she breathed a sigh of relief. She knew she would have made a rotten spy. She quickly e-mailed the address to Harvey, and knew that all they needed to do now was wait.

On Monday they started the search for Em. On Tuesday they found her. A contact of James's had been able to trace her details. Although the public was constantly being told how secure the Internet was, the truth was it wasn't *that* secure. They had found out the following information:

Name: *Emily Stratton*
Age: *Thirty-one*
Occupation: *Publican*
Address: *The Flying Fox, Putney High Street, Putney.*

When Bob revealed the information, Tanya and Lucy were sitting in the office along with Harvey and Cherry.

'Christ, she's a publican. David will be pleased,' Tanya said.

'She's young enough and obviously a she,' Cherry added.

'But we don't know much do we?' Lucy pointed out.

'We know enough. Anyway you and Tanya can go and fill in the blanks tonight,' Harvey replied.

'What you mean, go to her pub?'

'Yes, go and ask questions. Make it look like you're interested customers. Use your imagination Lucy.' Harvey smiled.

'Excellent, it will be like spying.' Lucy had called the housemates dramatic, but it was also one of her main traits.

'What happens if she and David do get it together and she recognises me and says I was in her pub asking loads of questions?' Tanya asked.

'If she does, say it was a coincidence, it's a pub Tanya and a pub not a million miles away from where you live. It's hardly that surprising that you would be there.' Harvey was exasperated. He wanted them to get on with things.

'You're right. OK, let's go. Harvey are you disappointed that she's not a man?' Tanya asked.

'I wouldn't jump to any conclusions if I was you.'

Tanya and Lucy took a cab from Knightsbridge straight to Putney. They had spent most of the day discussing all the story requirements with Harvey and Cherry. Harvey, who hated details, asked Millie to take charge of the details for all the other plots. Tanya tried to protest, she didn't have enough faith in Millie to give her such responsibility, but Cherry wouldn't hear of it. Cherry seemed to believe that Millie was the golden child.

'How should we play this?' Tanya asked, as she sat in a taxi with Lucy. She took out her lipstick and applied it.

'Let me ask the questions. That way, if there is any possibility that she remembers you it will be me who was nosy. If we don't find out anything much, then we'll need a plan B. Maybe we'll have to be regulars. Anyway, let's play it by ear. Now, what do we need to know?' Lucy grabbed the lipstick off her and used it.

'We need to ask her if she has a boyfriend, we need to know that.'

'And if she does?'

'Then we'll write her a letter telling her we know the truth and if she doesn't tell David then we will.' Tanya had already decided that Emily was cheating on her boyfriend with David, in a kind of cyber-cheating way.

'So we find out about her love life. But Tanya, leave it to me. You can't storm in like a bull in a china shop.'

'Fine.' Tanya sulked. She was trying hard to believe that she was giving David a helping hand, but she couldn't help feeling that all she was doing was meddling.

The taxi driver pulled up outside the pub. It was a large modern pub. It had the name of a traditional pub but the look of a trendy bar. As Tanya and Lucy got out of the taxi they were both staring at it as if it would offer answers.

It was relatively empty; it was early. Tanya followed Lucy as she walked up to the bar confidently. Behind the bar were a man and a woman. The man was young, he looked as if he was just reaching twenty. The woman looked several years older.

'What can I get you?' she asked as she walked over to where Lucy and Tanya had settled.

'Two glasses of red wine please,' Lucy replied, smiling. They both turned their backs to the bar.

'How do we know if it's her?' Tanya whispered.

'Let's keep quiet, we'll hear them talking.' They turned back to the bar.

'Gary, can you collect some glasses?' the girl asked.

'Sure Michelle.' This was not their woman.

Lucy lit a cigarette and Tanya grabbed one. They looked around them and at each other but they didn't speak because they were too scared of missing something. After about fifteen minutes another woman emerged from the back of the pub. She looked about the right age; she had blonde hair which fell around her face; she had pale skin and big blue eyes. She also looked as if she was very, *very* pregnant. Tanya and Lucy spun round again.

'Shit, what if that's her?' Tanya hissed, the idea was one she was unable to contemplate.

'How long have they been having this romance?' Lucy asked.

'I have no idea, why?'

'I was wondering if you could get pregnant from cyber sex.' Lucy giggled. They turned back to the bar.

Lucy had grown bored of the subtle approach. Although the pregnant woman was chatting to Michelle, they still didn't know her name. 'Excuse me,' Lucy said. Both female bar staff looked round. 'Excuse me, but would it be possible to speak to the manager?' Lucy asked.

'I'm the manager.' The pregnant woman stepped nearer to them.

'Hi, I'm Lucy and that's Tanya.'

'Hello,' the pregnant manager said. 'I'm Emily.' Bingo! A chill ran down Tanya's spine. Why would a woman refuse to meet the man she had been e-mailing? If she thought he was a weirdo; which she obviously didn't because, according to David, they were soulmates. If she was hideously ugly; which Emily clearly wasn't. Or if she was about to pop another man's child out of her loins. Tanya grabbed hold of the bar to steady herself. She felt sick. Lucy, however was completely composed.

'Wow, you don't look old enough to manage a pub,' Lucy told her. Tanya groaned inwardly. David was in love with a pregnant woman. How on earth could that have happened?

'What can I do for you?' Emily was obviously not the type to take any nonsense.

'I wondered if you might have any work going?' Lucy asked. Tanya felt her senses return and shot her a look. Lucy's improvisations were making her nervous. At this rate Lucy would be a barmaid before they had got what they wanted.

'I'm sorry, but no vacancies.' Emily smiled for the first time. Tanya decided she was pretty. *She was pregnant*, her head screamed.

'Oh that's a shame, I really like it here,' Lucy replied, 'and, well no offence, but I guess you can't work much at the moment. It can't be a healthy atmosphere for a pregnant woman.' Lucy smiled and Tanya flinched.

'I know, it worries me a bit, but the thing is I do have a lot of staff, these guys here will be joined by reinforcements by the time we get busy. I usually only work when I have to.' She smiled again. Tanya couldn't believe that she wasn't offended.

'It must be hard work.' Lucy's voice dripped with sympathy. Tanya flinched again. She was hardly the subtle type herself but Lucy was a sledgehammer, a double sledgehammer.

'It's because I am terrible at letting go. I generally keep an eye on things, which must drive everyone mad because I'm sure I'm more a hindrance than a help.' She laughed. Tanya was surprised by her openness, but then Lucy had that effect on people.

'Do you own this place?' Tanya asked, finally finding a voice.

'No, I lease it.'

'When are you due?' Lucy asked. She had a way of looking at people which ensured that they didn't mind her questions. She had a quality which made her appear unintrusive, when she was precisely the opposite.

'Two months, although I look like it could be any minute. Then, as it's my first, they say it might be late. Imagine, I might get even bigger, it's terrifying.'

'Does your partner work here too?' Lucy asked. Tanya kicked her lightly but Lucy didn't bat an eyelid. Lucy was on a mission, and frankly she found Tanya was most unhelpful.

'I don't have a partner. Before you ask, the baby's father is a man who no longer wants anything to do with me. So, I'm going to boost the single parent statistics.' When she said this, there was an edge of bitterness in her voice, tinged with a control which told everyone around that, whatever happened, Emily would cope.

'I'm sorry,' Lucy responded as Emily, with no prompting, pulled a bottle of red wine from behind the bar, took three glasses and invited them to sit down and have a drink with her. The other barmaid looked surprised, but not as surprised as Tanya. Lucy, however, acted as if this was exactly what she expected.

'We'd love to, Emily.' Lucy smiled and shot Tanya a look. 'Can you not make more of an effort?' she hissed. Tanya shrugged, how could she make an effort under the circumstances?

They sat around a large wooden table as Emily poured out drinks. 'I've been told by my doctor that I'm allowed the odd glass of red wine and I bloody well believe him.' They discussed pregnancy. Emily furnished them with details of morning sickness, getting fat, cravings and scans. Tanya felt a little sick herself.

'It must be hard, going through it on your own,' Tanya said, finally.

'It is, but I have friends who help me out, and well, there is someone special in my life.'

'Who?' Lucy asked.

'You see I use the Internet a lot and I met someone though a chat room, well, I was lonely when I first found out about the baby. I can't believe I'm telling you this. Anyway this guy turned out to be so wonderful and I could talk to him about anything.

And he could do the same with me. The thing is, I didn't realise how strong the bond could be. He wants us to think about meeting but look at me. I haven't told him about the baby, of course I haven't. I talked to him about everything except the baby. I mean he would have stopped mailing me straight away. You see he's a bit younger than me.' Emily looked sad. Lucy nudged Tanya in the ribs.

'Ow.'

'What Tanya meant to say is that she has a friend who is a real Internet fiend,' Lucy prompted.

'Yeah, he is, and funnily enough he's having an e-mail relationship pretty much like the one you described. Although I think he has cyber sex.' Tanya smiled. Lucy scowled. Tanya realised she shouldn't have mentioned the sex.

'Really? No, it would be too weird, far too weird. I mean it would be a massive coincidence wouldn't it?'

'He's called David Munroe,' Tanya blurted out. Emily turned white. Lucy thought the shock might send her into labour. She scowled at Tanya again. Tanya had become even less subtle than she was.

'My God,' Emily said.

'Are you OK?' Lucy asked.

'He's called DavidM. It *can't* be the same guy.'

'Emily,' Tanya said softly. 'What name do you use?'

'Em.'

'It is you,' Tanya whispered. Although they already knew it was.

'Shit,' Emily said. 'Shit, shit, shit. It can't be him. It just can't.'

'OK, tell me something you know about David,' Lucy coaxed.

'Is this some sick joke?' Emily asked.

'What?' Tanya asked, thinking the same thing.

'He is all I've got, and now you come in here and claim to know him. I know, his cousin is called Leigh.'

'Leigh's my best friend,' Tanya whispered. She suddenly felt desperately sorry for Emily.

'Oh no, this can't be happening.' Emily had abandoned her drink and her head was in her hands.

'Why?' Tanya asked.

'Because you'll tell him and I'll lose him. I don't think you understand how much I need him.'

'But Emily, do you honestly think that you can keep up this relationship with him for ever? At some point he'll want to meet you. Don't you think it's worth risking the likelihood that he won't run away?' Lucy asked.

'I've known David my whole life. He isn't shallow. But you have to make him understand. He'll be hurt that you lied to him,' Tanya explained.

'I can't tell him. But I can't lose him either.'

'Emily, do you believe in fate?' Lucy asked. Emily nodded. 'Well then don't you think this is fate? I come in asking for a job, Tanya was with me and she turned out to be living with David who you've been communicating with by e-mail. All this happened for a reason, and I think that it's a sign that you should come clean once and for all with David.' Tanya had to concede that Lucy was good. Bloody good!

'How should I do it?' Emily's eyes filled with tears

'E-mail. Emily, tell him the whole story, don't say you met me, but tell him everything and tell him you want to meet. Tell him you hated lying to him but you were terrified of losing him. It's time for honesty.' Lucy patted her hand. They had almost finished the bottle of wine. Lucy felt that her job had been done. She had the story she wanted. It was time to leave. 'We have to go Emily, but please think about what we've said, and don't worry, Tanya won't say anything to David. That's your job.' As Tanya and Lucy stood up, Emily smiled, weakly

'It will be fine?' she asked.

Tanya nodded. 'He doesn't have to know about us meeting unless you want him to.' Lucy gave Emily a hug. Her bump was so large that she was unable to get her arms fully around. They left.

Tanya wanted to walk home. 'I can't believe she's pregnant. What is David going to do?'

'I was going to ask you that?'

'I don't know, he is in love with her. Or he's in love with the e-mail version of her. David is very protective, very honourable, there is always the chance that he'll see her as someone who needs taking care of, and he'll want to take care of her. I don't know if that's a good thing or not. What troubles me is whether he is in love with her or his own version of her and she with him.'

'I know, but I don't want to see David hurt. Mind you I guess this would have come out at some point.'

'Exactly. I'm going to call Harvey. Do you think he'll be disappointed?'

'No.'

'Yeah but it's a shame that she didn't get pregnant as the result of cyber sex, imagine that!' Lucy exclaimed.

'Lucy, you are totally insane,' Tanya snapped. She was just getting over the shock and now the enormity of the situation was beginning to sink in.

'Oh well. Listen I better hail a cab when we get near your place, I don't want to come in.'

'Why not?'

'I don't think it's a good idea for me to meet your housemates face to face. I need to maintain some professional distance.'

'Fine,' Tanya replied. Lucy was definitely something else. 'Tomorrow we'll work out how we fit the other stories into the framework.'

'Call me.' Tanya kissed Lucy's cheek and left her waiting for a cab.

Lucy called Harvey from the cab. When she explained fully what had happened when they met Emily Stratton, Harvey was delighted. 'I don't know what he'll do, but Tanya seems to think he might really go through with it.'

'What marry her?' Harvey asked.

'Who knows? Apparently he's totally smitten and he's an honourable sort of bloke, but imagine being faced with the decision that the woman you think you're in love with, but have never met, is eight months pregnant with another man's child. It scares me.'

'But he would have found out at some point,' Harvey said.

'I know. We haven't actually done anything except speed it up, hopefully. I just hope we've done the right thing.'

'As if we ever know what the right thing is.' Harvey hung up.

He walked into the sitting room where Cherry was watching television. Bob was still at the editing suite.

'Lucy called,' he said.

'So what happened?' Cherry asked, turning away from her programme. The film had taken over from her love for reality television. It was far more exciting. As Harvey explained the Emily situation, Cherry turned pale.

'Poor David,' she said.

'Maybe, or maybe not. After all she's still the person he fell for, she just isn't quite what he is expecting.'

'But can you imagine the complex feelings this will trigger in him? He is such a nice guy.' Cherry felt like crying, although she wasn't sure why. Harvey couldn't believe that Cherry was this upset for a man she'd never met.

'Well it is good for the story,' Harvey stated.

'Harvey, for one minute, fuck the story. This guy's life is about to be turned upside down. How on earth would you cope in his situation?'

'Cherry, listen to me. We didn't do this. We didn't arrange for him to fall in love with a pregnant woman. All we did was to intervene slightly. Like we did with Gus and Natasha.'

'Well maybe in this case we shouldn't have done. I can't help thinking that it wasn't the right thing to do.'

'As if we ever know what the right thing is,' Harvey replied, wearily, using the line a second time.

Harvey and Cherry never argued. Or Cherry never argued with Harvey. But as she sat on the sofa, thinking about David, poor, poor David, she wanted to lash out. Everything seemed wrong. Life was complicated enough and here they were playing with it. Life should never be played with. She had supported him, wholeheartedly, ever since she had first met him, but she didn't know if she could now. The justification for what they were doing was fading, and she shuddered as she knew that this was just the beginning. Fear trickled through her. The poor, unsuspecting people. Because that was what they were, they were just people.

Harvey could almost read her thoughts, he could almost feel them. The one person who had always been there for him was Cherry. His confidence, or arrogance, depended on her. He depended on her. It was his one weakness, or his most prominent one. If Cherry didn't *support* him, if he *lost* her. Fear trickled through him. He could never lose her.

'Cherry, if you want us to stop we will. I can't do this without you. I can't do anything without you.' He looked at her and tried to see into her. If he could understand, then he would fix it. But as he said, he really had no idea what the right thing was.

'Harvey, we've come too far, I know that. But I'm scared. I'm scared for them. I've never met them but they're like my favourite characters. I love them. I love Leigh who I just want to hug all the time, I love Gus for his romanticism, I love Eric because he makes me laugh and I love David. Serious David. As characters I care what happens to them. Don't you see? They're not real to me, they're like a soap opera, and I need them to have a happy ending. I need that.' Tears ran down her cheeks.

'Then we'll make sure they do. We'll give them happy endings.'

'But who are we to do that?'

'Honey I have no idea. But we have to. We've come too far.' As Harvey scooped Cherry into his arms, he began to have doubts. He acknowledged that he should have had them sooner perhaps, he should have thought about consequences. However he didn't, because when you are an ideas man you don't. If you thought about consequences then ideas would be cut dead. He actually felt ashamed. He looked at Cherry's face, her tears looked like diamonds, he wanted to tell her he loved her. He wanted to take her in his arms and tell her that everything would always be all right. Even if he didn't know that it would. But he couldn't. The problem with being seen as a manipulator was that it was difficult for your actions to be seen as genuine. And Harvey would never hurt Cherry, he would only tell her he loved her when he was sure he was telling her for the right reasons. The way the darkness arrived so suddenly in London, darkness entered his head. Harvey Cannon was confused.

Everyone was at home when Tanya walked through the door. Eric and David were in the sitting room; Gus and Leigh were in the kitchen. Tanya wondered if they were two divided camps. Having given up long ago trying to penetrate the conversations between Gus and Leigh, she went to join Eric and David.

'Hi,' David said, he smiled at her tenderly.

'Hey,' she replied and went over to ruffle his hair.

'Where have you been?' Eric asked.

'Just out with a friend,' she replied, and she took a deep breath. 'No Internet tonight?'

'You know I only talk to Em late on. I don't know what she does but she works most evenings.'

'Hey, maybe she's a stripper,' Eric suggested, his face lighting up with the suggestion. David laughed.

'No way. There is no way. If she was then she'd have told me. I think she would. She doesn't keep secrets.'

'But you don't know her job?' Eric questioned.

'As I said, I know she works most nights. I think she's a waitress. I didn't really feel I needed to know and she didn't tell me.'

'Does she know what you do?' Tanya asked.

'No, well she knows I work with computers. Those are details, they don't seem important.'

'Maybe not in an e-mail relationship, but what about a real relationship? How far do couples get without knowing what each partner does for a living?'

'Tanya, I know you don't understand, so don't question it. I'm happy, happier than I've ever been. Isn't that enough?'

Tanya looked at him. 'I hope so,' she said quietly, before leaving the room.

'What's with her?' Eric asked.

'I don't know. I've long since given up on trying to work her out. I think she probably misses Howard.'

'You know, for the first time in ages, I am happy with what's happening in my life. You know, I'm not going to spend so much time worrying about everyone else.'

'Good for you mate.'

Tanya shut her door and tried to shut out the feelings that she'd had in the sitting room. They refused to be shut out. She was terrified. When she looked at David, when she heard him, then she thought of Emily, and she thought of how Emily would now be somewhere in her pub, worrying, torturing herself about how she could tell David of her pregnancy. Getting Emily and David together, in theory was a good thing, but was it really? Should their relationship have been left alone? *They* should have decided when they wanted to meet, or when she wanted to tell him the truth.

Bob and Amanda were discussing the news that Harvey had imparted to them.

'I don't mean to sound like a typical man, but at David's age I wouldn't feel too chuffed being faced with a decision like that.' Bob shuddered.

'Is it a decision though? Think about it. They have only e-mailed each other, it's like they're just pen-friends. What else have they hidden from each other? I can see how you could have the perfect relationship that way, but it's not real. How can it be real?' Amanda responded.

'But it's real to them and in the whole reality issue, we've learnt a few things lately. Real is a feeling isn't it? A feeling as well as a state. David is in love with her, and who is anyone to say how "real" that love is? Like with LeeLee. How real is her love for Gus? It doesn't matter, because to her it's real.'

'You're right. Whatever happens, it's going to be tough for him isn't it?'

'It sure is. I can't help thinking that maybe this should have been left alone.'

'Do you think we've done the wrong thing?'

'I don't know, but I'm scared we may have done the wrong thing.'

They talked late into the night, long after the footage had finished. Bob admitted to himself that Amanda confused him. Relationships between him and women had always been based on physical attraction alone. But he could talk to Amanda and he enjoyed talking to her. He wondered, fleetingly, if she was his Em.

Chapter Forty-Three

A meeting was arranged for the next afternoon. Lucy had decided that, as the whole David/Emily thing was out of their hands, they should distract themselves from the awfulness of the situation by moving on with other stories. Before they all changed their minds. The mood around the table was sombre.

'Let's not talk about the events of last night,' Tanya pleaded.

'Fine by me,' Harvey agreed. Tanya looked at him, she was puzzled. He looked tired, devoid of his usual cheer and she thought that he of all people would have wanted to discuss Emily.

'I want to move the other stories on. We'll go through each character. Starting with Leigh's secret admirer.'

'I want to do something nice for her,' Tanya started, 'and as we can't arrange for Gus to fall in love with her, we have to make sure that this admirer is lovely.'

'There is no admirer,' Cherry pointed out.

'But she doesn't know that,' Lucy said. 'Anyway, I've made a list. I thought we'd start by sending her some flowers, pink of course, that way her admirer knows her. We send them to work, because, let's face it, she doesn't seem to know anyone outside the house, she only knows people at work and they wouldn't necessarily have her home address.'

'Aren't you worried that she'll think it's Gus?' Bob asked.

'No, because she knows that Gus isn't the sort to do anything secretly. If he admired her, he'd tell her. Right?' Lucy replied.

'Yes, he would.' Tanya smiled, sadly. If only she could make Leigh happy.

'So, flowers, notes, which I'll compose, but we need a man to actually write them. Harvey? My writing is a bit girly and people can generally tell men's writing from women's. I'd like to send her some gifts too. We'll send her some perfume, maybe a teddy bear, sweet things, sweet like Leigh. I want the flowers to go one week, then I thought a gift a week, or a note. We don't want to flood her all in one go because then it'll be over straight away. Now, my thinking is, and don't ask me why, that there are probably a few men who work with her and fancy her. She is really cute after all, so this might actually prompt her to look at other men. It might help cure her of Gus.' Lucy was better at justification than even Tanya.

'That would be brilliant. Send her roses, roses are so Leigh. I'm not sure about a teddy, that's a bit sad, and if a man sent me a bear I wouldn't be chuffed. What about sending her a box of *Love Hearts*, that's right up Leigh's street. What will the notes say?'

'I'll show you when I've written them. But nothing too romantic, because that's Gus's style, so just notes that tell her that she's fancied.'

'Isn't that a bit close to what we're doing with Eric?' Harvey asked.

'No. Because Eric gets prizes. He wins things. I've made a list of fake competitions. Millie, have you got a list of prizes?' At her cue, Millie stood up and distributed a typed list. She had spent ages on it and she was rather proud of herself. They all took a copy, and Millie started to read.

'A box of chocolate bars because I have never known anyone to eat so much chocolate. I thought we could find out what's new and then send them because they always give away new chocolate in competitions.' How she knew this, she had no idea, but she wanted to sound as if she did. 'T-shirts, I don't know what sort, but I thought the sort of skate look that Eric seems prone to, so I'll send him a bunch of T-shirts. The thing is, I thought that perhaps we would start off with little things, that way he won't be too suspicious.'

'Can I just say that I'm not sure about this now? He'll know he never entered all these competitions,' Tanya objected.

'But you said he's really forgetful,' Millie said. 'Anyway. Then there's a fishing rod.'

'A fishing rod?' Tanya screamed. She knew Millie was dumb, but a fishing rod?

'It'll be funny because he doesn't fish.'

'But surely even with his shot short-term memory he'd know he never entered a competition to win a fishing rod,' Tanya stormed.

'Look, this is meant to add humour. Can we at least give it a try?' Harvey asked, rubbing his temples. He had a headache and this wasn't helping.

'If this results in us getting caught, well, I just think it's a bit off the mark.' Tanya pouted.

Millie continued. 'A guitar, because I've noticed you never have any music in your house and I thought that if Eric learned to play the guitar it might be fun and distract him from his smoking.'

'We do have music. Whenever we have dinner we have music,' Tanya protested. She knew she was being deliberately obtuse; but that was because she found Millie irritating now as well as stupid.

'Please, can we just get on? He's winning things Tanya, does it matter what he wins?' Harvey was losing patience. Tanya shrugged.

'A pinball table, a box of aromatherapy oils, a box of condoms, some videos, socks, because I noticed he needs new socks, and a speedboat.'

'What?' everyone chorused.

'Maybe I went too far with the speedboat. How about a Jacuzzi?'

'Millie, where exactly would he put a Jacuzzi?'

'In the garden, you never use your garden. Remember Big

Brother on TV? They put in a Jacuzzi and it spiced it up no end.'

'We never use our garden because to get to it you need to go through David's room and anyway it's tiny. It's more like a patio than a garden. Besides we haven't got any cameras there.'

'Well that's silly because it's summer soon.'

'Shit, that's a good point. How about replacing the Jacuzzi idea with a barbecue and we'll get cameras in the garden?' Harvey suggested. Bob groaned. 'Surely the garden is big enough for that?' he finished.

'I suppose so,' Tanya said, annoyed that Millie had thought of the garden and she hadn't. 'But there is no room for a pinball table.' Millie pulled out her pen and huffily put a line through speedboat and pinball table. Then, because Tanya was being such a bitch, she put a line though guitar.

'That's great, Millie,' Harvey praised. 'You've done a great job. So you can be in charge. You arrange to have them sent, on Lucy's say so, and she'll give you the details of the competitions so you can send a card with them saying congratulations you have won blah blah.' Harvey rubbed his head some more. Millie went pink and basked in his praise, which upset Tanya further.

'What about Gus?' she cut in to take the attention away from Millie.

'The stalker? The more I think about it the more sense it makes. Gus has this unrealistic idea about love, right? So when a woman stalks him, and follows him, she would have to follow him home from the hospital, at a distance or whatever, then he might start to review his ideas,' Lucy explained.

'I don't see it,' Tanya said. Cherry agreed with her.

'Well then he gets fed up with being followed around and it brings him to his senses a bit. Shakes him up.'

'I'm not sure,' Tanya said. 'It could be a problem. What if he calls the police?'

'I tend to agree with Tanya on this one. We've got Leigh suddenly finding herself with an imaginary admirer, Eric winning prizes and Gus being followed. It all seems a bit "samey",' Harvey added.

'Well then we need to think of something else for Gus,' Lucy said.

'But do we? We've had enough drama with him already. Perhaps Gus can just sit back and enjoy the rest of the filming by reacting to the others. After all, when Leigh gets this admirer, she's going to turn to Gus to discuss it with. Eric will probably turn to him when he gets all these prizes, why don't we leave him alone?' Harvey suggested. Everyone looked at him with surprise.

'I agree, and if we feel it still needs some padding, then we can do something later.' Tanya smiled.

'What about Tanya?' Lucy said; she thought that although they agreed not to be too dramatic, now they weren't being dramatic enough. How interesting could a few flowers and a few chocolate bars be? If she were writing this as a story she would definitely add more spice.

'I *had* Howard,' Tanya pointed out.

'What, and Howard has put you off men?' Lucy retorted.

'Yes, not a bad idea. My storyline could be that Howard has made me wary of men and I could discuss it.'

'Not bad,' Harvey concurred. 'How about we just do this and wait and see what happens for a while? We've got four months of filming left, enough time to add ideas if we need to.' Harvey felt the pragmatic approach was needed. He couldn't help but feel that what had happened to David had put a damper on the proceedings. Perhaps when David and Emily sorted things out, *if* they sorted things out, then there would be more room for creativity. He had a sinking feeling that he had already had enough of this.

'What about David?' Lucy asked.

'We'll wait and see what Em does,' Tanya said, quickly. She was still not ready to discuss it.

'In the meantime we've arranged for David to receive some Internet porn though his e-mail.' She sat back and awaited the onslaught.

'You've done what?' Tanya shouted.

'Gay porn actually. Come on Tanya, he spends far too much

time on that damn computer, if we send him some gay porn, which by the way isn't really pornographic, it's just men kissing and stuff, nothing sick, then maybe he won't be so keen to sit at the thing all the time.'

'Lucy, you should have cleared this with Tanya,' Harvey said. She had actually already cleared it with Harvey.

'I know and I am sorry. But it's too late to pull the plug. I thought it would be funny.'

'Nothing sick, no animals, no sex?'

'No, actually we've just subscribed him to some gay sites so they send him pictures of men, apparently they're a bit naked that's all.'

'Why?' Tanya asked.

'I told you. It'll be funny.'

Tanya thought for an instant and decided it might be funny. Last night forgotten, she laughed. It was as if they were playing a computer game. The players were sat around the table; the characters were her housemates; the subject was life. They were playing it constantly, it was becoming an addiction. The same as computer games.

Lucy sat down alone with Millie and went through her list. First Leigh would hear from her admirer. Two weeks later, Eric would win his first prize. Three weeks later, David would get some gay pictures. Lucy felt that it was her turn at the controls of the video game of the lives of the people in the house in Fulham, and no one would wrest the controls from her until she had completed her turn.

Harvey wasn't playing the game. For the first time since the filming started he had become detached. The reason was that now they were putting storylines in, there was a need for direction. Harvey had a job to do. He had been thinking about the way the film was fitting together, but whenever he found his main theme another one would come along. He needed to make something that the Studio would love and that people would pay to see. Therefore he needed to pay attention. Lucy could come up with the stories; but he would have to come up with the story.

Chapter Forty-Four

Millie messed up. It came as no great surprise to anyone when she did. However, it came as a big shock to Millie who didn't realise she was capable of such incompetence.

She had been so concerned to get the details of the plans right: Eric's prizes; Leigh's gifts; the mailing lists for David's porn; that she managed to get the dates mixed up. Instead of it happening the way Lucy had planned it, everything happened almost at the same time.

Leigh received a bunch of pink roses at work on the same day that Eric received a box of Soprano chocolate bars. Tanya took the box and left it on the coffee table for Eric when he came home. She thought it strange that Eric had received a prize when Leigh was supposed to be the first, but because she was due at the editing suite, she promptly forgot about it.

Leigh had been delighted when the receptionist called her and told her there was a bouquet waiting at reception. She rushed out to collect it and tore the card open. The card read: '*Dear Lee,*' (the florist had spelt her name wrong and putting LeeLee on the card was too dangerous) '*you are truly as beautiful as a rose.*' The florist had also got the message wrong. It was supposed to say: '*The beauty of these roses reminded me of you.*' It was a surprise that Millie and the florist weren't related. It wasn't signed. As Leigh took them back to her desk, the rest of her team crowded round her.

'They're beautiful, who are they from?' Zsa Zsa demanded.

'I don't know, it isn't signed,' she replied, she was almost as pink as the roses. Sukie saw them and sprinted from her office.

'LeeLee, are they from him?' she asked, breathlessly.

'No. Definitely not. He would have put his name on.' Even the fact that they weren't from Gus couldn't dampen her spirits. She spent the rest of the day dreaming about who could have sent them. She decided to keep them on her desk. She wanted to have them in full view of the office, no one had ever in her life sent her flowers at work.

The first person to come home was Gus. Tanya had returned from the editing suite and was in the sitting room watching television.

'Don't you go to work any more?' Gus teased.

'I *am* working Gus, television is my job,' she retorted.

'*Countdown?*'

'Everything. Anyway you're back early.'

'That's because I have to go back in later. What's that?' he asked, picking up the box.

'Something for Eric,' she answered, casually.

'Right. I'm going for a shower.' Once again she was alone. Two hours later, David came back and sat down next to her.

'You all right?' she asked him.

'A bit tired. This thing with Em is making me tired permanently.'

'Why?'

'We spend hours talking to each other. It's wonderful, but draining. You know how unemotional I am, but when I write to her all my feelings just rush out. I'm like a different person, Tanya. It's probably harder work than a normal relationship.' David laughed, Tanya cringed. He didn't know the half of it. They lapsed into silence until they heard the door open and Eric appeared.

'Hi,' Tanya said. 'There's a parcel for you.' Eric looked at the package suspiciously. Then he picked it up and shook it.

'Just open it,' David suggested.

'All right, I will.' He started to open it, which was no mean feat, it had been taped securely. When he finally succeeded, he peered inside at row upon row of chocolate bars. He pulled out a card. A puzzled look crossed his face.

'What is it?' Tanya asked, innocently.

'It says that I have won these brand new chocolate bars from my prize-winning entry to a competition that I've never heard of.'

'Let me look.' David snatched the card from Eric. 'It says you entered a chocaholics competition,' David said. 'Did you?'

'I suppose I must have done. Anyway, let's see what they're like.' He picked out three bars and distributed them. After they unwrapped them and started eating, they all grimaced.

'They've got strawberry fondant in the middle, yuk.' Eric threw his down.

'What a shame, winning all those bars and finding out they're horrible,' David lamented.

'They're disgusting,' Tanya finished. They all looked at each other and laughed.

'I guess I ought to be more careful about what competitions I enter,' Eric said as he took the box out to the kitchen.

'Trust Eric to win a prize he never remembered trying to win,' David said.

'But he must remember,' Tanya replied. 'It's crazy.' She was back to being an actress.

'Maybe he enters competitions all the time, like those housewives you read about who don't want to admit it,' David suggested.

'Perhaps you're right.' Tanya smiled. Lucy was right, this was easier than anticipated.

As Eric returned, minus the chocolate bars, Leigh arrived home.

'You'll never guess what happened to me today,' she started.

'You'll never guess what happened to me,' Eric cut in. Tanya rolled her eyes, and cursed Millie. She felt herself going red. She was angry. Here were Leigh and Eric having both received surprises on the same day. She baulked as she thought that David might get his first e-mail. She could just imagine that everyone would realise that it was all a set-up – not a coincidence. She wanted to extricate herself and call Harvey. But couldn't. She tried to act as surprised and as interested as they were. Again she cursed Millie and vowed that she would not let her get away with it.

'What?' Leigh was taken aback.

'I won a box of strawberry fondant chocolate bars in a competition I don't remember entering.'

'Horrid,' Leigh said. 'Anyway, I got flowers.' Tanya's fears were confirmed.

'Where?' David asked.

'What do you mean where?' Leigh replied.

'Where are they?' he asked.

'They were sent to work. Pink roses, they're heavenly.' She smiled.

'Who from?' David asked.

'That's the thing, I don't know. The card was unsigned.'

'Shit LeeLee, you've got a secret admirer,' Eric said.

'Oh my God. I have haven't I?'

Gus returned with his hair glistening from his recent shower. They went through the events again. He laughed at the chocolate but he was thrilled for Leigh. Her housemates were in danger of turning into *The Waltons*.

For some reason, the excitement brought them together. They ate together and stayed together until it was time for Gus to leave. Then everything fell apart. David had urgent computer business to attend to. Eric, who was still moaning about the horrible chocolate, had urgent joint business to attend to. Tanya and Leigh remained.

'Maybe we should make a list,' Tanya suggested.

'A list of what?' Leigh asked.

'Who could have sent you the flowers,' Tanya replied.

'Oh no. I have no idea and I like the mystery of that. I know

it's not Gus, before you say anything, even if I had a tiny hope
that it was, his reaction told me it definitely wasn't him. As
there's no one else I'm interested in, I'd rather keep it as an
unknown surprise.' Tanya decided not to argue.

She had to endure an hour of Leigh giggling and talking
about her pink roses. She didn't mind; the Leigh with the
admirer was preferable to the Leigh with the crush, although
Tanya guessed her crush hadn't abated. When Leigh finally
retired to bed, Tanya went to her room, shut the door and called
Harvey on her mobile.

'You will never guess what that moron has done,' Tanya
stormed, when Harvey answered the phone.

'Which moron is that?' Harvey asked. Bob had already called
him and told him that Eric's and Leigh's stories had clashed.
Harvey didn't see it as a huge problem and thought that maybe
this would mean they could get the filming over a bit more
quickly, which, he had finally admitted to himself, was what he
wanted to do. Cherry managed to convince him and herself that
it was a good thing. That way, Millie didn't have to face being
chastised.

'Millie. Millie the fucking moron Harvey. She sent Leigh
flowers and Eric chocolate on the same day.'

'I know it wasn't the plan but I don't see it as a huge
problem,' Harvey responded, calmly.

'Not now maybe, but what happens if David's porn starts
today? It will look like they are all victims of practical jokes or
something, and as nothing is happening to me they'll know,
they'll guess.' The level of hysteria in Tanya's voice was rising by
the second.

'Tanya, how *can* they know? Gus doesn't have anything
happening to him either, so it's not just you. And maybe Millie
got David's e-mails right, you never know. The point is that's it's
done now and we just have to roll with it.'

'I want her fired.'

'We can't fire her, she is very useful and I think you'll find
that it is all going to be all right. Tanya, I am sorry that it isn't

going according to plan but we need to make the most of it and we need to ensure that we don't slip up.' Tanya baulked at his words. So it was fine for Millie to slip up. I see. 'Listen, honey, I'll call Lucy, and get her to call you. You guys put some damage limitation in place and I will have words with Millie. It's probably our fault, we shouldn't have given her so much responsibility.' Tanya couldn't argue with that.

Harvey was almost pleased that Millie had got things mixed up. As it wasn't dramatic, one story at a time would have just dragged the whole thing on. His idea, or Lucy's ideas, were only there to provide him with *wallpaper*. He had his main stories, they were obvious. The admirer, the e-mails and the prizes were going to add, sure, but they were never intended for anything more than that. As he watched the footage that Bob brought home for him he began to see the film forming in his mind and he was happy. He just needed to wait for David, and keep Tanya on side.

Harvey did exactly what he said he would do. He called Lucy and told her to pacify Tanya. Lucy groaned and tried to protest; she seemed to get all the worst jobs. '*I'm a writer not a fucking babysitter*,' were her exact words. However, as Harvey had predicted, Lucy did call Tanya, did manage to calm her down, and even persuaded her that the slip-up could be a positive thing. He then called Bob and told him to step up the editing meetings. He wanted Tanya to spend two days a week with them, not only to keep her busy but to ensure she saw the film coming together, because it was, it was coming together. He told Cherry to check everything Millie did in future, and Cherry agreed as long as she didn't hurt Millie's feelings. He wasn't just 'directing' a film he was trying to keep his team happy, which, he guessed, was all interlinked and part of a director's job. But it wasn't easy. As he prepared for sleep that night, he felt that he might just have pulled everything back under control. The only thing out of control was the situation with Emily and David, but even Harvey could do nothing about that.

Chapter Forty-Five

It was a long two weeks later that Emily decided to tell David the truth. Everyone involved in the film had been tested. They were waiting, they were scared. They knew it was coming but they were powerless to intervene. They had tried to bury themselves in the other stories. Leigh had received her first note, which was simple:

> *I know you don't know who I am, but please believe me when I assure you I'm not some weirdo. I like you, I want to talk to you but at the moment I need to do it from afar. Leigh, you are the sweetest thing, and your smile is everything to me. I am nothing to fear, but something to look forward to xxx.*

When Leigh showed it to her Tanya thought that it was dreadful. If she had received a note like that she would have definitely thought that it *was* from some weirdo. She also recognised the writing as Bob's spidery scrawl. It was barely legible. But Leigh was happy, she had reacted the way one would when someone, anyone, showed an interest. She was so vulnerable and her self-esteem so low that she was affected in a positive way. Her eyes shone a little brighter, she had a spring in her step. Someone liked her, which gave her the ego boost that she needed.

Eric had received four *Mambo* T-shirts and a box of socks on the same day. The T-shirts said he'd won second prize in a skateboard competition; the socks that he'd won a foot odour slogan competition. Tanya thought Lucy's imagination was out

of control, but again couldn't do anything about it. Eric took it
on the chin, despite his inner confusion. He shared the T-shirts
with David and Gus, and he put his socks into a drawer where,
unbeknown to anyone else, he would stare suspiciously at them
every now and then. David was totally convinced that Eric was
addicted to competitions; Eric was convinced his memory had all
but disappeared.

Everyone watched, but couldn't enjoy. They all tried to push
it away, but Emily Stratton and her secret kept pushing right
back. Tempers were fraught. Relationships strained. The film
had taken over their lives. How it had happened, they had no
idea but the effect was all-encompassing.

They had all tried to distract themselves. Harvey kept Cherry
and Millie busy with things that didn't really need doing. Lucy
had decided that she would develop an idea for a new novel and
she tried to busy herself with that. The editing team spent the
time they weren't watching footage developing ideas and stra-
tegies, and although most of them were preposterous, they kept
at it to occupy their minds. As Harvey had requested, Tanya was
bought into the editing suite to spend more time with them. Bob
and the others were instructed to show her the footage in such a
way that she could see the film framework forming. They did
this and Tanya did see the film coming together. She spent more
and more time with them, and the excitement was almost enough
to keep her thoughts from David. But almost was not what she
needed.

For David the timing was, at best, unfortunate. Em chose to
make her confession on the same evening that he received his
first picture from a gay website he had never heard of. It was a
picture of two naked men kissing. He realised immediately that
someone must have put his name on a mailing list. He had no
idea who or why. When he told the others, they thought he was
obviously on the receiving end of a practical joke, but David and
Eric refused to find it funny.

David was waiting for Em to write to him. He had sent her an e-mail, as he usually did: Em, I can't wait to hear from you tonight. As soon as you log on and get my message, reply.

It was short and sweet, as were most of David's messages, but as he watched his inbox for a reply, he was filled with anticipation.

David. I have something to tell you. Emily had sat at her computer, trying so hard to find the right words. She had none. Although she hadn't heard from the two girls who knew David (and still she didn't understand why she had spoken so freely to them), every day she had worried that Tanya might tell him, and she would lose him. You know how much I feel for you. She continued, You've become the closest person in the world to me, which makes what I've done to you even worse. I wouldn't meet you and you didn't push it, but I can't put it off for ever, especially as I want nothing more than to see you. I never thought that our relationship would run so deep, that I could care so much for someone I'd never met, but I do. Please believe that I do.

The thing is that I'm pregnant. I'm more than eight months pregnant. The father of the child is no longer in my life and I haven't been lying to you about being single. I am single. But I'm not alone. I have a child growing inside me and the child has grown with our relationship. She stopped to wipe the tears from her eyes and to rub her stomach. I want to talk to you face to face, to tell you everything, to explain, but I know you won't want anything more to do with me. As a single mother of thirty-one, I know I'm not an attractive proposition, and I've lied to you. I can't convey how awful I feel and how scared, that, ever since we first wrote, you have become so important to me. I am terrified of losing you, but know I probably will. E-mail me when you are ready, take as much time as you like. You can tell me to get lost, but please write. I couldn't cope with silence from you. Please David. Believe I am sorry. Em xx.

At first David thought it another cruel joke, like the gay e-mail, that someone was out to get him. But when he read it for the *fourth* time, he knew it was no joke. Her words were true and he had fallen in love with a woman he didn't actually know. Tanya was right. Their relationship wasn't real. So why did it feel like the reallest thing he had ever had?

He switched off the computer. Even if he had wanted to reply, he had no idea what to say. He sat staring out at the blackness of the garden and smoking cigarette after cigarette. Was his heart breaking? He wanted to ask Gus. He had no idea what the emotions he was experiencing meant. How could he ever reply to her? How could he ever find the right words?

That night he went to bed hating the one thing he'd always loved: his computer. How could the thing that had become so central to his life that he would swear he couldn't live without it become so cruel?

His energy had been sucked from him. If anyone thought he was being over-dramatic (which was, after all, what Harvey was relying on), they should realise that he had never been this close to love before.

The following day he stayed in bed. He called work to say he was sick. He didn't leave his room.

Oblivious to this, he was the main topic of conversation between Lucy and Tanya.

'Do you think we should pay her another visit?' Lucy asked.

'No, we've interfered enough,' Tanya replied.

'She had better hurry up or she'll be telling him from the maternity ward.'

'Lucy shut up. Let's talk about something else.'

'Well everything else seems under control.'

'It would be if Millie could get the days right. That girl is so stupid.' Tanya's anger and frustration with David's situation had found an outlet: Millie.

'I know.' Lucy had heard Tanya complaining about Millie so many times lately that she couldn't be bothered to argue.

'If we get found out, it's all her fault.'

'I know, I'll speak to her. Relax.'

'It's hard to relax while we're waiting for the bomb to be detonated,' Tanya finished. Lucy, who had been put in charge of making sure Tanya retained her sanity, was exhausted. She was waiting for the bombshell, too, after all, it was her idea to find Emily. She was a little worried that if it all went horribly wrong she would find herself living with guilt for the rest of her life. She had visions of ending up alone as retribution for what she'd done. Although, at the moment, Lucy liked being single, she didn't want to stay that way forever. Then she tried to shake the thought away and look at it in a positive way, but she couldn't. With her potential ruin in mind, and trying to keep Tanya sane, she was fast running out of energy.

'Harvey, I can't bear it. David was so happy. It's really got to me.' Cherry was also devoid of her usual abundance of energy. She and Millie had become more like coffee morning companions (not that Cherry knew what a coffee morning was) than boss and employee. Every day since they'd found out about Emily, they had spent hours discussing every possible outcome. They were both on tenterhooks.

'I know honey, but we have to wait. She'll tell him in her own good time.'

'What if she doesn't? What if she just disappears?'

'She won't, she'll tell him, I just know it. Relax.'

'How can we relax when we're waiting for a disaster?'

That night, Bob and Amanda sat in front of the screens. Bob was slumped in his chair. He was shattered.

'I'm worried about David. He's going to take it really badly, I just know he is,' Amanda said.

'What can we do?' he replied.

'I don't know. Nothing. I feel so powerless. I've grown very fond of him you know, he's so caring and kind. I can't cope with seeing him heartbroken.'

Bob hugged her. 'You're special for caring so much. Come on, let's play hookey, go and get some dinner and try to relax a bit.'

'I'm sure I can't relax. Not with this about to happen.'

David, unaware of the interest his life had generated, stayed in bed. That evening was the first hint anyone got that something was wrong. When she came back from spending the day with Lucy, Tanya realised he hadn't left the house. She told Leigh, who went to David's room. The door was locked. (Tanya would sometimes curse the locks that she had had installed.) Leigh knocked and David told her he was just really tired and wanted to be left alone. He wouldn't allow her to push him further, although she knew something was wrong; she had known him for such a long time. David wasn't the type to stay in bed. They all discussed it and decided to give him space. Tanya shuddered at the thought that it had actually happened.

David was trying to come up with words for Em. He was trying to work out how he felt. He had made progress of sorts; he understood why she lied to him. If they were having a face to face relationship she couldn't have hidden the pregnancy, but they hadn't met and the more their relationship grew, the harder it became for her. He realised suddenly how little they knew about each other. They had founded their relationship on talking about feelings, not things. They knew how they felt, but they didn't know what they did. It was not real. He knew that now. They had the best parts of the relationship without the worst. Well, the day of reckoning had arrived and he had no idea how to deal with it.

The following evening, Leigh called an emergency house meeting. At work that day she'd received a box of Love Heart sweets, which had annoyed her. Because she was worried about David she was in a bad mood and then, out of the blue, having a secret admirer had gone from being exciting to being irritating.

Flowers, a note, sweets, nothing more. It wasn't real. She called David at work and found that he'd called in sick again.

Back home they discussed what to do to rouse him.

'I think we insist on going in. He might say he wants to be alone, but we don't know what's caused this and we need to make sure he's all right,' Leigh said, surprisingly taking control.

'He might be ill,' Tanya suggested.

'Or he might still be upset about the gay picture he was sent,' Eric added.

'I'll go,' Gus offered.

'Oh would you? He might listen to you,' Leigh replied, thinking anyone would listen to Gus.

He knocked on the door. No response. 'David, it's Gus. Please let me in, we're worried about you.' He waited a while before he heard David move and come to open the door. Gus nearly baulked at the sight of David. He looked awful. He was wearing a pair of jogging bottoms and a T-shirt, he was unshaven, and his hair was sticking up in all directions. He looked pale and ill.

'Hi,' Gus said, tentatively. David turned his back and went back to his bed. Gus went in. 'Are you ill?'

'It's Em,' David said, his voice full of emotion. 'She's pregnant. Eight months pregnant. She told me the night before last. She said she was sorry.'

'Is she married?' Gus asked, as he tried to digest the information. It wasn't easy to take in.

'No. She's single. I don't know who the father is, but she said he's long gone. She said she loved *me*.'

'Do you love her?'

'I thought I did, I do, but I don't know her do I? I've been fooling myself that I was having a relationship but I wasn't.'

'You were, sort of. I know you didn't know everything about her, and you'd never met her, but you shared things. Most relationships are about sharing things.'

'I guess. I thought that out of everyone you might understand. I don't know what to do. I have to write to her, to say something, but I don't know what.'

'I can't help you. I can't tell you what to do. I just don't know what I'd do if it was me. If you continue your relationship as it is, or if you meet her, and whatever you decide, there will be a baby as well. Shit mate, it's a difficult call.'

'It isn't fucking fair. You know, I was thinking, so much seems to have gone wrong since we moved into this house. First Natasha, then Howard, now Em. It's like there's a curse.'

'I know, but there isn't. It's just life and life sucks at times, believe me, I know.'

'Gus, do me a favour? I need to think this through, although God knows how, and I need to come to some sort of conclusion. But I can't do that yet and I can't face the others. So tell them for me, and tell them that I know they care, but at the moment I need time to think.'

'I understand. If you need to talk, please come and find me.'

'I will, thanks.' David managed a weak smile.

'Why don't you have a shower and something to eat?'

'No. I've got no energy for that.' Gus patted his shoulder and left the room. As he walked away he heard David lock the door behind him.

He returned to the sitting room where four anxious faces looked up at him. He took a deep breath. 'Em's pregnant,' he said.

'My God!' Leigh shrieked.

'How?' Eric asked.

'Eric, what a stupid fucking question, you know how,' Tanya snapped.

'I mean who with?'

'Well not David, mate. Apparently the father-to-be has scarpered, he doesn't know the details, but she's nearly due.' He went on to impart all the information he had.

'I know David, this will hit him so hard, it already has. He loved her Gus, he did. What's he going to do?' Leigh sobbed.

'I don't know, he doesn't know. He needs time to think, we can give him that.' Gus stroked her hair.

'What a bitch,' Eric said.

'How do you know she's a bitch?' Tanya snapped, again.

'She's been leading him on. She's been e-mailing him every night, even having fucking cyber sex or whatever you call it. She told him she loved him, he told me that.'

'She must have be so scared,' Tanya replied.

'That's particularly understanding of you,' Leigh sneered.

'LeeLee, I'm just as worried about David as you are, it breaks my heart to think of him, but I'm just saying, she's not necessarily a bitch.'

'Well fuck you Tanya, because she has hurt my cousin, lied to him, and that makes her a bitch in my mind. And as for breaking your heart, well you'd need a heart for that to happen, wouldn't you?' Leigh fled the room. Tanya shrank into the chair. She felt as if she'd been hit. Leigh had never spoken to her like that in her life.

'Tanya, she's just upset, I'll go after her,' Gus said. Tanya started crying as he left the room.

'Oh God, why do women always cry?' Eric asked, awkwardly.

'I'm sorry, but Leigh never shouts. It's David I feel sorry for, but in this house it seems that every problem becomes everyone's problem.'

'We all care. Listen Tan, I know you've got a heart and you might be right about Em, but Leigh needs to hate her, because she's hurt David.'

'I know. God you can't trust anyone can you? Look at us, all of us hurt by other people. Well not you and Leigh but I am never getting involved with another man again.'

'You will. You will.' Eric went over to her and held her as she cried. She wouldn't let him let go.

Chapter Forty-Six

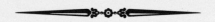

They met at Harvey's instigation the following day. Tanya still hadn't seen David; Leigh wasn't talking to her; Eric was trying to take care of her while Gus took care of Leigh. Bob was upset. He was upset because he hadn't seen for himself if David was all right. Cherry felt the same. Harvey both relished the tension that the bombshell had caused, and also hated the way it seemed to affect everyone. Lucy was angry, so she took it out on Tanya.

'You weren't supposed to use your storyline so quickly,' she chastised. She had tried to find something in the footage that she could hold onto to take her away from thinking about David.

'I don't know what you mean,' Tanya responded.

'The thing about being off men. It was meant to be more a feature, not just a throw-away line to Eric.'

'I wasn't thinking of my storyline, I was reacting to events.'

'Well maybe you should have thought.' Lucy and Tanya locked eyes.

'Come on, Lucy, I think it was a bit understandable under the circumstances.' Harvey sighed.

'What you have to remember is that I am living this whole film as well as living it with you. I'm part of it and I can't always act in my life, because no matter how much we mess around with it, it is my life,' Tanya shouted. Lucy spent the rest of the meeting pacifying her. Harvey looked even more tired, even Millie refused to smile.

'I can't smile until I know how he's going to deal with it,' Millie had told Cherry earlier.

'Neither can I,' Cherry had agreed.

David received another e-mail from the same porn website. He deleted it in anger. At least, if nothing else, he had something to vent his anger on. He sent an e-mail to the site demanding to be taken off the mailing list, and threatening to sue them. It was an empty threat, but as Lucy hadn't thought of him doing it, it marked the end of the e-mails.

Em had e-mailed him again, she had told him everything about herself that he didn't already know, or everything she could think of. She told him of her upbringing in a pub in Hertfordshire. She told him she had worked in bars all her life and that she was successful, or as successful as she wanted to be. She told him how she hadn't been in love with the father of her child and how she hadn't been too upset when he ended their relationship. Then she gave him her address, which he memorised, but had no idea why, and told him that, although she'd never seen him, she had never felt so strongly for anyone as she felt about him.

Part of him wanted to tell Em to leave him alone. He wasn't ready to begin a relationship with a mother, or a mother-to-be. Part of him wanted to call her and see her straight away as if seeing her would tell him what to do. Another part of him wanted to pour his heart out the way she had, and to tell her he would take care of her and the baby. He couldn't make sense of his feelings.

As he sat in the room he had loved so much, he moved only from his desk to his bed and back again. If only he had been normal like Gus and dated real women, none of this would have happened to him. He blamed the computer.

In the distance he heard the doorbell. He heard Tanya go and answer it. He wondered fleetingly why Tanya never went to work any more, but then remembered she had been out and come back. He scratched his head. He was thirsty. Gus had brought him water the other night and left it outside his door. He was hungry but he didn't have the strength to eat. He looked at the empty cigarette packet and realised he needed more. His addiction to nicotine was the only thing that would get him out of the room.

He finally emerged and found Tanya standing in the hall holding a long thin box.

'Hello,' she stammered. She was shocked by his appearance. She hadn't expected this. David, more shaggy than ever, smelling like he needed a bath, looking like his spirit had left him. How could an unreal relationship do that to anybody?

'Hi,' he replied. He walked past her and the parcel without seeing them properly and went to take a shower. Afterwards, he had to admit he felt better. He found the energy to shave. He went back to his room and got dressed. Then he left the house.

Out of a sort of respect for him, Tanya had gone to her bedroom, locked the door and watched his movements onscreen. After an hour he returned to the house and he went to the kitchen, where he pulled some bread and cheese out of a carrier bag. She watched him eat it, then make a cup of tea. She thought about going to see him but she didn't, she just watched. He sat at the breakfast bar eating his sandwich slowly, as if he was just discovering how to eat. Then he went to the sitting room where he put a game on the Playstation. Still Tanya watched.

She was so engrossed in watching him, that when someone else walked on to the screen, she jumped. It was Leigh.

'David,' Leigh's little voice said. He turned round.

'Hey.' Leigh went and sat down next to him.

'You want a chat?' she asked.

'That would be nice.' He leaned over, took her hand and squeezed it. 'I've been a bit of a mess.'

'We've been worried.'

'Well if I was you, I would have been too. I fell in love with a woman I've never met and she's about to give birth.' He laughed, but the laugh sounded more like a cough.

'I know. But the point is you did fall in love with her.'

'But how could I? No one falls in love like that.'

'Don't they? I have no idea. But you did.'

'Do you think I'm mad?'

'David, you may never have met this woman, but she felt the same about you. I've spent months being in love with Gus, who, although I've met him, doesn't feel the same about me. Now tell me who's mad. Oh David, come here.' She enveloped him in her arms. 'We all love you so much.'

Tanya just watched.

She was still watching when Eric came home and found another parcel. After tentatively saying hello to David and Leigh, he turned his attention to the parcel.

'This is getting out of hand, now what have I won?' He tore it open and pulled out a fishing rod. 'OK. Enough is enough. I have never been fishing, why would I have entered a competition to win a fishing rod? And I've never heard of Floaty Bait.'

'Floaty what?' Leigh asked.

'Floaty Bait. That's who sent me this prize.' Eric stood with one hand on his hip and the other wrapped around the rod.

'Well you did buy this fishing game,' David pointed out, glad of a distraction.

'Do you think it's connected?' Eric asked. David shrugged, Eric put the rod in the corner of the room. 'I don't get it, I really don't. Not remembering is beginning to piss me off. Do you think I've got amnesia?'

'You remember most things don't you?' Leigh asked.

'I think so, but how do I know? If I have got amnesia, how do I know what I forget? You all right?' he asked David, suddenly changing his attention.

'Nope. Haven't a clue what I'm going to do, but I have to rejoin the world, right.'

'Right. And in honour of rejoining the world, let's have a beer and a joint.' Eric went to get both.

Tanya just watched.

Gus walked in as they were drinking and smoking. He greeted everyone then went to get himself a beer.

'OK David?'

'Yeah, I guess.'

'Why have we got a fishing rod in the corner of the room?' he asked, staring straight at it.

'I won it,' Eric explained.

'But you don't fish.'

'I know, it's stupid. Why would I, who never fishes want to win a fishing rod?'

'Search me. LeeLee, any word from the secret admirer?'

'No.'

'You have no idea who it could be?' David asked.

'I'm beginning to think it's some sick joke. If it is, then I no longer find it funny and I'm no longer enjoying it. Everything is getting too weird.'

'Shit, you're right. You get a secret admirer, I win competitions, David gets gay porn and now this thing with Em. You don't think it's a joke do you?'

Tanya watching in her control room, froze.

'No. Can't see how.'

'Where's Tanya?' Gus asked.

'In her room I think,' David replied.

Tanya just watched.

She was watching and watching, and watching. Like an addict she couldn't pull herself away from their lives, she was hooked. She didn't want to be part of it, she wanted to watch it, and so she did.

David went to his room later that evening and sent Em an e-mail. I need to talk to you properly, give me your phone number. It was midnight before she replied. He punched the number into his mobile phone, his hands were shaking.

'Hello,' a voice said.

'Em, it's David.'

'I know,' Emily replied.

They spoke for an hour – or maybe it was longer. Her voice made David feel warm inside; his did the same for her. He made her an offer.

'Em, I can't promise anything. I'm still confused by what's going on, but I can be a friend to you, that's something I can do. You were a friend to me whenever I was upset and I'll do the same. But not over the Internet, for some reason it's lost its charm. I'll come and see you, on Friday, and we'll talk properly.'

'Thank you,' she replied. They arranged a time and said goodbye.

When David told everyone (including the cameras) of his decision the following evening, Harvey was surprised by his reaction as he found himself feeling anxious. Cherry was distraught, convinced that David was too young to be an instant father. Bob took the technical view. He thought of the practicalities of David having to move into the pub, give up his job, become a landlord and a father at the same time. Amanda thought that it was a decision he would live to regret. Lucy approved because she had liked Emily when she met her. Millie was convinced that they would fall in love and get married.

Tanya watched David's news; she wasn't there in person, but she felt relieved. The fear that had kept her in her control room abated. She was ready to rejoin the house. She did so and listened to David's news as if she was hearing it for the first time. She hugged him with gratitude that he would never understand.

David's friends all took different views, which they shared with him (and the cameras) over the next couple of days. Gus told him that if he found his feelings as strong after he met her as they were when he spoke to her on the Net, then he would have to listen to them. Gus made him promise to listen to his heart.

Leigh conceded that being her friend wasn't a bad move. Leigh didn't want him to be hurt; but the thought of him becoming an instant father was unnerving.

Eric thought David was mad. He had never met this woman; how could he even consider being a father to her child? He thought that David had convinced himself he was in love with her and that he would get caught up in the romanticism of the whole thing and the next thing you knew they'd be married.

Tanya still thought David more sensible than anyone else in the house. David took the only possible route, not cutting her out of his life, but not fully letting her in either. She was proud of David for his decision and she made sure that he knew this.

David didn't mind the advice, but he knew he didn't need it; he hadn't asked for it. As soon as he had decided that he would meet Emily, his need for advice had ended. He'd made his decision, and, being David, it was a cautious one. He would play the rest by ear. But his good nature meant that he would listen to the opinions and advice of the others; he knew in the end he would do the right thing. As soon as he knew what the right thing was.

Chapter Forty-Seven

Harvey was feeling claustrophobic. Everything was closing in on him: the film, the office, the flat. He had never spent so much time confined to one place, and, even though it had been his choice, it was now affecting him adversely. It wasn't just the flat, it wasn't spending so much time with Cherry, it was – everything. It was the way that they had started the storylines, it was Tanya, it was the effect the household was having on all of them. When people in the house were sad, everyone was sad. When they were happy, everyone was happy. Harvey might have intended pulling their strings, but he couldn't help but feel that they were now pulling his. The only way he could start to put things into perspective was to suppress the feelings and concentrate on the film.

They sat around the table. Harvey started proceedings: 'At the editing meeting this week we realised that we have increased the footage greatly. We have the new story with David and Em, and I love the way that everyone went to him separately to give him advice. I asked Bob to cut it to make it a sequence. Bob, can we watch that now so everyone else can see what we mean?' Bob nodded. Everyone gazed at the screen.

'Well what do you think?' Harvey asked no one in particular.

'I think it looks good. Great in fact,' Tanya replied. She was smiling.

'Good, well done. Well let's move on? I want to talk about the progress in general. I think the David/Em situation is working out well, and we'll just have to see how it develops. For the film I'm glad that David is going to see her, actually I think it's the best thing for him. I guess it would be better if he brought her to the house, but we can't have everything,' he laughed. 'So, we'll wait and see. I am a little worried about Eric and Leigh. He was suspicious a while ago, but then Eric seems to be suspicious by nature. What worries me is that Leigh isn't enjoying her secret admirer, and soon we're going to have to stop. The admirer will disappear into thin air which I'm not sure I feel comfortable with. But I also think that her reaction is great for the film, you know how she was excited first and now she's frustrated and angry and I'm not sure if it's good for her,' Harvey finished.

'But at least she talks about something other than Gus now,' Lucy cut in.

'Yeah, but what happens when the guy disappears without revealing himself? Then she will probably have the worst kind of relapse,' Harvey surmised.

'Shit, why didn't you think this through?' Tanya asked.

'We took joint decisions, don't point the finger at me,' Lucy sulked.

'OK, OK. Let's not start arguing.' Cherry was fed up of arguments.

'Let's leave it until we know what happens tonight. After all, for David and for all of us, tonight is the big one.' Tanya looked in amazement at Harvey as he said this. He spoke as if it was them being affected personally by the situation. Harvey had his reasons for feeling anxious about David. He had been spending all his time lately trying to find out what his film was about. Initially the fact it was real had been enough, but it wasn't. Ever since the manipulation had started the film had been presented with a number of hooks. Leigh's crush, Gus's love quest, Natasha, Howard, Emily. The film was gaining stories at a rate of knots, but there still wasn't one that he could build his film around.

* * *

Leigh had a bottle of Chanel No. 19 with a note delivered to her at work. As she opened the gift her colleagues crowded around her.

'I never wear Chanel. Obviously this person who is harassing me doesn't know me that well.' She put it on the desk and stared at it hoping for a clue.

'Maybe he does know that, but *he* likes the perfume,' Kitty suggested.

'Good point, it could be that,' Sukie concurred.

'I wish he would reveal himself. At first it was exciting you know having a secret admirer, but now it's tiresome. Do you know the last time I had a date? Well I can't remember it was so long ago. If this man really likes me then it's about time he showed me.'

Eric won another competition; this prize sat waiting for him on the breakfast bar. It was a rather large, square box. Tanya had signed for it before she left for her meeting.

By the evening Leigh was in a foul mood, David was a bag of nerves and Eric came home to his package. Leigh was in the sitting room with Gus. She had managed to spend the entire afternoon and the tube journey home tying herself up in knots over the gifts and notes.

'I can't believe that any man can be that gutless: OK, so send me flowers anonymously, even send a note, but I've had flowers, sweets, two notes and now perfume. That's sick. If he is real and he likes me then he should have told me who he was by now, this is driving me nuts.'

'What if he's shy?'

'He's not shy, he's a fucking idiot. Sorry I mean that's the thing isn't it? He is having a one-sided relationship with me. It makes me think it's like one of those creepy films, like this guy is going to murder me.' Leigh shuddered.

'Don't be silly, LeeLee, I know it's a bit weird, but I'm sure this guy just thinks he's being romantic.' But Gus was worried about this secret admirer but he couldn't tell Leigh that. She was upset enough.

David ran, breathless, into the room. 'Have you got time to help me?' he asked, eyes wide with panic.

'Of course,' Gus replied.

'Can someone iron a shirt for me?' he puffed.

'I'll do it,' Leigh said. David looked in such a state she forgot about her murderer for a minute.

'Thanks,' he said, throwing a blue shirt at her. Leigh went to get the iron.

'Gotta go, gotta get ready.' David turned to run out of the room again.

'David, calm down,' Gus said. 'Now, do you need anything else.'

David stopped and turned around. He hesitated, then spoke. 'I was going to wear my dark blue Levi's, you know the smart ones, and the blue shirt that Leigh is ironing, but I hadn't thought about shoes. I only have trainers. Which ones should I wear?'

'Don't you have *any* shoes?'

'No, only boots that I used to wear when I was at college, but they make my feet look massive.'

'What size are you?'

'Ten.'

'You're in luck. Come on we'll go to my room and I'll lend you some.'

'Thanks, Gus, you're a star.'

Leigh walked back into the sitting room with the ironed shirt, at the same time as Gus and David came back, David clutching a pair of Gus's shoes.

Eric walked in. 'Hello.' He looked at David and smiled. Eric went to get a beer. Seconds later, he walked in clutching a box.

'Oh God, I forgot about that, it looks like you got another prize,' Leigh said.

'You must be the luckiest guy in Britain,' Gus pointed out.

'Yeah well I don't feel it. It's really pissing me off. I keep winning prizes I don't want from competitions I don't enter.' Eric tore open the box and stared at the contents.

'Why the fuck would I enter a competition to win a box of children's videos?' Eric shouted, putting them down roughly. That was the moment that Tanya entered the house. She walked into the sitting room and into the confusion.

'That does seem a bit odd,' Gus concurred, thinking that Eric's addiction for competitions must be worse than they first thought.

'Eric, maybe you were trying to win something else and you won that because it was second prize. What competition was it?' Leigh asked. Eric reached into the box and pulled out a card.

'I won a *Kiddies* Saturday morning competition. I don't even watch it. I don't even fucking know what it is.' Eric's voice was raised. Leigh was surprised at how riled he looked. She thought that maybe his cannabis addiction had spurred his competition addiction and this rage was one of the side effects of both. She didn't voice this until she was alone with Gus. David walked in.

'Should I wear aftershave? Do I need it? I mean this isn't a date and I don't want to appear like I think it is. What should I do?'

'David, you look fine and you smell fine. What am I going to do with all these videos?' Eric moaned.

'At least you don't have a man who is too frigging gutless to show himself,' Leigh added. Gus rolled his eyes. Tanya decided to take control.

'David, no aftershave. Eric, we'll give the videos to a charity shop. Leigh, next time you get a delivery from your secret admirer refuse to accept it. Send the florist or whoever back with the goods and the message that if you don't know who the person is you won't accept the gifts.' Everyone stared at her.

'OK,' David said.

'Sure,' Eric added.

'Good idea,' Leigh finished.

David looked ghostly as he left. Tanya almost suggested going with him, just to ensure that he got there. They waved him off and anxiety filled the room.

'I'm so worried,' Leigh said.

'We all are, but he'll be all right,' Tanya responded.

'You believe that do you?' Leigh snapped.

'I am trying to.'

'How about we don't argue?' Eric suggested.

'OK,' Tanya agreed. They had some wine to calm nerves. No one could fully understand the oppressive atmosphere, but it was suffocating.

Leigh shivered, 'I hope he's going to be all right.'

'There's nothing we can do now,' Tanya gave Leigh a hug. 'All we can do is wait.' They all waited.

'I can't believe he looked so dreadful,' Amanda said.

'Poor bloke,' Bob agreed.

'It's going to drive me crazy, not knowing what's happening.'

Bob smiled, 'I know honey, but that's exactly what we have to do. We have to wait.'

'Are you sure Bob will call us as soon as David gets back?' Cherry asked.

'Of course he will, he promised,' Harvey replied.

'Do you think it might be better if we go to the editing suite?' Cherry asked. She was angry with herself because she had started biting her nails, a habit she had shed a long time ago.

'Honey, I know you're anxious, we all are, but we agreed that we wouldn't interfere when Bob was editing.'

'But this is different, this is David. I don't know if I can bear it.'

'How about I take you out to dinner, and we'll eat and drink and when we get back hopefully we will have some news?' Harvey was agitated; he didn't know if he could eat. Cherry thought about the offer. She was sure she wouldn't be able to eat. She nodded.

'I'll get changed.'

As Cherry was changing, the telephone rang. Harvey

snatched it up, although he knew it couldn't possibly be news of David. 'Hello.'

'Harvey, it's Lucy. Listen, I'm going mad here, what is happening?'

'Well he went out to see her but that's all we know.'

'I've been trying to call Tanya's mobile, but she's not answering.'

'She's hanging out with the others. Look, I'll call you as soon as we have any news.'

'When will that be?'

'I have no idea, he might stay there all night.'

'Don't say that, there's no way I can bear it if I have to wait all night.'

'Relax, I'm sure we'll hear something, and as soon as I do I'll call you.'

'I'll go drink a bottle of vodka and wait.'

'Good idea.' Harvey hung up, lost in his thoughts.

He tried to work out where it had turned on him. Where the project he controlled had started to control him. The film was controlling the director not the other way around, and, although this seemed to be a temporary blip and he was sure that it was just temporary, it was also startling. Nothing ever controlled Harvey, but this was doing so. They had changed from the puppet masters to the puppets. Harvey had no idea who or what was pulling the strings. And all he could do was wait.

David walked to Em's pub, putting all his thought and effort into guiding one foot in front of the other and moving forward. He thought about turning back a number of times, but he didn't. He told himself that he was a man, and although he didn't often act like one, he needed to now. He was ashamed of being so weak. It was time now for him to pull himself together and stop behaving like a frightened child. After all he was twenty-nine, nearly thirty.

David had never been afraid of commitment or responsibility; he just hadn't had to face it. It was down to his fear of reality; he had hidden so effectively from reality that he had inadvertently left himself ill equipped to deal with it. All that was going to change. Whatever happened with Em, it was time for him to move his life forward.

He didn't take much note of his surroundings as he walked down Fulham Road, over Putney Bridge and up Putney High Street. He focused on walking. He didn't stop until he got to the pub. He looked at it and felt grown up. Then, for some inexplicable reason he felt proud. His Em ran that pub.

He walked in and up to the bar, then he stopped. He saw a woman and knew instantly it was her. She was tall, almost as tall as he was. She had straight light blonde hair cut neatly around her face. Her complexion was pale, but rosy. Her eyes were light blue. He couldn't see her 'pregnancy', it was hidden behind the bar, but he knew it was her. More importantly he wanted it to be.

'Em,' he said as he stood at the bar.

She smiled, 'David?' As he saw her look at him, he prayed that she liked what she saw.

'Yes, in the flesh. Is this a pub or what? I'm dying for a pint.' As soon as David spoke, his nerves dissipated.

Em laughed, 'I can get you a pint here, or we can go straight upstairs and have some wine.' David noticed how her eyes seemed to close a little when she smiled.

'OK, wine it is.'

Emily's bar staff watched them go upstairs and thought the whole thing strange. They had been told that David wasn't the baby's father, but that he was a friend. Michelle noted that the way he looked at Emily had been more than just friendly.

Emily poured the wine. He sat on the sofa; she sat opposite him in an old leather armchair.

'This is weird,' she said.

'Isn't it? I know the situation is weird, but this doesn't feel anything but normal to me.'

'You know that's what's weird. It feels so normal.'

'I can't believe I acted like such a headcase all last week. I should just have come straight over because it doesn't feel like a big deal any more.'

'What doesn't?'

'You being pregnant, you lying to me, but that doesn't matter now.' David stopped and smiled. Emily coloured slightly. 'The fact is that I don't know where we go from here, our timing is lousy.'

'So what do we do?'

'Get to know each other I suppose. Spend time together, and be friends. I suppose you can use a friend right now, and I know I could.'

'You're not going to turn your back on me?'

'Not on you or the baby. If we're friends, the baby will have to be part of that and I can do this, Em, I really can.'

'You know, after I met your friend I wasn't sure how this would turn out.' Emily turned to look at David, whose smile had frozen on his face.

'What? What friend?'

'Tanya. I met Tanya. Well I met her and another girl . . . Lucy? She wanted a job here. Anyway, we got chatting, mainly me and Lucy actually, but for some reason I told them about you and they put two and two together.'

'She didn't tell me,' David said, his brow wrinkled in confusion.

'I asked her not to, I wanted to tell you myself.'

'But she should have told me.' He couldn't believe what he was hearing and felt upset. Tanya had given him advice for God's sake, advice about Em. She had told him that he had made the right decision; she acted like she was concerned. Why didn't she tell him?

Emily shrugged, 'David, I don't know, maybe I shouldn't have mentioned it, perhaps she thought you'd be pissed off that she didn't tell you straight away. Can we not dwell on it? Not now when we were beginning to get somewhere.'

'You're right, I'm sorry. I didn't come here to talk about Tanya, I want to talk about you, about us.'

And that is exactly what they did. For hours.

Emily found him the easiest person in the world to talk to. David gulped his wine, Emily only sipped. She prepared some cheese and biscuits – her most enduring craving – and they nibbled at them in between talking. They discovered as much about each other as time allowed. David was falling rapidly in love with her but this time in the flesh.

She started yawning, against her will. She wanted to stay up and talk to him all night, but she was fighting exhaustion. David sensed this.

'I'd better get home, it's late.'

'I'm sorry, I'm so tired but I really don't want you to go.'

'You need to rest Em, but I'll call you tomorrow, I promise.' He stood up and pulled her to her feet.

'I'll show you out.' As he followed her downstairs and through the empty pub he realised how late it was.

David turned to look at her. 'Is it safe, you being here on your own?'

'I've been here for two years and I've been fine. Where is safe nowadays anyway?' She smiled at his concern. He kissed her on the cheek and held her for a few seconds before he left. As he walked home he felt so relieved and glad that he had done this. Emily was just as he had hoped she would be. For the first time in his life David felt that he was truly happy. He felt a warm glow consume his entire being.

When he arrived home everyone held their breath. As he seemed to float into the sitting room, they relaxed visibly.

'So?' Leigh asked, as David sat down.

'She is everything I thought she would be. It was great. But we're not rushing anything; we're going to spend time together and get to know each other properly before we take any steps.' David grinned widely.

'What about the baby?' Tanya asked.

'It'll come along soon and we'll deal with it then. I know it all sounds really weird, me falling in love with someone I hadn't met, then finding out she was pregnant, then meeting her, but life can't always be simple, right? I do love her, I'm sure of that now.'

'Ah, love . . .' Gus said, wistfully.

'I want you all to meet her and I don't want you to make a big deal out of the baby, I mean if I'm not making a big deal out of it why should you, right?'

'Fine by me,' Tanya said. She was relieved. Again, she had intervened but David was happy, happier than she'd ever seen him, so she had done the right thing.

'David, you know we only care about you, and if you're happy then that's fine,' Leigh agreed.

'There is one thing though,' David said, his eyes clouding over slightly. His happiness had pushed it to the back of his mind, but seeing Tanya reminded him.

'What?' Eric asked.

'Tanya, you knew about Em and you didn't tell me.'

'What!' they chorused.

'Why didn't you tell me?' David continued,

'She asked me not to,' Tanya was immediately defensive; everyone was looking at her suspiciously.

'Tanya, you knew this was so important to me. You should have told me.'

'You didn't tell any of us,' Leigh whispered.

'Hang on. I thought it would be best for you to hear it from her and when you did I didn't want to get involved in case I ruined things. It wasn't my business.' Tanya defended herself.

'Since when did you ever keep out of anyone else's business? You are such a hypocrite. I know, you couldn't deal with it so you thought you'd pretend you'd never seen her. You couldn't deal with the way it would make me feel because, Tanya, you are THE most selfish person I have ever met. You could have saved me some pain but you didn't. You're the same with Leigh; the way you treat her sometimes is just terrible. Well, you know we have always been there for you, with the older man, with Harvey and with Howard, but this, this makes me wish I hadn't bothered.' David stormed out of the room.

'Shit,' Gus said, for want of something to say.

'I'm going after David,' Leigh proclaimed shooting a hurt look at Tanya.

'But . . .' Tanya started to protest.

'Save it. David needs *friends* at the moment.' Leigh walked out of the room quickly followed by Gus.

Bob flinched as he watched the exchange. He turned to Amanda.

'We went too far with this, I knew it and I told Harvey, but did he listen, did he ever listen?'

'This isn't good, but there's nothing we can do now, nothing at all.'

'I'm calling Harvey.' Bob pulled out his mobile phone. Hi,' he said as Harvey answered his call. 'Listen this has gone way out of hand. Everyone is blaming Tanya and David is real mad at her, although you might be pleased to know that his meeting with Emily apparently went well. Shit, Harvey I don't know, this is not good. Not good at all.'

'Hold on. You said the meeting went well, Christ Bob we've been on tenterhooks all evening for this. Shit, even Lucy is calling me every five minutes.'

'Christ Harvey, you've turned Tanya into a monster and she is going to lose all her friends.'

'I didn't turn her into a monster, she acted that way, it was her choice. Bob, let's not fight now. I'm not entirely pleased about how things turned out and I do accept my share of the blame.'

'But that doesn't mean I have to be happy about it.' He hung up.

Harvey imparted Bob's news to Cherry and then called Lucy. He was feeling bad.

'At least he and Emily got on well,' Lucy pointed out. 'David's just lashing out at Tanya for keeping it a secret, but he'll get over it. He really likes Emily, which is what we wanted, and the best thing is that means she will become another character in the film.' Lucy had taken over from Harvey when it came to being positive.

'I guess so.'

'Listen, I'll call Tanya in the morning and I will personally make sure she is all right.' Lucy smiled, and hung up.

Eric looked at Tanya, who promptly burst into tears. 'I keep messing up,' Tanya lamented.

'You do,' Eric replied. Tanya looked up at him. He noticed how vulnerable she looked, he noticed how her eyelashes glistened with the residue of her tears, and he realised at that moment how much he wanted her. He was panic-stricken. Yikes! He liked her, he really liked her, and although his aversion to her had been because she was bossy and stroppy and difficult and selfish, she was also sexy, and beautiful and funny and intelligent. Yikes! he thought again, what the fuck is happening here?

'Eric, please don't shut me out, not you,' she begged, bringing him back to reality. He took a deep breath. Then another. Erotic thoughts had crept into his head and he tried to send them away. He hadn't felt like this for years, or maybe not ever. He tried to compose himself.

'Tanya, I am possibly the only person who won't shut you out.' He looked at her and took a deep breath. He felt slightly nauseous and he needed a smoke. He rolled a joint. Although his hands were shaking, it offered a distraction.

'Eric, I *am* sorry. I thought that by letting her tell him herself I was doing him a favour. I thought that it was the right thing to do, well I didn't know what the right thing to do was, but I thought I should let him and her, you know, it's not my business, but of course I worried about him and I spent two weeks worried sick for him because she didn't tell him and . . . oh my God . . . I am just the worst person ever. I hate myself, I really do.' She started crying again. Eric concentrated on his joint, which he finished rolling and lit.

'Tanya, you should have told one of us, we could have helped then, but you didn't and I think it was bad judgement rather than an indication that you are a bad person.' Eric tried not to look at her, he was worried about looking at her, as if she might turn him to stone.

'I fucked up, it's that simple.' Tanya sighed, she wished that he knew the truth. She decided then and there that no one should ever know that she had tracked Em down. No one would forgive her for that. They might never forgive her for the whole thing, but she couldn't let them know the truth. Never. 'Why aren't you shouting at me?' she asked.

'I'm not good at shouting.'

'Sometimes I think you're the only friend I've got left. I seem to do nothing but upset everyone else. You always talk to me, or you do now. You used to run away every time you saw me.' Tanya sniffed, then laughed. A small, tired laugh. Eric smiled at her. Could it be . . . ? he thought. No that's real stupid . . . Could I be in love with Tanya? The thought hit him like a thunderbolt! If he had to fall in love with anyone, he wouldn't have chosen Tanya. What *is* happening here?

'*Smoke more and maybe it'll go away,*' a voice said.

'*Face up to it like a man, for pity's sake, you are going to end up a sad individual if you don't do something,*' another said.

'Eric, is something wrong? Please don't say you're mad at me too,' Tanya pleaded.

'No, I want to kiss you,' he replied. Fuck.

'*Idiot, now she will knock you back and you'll feel a prat,*' the first voice rebuked.

'*Well done, that's possibly the bravest thing you've ever done,*' countered the second.

'Did you just say what I thought you said?' another voice asked. It was Tanya.

She knew she hadn't misheard him, she could tell by looking at him. He was staring really hard at the table, where his joint lay, abandoned in the ashtray. His head stooped, but she could see the trepidation in his eyes. What surprised her was the warmth that filled her body. Her tears all but stopped. She didn't feel horror, revulsion, and all the things that she thought she would.

She felt warm. How could she feel happy? It was Eric. Eric who teased her. Eric who annoyed her. Eric who was far too obsessed with cannabis to ever be acceptable. Eric who made her laugh, who hugged her so nicely, who had the cutest hair and a really good upper body. Eric whom *she* wanted to kiss too.

Slowly Eric lifted his head and looked at her. She was gazing at him. They locked their eyes, they both swallowed. Tanya saw his Adam's apple move. She moved. Eric. Then they kissed.

'Holy shit,' Bob said, his eyes wide.

'Unbelievable,' Amanda agreed.

'I would never in a million years have guessed this would happen.'

'Shush.'

The kiss lasted for what felt like an age.

'What now?' Eric asked.

'I have no idea. I never even imagined this would happen.' Tanya stroked his face. 'Now it has I think I'd like it to happen again.' Eric obliged.

'I'm calling Harvey,' Bob said and jumped up.

Amanda looked at Bob with a wistful look on her face. She wished that he could look at her the way Eric was looking at Tanya.

'You *are* joking?' Harvey said.

'No, I'm not. They're kissing as we speak.'

'Shit.'

'Harvey, this is real,' Bob said.

'My God.' Harvey laughed and as soon as he hung up the phone, he went to tell Cherry.

Her face lit up as he finished. 'For real?' she asked.

'Yes honey, I mean we haven't seen the footage yet, but Bob said that it looks pretty much as if they've both really fallen.'

'I can't believe we didn't notice. *You* normally don't let things like this pass you by.'

'I know, maybe I'm losing my touch. Or maybe it's just because they acted like they hated each other.'

'They always say that that is a sure-fire give-away.'

'Come here. I think maybe with this we can believe things are looking up.' He engulfed Cherry in a big hug and smiled, really smiled for the first time in ages.

'I've got to tell Lucy.' Cherry reached for the phone.

Lucy answered.

'It's Cherry.'

'Hi,' Lucy replied.

'I didn't wake you did I?'

'Shit no, I am not being blessed with the luxury of sleep right now.'

'Tanya and Eric kissed.'

'I take it back, now I know I'm asleep because this would only happen in one of my wild dreams.'

'Wrong buster, it is happening for real.' Cherry couldn't help laughing.

'My God, Tanya and Eric? She can't stand him. He's terrified of her. Shit, I should have seen it coming, it was obvious. I couldn't have written this story better myself.'

'Talk tomorrow,' Cherry said.

'Absolutely, 'bye.'

The story still had a life of it's own.

'What do we do now?' Eric asked again. He felt timid, nervous, not scared exactly but not confident either. He was still having trouble believing what was happening, but he felt really good about it. He liked it.

'Eric, this feels so right. I'd like you to stay with me tonight, I don't want to have sex but I want you to hold me and I want you to come to bed with me.' Eric kissed her lightly.

'I think that sounds OK.'

'Only OK?'

'Well I'm a man, I'd rather have sex.' Eric had found himself again.

'Well you can't, and if you try anything I'll cut your thingy off.' The old Tanya was back. They laughed, kissed and went to bed.

'Tanya is something else,' David said. Leigh and Gus had joined him in his room.

'I know, but I don't think she meant to hurt you,' said Leigh, who, although angry with Tanya, had had time to think. 'She just found herself in a really awkward situation. She made a mistake.'

David just folded his arms.

'It must have been difficult for her, knowing what she knew and keeping quiet, I think she didn't want to be seen as a gossip. Remember with Natasha, she kept that quiet too. Perhaps we're being a bit harsh.' Gus looked at David, then at Leigh. He felt relieved when he saw their features soften.

'I am still angry though'.

'I can understand that. But things have turned out OK, haven't they? After all you and Emily got on didn't you? Maybe, just maybe, Tanya was right not to interfere.'

'It was brilliant.' David proceeded to tell them all about the evening.

As Eric and Tanya lay in bed, kissing and hugging, he said, 'What about the others?'

'What about them?'

'Should we tell them?' She hadn't thought about that.

'No . . . I don't know . . . but I get the feeling that this might be best left between us for now, we'll tell them, but not just yet,' she replied, kissing him.

Chapter Forty-Eight

Tanya awoke the next morning with the most delicious feeling. When she looked over and saw Eric sleeping, she remembered why. She didn't want to wake him, but she stroked his hair gently. She felt different. She didn't know how exactly, but calmer. She looked at him again and hoped that she wasn't with him for the wrong reasons. She hoped she wasn't with him because she was lonely, or because she felt guilty, or because he was the only person who was nice to her.

She dreaded to think about how complex this made things. Even if Eric did like her and she did like him, which she thought was the case, this was so complicated. It almost didn't bear thinking about. She was deceiving her friends, and now she was deceiving the man who kissed her, who was now lying beside her. Would he still feel the same when the filming was over?

Eric stirred and looked at Tanya. He smiled at her. He really did think she was beautiful; he always had. He knew that he had fallen for her in a big way and he was powerless. He didn't exactly know how things would turn out, after all, Eric wasn't the world's biggest expert on relationships. In fact he sometimes thought he had never had a relationship although he had had sex, and when he was younger there were girlfriends. He hadn't been in love, of that he was quite sure. He felt he might be falling in love now.

They looked at each other, then they moved closer and kissed again. Everything felt right.

Tanya had never known a man to feel 'right' before, but she knew that Eric did. Eric didn't even know that a woman could feel right; but Tanya did.

'It might be hard keeping it quiet,' Tanya said, thinking aloud. Eric stroked her cheek.

'Maybe.'

'Should we tell them after all?' Tanya didn't want to. In the spirit of her old self she was pleased that, for once, she had someone in the house to herself and she didn't want to share their relationship with anyone.

'I suppose they might guess, and if they do you know how they'll interfere.' Eric frowned. He realised that he didn't want Gus's advice, or David's words of wisdom, or Leigh's opinion. He just wanted it *to be*. Although it would involve sneaking around, he didn't mind. He wanted privacy.

Tanya shivered. More secrets. Her life was being built on secrets. But because that was the big secret, she couldn't share it with Eric. 'We'll have to be careful,' she pointed out.

'I know.'

'You'll have to sneak back to your room now.'

'Right now?'

'Well, it is Saturday and I have a lot to do, so although I would like to spend the day in bed with you, I can't. And also, as everyone else hates me, they'll probably be looking for you to moan about me.' Tanya found she didn't care about being hated. She wondered how she could be so fickle. All she wanted was someone to like her, and now she had that she forgot about everything else. She had Eric, and for some reason she felt as if she had just won the Lottery.

They giggled as Tanya stood on the stairs and made sure that the coast was clear. Tanya stood in the doorway of her room beaming, as she watched Eric, wearing only his boxer shorts, and carrying his other clothes, enter his room. She hugged herself tightly. She was seriously in danger of becoming like Leigh.

She thought about Eric and nothing else as she dashed into the shower. She thought about him while she showered. She thought about him while she dressed. She thought about him while she applied her make-up. She stopped thinking only when her mobile rang.

'Hello.'

'Fucking unbelievable.' It was Lucy.

'Hi, Lucy.'

'Tanya, please tell me what happened. I mean I watched the footage today and it looked like a love scene. My God, you two almost had me puking. What happened?'

'I guess we realised we had a strong mutual attraction. I don't know, I mean gosh, Lucy would I ever have said Eric was my type? No way, I always thought he was a pain and definitely not sexy. Now I can't stop smiling.'

'So it's for real?'

'Yup, more real than anything. Which reminds me, I need to chat to you and the others.'

'OK, well come over and pick me up and then we'll go to Harvey's.'

'I'll be there shortly.'

When Tanya flew down the stairs she found Leigh and Gus in the kitchen.

'Hi,' Leigh said, warmly. She had already forgiven her.

'Hello,' Tanya replied, suspiciously.

'David's gone out, God knows where but he's taken his car. I think he wanted to apologise to you for, well, you know.'

'Hey, I admit I was wrong, but I made a mistake.' Tanya shrugged.

'Yes, but that doesn't mean he had to be so nasty, or me. I'm sorry too.'

'It's fine. Please, let's just forget it.'

'Tanya, you are very gracious,' Gus laughed. 'Have you seen Eric? I bet he's still in bed.' Tanya coloured slightly, but no one noticed.

'I've no idea. Anyway, guys, I'm going out now, I have some

work to do. I might be back late.' She smiled and left the house.

'I don't believe it,' Leigh said, after Tanya had gone. 'It really isn't like her not to milk an apology for all it's worth.'

'I guess she still feels a bit guilty.'

'Mmm, but Tanya doesn't do guilt.'

Lucy questioned Tanya for the whole journey to Harvey's flat. Tanya, instead of getting annoyed, actually enjoyed answering Lucy's questions. Lucy was amazed — she liked the new Tanya even more than the old one.

'So anyway, how many times did you watch yourself kissing?'

'Actually I haven't.'

'You haven't seen the footage?'

'No Lucy, I bloody well haven't, OK. I was there, I don't need to watch it. It was lovely, I know that.'

'Well you'll have to watch it at some point, like when it's on the big screen.'

'Oh, shut up.' Tanya giggled and swiped at her. Things were looking up.

They all sat in Harvey's office drinking coffee. He had spent the morning in a coffee shop trying different types of beans and he was experimenting with them at home. Harvey was bored. He had learnt that there was a reason that he was an ideas man rather than a director. Ideas were fun; carrying them out was not. It got boring. It was hard work. He had to look after his entire team in a way that he had never had to before. If he had left the film to someone else to make after he had the initial idea then he wouldn't be bored because someone else would be dealing with the shit. He loved the idea, he loved his cast, but he wanted to fast-forward to the end. He wanted to see it finished, because, well, because he'd had enough. Due to that boredom he had, for some bizarre reason, been channeling his energy into coffee.

'Nice coffee,' Cherry observed, knowing about Harvey's obsession. 'Tanya, what on earth happened last night?' she laughed.

'I kissed Eric, and I know you are all going to go on about it but can we not?'

'Great for the film,' Harvey said.

'Fuck the film Harvey, it's great for me! I really like him, which is why this subject is closed.'

'So why the meeting?' Harvey asked.

'OK, I think that a lot is happening; David and Em, me and Eric, and I think it will carry the rest of the film. I'd like to talk about ending it.'

'What, now?'

'No, not now, but I feel, especially with the time I've spent with Bob, that there is a film in there and I don't think it's so far off completion.'

'So you're not trying to censor you and Eric?' Harvey asked.

'As if I could get away with that. No, Harvey but I want us to drive this to the end.' Tanya smiled. 'Listen, it was hard enough lying to everyone when they were my friends, but now, I'm lying to Eric. So I think that I'd like to see it come to its conclusion sooner rather than later.'

'I agree.' Harvey could see the end and that made his boredom lift a little.

'How do we get this to the end?' Lucy asked.

'Here goes. Right. Leigh is upset because of her admirer, which I think is probably Millie's fault. Anyway, she needs to get a couple more notes and some flowers and then we need to come up with some way of ending it. Maybe he can send a note saying he's emigrating or something romantic like that. Shit, Lucy, you're the writer. She isn't over Gus and now she's fed up about this admirer. We need to do something.

'Eric is going mad about his prizes and I would like to say stop, but I guess that's favouritism. But can we get him the barbecue, because God knows it would be useful for us to have something to bond around, and the weather is almost good enough at the moment. But then can we stop the prizes, I don't want him to get any more and I'll tell him that he had a run of luck but it's obviously over, and that will be that. I mean now he's with me he's got a storyline anyway.

'Then Gus, well I think we were right to leave him because between Leigh and David he has his hands full. Which brings me to David. Emily is going to join the cast. So that's perfect. I figure that it will run for another two months tops.'

'I agree, but there are a few more things we need. Tanya your relationship with Eric needs to develop on screen. As you're intent on keeping it secret from your friends you'll have to ensure that you and Eric spend time in the communal areas.' Harvey waited.

'You mean direct my relationship?'

'Yes. It could be the breakthrough we need. With Leigh's secret admirer, I'm not sure we are finished, so that needs to be worked on. Her reaction is great, but we need to keep it going a while longer. Lucy, get more personal with her so she believes that he knows her. Also, we need a dramatic conclusion to Eric's prizes. We'll get him his barbecue and take it from there.'

'It sounds malicious,' Tanya said.

'No, Tanya, dramatic. It's what the film needs so it's what we've got to do. Does anyone have anything to add?' Harvey asked. This was going better than he had ever hoped.

'Actually I do,' Lucy answered. 'I thought about a really good thing last night. How about we interview the housemates?'

'What?' Tanya asked.

'OK, here goes. We get someone to interview you because they are writing a magazine piece on young professional people who share flats et cetera. You guys are perfect. Then they interview you, on your own and all together and the interviews will be filmed so we can slip that into the film.'

'I love the idea but I don't want a journalist getting anywhere near this,' Harvey said.

'I agree,' Tanya concurred.

'Use Millie,' Cherry suggested. Everyone looked at her.

'No way,' Tanya stormed.

'But Tanya she hasn't had a role, she'll be able to pass herself off as a writer on one of these women's mags or something.

Think about it, she'll be really pleased.' What Cherry didn't say was that Millie had begged her for a part and she had promised her that she would do her best.

'I think Millie would be fine. I'll work with her and make sure she knows exactly what she has to do. It'll be fine.' Lucy almost adored Millie as much as Cherry, and besides, Millie was pretty and had a lovely manner, she wouldn't need to be hired, it would be an altogether quicker process.

'I agree. Millie would be perfect. Tanya, I know she messed up over the dates but other than that she's doing a great job. This would be like a great opportunity for her.' Harvey was actually thinking that she would be cheap.

'I guess I'm outvoted. But remember, when she fucks up and gives the game away, I voted against her.' Tanya folded her arms and laughed. She was finding it impossible to be angry about anything for longer than a minute. Which went against her nature. 'What I mean is that you'll need to give her a makeover, even if she is a features writer rather than a journalist she needs to look a bit more modern. (Millie dressed only in navy blue, Tanya thought she looked like a member of the pony club. This was why Cherry liked her so much.) And you'll have to script it, well script the questions. And make her rehearse. It'll take time.'

'Sure, you're right. Which is why Lucy is going to get on to it straight away.' Harvey grinned, he liked the new Tanya and he liked the fact that he could at last see an end to his movie.

'Right, Tanya, this is what you need to know. First Millie will interview you and Leigh in the sitting room. Then she'll interview the boys in the kitchen. Then she'll interview you all in the sitting room,' Lucy explained.

'It sounds staged,' Tanya said.

'But only to you. Actually I think she should have a camera so she can take some photos.'

'Won't she have a photographer with her?' Tanya asked.

'No, because she works for a new magazine which hasn't even been launched yet and will be on a tight budget.' Lucy folded her arms, defiantly.

'It doesn't sound very believable.' Tanya pouted.

'Hey listen, can you two sort out the details later, I'm kind of busy,' Harvey intervened. They both looked at him. 'I'm happy to leave it to you,' he added.

'That's not like you,' Tanya said.

'So far everything is perfect. The editing efforts are making this into a film. I love it all. So off you go.' Harvey smiled. He needed to think about what he was going to do next. This was almost over, and that meant that he could come up with another idea, which is what he wanted to do. When the film was over, the editors would put it together, then he'd get the title. He knew that, although it had eluded him so far, the title would come to him when it was ready.

The meeting over Lucy and Tanya spent most of the day together. While they were finalising details Tanya's mobile rang, it was Eric.

'Hi,' he said shyly.

'Hello. Are you all right?' She felt uneasy.

'Yes, I just wondered what you're up to. Leigh and Gus are around, but David is at Emily's. It looks like we've lost him.' Eric laughed.

'So you're bored?'

'No, I didn't know what you were doing, and I thought we might go out tonight.'

'I'm working at the moment, but I'll be back by about seven. Do you mean go out like on a date?' Tanya giggled, like a teenager. Lucy who was listening to Tanya's part of the conversation looked on in amazement. Tanya had gone from being a woman in control to someone who looked as if she was on happy pills.

'Yes, a date. Well a secret date. I wanted to go out for dinner or something. I already told Leigh I was going out, and we could meet somewhere but I thought that I might need to book, it's so long since I've been out for dinner on a Saturday night, so should I?' Eric was flustered. He wanted everything to be perfect, but he was a little unsure of how to go about it.

'You should. I'd love to have dinner with you. Why don't you book somewhere and when I come home you can put a note under my door with the time and place and I'll meet you round the corner or something.' Tanya giggled again. God she was becoming more like Leigh by the day.

'I'll do that. See you later.'

'Bye.'

'You're going on a date then,' Lucy observed.

'It doesn't take a genius,' Tanya replied, sarcastically.

'First date.' Lucy was nonplussed by Tanya's last remark.

'Yes, it's sweet really isn't it? I never thought Eric would be the type to try to arrange dinner.'

'What are you going to wear?'

'Hadn't thought yet. Probably a skirt, you know a bit sexy. I think I might have sex with him tonight.' Tanya was not the type of girl to worry about what she wore. She had enough confidence to know she had a hot wardrobe and even under the blanket of love, that confidence remained intact.

'So much for taking it slowly,' Lucy replied.

'Lucy, shut up, you would do the same.'

'Shit, if I were in your position I would have already done so. I told you that I thought he was sexy.'

'You know, now I look at him I think he's sexy, but before, I thought he was dorky. What happened?'

'Maybe nothing. It's obvious that you were right for each other. He is the only person who stands up to you.'

'Which I think I actually quite like.'

Leigh and Gus were sitting at the breakfast bar with their heads nearly touching when Tanya got home.

'What are you up to?' she asked.

'We are discussing holidays,' Leigh answered, beaming with pride. She could barely believe it when Gus had suggested it. They would be together for two whole weeks. Even if he wasn't going to fall in love with her, they would be together, which was

the next best thing. She couldn't wait to tell Sukie and shop for
pink bikinis.

'You're going on holiday?' Tanya bit back the anger that,
irrationally, this piece of information caused.

'Well, I need a holiday, I seem to be working longer and
longer and I'm wiped and when I mentioned it to Leigh, we
realised that none of us have had holidays so we thought we'd go
together. I can't get time off for a while, but I've requested it. We
could all go, but Eric said he's too busy, doing what I have no
idea, and David said he wants to be around for Emily.

'Anyway, I have oodles of holiday to take and I haven't taken
any since I started my job. So we're discussing destinations. I
want to go to the Caribbean. What do you think?'

Tanya swallowed her feelings. 'I think that Barbados would
be fabulous and I think that you two could really do with a
break. Go for it.'

'What about you, you could come?' Leigh suggested, mag-
nanimously. She wanted a holiday with Gus, but she wouldn't
exclude Tanya.

'No, I have so much work on right now that I need to be
around. But I tell you when this project I'm working on is
finished, I will take a long holiday.' This made her think of Eric.
Eric would find out and their relationship would be over. Then
she would be alone. And what if, by some amazing fluke he
didn't end it? Then she would have to decide if she was going to
move to LA or not? Then she realised that she was looking at the
whole picture and she wanted Eric to be a part of the whole
picture. This wasn't like any feeling she had experienced before.
She really wanted him.

As the panic started squeezing her she took herself out of the
room, ignoring the stares of Gus and Leigh, who looked puzzled
as they noticed the slightly green shade of her face and the deep
frown that she wore, and she ran upstairs to her room.

As she unlocked the door her hand shook. She noticed that
Eric had left a note. It said that he had managed to book a table
at the Atlantic Bar for nine that evening. He also told her that he

would meet her at the corner shop on the adjacent road at eight. Tanya smiled; he *was* the cutest. Then she remembered her panic.

She picked up her phone and dialled.

'Hello.'

'Lucy, it's me.'

'Christ, you've only just left me.'

'Listen, this is serious. I just realised what I'm doing. Eric doesn't know about the film. When he finds out he'll kill me or dump me, and either way I lose him.' Tanya was hysterical.

'Calm down. Babes, you need to make a decision. Harvey would kill me if he heard me saying this, but there are some things which are more important than his damn film.'

'No. Don't you see that the reason I've got this far is because the film is the most important thing. I want to be at the Oscars, the Baftas, Cannes. I want it all so badly and that was more important than anything. You know, I'm a bad person. Before, I could never see the point where we told them, but you know it's soon, really soon, and they'll all know and, oh my God, I can't bear it.' Tanya wasn't crying, she was screaming.

'OK. I understand. Now first get a hold of yourself. I know it seems impossible but everything will work out. If you think that Eric should know now, then you tell him. But if you think that it would be better to wait, then wait.' She laughed uneasily. 'If you want to go through with the film, which I know you do, then concentrate your efforts on that. After all the sooner it's over the sooner you can sort things out with Eric. But you need to be calm before you make that decision, and you need to be calm now because you are soon going to be on your first date with Eric.'

'You're right, Lucy, thanks, I have no idea what I'd do without you. OK. I'll get dressed and ready and I'll have a great evening, and then I'll decide.'

'You can call me any time you need to, but, whatever happens, do not do anything rash.'

'I promise.'

Lucy called Harvey. She didn't want to betray Tanya, but of

course the whole project was based on betrayal and she realised that everyone betrayed everyone else. She called him and told him what Tanya had said. Harvey wasn't surprised, he knew that that was what would happen. His advice to Lucy was to follow the path she had embarked on. Because of her reaction (which was in fact genuine), they were both sure that Tanya would speak to her before she did anything, or made any moves. That was all they needed. Just to ensure that they were aware of any possible moves. They also arranged to meet to discuss the other story-lines, without Tanya.

Harvey told Cherry and they discussed the fact that they had made the right decision to get the film to the end. As they sat in their flat in companionable silence, watching footage from their film (something they did increasingly lately), Harvey casually put his arm around her and it didn't go unnoticed.

Bob and Amanda were in their usual positions watching the footage. They were having a good night. David hadn't appeared, but had called, and delightedly told Leigh that he had learned to pull a pint. Gus and Leigh had decided to stay in for the evening, and Gus sat surrounded by holiday brochures as Leigh cooked something that was supposed to be shepherd's pie, but looked more like mince in gravy with some runny mashed potato on top. Although Leigh had become feminine, she still wasn't the greatest cook. But Gus ate it, and, although it looked dreadful, he seemed to enjoy it. They had watched as Eric left the house, looking smart and clean, telling them that he was meeting friends. No one questioned him, or asked for more detail. When Tanya left, about half an hour later, she announced she was going out with friends. She looked gorgeous.

'I guess that's about all we're going to see tonight,' Bob said, when Leigh and Gus had finished washing up and were discussing their holiday.

'Until Eric and Tanya get back. I wonder what they'll do?'

'Probably go in at separate times in case anyone else is there.'

'I feel so proud of them. Did you see how smart Eric looked?'

'He did, and Tanya looked so happy.'

'I'm glad they're together.'

'Me too.' Bob and Amanda shared a moment.

Tanya and Eric had a wonderful evening. Wonderful would be the word both used to describe it later on. They talked, they ate, they laughed, they held hands, they kissed and they talked some more. They had drinks in the bar, followed by dinner and then more drinks in the bar. Neither seemed to want the evening to end. They took a taxi home. As Bob had predicted, Tanya went in and Eric hid behind a bush in front of the house. When she realised the house was quiet, she ushered him in. They kissed passionately. Tanya led Eric to the sitting room. She switched on the main light. Eric went to turn it off, but she stopped him with a kiss. Keeping her thoughts on the cameras she led him to the sofa and pushed him down. She then kissed him knowing that the cameras would capture them from the best angles. The reality of what she was doing made her feel bad, so she pushed the thought away and replaced it with a picture of how good she'd look on screen. The success of the film was paramount. Her future career depended on it.

'I had a great time tonight,' Eric told her.

'It isn't over yet,' Tanya replied, kissing him some more. Eric reached out to pull at her top which was when Tanya realised that the scene was over. She, unlike Natasha, would not agree to nudity. She whispered in his ear and they stood up and went upstairs.

The evening's viewing was over.

Bob and Amanda went home. Tanya and Eric went to bed. He seemed nervous, she was nervous. They were so considerate with each other. Then Eric had to ask about condoms; Tanya looked embarrassed as she produced some. Eric tried not to think of her and Howard. Tanya willed Eric not to think of her and Howard. She desperately needed to do something to lighten the mood.

'How long is it since you last had sex?' she asked.

'About three years.' Eric blushed.

'Are you sure you know how to do it?' Tanya teased.

Eric laughed. 'I can assure you I have a perfectly healthy sex drive and a perfectly adequate technique.'

Tanya giggled. 'Well I guess that after three years' celibacy the very least you'll be is keen.'

Eric proved that was the case.

Tanya wore a smile the following day, as did Eric. David returned (having spent the night with Emily but not in the same way as Eric and Tanya; his relationship with Emily was still non-physical), with the same smile. Gus and Leigh were the only ones who hadn't undergone a transformation, but they were also so involved in their own worlds that they didn't really notice. Leigh was still in denial about David and Emily having a relationship, although it was impossible to deny that David did want one. Gus was so convinced that what David and Emily had was real love that he failed to notice two other people who had it too. The atmosphere in the house was one of happiness. Leigh was excited about her forthcoming holiday, as was Gus; they were behaving more like a couple than ever. The thoughts of the holiday pushed all thoughts of the secret admirer away. Once again, Gus was Leigh's only focus. For the first time in ages, everyone was happy.

The observers of the housemates: Harvey, Cherry, Millie, Bob, Amanda, James, John, Sally and Lucy, all thought that love was the most amazing thing. Watching the house in Fulham made them all believe it really did make the world go around.

Chapter Forty-Nine

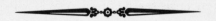

Tanya's request to get to the end and Harvey's desire to do so seemed to speed everything up. The film was almost on fast forward. Harvey had made the decision that all he wanted now was to meet Emily, to have the secret admirer and the prizes resolved, and to tape the interview that Millie would conduct. As far as he was concerned, it would then be over. Bob and his original team of craftsmen and experts had revisited the house to fit cameras in the small garden. This happened swiftly, as everything they did seemed to. Once complete, Eric received his barbecue, and because of Millie's incompetence he had received a large box of condoms at the same time. He had won so many prizes, but he loved the barbecue most. Somehow, this not only alleviated Tanya's guilt, but also made her forget about telling him what was going on. As long as he was happy, she felt that she could keep the secret. That was Tanya's own logic. The fact that Eric had confided in Tanya that he thought he might actually be going mad, was something she managed to deny.

Leigh received another note from her secret admirer. This time, Lucy, who had been feeling mischievous and bored, told her that 'he' thought she would look lovely with short hair. He also said he hoped they would meet soon. Lucy hadn't thought of a conclusion to the story, which was frustrating her. She was almost tempted to use the emigrating idea. Leigh, who (unbeknown to Lucy) was seesawing between feeling vulnerable and wrapped in self-loathing, to feeling happy about Gus and her being together, found a commendation from anyone, even someone she didn't know, enough for her to go and get her hair cut. When she looked in the mirror at her reflection, she burst into tears. Her long 'springy' hair was really quite spectacular. She moaned about it, but it did suit her; she was insecure about it, but then she was insecure about everything. Now, her corkscrew curls seemed to grow out of the side and top of her head. It was awful. So, she cried, the hairdresser (suffering severely from PMT), burst into tears and although this led to the manager of the salon giving Leigh a free haircut, it didn't really cheer up either the hairdresser or Leigh.

She walked back to the office, dreading the reaction she would get. Not the teasing, but the sympathy. As soon as she saw Sukie, she burst into tears. Sukie sent Kitty out to buy her a pink hat. Everyone tried to console her, but no one could convince her or themselves that her hair looked anything but awful.

Leigh took her bad hair home. David was the first person she saw and he didn't notice at first.

'Look at my dreadful hair,' she screamed. David jumped then looked. He hugged her as she burst into tears.

'It's not that bad, I quite like it,' he lied.

'It's awful.'

'Why did you do it then?'

'Because I wanted to. No. Because I got a note from my secret admirer and he said that he liked short hair. I guess I kind of went mad, because the more I thought about it the more it seemed like a sensible thing to do.'

'It'll grow back LeeLee.' Leigh looked at David, witheringly. Why did everyone say that? Of course it would grow, it was hair and that was what hair did.

Tanya nearly fell over when she saw Leigh. 'What the fuck have you done?' was her ever subtle response.

'He told me to,' Leigh sobbed.

'Who did?'

413

'The secret admirer.' As her words sunk in, Tanya excused herself and went to shout down the phone at Lucy.

Eric, who learned of the hair disaster from David, just didn't mention it and by the time she saw him, Leigh had run out of tears. So when Gus came home, looked at her and turned slightly green, she was ready for him.

'I know it looks crap, and Gus, you're my friend so please don't tell me that it doesn't. Anyway, I went a bit crazy I guess, maybe it was my hormones. Anyway it'll grow back and until it does Sukie gave me a hat.' She smiled and gave Gus a hug. The imminent disaster was over.

'She's taken it quite well, after the tears,' Amanda said. She was a little shocked by the hair and she was angry with Lucy.

'Poor thing, she looks awful.' But Bob found the whole scene amusing. He couldn't stop laughing.

'What has she done?' Cherry said when she saw the footage.

'Lucy,' Harvey said, and laughed. Cherry looked at him sharply.

'I am going to have words with that young lady.'

Leigh was in the midst of her worst spate of confusion. The hair only added to this. She was confused about Gus, and couldn't help but think that he asked her to go on holiday because he liked her in the way she wanted him to like her. Then she thought that he asked her for totally innocent reasons, friendship reasons and this thought was almost too much to bear. She didn't know why she had cut her hair off on the say so of someone she'd never met. She had no idea how, with no encouragement, she still thought there was a chance with Gus. Tanya was another cause of her confusion. She was increasingly angry with her; she felt increasingly isolated from her. She was trying to desperately cling to their friendship while seeing her as a stranger. All her thoughts and feelings were pulling at her in different directions. She didn't know which was the direction she should take. She didn't even see it as a decision that was hers to make.

Harvey, Cherry, Lucy and Millie met to tie up the storylines. After being told off by everyone for Leigh's disastrous hair, Lucy was feeling a little guilty.

'I was bored,' she admitted.

'Well we need to put an end to this secret admirer, any ideas?' Harvey asked.

'We've got two choices. Either we write a last note saying that he's going away, or we just let him disappear.'

'If this was a scripted film then it would have a proper conclusion. We can't just let this taper off.'

'Why isn't Tanya here?' Lucy asked.

'I thought that since she's so absorbed with Eric, it would be more effective to sort this out between ourselves,' Harvey replied. Lucy raised an eyebrow, they were playing double deception, but she kept quiet.

'She could always meet him,' Millie suggested.

'Millie, honey, there is no him,' Harvey pointed out.

'That's not bad, Millie you're a genius,' Lucy exclaimed.

'Go on,' Cherry said.

'Well we finally arrange a date, then Leigh can meet her secret admirer. What we can do is to have her see him and feel so physically repulsed by him that she runs away.'

'Not a bad idea,' Harvey agreed.

'Think about it. We hire some fat, old ugly man to turn up to the bar, and then when Leigh sees him she'll leave straight away and at the same time she won't feel rejected.' It was a bit of a long shot, but Lucy had managed to convince herself that this could work.

'Cherry, find someone to fit the bill and sooner rather than later. Also, there is no need to tell Tanya.'

'She'll go mad,' Cherry warned.

'Of course she will, but if we tell her that it was a last minute decision, made by Millie and set up by Millie we'll all be in the clear.'

Millie paled at the suggestion. 'No way.'

'Look honey, think about it. Your conscience got the better of you and you thought that the nicest thing you could do was to help Leigh out. Afterwards she might even be grateful.'

'Or she might hate me even more.'

'We'll protect you from her.'

'Do I have a choice?' She was torn between her fear of Tanya and quite liking the idea that she would be credited with initiative.

'No, but I promise you will be safe. Your job will be safe and your role in the film will be safe. Which brings me to Eric. You might want to conclude that as well.' Harvey was visibly excited.

'What?'

'He means that you might want to use your initiative and Harvey's credit card to get Eric his speedboat,' Lucy answered. They all looked at each other and broke into huge smiles.

Chapter Fifty

A note was dispatched to Leigh's office inviting her for an after-work drink on Friday night. Millie and Cherry had chosen a sixty-year-old, fat, bearded actor. Millie said he was the ugliest man she had ever seen. Cherry said she almost felt guilty because she had chosen him for his bad looks. They consoled themselves with the thought that he was getting paid.

The note Leigh received had been hand delivered. She looked at it despairingly before she opened it. When she read it she felt relieved. At last he finally wanted to meet her. As it suggested a bar near her work she felt a bit spooked, and it also suggested she wear her pink hat. She knew that he must be someone she worked with, otherwise how would he know about that? He finished the note by saying he would be wearing a red baseball cap. There was still no name.

Leigh decided she would go. Then she changed her mind. She was going to ask Sukie for advice but knew that Sukie would insist on going with her. Then she thought of Gus, but she knew he would say the same. David and Tanya would also either tell her not to go or tell her not to go alone.

For the first time, Leigh acknowledged that she wanted to make the decision herself. The secret admirer was the only thing she had that was hers alone. So she would go, yes she would go, and she would go on her own.

On Friday evening she left work at six, wearing her pink hat and made her way to the bar. It was a bar after all, what could happen to her in a bar? She had studied the men in her office and tried to decide which one it might be. As she hoped he would be single, she thought only of them. She knew of only five men in her office who were single and straight. She didn't want it to be any of them. She was, again, swaying between elation and depression.

Just before she approached the glass-fronted bar she made a last minute decision to take off her hat. He knew who she was, so why she had to wear it she didn't know. Clutching her hat to her chest she opened the door. The bar was packed. She scanned heads until she found the one, solitary, red baseball cap. She shut her eyes tightly and then opened them again. Then she looked at the person underneath the cap.

Her instinctive reaction was to scream. Any one of her colleagues would have been preferable to this. The man – a man she had never seen before in her life – was old. Older than her father. He was also fat. So fat his body was spilling out of the wooden chair he was sitting in. He was bearded. A beard that you could store things in. He was wearing brown trousers and a matching shirt. He was totally gross.

She fled from the bar, knowing she could never have spoken to him. It was a total injustice. She felt sorry for him, although she had no idea who he was. Then she felt sorry for herself. If that's the best I can do, I would rather be alone, she said, before running to the tube. She was devastated.

Chapter Fifty-One

On Saturday, the sun shone. Everyone was in the house. David was bringing Emily that evening to meet his housemates for the first time. He was at home to ensure that everything was perfect for her. Because the sun was shining, they were going to have their first barbecue.

Eric, who had slept with Tanya (as he had every night since they'd been together), woke early, and left her side to get ready for the barbecue. Tanya pointed out that it was only nine in the morning, so he had plenty of time, but Eric insisted that it was a boy's thing and she wouldn't understand. As he crept back to his room, she smiled. He was crazy.

Later, as she and Leigh sat in the kitchen drinking coffee, Eric, Gus and David were assembling the barbecue. Tanya was pleased to note that Millie had sent Eric a horribly complicated looking self-assembly one. She wanted to go upstairs where she could now watch the garden from her control room, but they were having a very important chat.

'I am not over him, but I realise that it's a fantasy and it's never going to happen. I can't spend the rest of my life pining after a man who is my friend but who doesn't want to be more than that. I could tell him I guess, but that would bring it out in the open and might be awkward, besides, look what happened to me, I wore pink all the time, I giggled like an airhead, I talked about knitting for God's sake. I mean, I know I'm pretty sweet

but no one is as sweet as I was. So now my hair is gone . . .
Actually do you think I'm like the reverse of Samson? Like he
lost his strength when his hair was cut off and I found mine?'
Leigh looked at Tanya, questioningly. Tanya gaped back at her.
'Well whatever, it makes me feel better. We've got the holiday to
look forward to, two weeks of sun in Barbados. The thing is, we
have to share a room so it would be awful if I haven't sorted out
the fact that I'm not going to sleep with him, don't you think?'
Leigh tried to hide the pain that her words were causing.

'Christ, you seem to have an awful lot sorted out since last
week. Hey the holiday sounds great, send me a postcard and
bring me back some booze.'

'Rum, I guess that's what you have to have. Anyway, I have
sorted things out because, you'll never guess what, my secret
admirer revealed himself to me.'

Tanya had to grip hold of the breakfast bar because she
nearly fell off the stool. 'How?' she asked.

'He asked to meet me.' Tanya nearly exploded.

'How?' she asked.

'Sent a note.' Leigh was confused by the question. 'Anyway, I
went to this bar last night and he was waiting for me. But Tanya,
he was a hundred years old and really fat. He even had a beard. I
had to run.'

'Why didn't you tell me, I'd have never let you go.'

'That's why I didn't tell you. Anyway it's over I guess. I doubt
he'll ever contact me again now I've stood him up. Unless he
wants to know why I stood him up.' This thought had only just
occurred to her.

'What will you tell him?' Tanya was confused and angry,
although she didn't know yet who to blame, but she had an
uncontrollable urge to laugh.

'That he wasn't my type?' Leigh looked at Tanya; hysterics
ensued.

'What's going on?' Eric asked, smiling. He was finding it
increasingly hard to act as if he wasn't in love with Tanya in
front of everyone else. He kept wanting to touch her. He looked

at her laughing, and saw that a strand of her highlighted hair had fallen across her eyes. He had to physically fight the urge to push it out of the way.

He enjoyed the secrecy of their relationship because it meant they had space to develop it without the interference of anyone else, but he was also surprised by the intensity of his feelings. Eric wasn't a needy man; he rarely even felt the need for female company; sex. But now he had changed and become addicted to Tanya. Addicted to her; addicted to kissing her; addicted to talking to her; addicted to sleeping with her. It didn't terrify him, he had benefited from an education from Gus; he knew that he was in love and he knew that love was brilliant.

'I don't know, we just heard a good joke,' Tanya replied when she finally regained composure.

'So tell us the joke,' Gus prompted.

'Oh you wouldn't like it. It was a bit anti-men.' Leigh giggled.

'Anyway how is the barbecue? After all we've only got six more hours until we need to start cooking.' Tanya laughed.

'You are such a bitch. Actually it's going reasonably well,' Eric responded. Tanya looked at Leigh. They stood up.

'I think we'll go see for ourselves.' They ran off with Gus and Eric hot on their heels.

They walked through to the small garden where the barbecue was laid out in about a thousand pieces. David was standing with a screwdriver in one hand, a piece of paper in the other and a worried expression.

'It looks like you're doing well,' Tanya said.

'Very well indeed,' Leigh added.

'The instructions are wrong,' David moaned.

'There are parts missing,' Gus complained.

'The instructions are wrong and parts are missing,' Eric finished.

'Give them here.' Tanya took command. Leigh sat down, where Gus joined her. They sat, soaking up the warmth while Tanya bossed Eric and David around. It still wasn't easy, but two hours and a lot of expletives later the barbecue was assembled.

'See, all you needed was some common sense,' Tanya pointed out.

'It still took you two hours,' Eric shot back.

'Children, stop rowing, it's done and that's the main thing.' Gus stood up and went to admire their handiwork.

'So we've got a barbecue, we've got sunshine, we've got food and we've got drink.' Leigh joined him. 'But we've also still got hours before we get to cook. Who wants lunch?'

They went to a bar down the road to have some lunch.

Bob and Amanda, who had started doing the weekend day shifts as well as the night shifts, were watching the garden. Although Bob didn't admit it, he had suggested more shifts as a way for them to spend more time together. He didn't know that Amanda welcomed them.

'This is hilarious. You've got five smart, well-educated people. A doctor, a pharmacist, a computer technician, a producer and an advertising manager. You would think that they would be capable of putting a barbecue together,' Bob exclaimed.

'Well at least Tanya sorted it out in the end,' Amanda replied.

'I bet it'll rain,' Bob said.

'Oh, that's such a horrible thing to say. Look how happy they all are. Look how far they've come. All that is left is for Gus and Leigh to find love – preferably with each other.'

'I guess it really is nearly over,' Bob concurred.

'I'm going to miss it, I really am.'

'Hopefully there'll be a grand finale, you never know.'

Millie was with Lucy, who was training her. She had a list of questions, and, as she was posing as a journalist, she could get away with using them during the interviews. Lucy was more concerned with making sure that Millie fully understood what it was she wanted from the exchanges. Millie, after the mix up with the dates, was being more attentive than she ever had in her entire life.

As Lucy and Harvey agreed, the way the film was being edited gave it that movie 'feel' which meant that it didn't look like a documentary, which is what they wanted; but, at the same time, Harvey wanted a hint of documentary 'feel', which led Lucy to develop the idea of interviewing the housemates both separately and together. This meant that Millie would achieve her aim of actually appearing in the film. She was already imagining herself as a film star.

Harvey and Cherry had hired a car and a driver and gone to Brighton. It was Cherry's idea. She thought that, as the sun was shining, they should explore a bit. Brighton was the only place that Harvey would agree to visit. He was curious to see what a British seaside resort was like. They looked out of the windows on the journey down, they chatted and they laughed. Harvey knew that his feelings for Cherry had grown in the time they were in London. He wasn't trying to ignore them, but he knew that he had to wait for the right time. He had no idea when the right time would come, but he knew two things: that it would come, and that he would know it when it did.

They were dropped on the seafront. They walked together, laughing at how it was nothing like LA but with a touch of Atlantic City about it. Cherry thought it was 'charming', Harvey saw how happy she was and agreed with her. They went on the pier, played the slot machines and ate chips soaked in vinegar. They were away from making the movie and it was such a relief. They spent the afternoon browsing in The Lanes, looking in antique shops, buying nothing. Cherry loved it.

'OK, so it's a bit run down as a beach place but it is incredibly cute,' she said.

Harvey smiled. 'You look good today, honey.' He hadn't planned on saying that, it seemed like his 'right time' had come.

Cherry looked at him. They were on the promenade gazing across at the breaking surf.

'So do you,' she replied. He kissed her, the kiss she had longed for so much. It didn't disappoint as her entire body shook with fear, desire and love. She was too scared to analyse it.

It followed that they didn't want to return to London that day. When they met their driver they instructed him to pick them up the following evening.

Harvey had a few problems finding a hotel, because it seemed as if, as soon as the sun came out, everyone went to Brighton, but he did manage to persuade a hotel manager to give them a room for an exorbitant amount of money.

They didn't notice the room. They didn't remember it, as they went to bed together for the first time.

That evening, David went to pick up Emily from the pub and bring her back to the house. They were having the barbecue at seven, but the evening had been scheduled to start at six. When they arrived back, everyone was in the kitchen preparing the food.

'This is Emily,' David said, proudly.

'Wow, you are so pregnant,' Leigh exclaimed, then regretted it.

'Still got another month to go, I don't know how I'm going to manage; might explode first.' Emily laughed. 'You must be Leigh.' Leigh blushed.

'Hi again,' Tanya said warily.

'How are you Tanya?'

'I'm fine, and you're blooming.'

'That's a nice way of putting it. How's Lucy?'

'She's fine,' Tanya replied, and then she introduced Emily to Gus and Eric to steer the conversation in another direction.

As drinks were distributed, everyone chatted easily. No one could fail to notice that David came to life when he was with Emily. That they would reach over to touch each other, on the arm or the hand, frequently. Leigh realised that the baby wasn't a reason for David not to be with Emily, they were in love, that was clear. David was twenty-nine, he had a good career, and even if his experience of women had been limited, at least he had some experience. Therefore, Leigh reasoned, he would make the perfect father, and, she assumed, husband.

Eric took a tray of meat, Leigh had a tray of bread and salad, Gus had drinks, Tanya carried condiments. David steered Emily in the right direction. The minute they stepped outside, the rain arrived.

'Bloody hell, I don't believe this,' Eric cried.

'We should have guessed, after all this is England,' Emily pointed out.

'Well I am bloody well going to cook a barbecue if it kills me,' Eric continued, wondering just how he was going to manage that.

'I know. We get a big umbrella, cook the meat out here and bring it back inside where we can eat in the dry,' Tanya suggested. Eric resisted the urge to kiss her.

'You're a genius,' he whispered. She blushed. This time, it was noticed.

So they launched plan B. Eric and Gus stood under an umbrella and cooked, while the others watched from behind the closed patio doors in David's bedroom. Later they ate and drank. When the evening had drawn to a close and Emily asked to be taken home, she had become part of their unusual fold.

Cherry made Harvey call Bob in the evening after they had decided they would eat in their room. Bob didn't ask why they were staying in Brighton and he didn't sound confused by their decision. He just said he'd see them on Sunday, and told him about the abandoned barbecue, which prompted Harvey to look out of the hotel room and notice the rain for the first time.

He hung up and took Cherry's hand.

'This isn't a fling, Cherry, this is for keeps.'

'I should hope so.'

'I know it's not the most romantic of settings, but I want to marry you.' Harvey looked at her. He saw her sweet blue eyes light up and he knew that he was her spark.

'It will make me so happy,' she replied.

'I'll take that as a yes, then?'

'Harvey you are the only man I've ever wanted, and lately, I thought maybe I was as crazy as Leigh because I always thought you felt the same but with the work thing you kept me at a distance. But I always knew that we belonged together.'

'How did you know that?' he asked.

'Because we fit.'

'What does that mean?' He smiled.

'It means that we fit together, that's all and what fits together, stays together.' They embraced and in her mind was the wedding, the plans, the dress and the way she would sign her name when she became Cherry Cannon.

They called room service, and went back to bed.

'Harvey's staying in Brighton, and, as Emily and David have left I guess we can call it a night.'

'Do you want to get a drink or dinner?' Amanda asked, willing him to say yes. She felt a spell had been cast over her, and as she watched the young people accept love so gracefully she thought she had learned a valuable lesson.

'Sure. I tell you what, watching all that barbecue food has made me kind of hungry. Why don't you come to the apartment, we've got enough to make a proper English breakfast.' He wanted to be in the apartment because he was suddenly nervous about what might happen.

'I'd love to,' Amanda replied, and, not knowing why, Bob took her hand and led her out of the editing suite. They smiled at each other awkwardly as they got into the cab, and Bob started talking about work. It was all he could think to do. Amanda tried to listen, but she could only hear her heart beating. She wanted to seduce him, but she wasn't an accomplished seductress.

They walked into the apartment and Bob immediately went to make food. As Amanda sat on the sofa, she was overcome by an insane desire to take her clothes off. Bob, safely ensconced in the kitchen concentrated on cooking. He called out to her every now and then asking her if she wanted this and that. Amanda, answered him.

At the same time as answering him, without knowing exactly why, she was taking her clothes off. Her hands shook as she took off her blouse, then her bra. She sat on the sofa again, trying to look appealing – seductive – and bit her lip nervously as she waited for him.

When Bob emerged, he took one look at her and dropped the food. He stood rooted to the spot. It wasn't that he didn't know what to do with a naked woman, but for some reason he couldn't remember. Amanda walked over to him, trying, but failing to feel confident. As she stood in front of him, he awkwardly raised his arms and placed them on her shoulders. She moved in close and kissed him hard. Their teeth clashed. Then he pulled away slightly. The second kiss was much better.

'Bob, are you sure this is what you want?' she asked when they parted for a few seconds.

'Yes.' He was still puzzled, he wasn't sure if he liked this. He liked the good feeling it gave him, but it just wasn't technical enough.

'Bob, I've liked you for ages and I've been trying to flirt for ages. I can't believe you didn't notice.' They started kissing again and Bob felt brave enough to place one hand on her wobbly buttock.

'You know, I want you to have the best ring and the best wedding,' Harvey said as he lay in bed beside Cherry. She took his hand.

'Will you choose the ring? I'd like that, surprise me.'

'OK, but then you can't complain if it's wrong.'

'Why would it ever be wrong?'

'I'll call my jeweller in LA on Monday.'

'You have a jeweller?'

'Honey, anyone who's anyone has a jeweller.' He smiled his powerful smile and kissed her.

'David will you stay with me?' Emily asked when they got back to her flat above the pub.

'I usually do,' he replied.

'That's not what I mean. You always stay in the spare room. I want you with me. David, I know I'm not the sexiest woman in the world at the moment but I want you to kiss me.' Emily kissed him, before he could answer.

'Wow,' David said, when they parted. He kissed her again and again.

As they lay in bed holding each other, David spoke. 'I really care about you, you know.'

'Me too, David. I just feel so relieved that you're around, you know, not just with the baby and stuff, but I feel so happy when you are with me.'

'Em, we need to talk about the future.'

'It scares me.'

'There's no need. I'm here and I'm staying. I'm staying here every night until the baby is born and then every night after the baby is born.'

'Do you mean it?'

'You have to agree.'

'I do agree. But what about your house?'

'I'll carry on paying my rent for now, but as soon as the time is right, I'll have to tell the others I'm moving out.'

'But . . .'

'No buts. I don't know when I'll move in properly, but I will always be here and as soon as we feel settled, with the baby and everything, then we'll plan the future.'

'I love you,' Emily said.

'I love you too,' David replied.

Bob never realised he had so much passion in him. He had turned into an animal. As had Amanda. They lay side by side in bed, she was stroking his chest.

'That was amazing,' she said.

'I know,' he replied.

'Bob, there's no pressure from me. I really like you, you know that but I know there are all sorts of complications and I know you live in America and I live here, Oh God, I sound like a neurotic woman and I was trying to tell you that I'm not a neurotic woman.'

Bob laughed. 'Honey, stop worrying. I guess what I'm trying to say is that I've learned a lot lately, what with all that stuff going on the house. Seems to me that when it's good, you go with it. In fact we could thank them for what we have, or for helping us have what we have.' Bob wondered when he'd become so confident. He wondered when he had developed the ability to say exactly what he felt. This was a new experience.

'So you think we have something?'

'It's looking good.'

Eric finally climbed into bed beside Tanya. It had been the most difficult evening so far. After David and Emily had left, they were waiting for a suitable time to do the same. But Gus was so happy about David that he wanted to talk to Eric about love. Gus had decided that he was looking too hard for love and trying to define it too much. He had come to a major decision that he would relax more, because he now knew that love would find him when *it* was ready. This theory took three hours of explaining, and for Eric, three hours of listening.

Tanya was having a similar problem with Leigh. Leigh was a bit tipsy and wanted to analyse everything. Tanya was let off a little more lightly than Eric, because, after two and a half hours, Leigh realised she was really drunk and needed to go to bed. Tanya had gone to her room and waited for Eric.

It was funny that she had let him come into her room — control room and all, even though it was hidden. But Eric's room wasn't as nice as hers, and she didn't want Britney Spears watching them when they had sex.

When Eric finally crept upstairs, he jumped on her.

'God, I have been dying to do this all night.'

'I've been dying for you to do it too.'

Eric was unsure where the words came from, but he knew that he meant them. 'I think I'm falling in love with you.'

Tanya kissed him lightly. 'I know I'm falling in love with you.'

If anyone was directing the real story, as Harvey thought he was, they would have directed it, just as it happened. Unfortunately for Harvey's cameras the best action couldn't be filmed.

Chapter Fifty-Two

It wasn't until later the next day that Tanya remembered she needed to kill someone over Leigh's secret admirer. To avoid Eric's questions she said she needed to go to work, and taking her mobile with her she left the house. As soon as she got round the corner she called Harvey. The phone in the flat rang and rang before switching on to the answerphone. The office phone did the same, and his mobile was off. She felt paranoid as she called Lucy. Lucy answered.

'Hello.'

'It's Tanya. What the hell is going on?'

'What?'

'Leigh saw her secret admirer. She went to meet him. Lucy, that wasn't the plan.'

'I have no idea what you're taking about. Explain.'

'He was old and fat and ugly. You didn't set it up?'

'No.' Lucy was proving she too had acting abilities.

'Well who did then?'

'Have you asked Harvey?'

'No, he's not answering his calls.'

'Stay calm. Come round and we'll track him down.'

It wasn't until the evening that they finally got hold of him. They were both fraught. Tanya because she was lying to Eric; Lucy because of Tanya. Harvey, who was at home with Cherry, telling Bob about their engagement, and receiving news that Bob and

Amanda were an item, managed to convince Tanya that he also had no idea. Tanya felt increasingly unnerved but could only wait.

The following day, Harvey called Tanya and told her that Millie had arranged it.

'What on earth? You mean she did it herself?'

'She thought she was doing Leigh a favour. Saving her from rejection.'

'How fucking noble. How on earth did she do it without fucking up?'

'She did fuck up, as you so nicely put it. He was supposed to be a more attractive guy, and he was going to tell Leigh that he was married and then Leigh would reject him but at the same time think that someone desirable wanted her. She got the names of the actors mixed up. She's really upset.' He lied.

'My heart bleeds. Fire her.'

'We can't, she's too upset. Cherry won't hear of it.'

'And her acting debut?'

'Tanya we need her to do this, we've worked too hard.'

'There better be no more surprises.'

'Ah yes. Well there is something else . . .'

Tanya slammed down the phone. She had always resented Millie and couldn't understand how she was still around. But she had more important things to deal with at the moment. She went downstairs as the doorbell rang.

'Delivery for Eric Reed,' the man on the doorstep said. Tanya was tempted to refuse it. But then would it make a difference? Harvey had told her to go through with it and in the next breath he had promised that it would be the end of it. So, hands shaking slightly, Tanya reached for the clipboard and pen and signed for Eric's speedboat.

When the man got back in his lorry and drove away, Tanya stepped outside. Sitting on a trailer was a white boat, not huge but big enough to look sexy. There was a note attached to it.

Congratulations! Happy sailing! Thank you for your interest in Whitecliff Waterskis. Enjoy the speed.

Tanya shook her head, the note was stupid. Millie would have to go. Just as she was about to call Harvey and shout at him again, a traffic warden approached. He circled the boat, pulled out his handheld ticket machine and started logging it.

'What are you doing?' Tanya asked.

'It doesn't have a parking permit,' the warden explained.

'It's a boat not a car,' Tanya responded.

'But it needs a permit,' he persisted.

'For fuck's sake. It has just been delivered. It's a prize.'

'There's no need to swear. We have rules you know.' With that he pulled out the ticket, put it into a clear plastic wrapper and stuck it to the windscreen.

'Miserable fucker,' Tanya screamed as he walked away.

She couldn't reach Eric at work to warn him. She left a message on his Voicemail. He arrived home but hadn't checked his calls.

'Did you know there's a speedboat parked outside?' he said.

'It's yours,' Tanya replied, thrusting the note at him. He read the note, then he went outside. He looked in bewilderment at the boat, then he came back inside. Tanya felt helpless; she felt responsible.

'Do *you* think I'm mad?'

'No.'

'Well you're the only one who doesn't. Including me. I really can't remember and I've cut down on smoking but I still don't remember. It's getting worse, I must have something wrong with me.' Eric panicked. He knew about all the worst medical conditions and was convinced he was suffering from one of them.

'There must be some other explanation.'

'Like what?'

Tanya couldn't think of anything, then she grasped at straws. 'Mailing lists. You know, you put your name on one and everyone gets hold of them, they must send them on and you've obviously been entered in loads of prize draws. Fortunately – sorry, unfortunately – you got lucky.' It sounded almost feasible.

'Is that common?' Eric was ready to welcome any theory which would negate his own madness theory.

'I've heard of loads of cases. Maybe I could do a TV show about it.' Tanya was warming to her theme.

'Is that a line Ms Palmer?'

'It could be Mr Reed.'

Eric didn't really believe her but it was better than believing he was mad. 'So what am I going to do with a speedboat?'

'We could sell it?' Tanya suggested.

'What for money?'

'No Eric for beans, of course for money.'

'So we don't have to waterski?'

'No we bloody well don't.'

They were laughing again when Leigh and Gus walked in together.

'Where have you been?' Tanya asked.

'Shopping,' Leigh replied and sat down.

'I don't suppose you know who the speedboat with the parking ticket belongs to do you?' Gus asked.

'It's mine.'

'No way! Eric it's so cool.'

'I won it.' Tanya shook her head, now he was admitting to winning it.

'You must be the luckiest man in the world,' Leigh said. 'Let's go play.'

As they all ran outside, film-Tanya clicked in and she went to get her video camera. As Eric seemed to have come to terms with things, she didn't see how a bit of filming would hurt.

Gus and Eric climbed into the boat. They pulled Leigh up.

'It's really bloody high,' she said.

'It's not, come on. You can drive.'

People going past looked on in amazement at the three people who were pretending to drive a boat on a trailer. Tanya kept filming.

'Ship ahoy,' Leigh shouted.

'I think it's a shark,' Eric said.

'Turn the sail,' Leigh commanded having fully embraced her role.

'We haven't got a sail.'

'Gus, I'm the captain, and if I say we've got a sail then we have.'

'Aye-aye captain.'

'We should christen it. Have we got any champagne?' Leigh asked.

'Nope, but we've got Becks.' Eric jumped down, ran into the house and retrieved four bottles. He handed them round, then took the last one and smashed it on the ground.

'You're meant to hit the boat,' Tanya pointed out.

'What and devalue her? I don't think so. Anyway, I hereby name this boat *Ericgustanyaleeleedavid* and I would like to bless all who sail in her.' Everyone applauded.

Tanya put down the camera. 'Eric, you might want to go back into the house before someone phones for the whitecoats.'

'Spoilsport,' Eric retorted, but he'd had enough.

They went inside with their high sprits. Tanya thought that the speedboat was quite a good idea, even if it was Millie's. Eric was now quite pleased with his competition addiction, even if he couldn't remember it.

The following day, Tanya decided it was time to get her own back. She called Harvey.

'How much did the boat cost?'

'Eleven thousand pounds.'

'How the hell did Millie get that kind of money?' Tanya was angry again.

'I gave her a company credit card. It has a big limit.'

'The problem is that Eric got upset when we were in bed last night and I told him that I'd get rid of the boat for him.'

'OK.'

'But then I called him this morning and told him that I'd already sold it to my boss for eight thousand pounds.' Tanya's own initiative.

'But you didn't know how much it was worth,' Harvey started.

'I guessed.'

Harvey shrugged to himself. Because of the reaction last night, he knew it was worth the money.

'I'll bike you the money round.'

'Oh, and Harvey, I told him it would be collected today. There's a couple of parking tickets that need to be paid.'

'You drive a hard bargain.' But not too hard, he thought.

Chapter Fifty-Three

Lucy and Millie came up with a wonderful plan for the interview scene, and Lucy, although not in love or even in lust was feeling wonderful. She knew the end was near and that heightened her elation; she knew, after the film, that her life would change for the better.

Millie, who was also aware that the end was in sight, was also in high spirits. She had realised as she rehearsed with Lucy that she would prefer to be an actress rather than a secretary, and if her debut went well, Harvey promised to get her an agent.

Emily was blissfully happy with David, and also excited about the birth of her baby, now imminent. David was lost in Emily. He spent the bulk of his time at the pub, although Emily did insist on visiting his house, because she didn't want his friends to resent her. Their relationship was physical, but frustratingly so because neither felt that sex would be sensible, or even possible, while she was still pregnant. Emily told Tanya that as soon as the baby arrived she was going to have sex, sex, sex. As soon as the doctors said it was allowed, anyway. Tanya laughed.

Tanya liked Emily and she liked David and Emily's relationship. Leigh liked Emily, but told her in all honesty that she would always worry about David, because he was like a brother to her. Tanya also said that if David could fall in love with Emily when she was heavily pregnant, then he really did love her because that must be the strongest indication there is. Leigh wondered which planet had claimed Tanya for their own.

What worried Leigh more than anything was herself. She had said she would get over Gus; she had managed to provide a good public front, but she still didn't know how to let go. Sukie had even told her that the holiday was the turning point and she had to try to move on. Even though Leigh knew what she was saying was right, she didn't want it to be. Sukie became another person she felt she couldn't confide in. She actually felt that she couldn't talk to anyone. Leigh became the best actress of all. She had everyone fooled, bar herself.

David was too busy to notice anything different about Tanya and Eric, but Leigh and Gus weren't. It actually took them quite a long time, but at last they began to question what was going on.

'Gus, Eric doesn't seem to smoke much any more and he never talks about his causes. And Tanya has stopped shouting.'

'I know, I asked Eric why he was smiling all the time and he said it was because he was stoned all the time, but you're right, he doesn't smoke as much as he used to.'

'You don't think?'

'No.'

'Strange how it affected both of them.'

'At the same time.'

'Shit!' they both exclaimed. Leigh was wondering how on earth that happened, Gus was thinking about how much Eric moaned about Tanya. It made no sense, but then, love never did. They went back over the recent events; the way they had behaved at the barbecue; the way they behaved when they were around each other; everything fell into place.

'How do we find out for sure?' Gus asked.

'I know, let's trap them.'

'How?'

'Well, for instance you could say that you're going on this date but the girl you're dating wants to bring a friend and you have to bring a friend too.'

'Yeah, then Tanya will get mad and Eric will try to make

excuses and then we'll know.' They loved their childish behaviour, as well as their serious conversations. What had emerged was the strongest friendship Leigh had ever experienced, even if she couldn't shake the feeling that it wasn't enough.

When they were ready to implement their plan, David and Emily were there. Emily's presence disrupted their seating plan. She and David were given the prize of the sofa. Leigh sat in David's chair and Gus would sit on the floor. Eric was still in his beanbag and Tanya sat in the other chair. Leigh flicked her foot out which barely touched Gus. He looked at her questioningly, she looked back at him, and he remembered what he was supposed to be doing.

'Eric, I've got this date next weekend and well, Lisa has a friend who she wants to bring along, so I sort of said that you would come too.' Gus noticed the colour creep up Eric's cheeks. He stole a look at Tanya who was blushing. Leigh and Gus smiled.

'What a great idea, Eric it will definitely do you some good to meet a woman,' Leigh added. Then she giggled as she watched more horror spread over Tanya's face.

'I think I'm busy then mate, sorry,' Eric mumbled.

'Be unbusy, please Eric, I really need you to do this.'

'And at least she's probably going to be gorgeous. Gus only seems to know gorgeous women,' David added, which was very helpful although he had no idea what was going on.

'But I hate blind dates,' Eric protested.

'Have you ever been on one?' Leigh asked. She looked at Gus, they both burst out laughing.

'There's something I think you need to tell us,' Gus cut in.

'What?' David, Emily, Tanya and Eric asked, in unison.

'Well, call it a hunch, but I think that our Eric has a girl,' Gus explained.

'And we may be mistaken but we think that the girl he has is none other than our very own Tanya,' Leigh added.

'No!' David said, looking from Leigh to Gus to Eric to Tanya. Tanya was the colour of her nail varnish, Eric was only a couple of shades off.

'As I said, we might be wrong.' Gus laughed.

'OK, so we're seeing each other,' Eric said, feeling relieved and unburdened immediately.

'What I want to know is how did that happen?' Leigh asked.

'No!' David repeated.

Tanya and Eric proceeded to prove how much of a couple they were by telling the whole story. Tanya started, Eric told the next bit, then back to Tanya and so on. Everyone was amazed, and although Leigh and Gus had been convinced that that was what happened, they were still surprised by the confirmation and the story.

Bob and Amanda watched. They had developed a policy of keeping their physical contact to a minimum while they were in the editing suite, but as soon as they stepped outside they would kiss on the street. Then the physical contact rule was reversed; it was kept to a *maximum*.

'I'm glad they told, and I'm really glad that Leigh and Gus guessed,' Bob said.

'Why?' Amanda asked.

'It kind of makes them less self-absorbed. I had better call Harvey.'

Harvey put down the phone and walked over to Cherry.

'Honey, Tanya and Eric, it's all out in the open.' He kissed her and took her hand. 'I wish the ring was on that hand now.'

'It doesn't matter, I'll look forward to getting it when we get home.' Harvey had ordered a very expensive, very special diamond. The setting had been ordered and the ring designed, but Cherry insisted that she wanted to get measured in person before they finished it, and, whatever Cherry wanted, Cherry got. 'How did they take it?'

'Apparently Leigh and Gus guessed and set them up, which I think is quite cute in the circumstances.' He kissed her again.

'Harvey, our professional relationship is completely kaput now, every time we talk about work you keep kissing me.'

'Do I hear a complaint?'

'Absolutely not.'

Eric and Tanya slept for the first time in Tanya's room without him having to sneak in. They didn't have to wake up before everyone else. They liked being 'out', as Tanya said. He liked being 'in', Eric retorted happily.

Chapter Fifty-Four

Harvey decided that everyone should join him for lunch: the editing team, Lucy, Millie, Tanya, and of course Cherry. They went to a small Italian restaurant that Millie had chosen.

The mood around the table was jubilant. Harvey praised the work they had done on editing and told them that they were all geniuses. Tanya raised her glass and took her praise. He praised the way that Tanya had held it together through all the difficult times (even though she had often barely held it together). She again took her praise. He told them that they were a great team and had nearly completed the best movie ever. He said it was nearly over, and that sentence, which was one she had been expecting, gave Tanya a huge sense of relief.

'It's nearly over?' she echoed.

'Sure. We discussed it. We nearly have everything we need. We're still going of course. We need Emily to have her baby, we need to get Millie's interviews, and wrap up a few details, but what we are doing now is entering the very last phase of filming.'

'Thank you,' Tanya whispered.

'And I think we should raise a toast – to us. I would also like to announce that Cherry, who has stuck by me through everything, even against her better judgement sometimes, has agreed to be my wife.' Cherry blushed, Millie lunged at her and burst into tears of happiness.

'What a fitting end to it all,' Lucy said. 'Although of course you're not in the film. Shame really, this film could do with an engagement.' She looked at Tanya who laughed.

'Congratulations, that is really wonderful news, but Lucy, I am sorry to disappoint you, Eric and I are no way near that stage.'

'Couldn't you propose to him? That would be a great ending?' Lucy was teasing.

'No. There's been enough manipulation don't you think?'

'And I have an announcement to make.' Bob looked embarrassed as everyone turned to look at him. 'You may or may not know that Amanda and I have been infected by the same love bug that everyone seems to have caught. Well, Amanda has agreed to come back to LA with me.' There was a lot of back-slapping and congratulations.

'Christ this is becoming so cheesy,' Lucy moaned. 'And I haven't even had any sex in months, let alone love.'

'I'll oblige you,' James offered.

'Thanks James, but I like my men with hair.' James looked offended but then he laughed. 'So, any more surprises?'

'Not from me, but then, in Tanya's house, you never know what might happen next,' Harvey replied.

Harvey had scheduled for Millie to make her appearance that week. Tanya had told everyone at home that a journalist wanted to interview them about being housemates and they agreed because, even though Tanya had mellowed, she was still someone to be reckoned with. Bob and his team were working harder than ever, and Tanya was heavily involved. Steve Delaney from Poplar Films had been told they were close to completion. Even though Bob had originally asked for three months for editing, it had become clear that they wouldn't need that much. Harvey was itching to get home. He had had enough of London and he wanted LA, he wanted to get married. Bob felt the same, he wanted to show Amanda his home.

Millie was getting ready to go to the film set. It was Thursday. Cherry and Lucy had taken her shopping. They hadn't involved

Tanya because they knew that she would probably make Millie too nervous. They selected a pair of leather hipsters, and a light green cashmere cardigan. They bought her a pair of diamanté earrings, which dangled from her ears, with matching necklace. Black, high-healed sandals completed the outfit. She looked the part. They took her back to the flat, where Lucy washed Millie's hair, and then applied so much gel to it that it actually managed to do something other than just hang from her head. Cherry applied make-up.

'Wow, I look smashing,' Millie said.

'You sure do honey,' Cherry agreed.

They armed her with a big leather tote bag, a Dictaphone, a camera and her notes. She was ready. Harvey, Cherry and Lucy kissed her cheek, wished her luck and waved her on her way. The taxi headed off.

'I hope she'll be all right,' Cherry said, with the anxiety of a mother watching her child start her first day at school.

'With all the work we've done she'll be fantastic,' Lucy reassured her.

Millie stood on the doorstep trying not to shake. She pressed the bell and waited. Hello. My name is Millie Harcourt and I am a features writer for *Juice* magazine, she said to herself, silently, as she slipped into character.

Gus opened the door and fell in lust instantly. As he stood, mesmerised staring at this object of desire, she spoke. 'I'm Millie Harcourt and I work for *Juice*,' she said. 'I've come to interview you.' She smiled and looked at Gus, who she couldn't believe was even cuter in real life. Tanya came up behind Gus.

'Hi, I'm Tanya,' she said, looking at the girl she barely recognised as the pony club girl. 'Gus, let her in,' she snapped. Gus moved out of the way. He still hadn't spoken. Love at first sight. He believed that this was the girl for him. Luckily for the film, Millie couldn't read his thoughts because she would have fallen apart instantly. Tanya however, could. She wanted to kill

Millie for the effect she was having on Gus, but instead she held out her hand. Millie shook it. 'Shall we get started?' she asked.

Everyone else was in the living room. Millie was a picture of professionalism as she said, 'Oh, I thought there were only five of you.' (She had been pre-warned about Emily's presence).

'I'm Emily, I don't live here,' Emily explained.

'She's my girlfriend,' David announced, like a teenager would.

'Well congratulations, you look like it might explode out of you any minute,' Millie commented.

Emily laughed. 'It feels like it too! Anyway, I'll slip off and leave you to it.' Emily went to wait in David's room.

'Right. Well that's Leigh, Gus you've already met, David, and Eric,' Tanya made the introductions. She hated to admit it, but Millie was coming across wonderfully.

'Hi. Shall we get started? As you know I am doing a feature on professional houseshares, because apparently the trend has grown, something about people not getting married so much. Anyway, can I have the boys in the kitchen and Leigh and Tanya here?' The guys got up and left.

Because it was Millie's big moment, Bob had invited everyone else to watch it in the editing suite. Cherry, who had recognised Gus's reaction as one of interest was thrilled. Lucy was proud of the way Millie was behaving and Harvey beamed. They all sat around and watched.

'First, I'd like to ask you to give me some background into how you came to live together.' She pressed play on the Dictaphone and smiled. Tanya proceeded to tell the story, Leigh added to it and after a while, they finished.

'Great, how do you find it living with so many people? Is there a fight for the bathroom each day?' Leigh explained about their schedules. It was exactly what Harvey wanted. She asked them how they found living with men, she asked a bit about their jobs, she asked about their interests, she asked about house romances. Then she went to the kitchen and asked the men the same things. Gus was tongue-tied but managed to answer her questions, then he slipped into flirtatious mode and Eric and David watched with amusement as he turned the questions on Millie.

'He fancies her,' Lucy exclaimed.

'Looks like it,' Harvey concurred.

'What about Leigh?' Bob asked.

'Well I guess now that she is getting over her crush, maybe we can get the happy ending after all,' Harvey replied, thinking that it would be so neat.

'For fuck's sake, if I wrote this people would call it trite.' Lucy laughed. It was as if there was nowhere safe from this love thing.

For her finale, Millie reassembled the cast in the sitting room and asked them a few last questions. As she nodded, they heard a scream from downstairs.

'What was that?' Tanya jumped.

'Em!' David screamed and ran downstairs. Everyone, including Millie went to the basement.

'It's the baaaaby, it's coming!' Emily shouted as she grimaced in pain. David rushed to her side and then hurried to Gus, he ran around in a circle before going back to Emily. Gus took charge.

'Tanya, call an ambulance.' He rushed to Emily, felt her stomach and started timing her contractions. 'Emily when did your waters break?' he asked.

'Just now I think, it was quick,' she shouted through clenched teeth.

'Keep calm,' David said, then regretted it.

'You fucking well have the pain I've got and keep calm,' Emily replied. Then as the contraction subsided she half-laughed. 'I'm sorry, God I'm sorry.' She burst into tears. Gus looked serious.

'Emily, these contractions are quite close together. Normally it takes a long time for a first baby. Now listen to me. Did you go to ante-natal?'

'I went once but it was such a load of crap I stopped going.'

'Do you remember how to breathe?' Emily shook her head, violently. Gus started breathing with her, she soon picked it up. 'Eric, go and see what Tanya's doing.' Eric ran upstairs where Tanya was just hanging up the phone.

'They're a bunch of morons. It took me ages but they said the ambulance was on its way. Thank God for Gus.' Eric took her and held her briefly before rejoining the others.

It was pandemonium. Emily was swearing again as her contractions were getting stronger. Gus was trying to stay calm, but not having any pain relief for her he was worried. First babies should be born in hospital, or at least with a midwife present. He could deliver, he wasn't worried about that, but he was worried about Emily's pain. David was unsure about what to do, but he was talking to Emily, stroking her hand and doing a good job under the circumstances. Tanya and Eric rushed back.

'It'll be here soon,' Tanya said.

'So will the baby,' Gus replied.

'Shall I boil the kettle? Get some towels?' Millie offered. Everyone looked at her, then Leigh giggled, so did Emily, and everyone joined in, anything to relieve the tension.

'I think we should let them have some privacy,' Eric suggested as they witnessed another contraction. Eric thought he might faint. Everyone apart from Gus and David left.

Millie didn't suggest leaving and no one asked her to go. Leigh started crying, so Millie hugged her.

'I know it's not David's baby but watching him in there, I felt like it was and I thought that's my cousin's baby.'

'It'll be OK,' Millie soothed. She hoped that it would.

'Holy shit, she's going to give birth in the house,' Harvey said.

'At least we don't have to watch it,' Lucy added.

'It's so wonderful,' Cherry said, clutching hold of Harvey's hand.

After what seemed like an eternity, the ambulance arrived. Tanya let them in and ushered them down to David's room. 'Get a fucking move on,' she screamed. If it were her giving birth she would book herself into a hospital the week before she was due and she would lie there waiting for her epidural.

They went into the kitchen and waited. When they heard the first cry from the baby, Leigh burst into tears again.

'My God, she's had it!' Tanya said, unable to deny the emotion she felt. Unsure what to do, they waited. Gus finally emerged looking really soiled. Eric recoiled from him.

'It's a girl,' he announced. 'We're going to get them to the hospital now, but mother and baby are fine.' He smiled and ran back downstairs.

The ambulance crew carried Emily in an ambulance chair, she looked exhausted.

They stood around in the hallway.

'Congratulations,' Tanya said and went up to kiss her sweaty cheek. Tears streamed down Emily's face.

'Thank you,' she whispered. Leigh went to kiss her.

'You've done a marvellous job,' she said.

'I did a quick job. Thank you for letting me have your cousin.' Leigh and Emily embraced, both crying with happiness. Gus was behind them, carrying a baby wrapped in a blanket.

'Guys, no offence but we really need to get them to the hospital. You can all come visit tomorrow.' They all sneaked a look at the baby but let them rush out. David followed, carrying a small suitcase. He was beaming.

'We were so organised, we even had the overnight case but the little thing didn't want to wait.' He hugged and kissed everyone quickly, even Millie, before getting in his car and following the ambulance to the hospital.

*   *   *

'It's a girl,' Cherry said. 'Did you see her? Did you see how small she was?'

'Babies tend to be small,' the ever-cynical Lucy pointed out.

'What a wonderful way for the film to end,' Harvey said.

'It's a wonderful way for life to begin,' Amanda replied.

'Champagne anyone?' Harvey asked.

Millie remembered who she was, or who she was supposed to be.

'Right, well I came here for an interview, I didn't get my photos but I almost witnessed a birth. I think it's time to leave.' She laughed. She was holding her character well.

'I'll get a cab for you,' Tanya offered. They opened a bottle of champagne to wet the baby's head as they waited for Millie's taxi. When it arrived, Tanya showed her out.

'You were brilliant,' she said as she hugged Millie. Millie wasn't surprised. It seemed that anything could and did happen in the house in Fulham.

Chapter Fifty-Five

The baby was fine; David was as much in love with her as he was with Emily. They were kept in hospital for a few days, then David took them home to the pub. He had told his housemates that, although he would pay the rent, he had effectively moved out. He had already arranged to take two weeks' holiday from work (paternity leave, he joked). Leigh, Tanya, Eric and Gus had visited them in hospital, bearing gifts of teddy bears, clothes, flowers, champagne and balloons.

'You are all so wonderful,' Emily said, she was still very emotional. Everyone cooed over the baby.

'Have you named her yet? It feels a bit odd calling her baby,' Eric asked.

'David and I discussed it and although we wanted to call her after Gus, because he delivered her, we didn't think Gus suited her, so we've decided to call her Lucy Tanya Stratton, after the two people who brought us together.' Emily smiled at Tanya. Tanya looked indignant at being only credited with the second name, but then she realised how childish she was being.

'Hello Lucy Tanya Stratton, I'm you're Auntie Tanya.' Everyone burst out laughing. 'What?' she asked.

'The idea of you as an Auntie. It's just so, so unfitting,' Eric said.

'Well darling, if you want to take the piss, oops sorry Lucy, I didn't mean to say that?' Tanya went red.

'It's OK, I don't think it'll scar her for life,' Emily joked.

'Anyway Eric, you should humour me as an Auntie because it's better for you than me being a mummy.'

Eric turned white. 'Whatever you say, Auntie Tanya.'

The house finally lost one of its house members, although it had possibly lost David a long time before.

Leigh felt David's loss now. She was happy for him but she would miss him and she wished her life were as complete as his. Or just a little bit complete. She tried to think only of the holiday. After all, if she let herself think about anything else, she had no idea what would happen.

When Gus had recovered from the excitement of the birth, he asked Tanya if he could have the journalist's phone number. Tanya, at first, didn't know what he meant. 'Millie,' he explained. Tanya told him she only had it at work, and for a moment thought about not telling Millie. Then she remembered the cameras would have captured it. When she went to the flat she had a word with Millie.

'Millie, it seems that Gus has finally gone insane because he likes you.' Millie blushed.

'What, you mean fancies me?' Cosmetically she had changed a great deal. This had a knock-on effect on her confidence. Since the night of her brilliant performance, Cherry and Lucy had changed her entire wardrobe, got her to a decent hairdresser and Harvey was lining up an agent for her. She was no longer from the pony club.

'Yes you moron, he fancies you.'

'Tanya you're so nice.'

'For fuck's sake, just tell me, do you like him? Or could you?'

'What about Leigh?'

'He likes you, not Leigh. Which reminds me, the holiday is only a week away, so if you want to go out with Gus you'd better hurry up and tell me.'

'I'd really like to.' Millie was crimson.

'Then you shall. Anyway, give me your mobile number or something and don't forget, if you do go out with him, you have to pretend to be a journalist.'

'Tanya I am a good actress.'

'Yeah, well remember, like me, when this is out in the open he might just not appreciate you being a good actress, so don't get too attached.' Tanya squeezed her arm; she had no idea why she was being so nice.

Harvey was ready to call it a day. Or a wrap. David wasn't there, they had only got Leigh and Gus for another week and the idea of filming Tanya and Eric wasn't that appealing. He announced to everyone that it was the last week of the film.

When Gus told Leigh about his forthcoming date with Millie, she wanted to rip her insides out. Instead she smiled and talked to Sukie again. But this time when Sukie suggested that it was time for Leigh to let go, she knew that it was true. This didn't make it any easier.

'You encouraged me,' Leigh said to Sukie.

'I know and I feel so guilty darling. Shit, LeeLee, I thought it would work, I couldn't see that it wouldn't. I was wrong and I am sorry and I will do anything to make it up to you.' Leigh assured her that she was forgiven, and there was nothing more she needed to do, but at the same time she couldn't help but blame her. Sukie had been wrong and Tanya was wrong. Who on earth could she rely on now?

'At least we are great friends and we'll have a great holiday,' the actress Leigh said.

'That's my girl,' Sukie replied. But Leigh wasn't Sukie's girl. She wasn't anyone's girl any more and that thought filled her with dread.

Gus took Millie out for dinner and they got on better than anyone expected. And Millie was right, she was a brilliant actress because she managed to act surprised when he told her things that she already knew. They went out twice that week, and the second time she came back and stayed in Fulham. She wouldn't let Gus have sex with her, 'she wasn't that kind of girl', but she wanted to sleep in the film set. As Tanya said, he probably wouldn't want to know her when he found out who she was really, which was a shame, because she had always liked him, always fancied him, now she did just that little bit more.

As summer sprang fully into life, it was reflected in everyone connected to the film. Although as anyone who has lived through a British summer will know, they are not without their storms.

Chapter Fifty-Six

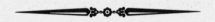

Tanya had been dealing so much better with things. This was because of Eric. She forgot her guilt because she was with him, although she should have felt guiltier because *of* him. She had no resolution. Her feelings see-sawed from relief to anxiety, from elation to despair. As she kissed Gus and Leigh goodbye, when they left for their holiday, she held them that little bit tighter. She behaved as if she would never see them again; she knew that they would never see her in the same way again. As the people who had installed the cameras got ready to take them out, Tanya and Eric were alone in the house.

Because the house was all but empty, Tanya stopped locking her door. She waved Eric off to work in the morning, she watched the last bits of footage, and spent every day in the editing suite. She was there that day. That day became the most horrible day of her life.

'Bob, this shot looks a bit odd, can we do something with it?' she asked.

'Sure, look.' Bob used a computer to light the shot differently. It looked much better.

'My goodness, we are so close,' she said.

'Tanya,' John called from his place in front of the screens. They didn't watch the screens much any more, especially since Gus and Leigh had left.

'What?' she called back.

'Eric has gone into your room,' John said, panic creeping into his voice.

'He was probably just seeing if I was there.'

'But he hasn't come out.' Tanya went to see John. Well, maybe he's just on the bed or something. Bob joined them.

'Or maybe he's found the control room,' Bob suggested, he was panicking too.

'Shit,' Tanya screamed. 'Has anyone got a car here?'

'Yes.' John jumped up and they ran to his car. He drove as fast as the London traffic permitted. After what felt like ages they got to the house.

'Do you want me to stay?' he asked.

'No, go back, it's only just after lunch, you'll know if anything happens. Keep watching.'

Tanya's hand shook as she tried to open the front door. Finally she got in. She looked around to see if Eric had left her room, but every other room was empty. When she walked, tentatively into her room she saw him sitting on her bed, staring at the empty screens in the control room. She froze.

'So you're back.' His voice was normal.

'Yeah.'

'I saw you walking up the stairs.'

'Yeah.'

'Interesting little set-up. You see I wasn't feeling so well so I came home. I was looking for you, seeing if you were working from home. Then I came in here and thought, as I didn't feel well, I'd get into bed and watch TV. I flicked on the remote control and this curtain type thing opened. Weird or what?' Tanya didn't know how to respond. His voice was normal, but his words weren't. He hadn't shouted at her; she wished he would. 'Do you think you might want to explain this to me?' he asked. 'Perhaps?'

'Oh shit.' Tanya sat on the other side of the bed.

'Right. Well if that's what it is . . .'

'Eric you know what it is.'

'That's where you're wrong. You see I know that this is a

bunch of screens which portray rooms in this house. No bedrooms, though. What I don't know is why they're there. Is this some kind of sophisticated security system that you installed when you went through your burglar-deterrent stage? Or is this the real reason you had a lock fitted?'

'Oh shit.' Tanya put her head in her hands. Her stomach was clenched with anxiety.

'Are you filming us for some television show you're working on? Is that it?'

'It's a film,' she whispered, rubbing her stomach.

'A film?'

'Yes,' she whispered.

'A film about us?'

'Yes.'

'Tanya, this is a bit of a shock to me. I come here and find that this house is riddled with secret cameras. Cameras that have captured, I guess, us, let alone everyone else. Do you think you could possibly find a way to explain to me in a little bit more detail?'

'Oh shit.'

'Stop saying that. Just explain.'

They sat there for a while in silence. Then Tanya found her voice and the whole story came tumbling out. When she finished, she was pale and her head was pounding. Eric was equally as pale.

'Why did you do it to us?' he asked.

'Because I wanted to work in films so badly, I thought it was more important than anything. Since you, well since I fell in love with you I know it isn't. Ironically, the whole film has taught me things that are far more important. But I know that isn't a good enough reason. I lived with the guilt; then because of the film and the new life I would get in Hollywood, I lived with happiness. Shit, I don't know.' Tears streamed down her face.

'It's really noble of you to cry. Tell me' – Eric was far more intelligent than he had been credited with – 'the weirdness, that was you and your film crew? Getting rid of Natasha; Howard;

Leigh's admirer; my prizes; you bumping into Em? Shit even David's gay porn. And me. It was all part of your little story.'

'No, not you. That was real. The rest yes. We paid Natasha to leave after I watched her conversation about Gus. I wanted to do something nice for Leigh so we invented a secret admirer. Howard was a paid actor. Your prizes were chosen by Millie.'

'Millie the journalist. Oh shit, now it all falls into place.'

'No, you don't understand. That was all we did. Yes we met Emily, but she and David did the rest, and Natasha was bad news so we got rid of her. And Leigh . . .'

'Fuck, Tanya you made her get that dreadful haircut.' Eric's face was red and blotchy as the full implications of what he was hearing trickled into his brain.

'No. That was Lucy, the writer; she didn't tell me she was going to do that.'

'Well, that's fine then. You tell me that our lives had a writer and you expect me to accept it. Did the writer decide that we should fall in love?'

'No, I told you that was real.' Tanya found some force in her voice.

'Can I believe that? You're my last prize aren't you? Well you were one of the best prizes, I'll give you that.' Eric's eyes were full of tears.

'I wasn't your prize. Us falling in love was as much of a surprise to me as it was to you. We didn't manipulate much, we didn't. We just put some additions in to make it more inter-esting.' As she finished speaking she realised how awful her words sounded.

'I apologise that we weren't interesting enough for you as we were. Tell me, how on earth did you think that we would ever let you release this?'

'Harvey said he'd pay everyone loads of money.'

'That'll be interesting, because I don't think they give you much money in jail.' Tanya shuddered at the harshness of his voice.

'It's not Harvey who will go to jail, it's me.'

457

'You?'

'Yes, I signed the contract, I took full responsibility.'

'You fucking idiot.'

'Why?'

'Because you will really hate prison.' Eric flinched at the cruelty of his words. He stood up and went to leave the house.

Tanya ran after him.

'Where are you going?' she asked him, as he was running down the stairs.

'To get out of here.'

'But . . .'

'Shut up. Just shut up. This is one huge mess and I need space.' He ran out of the house, realised he wasn't wearing any shoes and came back in. He ran up the stairs.

'Eric please, I'll tell Harvey that it can't be released. I can't lose you, don't you see?'

'Tanya, if I thought for one minute you meant that, I might just relent, but I don't.'

'I do, though, I love you. I want to marry you.' Eric stopped dead.

'What did you say?'

'I want to marry you? Not for the film, not for the story, for our lives. You might think I set you up, but if I did, then I'm a fucking good actress. You think I was faking it when I kissed you, when I touched your hair, your cheeks? You think I was faking it when we were in bed and I begged you not to go to work every day? You think I was faking it when I fell into your arms and told you I loved you? I might have had unforgivable secrets: I acted for my own ambition – yes; I was a selfish, thoughtless bitch – yes. But when I gave you my heart, it *was* my heart and now it's breaking. The thought of me watching you walk out of that door makes me want to die. I want you for ever, Eric, which is why I want to marry you.'

'Oh Jesus. Yes.'

'Yes what?'

'You're a selfish, deceitful bitch, but I do, for some crazy reason, believe you love me, and for an even crazier reason I do want to marry *you*.'

Thus Lucy got her proposal.

Bob and John were gripped.

'Holy shit.' Bob called Harvey and kept him on the phone the whole time, from when Eric started running down the stairs. When it ended with a proposal, they were all in shock. Cherry stood next to Harvey, who relayed all the information to her. She felt sick, until she heard about the proposal. She called Lucy and told her.

Tanya took Eric to her room.

'They're taking the cameras out.'

'I guess they got enough film then.' He hadn't forgiven her, but he did love her and when he thought about leaving the house he felt the pull of love dragging him back When she asked him to marry her, he thought it was a set-up, but even though he wasn't the most confident man, he knew that he and Tanya were real; and if they weren't, nothing was.

'What about the film?' Eric asked.

'Fuck the film. I'll tell Harvey to burn it.'

'You'd do that, for me? Even if you never got to work in films again.'

'Sure, I'll be unemployed and you'll have to keep me, but yeah I'd do it.'

'I like the idea of keeping you.' They went to bed to consummate their engagement.

The director said 'cut' for the first and last time.

Chapter Fifty-Seven

Post-Production

They were editing the film for real now but Harvey still had no idea how he was going to direct the footage. He didn't have time to deal with it; his immediate problem was Tanya. She had told Harvey that the film would never be released. Then she had changed her mind and told them that unless Eric agreed to it the film would never be released. Harvey had agreed that it would be his job to persuade him, and the best way was over dinner. As they were aware of Eric and Tanya's engagement; and Tanya told Eric about Harvey and Cherry's engagement, they made the invitation a dinner to celebrate two forthcoming marriages.

Tanya wanted them to behave as a normal couple, but that was exactly what they weren't. Ever since they had aborted the row and got engaged, they hadn't mentioned the film. Or Eric hadn't mentioned the film and Tanya had no intention of bringing it up. She didn't understand why Eric had suddenly forgotten about it, but she couldn't ask him. She felt trapped. Mentally and physically she spent the two days until Harvey's dinner as a wreck.

Eric noticed this but had no idea what to do. He watched with a detached interest as the workmen took out the cameras. He couldn't believe how sophisticated everything was; he was almost impressed. He saw that Tanya was barely eating, barely sleeping, and she looked ill; but he couldn't make it better for her. He didn't know how. He still didn't understand. How could anyone understand anything of this magnitude? He couldn't. At first he wanted to kill her, then he agreed to marry her. He was happy every time he thought of spending the rest of his life with her; he was angry every time he remembered what she'd done to him. The reason he didn't mention it was because he didn't know how. He had an awful feeling that he would just get angry again; he knew that there could be no justification for what she'd done. Yet he was being a hypocrite because he was still with her. However badly she had behaved, she was still the woman he wanted to marry; he wanted it more than anything.

They set off to Knightsbridge and to the dinner. Although Eric was suspicious, the only time he'd met Harvey he'd thought he was sleeping with Tanya and recently he'd discovered that that was just another lie. It was all more deceit. He was paranoid that if he went to the dinner, they would tell him more lies and he would never know what to believe, but there seemed to be a powerful hand in his back which was pushing him, so he agreed to go and he took Tanya's hand as she led him there.

Tanya had never been so nervous. The house was now a normal house. She was about to embark on final editing, if Eric agreed. That was it now. Her life was in his hands. For Tanya to relinquish that amount of control to anyone was unheard of; which was Harvey's main selling point.

They walked into the flat, and Tanya made the introductions. Eric said he knew who Harvey was, and he shook Cherry's hand. He felt uncomfortable. Harvey poured the champagne and everyone sat down.

'Eric, you must think we're all pretty unscrupulous,' Harvey said.

'I think you're mad. Why on earth did you come up with this idea?'

'I met you guys. Well, it was partly that, but mainly due to Cherry who got addicted to reality TV shows over here. Then I met Tanya, who had no idea what she was letting herself in for when I asked to meet you guys. The rest is history.'

'But did you have to interfere? I could almost accept it if you didn't interfere, well maybe I could, but the prizes, the secret admirer, Emily, Natasha.'

'Tell me one bad thing we did? OK, so maybe it was a bit wrong of us to make you think you won competitions you didn't enter, but I think that was probably the worst we did. Somehow, it all worked out. Natasha was using Gus and you didn't like her anyway, and don't tell me that Emily and David didn't both benefit from our intervention. I think that it might be better for them not to know the extent of our involvement; we didn't do much. I presume we should just let them think what they already think.'

'Don't you think that they will guess?'

'Maybe they will, but if we stick to our stories then they'll never know for sure.'

'More deceit.'

'White lies. The truth will only hurt them; we might have to tell Gus about paying Natasha because he'll wonder how she ever consented to being in the film. Apart from that we keep quiet.'

'I'm not sure; anyway this film will never be released and if it is who the hell would watch it?'

'You'd be surprised. Eric, I want to ask you one thing. Let us finish it; let us edit it. Watch it, then give us your verdict. The film can't be released without the consent of all the cast, but the rest of the cast don't even get to see it unless you agree.'

'What?'

'Well Tanya has made it your call. If you want you can pull the plug now, or you can wait until we've finished editing and then decide. It's up to you.'

'Right, so I am supposed to be pleased because you are going to make out that I'm in charge.' Eric was confused; Harvey calm; Cherry was pained; Tanya was green.

'No. I don't want you to be able to make such decisions. Tanya insisted. Look at her, she barely looks as if she has the strength to plan anything. I know you probably don't understand why she did what she did, but it was ambition; pure and simple. She had no idea that it would be so hard; that it would be as involved as it was. She, and we, didn't know the extent of what we were doing until we started doing it. She wasn't acting, not much, she didn't even have a script to follow, and if she was, then someone would probably have noticed and mentioned it don't you think?'

'I suppose so, but this isn't about blaming Tanya.'

'Isn't it?'

'No. Of course I blame her and I know she did it for ambition; I can understand, not about the ambition, but if someone said that doing this would further the things I believed in; you know, my legalisation of cannabis for medicinal purposes, then I might have agreed too. I don't know. I'm not sure if I would be able to lie that much. Tanya, sorry, but you did deceive everyone, including me, and I love you, and I want to marry you, and I even trust you – now – but the lies end here. One more and I won't be able to bear it.'

'I understand,' Tanya whispered. She had no lies left.

'Eric, it will promote your cause, there's loads of footage of you discussing it in that intelligent way of yours. You know, you guys will be stars; you'll be heartthrobs, not objects of ridicule. You are all intelligent, you all believe in different things, you've all built relationships in different ways in the film. It is mainly real. You know five people in a houseshare; five young professional people. Which is why it makes such compulsive viewing.'

'I'm not convinced, but I *am* hungry.' Eric remembered why he had come and he laughed.

'OK, we eat now, then Eric we make a deal. Let us finish the film, then see it; promise until you do not to tell the others; if you still want to kill it then you can, if you want the others to have the opportunity to agree to it then you can.'

'You make it sound as if everyone will agree to it.' Eric looked puzzled.

'I guess that depends on how much you want to be rich.'

'Rich?'

'You don't think we'd expect you to have gone through all this for free? Everyone will be paid a hefty fee, enough for you not to worry about ever working again.'

'How much?' Eric asked.

'I need to work on figures, but I'd say around a million.' Tanya went pale. (She had been promised double what everyone else got). Eric adopted her green look.

'Dollars?'

'Yes dollars, which at the current exchange rate isn't bad at all.' Eric tried to do some calculations but the only thing his head would allow was the word 'rich'.

'Let's eat shall we?' Cherry suggested and stood up to lead everyone to the dining table.

Harvey managed to steer the conversation away from the film for the entire dinner. Eric didn't bring it up again, which was unsurprising. Tanya managed to regain some composure, and after a while she actually looked like she was enjoying herself. Harvey was doing an incredibly good sales job on LA; he was trying to convince Eric that it was the most 'brilliant' place to live. He figured that once he'd got Eric to agree to the release of the film, all he needed to do was to get him to agree to move there with Tanya.

Eric began to relax. He remembered how much he liked Harvey when he first met him; his opinion of him, despite everything, was the same. Harvey managed to persuade him about the merits of the idea; the merits of LA and the merits of Tanya.

When they left, Eric was a little drunk and very happy. He had a woman he loved, and a sneaking suspicion that, despite the rights and wrongs of the whole situation, he was going to become quite rich.

Chapter Fifty-Eight

Harvey went back to concentrating on finding his hook. The editing wasn't as efficient as it should have been, they lacked direction and Harvey only had himself to blame. He was angry with himself. Everything had worked out but he was useless. He had great footage, but he didn't have a movie. The Studio would laugh him out of town. The most frustrating thing was that he knew the answer was there, he just couldn't find it.

This was unknown territory. He liked that, but that didn't mean he was able to handle it. He was the first to admit that his success was based not only on himself but on other people. His success was down to his ability to use the right people.

Ideas, Harvey knew, came because you were able to step outside the situation. That was why he had needed Lucy. But now, he was too far inside to see it clearly. Admitting he was unable to do it was not quite the same as admitting defeat. Defeat was not an option. Accepting that he needed help would save him.

He took himself back to the beginning and before. He relived every step to find his solution. Using this process, it didn't take him very long. The answer was Bill Harrison. He called him.

Bill felt on edge. Harvey always managed to do that to him. After he had asked him to put his name to a film he would know nothing about, after he had asked for his contact list, he was pleased to have nothing more to do with it. Bill had heard the rumour in Hollywood: that Poplar and Harvey, with their secret movie, had finally lost it. People were waiting gleefully for the day when they would crash. The problem was that Bill wasn't one of those people. He liked Harvey, he owed his success to him. He was nervous of him but he still wanted to help. That was why he had agreed to see Harvey straight away. Why he had cancelled all other appointments to see him. Why he was sitting in his office, feeling slightly sick but still ready to welcome him with open arms.

The first thing Bill noticed when Harvey walked in was that he looked tired. His physical presence, which normally filled the largest of spaces, seemed small. This made Bill feel sad.

'Harvey.' He stood up to greet him.

'Bill.' They shook hands.

'So what can I do for you?'

'I really need your help.' Harvey began to explain everything.

When he was alone later, Bill watched the tapes. He had been given them in chronological order, and with each one he felt his fascination grow. Harvey was unbelievable. It wasn't just that the idea was great, but also what Harvey had managed to do with it. The characters were strong; the storylines dramatic but real at the same time. It was amazing, truly amazing. As the footage came to an end, Bill realised that what they had could be the biggest movie of the year. It *would* be the biggest movie of the year. He called Harvey.

Harvey held the door open and ushered Bill into the apartment. If he was surprised to see him only twenty-four hours after their meeting, he didn't show it. Bill smiled, he could afford to. Not only would he be out of Harvey's debt, but he was also going to be a part of Harvey's latest success. He couldn't help but feel pleased with himself.

'We'll go to the office,' Harvey said, showing him through. Cherry, who was sitting behind her desk, stood up.

'So?' she asked, showing impatience that normally belonged to Harvey.

'So, is anyone going to get me coffee?' Bill asked. He was

teasing, they knew that, but he could. Cherry went to make the coffee feeling anxious. She drummed her fingers on the counter as she impatiently waited for the percolator to perc. She took the coffee into the office. Harvey and Bill were friends, supposedly, but the way they were looking at each other suggested otherwise. They were sizing each other up, they looked as if they would lock horns any minute.

'OK, we have coffee. Can we proceed?' Bill and Harvey both looked at her. They both smiled. She had diffused the tension and they were ready to play nicely.

'The movie is dynamite. Or potential dynamite. I have to congratulate you; it's a totally cool premise and the potential is more than huge,' Bill said.

'Thank you.' Harvey was bemused by the praise, Bill was actually a nice guy.

'You remember when we started this, I had to agree to pretend to be a co-director on the movie? Then we had a separate agreement for when they realised that I wasn't needed?' Harvey nodded, his face was taut. He had an inkling of what was coming next.

'I can sort your movie out for you. But I want a part of it.' Bill smiled. 'I want full credit as co-director.' This was the first time he had ever had the opportunity to control a situation with Harvey, he thought it might be his last.

'Sure.' Harvey smiled. It should never be said that he didn't give credit where it was due. After all the original idea was his and that credit was the most important thing. 'But you have to solve the problem,' he pointed out.

'Here's your solution. As with any movie, it's right under your nose. The problem is that you have a number of stories but not one main one. What you need to do is to strip the film bare and build it up again.' He paused and looked at Harvey.

'Go on.'

'Well, to find a hook in a movie there are a number of things you do. The first is that we find a main character. You choose not only the most obvious character, but also the one with the strongest story. In this case, you choose the original protagonist which is Tanya. She's the main one because she is the only member of the cast who knows what is going on. That is how you sell it. The film is real, but it was set up by one of the cast. She's the baddy, but she's also kind of good. She betrayed her housemates, which makes her an object of fascination. People will condemn her but they'll be intrigued by her at the same time. So we have a main character, but we need her main story to build the film around. Let's start with knowledge of the film. The viewer knows she knows because of her solitary conversations with the cameras. That is crucial to the film. We know she is lonely, we know she questions what she is doing, she admits her deceit but she justifies it with her loneliness.

'To take it further, we have her love affair with Eric. This is the perfect hook because she is genuine in her feelings for him but she is also directing their love scenes. You need to make this obvious but it's quite clear. We have the guilt she feels for him, then we have the finale where Eric finds out and she proposes. It's a brilliant way to end it. Everyone else, and everything that happens, including the birth of a baby, fits around it. What you have is a movie that could easily be just a crap romantic comedy, but it's not going to be. It's going to be a film about love, friendship and deceit. A killer combination. Use the fact it is real to sell it, but more than that, use the fact that Tanya is spying to sell it.'

'You're a fucking genius,' Harvey said, meaning it. It was obvious but it had eluded them all.

'No, Harvey, I'm a director. Anyway, what I propose is this . . .' Cherry took notes. Harvey nodded his head. With Bill's help, he really did have an amazing movie. Or he would have as soon as the editing team were on the case.

Chapter Fifty-Nine

Harvey briefed the editing team and they worked harder than they ever had done before. Tanya worked as many hours as she needed to, but she also had the job of ensuring that Eric didn't run out on her. They had the house to themselves; David had moved the last of his things out. Leigh and Gus were still on holiday.

Eric spent his days at his job where he had become increasingly disillusioned. This was due mainly to his daydreams of sunnier climates and a fat wallet. Eric wasn't a bad person; he hadn't got a bad bone in his body; but he was human and human enough to admit to himself that the life he was being offered was better than the one he had already.

They spent the evenings together. Sometimes they stayed in and cooked; other times they went to visit David and Emily. David had taken to bar work and fatherhood like a duck to water. He said it was too soon to make any decisions, but he thought he might leave work and help Emily run the bar full time. Lucy junior was proving to be adorable, but as noisy as her namesake.

They spent time with Jason and Serena; it injected normality into their relationship. They chose a ring, and decided that they wanted to be engaged for a year or two before getting married. They felt the engagement was all the commitment they needed, and both realised that, although they pushed the uneasy feelings away, there was still much that was up in the air.

Tanya loved the work; the footage was becoming a film; they

had told everyone of their engagement; they forgot about everything else. They learned to focus on the good times and ignore the looming black cloud that was Eric's decision and the subsequent decisions of the rest of the household.

Although the production team had been working hard, they still hadn't finished the rough cut by the time Leigh and Gus returned from their holiday all tanned and relaxed. Because of the situation, Eric and Tanya were the opposite – pale and tense. While Leigh and Gus enthused about their trip, Eric and Tanya tried to show the required amounts of enthusiasm. The problem was that they had spent all their energy by not arguing. They felt strained.

Tanya wasn't too exhausted to ask Leigh about the holiday when they were alone.

'How was it really?' she asked.

'Beautiful, amazing. Great fun. We hired a car, we went snorkelling, the hotel was lovely.' Leigh sounded like a holiday brochure.

'But how did you get on?'

'The same as always. Brilliantly. But since you introduced Gus to his latest girlfriend, I have to face the fact that we are only ever going to be platonic friends.'

Tanya felt stung. 'I'm sorry.'

'Not as sorry as I am.' Leigh looked at Tanya and felt empty. She was totally empty.

The time they had passed in the house, which didn't even amount to a year, had been one of the most confusing, frustrating and intense periods of Tanya's life. The cameras, the film, only added to this. And now it was over. Although it wasn't over because they still had to get the release forms signed.

Due to the mounting tension, Tanya concentrated on practical things. Eric buried his head in the sand. Tanya spoke to Harvey about the dilemma of David's room. Without his rent, the others would face a bit of an increase, and Tanya didn't feel right about that. So she took over his room as her office, and Harvey paid the rent. She could then at least look a bit more convincing with her 'working from home' story.

At this point, Eric and Tanya had an argument. The argument that had been brewing but that neither wanted to have. Eric said that she was addicted to being deceitful; she protested that she was only trying to do the right thing. Eric asked her how she could expect everyone to still be friends with her when the friendships were built on lies; Tanya asked him how he could be in love with her if that was the case; he told her that he had no idea, but obviously he had little choice in the matter; Tanya cried and told him that he did have a choice, he could leave her; Eric said that he couldn't leave her, he'd tried and he couldn't. He was unhappy with her, but he was happy with her. He was frustrated by her, he didn't understand her; but when he thought of leaving, the hole that seemed to open up at the thought was the biggest, blackest hole of his life. Therefore, although the situation wasn't ideal, there was little he could do. Part of him just wanted to see the damn film so he could make his decision. Instead, he could only imagine it, and even with his poor memory he couldn't think of anything that happened to them that would be worthy of a film. Maybe parts, but not an entire ninety-minute feature. It was incomprehensible.

Gus called Millie, who was beginning to feel the burden of guilt, and who told him she was ill. When Tanya confronted her she told her: 'You might have been able to let Eric fall in love with you when you knew all this was going on, but I can't do that to Gus. I refuse to see him again until I can be honest with him, and as I still work for Harvey I can't do that yet.' Gus, not being the best at playing hard to get, sent her Lucozade, flowers and even a poem. Tanya had to admire Millie's integrity, she wouldn't have minded some of it herself.

This caused another row between Eric and Tanya. He could live with her knowing what she had done to them all; just. But Gus had told him that he thought Millie might be someone he could come to care about; he wouldn't allow Gus to be affected by it, although he knew he would be. They all would be. Frustration built up once again, and he had no idea what to do about it.

Harvey was impatient once again. The editing wasn't taking as long as they thought it would, but it was still taking too long. He was bored with London now (an opinion he had voiced before), but also realised that he didn't want to make movies. He much preferred being an ideas man.

Bill was proving a more than adequate director. He even pointed out a possible problem with Eric's cannabis smoking that they had almost overlooked. Cherry got their lawyers on to it and the result was that they could use it without being liable for prosecution, 'after all the filmmakers weren't doing drugs', but from a moral point of view it would be a good idea for them to distance themselves from the issue by adding a strapline to the credits saying that they did not condone the use of drugs. They also suggested that it might be a good idea to get Eric to issue a press release saying he had given up smoking cannabis. Harvey chuckled to himself when he thought about what his reaction to that suggestion would be.

He was grateful to Bill, but also pleased with himself. He believed that the project had not just been about the film but it had been about self-exploration also. He knew himself so much better, or he knew his feelings better; London had changed them all. He knew it had changed them all for the better.

The problem with impatience is that it makes life difficult, there was nothing Harvey could do to hurry the process up, it was like being a child who is told to sit on his hands. Harvey was trying hard to sit on his.

He had directed it; he was just waiting for the rough cut.

Tanya, whose title of producer might not have been entirely accurate, had proved herself more than capable of working in films and was proving an asset. Harvey had Cherry draw up a contract to have her employment by his company continued. He would then second her to studios the way he seconded himself. It would be the best way for her to build her career, and that was what he had promised her when they started this. Now, more than ever, he wanted to ensure that she was taken care of.

Cherry sensed his boredom and devoted her last few weeks in London to making him happy. Cherry wanted to devote the rest of her life to making Harvey happy; she intended to do just that.

Bob and Amanda's relationship was purely professional, for about eighteen hours a day which is how long they were working. Amanda was his best editor so he and she would work long past everyone else. They were dying to spend some time together away from the screens, but they accepted the fact that their work was the priority. They looked forward to releasing their pent-up frustration.

Lucy's role had become rather like Tanya's, without the guilt and without Eric. She was working in the editing suite, seeing her stories being brought to life. At the end of the day she would go home, alone, and try to work out what she would do next. Lucy loved writing novels, it was all she had ever wanted to do; but now she thought that she might like to do something else. She wanted to go to LA, she wanted to see what the film business was like; she wanted some sunshine. Harvey had told her that he would fix her up with a job co-writing a script, which would give her the experience and the exposure to allow her to decide exactly what it was that she wanted.

Cherry joked that London would be empty by the time Harvey had finished poaching its residents. First Tanya, who now came with Eric, (hopefully); then Lucy and finally Amanda, who came with Bob. She was sorry that they couldn't persuade Millie to come with them, but she insisted that she wanted to take her acting classes in England and then see what would happen next. She promised Cherry there would be a reunion at some stage. Cherry even joked that if all went well, Millie might even bring Gus with her.

All the plans for the future offered a distraction; it allowed them to overlook the next hurdle and see only what was on the horizon.

Chapter Sixty

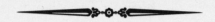

Tanya didn't tell Eric that she was about to go and view the rough cut; it would have made him more nervous than he already was. If any couple would make it then they would, Tanya reasoned, because their honeymoon period had definitely ended prematurely; although they were still so in love.

She met everyone at the editing suite. There was a large screen assembled; and the excitement in the room was tangible. They all took their places: Harvey, Cherry, Tanya, Lucy, Millie, Bob, Amanda, John, James and Sally. There was total silence as Bob started the film.

There was no soundtrack, but that didn't stop them from being mesmerised by what they were seeing. The first sequence had been taken from the video of the Lake District weekend when they had been drunk and running through the field – that was to be the title sequence. What followed was the story of the house. Tanya, who had been in on the editing, knew all the footage by heart, but when she watched it as a whole, she could barely believe what she was seeing. It wasn't just footage, it was a coherent story.

Harvey would sum up the story as being of love, friendship and deceit. Those were the main components of the movie; Tanya was its star.

Although Eric's causes and his 'habit' had a part in the film, Tanya was portrayed as his main focus from day one. David

475

appeared to be totally absorbed with his e-mail romance from day one; he appeared to be slightly distant to Tanya, although close to Leigh. Leigh's love for Gus ran throughout the whole film, and on screen it looked as if Gus's obsession with love was leading him to Leigh. The rows were more dramatic, the humour more humorous, the deceit totally incomprehensible.

Tanya had become the hook. Her relationship with her housemates, her betrayal of them, her guilt and her love for Eric *were* the film. Even the birth of Lucy junior hadn't taken the spotlight off her for long.

The conclusion belonged to Tanya and Eric. Eric's discovery of the film was played in full. That and the subsequent marriage proposal gave the film its dramatic conclusion. Although the film ended with Millie's interview, that was almost an epilogue.

The entire team who had made the film were stunned into silence. Then they prepared to celebrate. They had made a film; a film that was real, even if its links with reality were questionable.

Chapter Sixty-One

It took a short time for them to move from the rough to the final cut. Mainly because everyone believed they had a magical film. Harvey loved it, they had people of real quality here; a rare find. The cast was the film; the film was the cast.

Tanya shook with nerves as she took Eric to the editing suite to see it. She was relieved that this would be it. Whatever happened from here, Eric would be responsible, or he would take some responsibility. He would either put an end to it now, which they were sure he wouldn't, or he would agree to let them move on to the next phase in persuading everyone else to agree to it. If they did, she knew they had a big task ahead of them, but if Eric was on her side, she knew that she would be able to do it.

Eric was impressed by the editing suite, which was, after all, one of the most sophisticated around. At first he was quiet, although he managed to make one crack about everyone knowing everything about him, but him not knowing much about them. The same people sat in the audience for the final cut; Eric was the only addition. Harvey believed in safety in numbers and had instructed his 'audience' when to laugh and when to cry. He had to get everyone to agree, because Steve Delaney and his cronies at Poplar were salivating over having a final film which had, funnily enough, come in under budget and ahead of schedule: two rarities which were equally unusual in the film industry. Poplar still had no idea what the film was about, and any concerns voiced about the quality of the film were dismissed by enough people who had utter faith in Harvey.

Eric watched in silent amazement. He didn't have time to analyse the thoughts and feelings running around in his head; he was too busy watching and trying to equate what he was seeing with his life. The thing was he couldn't. He recognised himself, as he recognised his housemates. He knew that what happened, happened to them, but not in the way he was witnessing. He saw everything was funnier, or sadder, or more emotional; it was different. When it finished, he felt relief and detachment. That wasn't his life. Well it was, but it wasn't his *real* life. He turned around and found everyone was staring at him. He made a split-second decision.

'For a million dollars, I agree to it, so I suppose you should show the others.'

Of course they knew that Eric was different. For a start he knew about the film and he'd had time to come to terms with it. They also had the added advantage of Eric being in love with Tanya. Nonetheless it was another hurdle overcome, and although Eric wouldn't sign the contract until the others did, he did manage to forgive Tanya, almost, which meant that the rows stopped and they were able to talk about what had happened.

'How do you feel about it now?' Eric asked. He had felt a detachment when he watched it and that confused him.

'I still feel wretched, although I can't help but be excited. Is that OK?'

'I understand. I almost feel the same. I didn't mastermind it but now I agree to it. The thing is I don't know if I'm doing it for you or for the money.'

'Can't it be both?'

'It could be. But that doesn't make me feel less guilty.'

Now it was Tanya's turn. 'I understand,' she said.

*　　*　　*

The last decision they had to make was how to break it to the cast. Harvey pondered this and decided that he would get them to the editing suite, under false pretences, and show them the film. His decision was based on the following reasoning: if he told them first, they would probably fly off the handle and refuse to watch the film; this would prolong the whole situation. Show them the film, let them go mad; then go in and offer the money and do whatever it took to get them to agree. He would give himself a week from when they first saw the film to persuade them to sign the contracts: Harvey loved nothing better than a challenge.

Chapter Sixty-Two

Eric was worried, Tanya was terrified, but they both supported the decision and they were both involved in making the arrangements. Tanya felt better, she was no longer on her own in the deception; the downside was that Eric felt worse.

The invitation came from Tanya. It was an invitation that she and Lucy devised. Eric conceded that one more lie wasn't going to make much difference so he went along with it.

Harvey, perhaps, was now behaving like a director more than he had done throughout the film. He had stage-managed and scripted the whole event. Tanya issued everyone an invitation to a special one-off screening of her latest television series. 'The Real Life Show' was the name Lucy chose because Harvey still hadn't come up with a title. This title made Tanya shudder. Millie and Cherry got invitation cards printed – it looked professional. The plan was for the housemates to watch the film in the same room as everyone else had seen it; now known as the screening room. Eric would be with the housemates, Tanya would be in an adjacent room with the crew – in the event of a violent reaction. Sally was to be stationed at the door to stop anyone from leaving before the end. Sally was terrified, she was an assistant, not a bouncer. Harvey believed he had organised everything, but also knew it had the makings of a farce.

Because there was no music in the film, James and John had

put a make-shift soundtrack on the parts where there was no dialogue, to add a bit of atmosphere.

When the day of the screening came close nerves were fraught. Harvey snapped at everyone, then apologised. Cherry started biting her nails again. Millie burst into tears because now Gus would find out who she really was and probably never want to see her again, and she wanted to see him. Bob wore an even bigger frown than usual and kept running his hands through his less than adequate hair. Amanda pouted and refused offers of conversation. Even James and John were rendered silent by the situation. Sally was just in pieces because she couldn't see herself as a bouncer.

They all needed the film to be released. Harvey had done exactly what he said he would do. He had made a ground-breaking film; one which was not only entertaining and visually stimulating, but also had the added attraction of being real. He knew that the studio would be delighted when they saw the movie; he knew the marketing potential was huge. He expected it to be one of the biggest grossing movies of the year. It would put Poplar back on the map; it would make them all rich. He was proud of himself; he had proved himself right again and all that remained was for five people to sign the release forms; Eric (who had agreed), David, Leigh, Gus and now Emily. Emily hadn't been invited to the screening because she wasn't a main character, but if David agreed, then she probably would too. Harvey would do whatever it took, because his movie, this movie would make history and as he said before he started this project, that was what he wanted.

No one was fazed by Tanya's invitation and no one was suspicious. She had never invited them anywhere to see her work; but that didn't mean anything. It was a Saturday, they had been given notice and they were all waiting at the house in

Fulham for the taxi that Tanya had ordered to arrive. Tanya was already at the editing suite; Eric was with his housemates.

'I hope this isn't going to be too boring,' Gus said. He had so little time off that he wasn't sure he wanted to spend his Saturday watching some TV programme. He also wanted to call Millie, whose 'not serious' illness seemed to be lasting longer than it should. He wanted to talk to her from a personal and a medical point of view.

'I'm sure it won't,' Eric said; he was nervous and he felt sick. He didn't like being the only person who knew what was going on. He wondered if Tanya felt the way he did. If she did, he felt sorry for her; the guilt was far worse than anything that would happen to the others. Or maybe it wasn't, but it felt it.

'I hope it doesn't go on too long. I've got a pub and a family to attend to.' When David said this it was with pure pride.

'I'm sure it won't,' Eric repeated.

'Come on, we might enjoy it,' Leigh said, she was happy about going; it killed time and at the moment she needed to kill time.

'I'm sure we will,' Eric added.

The mood was jubilant as they got into the taxi. Leigh, David and Gus were blissfully ignorant of the real purpose of their journey as they gossiped and teased each other. Eric sat in silence, his discomfort growing by the second. Although he was quieter than ever, no one else noticed due to their own high spirits.

They stepped out of the taxi and into the building. Eric trailed behind, trying not to behave as if he had been there before. When they arrived at the editing suite they were met by Tanya. She kissed everyone, lingering on Eric. 'You OK?' she whispered. He nodded but looked anything but OK, as Tanya ushered them into the screening room.

It was the first time that most of the team had seen them in the flesh. As Sally came out she was introduced to everyone, Tanya asked them to take their seats.

'Gosh, this is quite exciting,' Leigh said.

'I hope you enjoy it,' Tanya responded, as she moved as quickly as her legs would take her into the adjacent room. Sally smiled nervously, and stood across the door and crossed her arms just like a bouncer. Everyone sat in their seats. Bob used a remote control to dim the lights and the screen sprang to life. The crew all crossed their fingers as the words, '*The Real Life Show*', came up on to the screen. Tanya prayed. The film rolled.

'It's us,' Leigh said as the Lake District footage played. They laughed. It wasn't until that had finished and they saw themselves in the house that they began shifting in their seats uneasily.

'What the fuck?' David was shaking his head, his eyes glued to the screen.

'That's me leaving for work,' Leigh said, she looked at Gus, then at David, then at Eric, who had hung his head.

'It's our house, our home,' Gus finished. They all looked at each other then back at the screen. They all felt sick, but they watched.

When Leigh's crush was revealed, she nearly screamed. Her complexion, which was normally pale, was ghostly. She hunched her shoulders. She looked at the door, she could barely focus on the girl standing across it as her eyes filled with tears. She turned back to watch.

Gus couldn't believe what he heard. He had no idea Leigh harboured those feelings for him, and he felt desperate that his finding out had to be so public. That on top of the nature of what he was watching made him want to throw up. He reached out and squeezed Leigh's hand. He didn't look at her, she couldn't look at him.

'I demand to know what is going on now,' David shouted. He was red-faced and he was on his feet. His fists were clenched by his side. Leigh and Gus looked at him, but were drawn back to the screen.

'Please, just watch,' Sally said, as she'd been primed to do by Harvey. David looked as if he would make a bolt for the door, then he stopped. He sat down and he watched.

Gus turned white when Natasha appeared. He looked at Leigh. Leigh, who could feel his pain, took his hand. They watched on. He thought he might faint as the kebab episode appeared; he looked at Eric, his eyes full of questions and pain. He turned back to the screen. He watched her telephone conversation, he watched himself being dumped. He looked at David with his clenched fists and his red face. He turned back to the screen.

Lucy held Tanya's hand as they stood in the next room. They heard David's outburst but they couldn't see any other reactions properly. They had to wait, while everyone else watched. As the film progressed, the grip she had on Lucy's hand tightened. By the time the film finished, Lucy said she had lost all feeling in it. Tanya had lost all feeling everywhere, except on her cheeks where she could feel the tears sliding down.

If she had been in any doubt as to how badly she had actually behaved (after all Eric didn't push it, and it was Eric's reaction she based the expected reaction of the others on), she was not now. She knew that what she'd done was unforgivable.

Sally's job was easy after David's first outbreak. They were all compelled to look at the screen, although they felt disgusted. They watched kisses, intimacy, tears, their lives, and although they wanted to run away, none of them could. But Sally felt awful. She felt horrible. She had watched their lives; she felt as if she knew them, but as she saw them reacting to the film she realised she didn't know them at all. She didn't know Leigh had tears that painful; she didn't know that David had such anger; she didn't know Gus could feel such hurt; she couldn't believe the extent of Eric's guilt. She felt like bolting from the room herself.

Harvey and Cherry looked at each other. They both knew that this was it. The finale. Whatever happened next would affect the rest of their lives. As such there was no room for regrets.

The editing team stood in a corner, almost cowering. Bob held on to Amanda's hand the whole time and James and John tried fruitlessly to crack jokes; there were no jokes. This was it, the moment they had been working towards for months. This was the end. And, as the words 'The End' spread across the screen, no one moved.

Finally, after what felt like hours, Leigh spoke.

'That was us.' It wasn't exactly what she was thinking, but it was the best she could do.

'Our house,' David added.

'Fucking hell,' Gus finished, with more vehemence than his voice had ever betrayed. They turned slowly to look at Eric. 'You knew?' Gus asked.

'Not all the time, only recently. Listen guys, you need to let her explain.' Eric was flustered, the tips of his ears burnt.

'Who is *she*?' Gus asked.

'Tanya,' they all replied in unison. Tanya's cue had finally arrived.

Leigh stood up as Tanya entered the room. 'I can't believe it. I won't believe it. That was us,' she cried. Gus and David moved so they stood either side of her, protectively. 'And you,' she pointed at Tanya. 'You were supposed to be my best friend.'

Tanya looked at Leigh. She opened her mouth and closed it again. Harvey and Lucy moved to stand either side of her. Eric stayed in his chair. His eyes were closed.

'I *am* your best friend,' Tanya whispered. They stared at each other. Tanya felt the familiarity of her eyes. Eyes that she had grown up with. She knew now, she saw just how much of a betrayal it was. The realisation left her without air, she struggled to breathe. How could she have done this? How could she have done it to the one person who would never hurt her? 'I'm sorry,' she stammered, feeling the full inadequacy of her words and the futile tears that were running down her face. Everything was too late.

Leigh looked into Tanya's eyes. Here was the girl who had saved her when they first met. The girl who had always protected her, helped her, loved her. Tanya was so much a part of Leigh that Leigh never questioned the rows, or the disagreements; she trusted her with her life. If there was one person whom Leigh trusted to know the right thing to do, it was Tanya. For twenty years she had relied on that. And she was wrong . . . so, so wrong.

'You stole our lives,' Leigh shouted. It was as if a light had switched on inside her. The Tanya she was staring at with the familiar eyes was someone she no longer recognised.

Gus and David looked at each other. David wanted to shout and scream and ask her why? But he looked at Gus and Gus indicated for him to let Leigh deal with it. Gus knew that, whatever had happened, Leigh needed this.

'I am not going to ask you what you were doing. All the lies. You told us that Harvey was your boyfriend, not Judas. You said that you were still working at the same company. You even had digs at me for spending too much time with Gus and neglecting you. Is that what this is all about? You felt neglected so you filmed our lives?'

'No; yes; I don't know. I was angry and I guess honestly that it made the decision easier.' Tanya's voice was barely above a whisper.

'I am so glad we made it easier for you, or I did anyway. You knew how screwed up I was over Gus, yet you let that be filmed, you even coaxed it out of me. You knew that Gus was in love with Natasha but you filmed his heartbreak, you knew how David felt about Emily but you filmed that. You even filmed—' Leigh paused. Tanya opened her mouth to respond.

'Don't you say a fucking word.' Leigh had warmed to her task. 'You violated us, you invaded our privacy, you watched our lives, you even watched Gus having sex. Fuck.'

'Fuck,' Gus echoed going red. He looked as if he would keel over.

'You watched everything. And now you are dirty. Soiled. How could you be anything but . . . when you watched us? How can you even stand up straight? You are the most disgusting person I have ever met.' Leigh paused again. Tanya opened her mouth again. 'Don't even think about it,' Leigh screamed. 'And you behaved so normally, are you human? Are you even human? Because you don't have a heart as sure as hell you don't have any feelings.' Leigh was screaming now and Gus had his arm around her waist. He looked at Eric, he was scared for Eric. Both Tanya and Eric opened their mouths to retaliate, but Leigh again stopped them. 'I will tell you when I've fucking well finished, but it's not yet, so shut up!' She turned to Eric. 'Tell me, although I am not even ready to start on you, tell me when you knew?'

'About a month ago, I guess, when it was finished anyway.'

'What, after the cameras were removed?'

'No, not quite.'

'Great. Anyway you can wait. Tanya, I will never, ever forgive you for this, never. Not only the lies, the deceit, the betrayal, but also for this, for dragging us in and making us sit through this. And you' – she pointed to Harvey and Lucy – 'you are sick, understand – sick. The whole lot of you should be locked up.' Leigh looked at David, who nodded at her, his face was contorted in rage and he couldn't find any words. Gus looked sad, he still held on to Leigh, although it was unclear from his face now if he was supporting her or if she were supporting him.

'Please, please let me explain,' Tanya whispered, tears still falling.

'No. No. Do you know how many times I have let you explain, apologise, manipulate me? Christ, we just watched the crappy way you speak to me and I let you. We all forgave you anything, but this, never. How can you explain, how do you ever think you'll explain? Is there a good reason you hid cameras in our house?' Tanya shook her head. 'Is there a good reason why you sold us to the devil over there?' Tanya shook her head. 'Of course not. Because, correct me if I'm wrong, but you did it for yourself. For your ambition which has always been more important to you than we were, and for money I guess.' Tanya nodded. She looked at Harvey who was watching the exchange intently. He couldn't believe how ballsy Leigh was being. He wanted to congratulate her but luckily remembered himself in time. Lucy felt the same.

'Please let me,' Tanya begged.

'No. No. In fact if I have to look at your face one second

longer I am going to punch it. Get her out of here, get her the fuck out of here.' Leigh exploded in hysteria and Lucy and Harvey led Tanya back into the other room. Cherry looked at Harvey questioningly, he gave Tanya to her and shook his head. They had all heard almost every word of Leigh's diatribe. Harvey and Lucy returned to the room. Sally, who was trembling slightly, was still standing across the door.

Eric stood up. He saw Harvey and he shrugged.

'I don't think you're wrong you know,' he said, to Leigh.

'Well if you did you'd be a fool,' Leigh replied, more softly, she couldn't quite bring herself to hate Eric.

'It's just that I had to forgive her. I love her you see. She makes me happy and I couldn't give that up. It was easier to forgive her.'

'I understand,' Gus said and he went over and hugged him. 'I understand, you know that, but you have to see that the decision isn't like that for us. We loved her as a friend and she betrayed us. You didn't, you were betrayed as well, and I know that as soon as you found out you would have done your best to protect us, I know that. Eric, you aren't to blame. But you know now that whatever happens we can't forgive her, you understand that don't you?' Leigh started crying as she saw the friendship and the hurt and the confusion in the eyes of Gus and Eric.

'I understand mate,' Eric said. They looked at each other, eyes glistening with tears, then they hugged again. Leigh turned away and threw herself into David's arms.

'Look what she's done, look what she's done to all of us,' she sobbed. David held her.

Harvey Cannon was lost for words. True, he had no way of turning back and he needed to get them to agree, but even he hadn't been prepared for what he was seeing. He was watching them being pulled apart, he was watching them falling apart. And he felt worse than he ever had done in his whole life.

Eric walked into the other room to join Tanya. He needed to hold her and he needed to tell her he loved her. He understood

the others, he understood Leigh. He understood that his friendship with Gus and David could never be the same again. But he
needed to hold Tanya, to kiss her to tell her he loved her. That
was how he knew he was doing the right thing.

'Guys,' Harvey said when Eric had left. The room was
depleting. The camp was divided and Gus, Leigh and David
were feeling as if they were on their own. Sally still stood across
the door. She felt sick and was sure, now, that her job description
didn't stretch to this.

Millie had kept quiet and stood silently by Cherry's side. She
saw the state that Tanya was in, but she feared for Gus. Eric
came into the room and held Tanya.

Millie looked to Cherry and Lucy. 'Can I go and see Gus?'
she asked.

'Honey, wait until we hear how they react to Harvey.' They
all waited.

'Guys,' Harvey repeated. They stared at him coldly. 'This
wasn't all Tanya, it was my idea.' As soon as he'd said it, he
realised how feeble it sounded. How could they, the computer
geek, the pink fairy and the poet make him sound and feel feeble?
He could deal with studio heads, top finance people, high-
powered lawyers. So why was he seemingly unable to talk round
the three people in front of him.

'We don't doubt that it is your fault too,' David responded,
coldly. 'But Harvey, how on earth do you expect us to deal with
this? You all did this to us, but only *she* knew us.'

'Do you want me to tell you the whole story? Will you listen?'

'Is it a story, or is it the truth?' Gus asked. He was tired and
furious. It was as if he had no idea whom to trust, apart from
David and Leigh.

'I'll tell you the truth,' Harvey replied. They all sat down.

Harvey took himself back and started in LA. He told them
about Poplar, about coming to London, about everything. He
told them about Tanya making the decision easily, but not being
able to live with it easily. He didn't tell them about the
manipulation, and as their brains were a long way back in

the processing of information, they didn't quite think to ask. When he had finished, everyone sat still; in the other room, they were just as still. Cherry was thinking back to the simplicity of LA. Bob was thinking about the rain; Tanya was thinking about how awful she felt; Eric was thinking about his friendship with Gus; Millie was thinking about Gus; Amanda was thinking that if it wasn't for the awful betrayal she would never have met Bob. James was worried; John was worried; Lucy thought that Harvey was in trouble. She was convinced that they would tear his film to shreds and throw it away.

The silence seemed to last an eternity; Leigh broke it.

'It's a great story, Harvey, and if you assure us that it's true, then it's true. But that doesn't make it any better. You saw me cry, you saw me laugh, you heard my secrets. The others went through the same. You've turned private moments into a public spectacle. Is that legal?' she asked, turning to Gus, then David.

'I don't think so,' David replied.

'Thought not.' Leigh looked at Harvey threateningly. Harvey sighed. He couldn't think of the words to bring them round. He decided they all needed time.

'Can I ask you to think about it? I know how you feel now but please think about it before deciding finally.' Harvey was pleading with them.

'Not that it'll make any difference,' David said.

'We'll never come round,' Gus said.

'I'd see you burn in hell before I'd let you release that,' Leigh said. Harvey wondered how on earth he had made them such a terrifying threesome.

They stood up to leave and a number of people surged into the room. First Tanya, with Eric in tow.

'Please, LeeLee, please give me a chance,' she cried.

'Never,' Leigh said, calmly, taking hold of David's hands.

'David? Please,' Tanya cried. David shook his head and turned away. Then Millie appeared. Gus seemed to remember, then, who she was.

'So, you don't work for a magazine,' he said, tiredly. Everything was too complicated, he wanted to sleep for ever and not wake up until the whole thing was over.

'That's why I kept away. It wasn't fair.' Millie looked at Gus and prayed that he would forgive her.

'Millie, I can't take this in. I feel like I'm in the middle of a huge joke. First Tanya, then Harvey, then you. I can't cope. None of us can cope. Leave me alone.' He looked at her coldly, and led the procession out of this studio of horror.

'Well that didn't go badly considering,' Lucy said, once they'd left. Everyone stared at her aghast.

Leigh refused to go home and David suggested they stay at the pub. They needed to stay together. To get them through the shock of what they had just heard, they would need drink, and plenty of it, so they decided the pub would be a very good idea.

They stopped off at home to pick up their stuff. Tanya and Eric weren't there. Leigh shuddered as she walked into the place that had been their home.

'It makes me feel creepy. Imagine, they saw us walking into the kitchen, everywhere. This place doesn't feel like a home any more.' Tears returned.

'It's all right, we don't have to come back, I'll call Brian, I'll terminate the lease. We'll find somewhere else.' Gus desperately wanted to make things better, for all of them.

'In the meantime, you can stay with us. There's a spare room, which you'll have to share, but it's quite comfortable. Stay as long as you want,' David offered. He was already wondering what Em's reaction would be.

'Thanks David. I don't think I could stay here.'

David drove them to the pub and they said goodbye to the house in Fulham. All their belongings were still there and they would go to collect them; but they would never live there again.

They sat in the flat above the pub. Leigh, David and Gus were nursing stiff drinks, Emily was nursing Lucy. David told her the whole story. As David spoke, everything became a little bit clearer to him. As Gus and Leigh listened, they felt the same. Em had no such luxury, she was learning everything for the first time.

'You mean you see me pregnant?' she asked when David finished. He nodded. 'And you hear me giving birth?' He nodded again. 'And you see Lucy?' Her eyes were incredulous.

'That's not all, you see David pining for you, Gus almost naked, and me crying and wearing pink all the time. It's so embarrassing. But it didn't happen like it happened, and that confused me.'

'Shit,' Emily said.

'Exactly,' Gus agreed.

'And Eric is obviously in love with Tanya because he is sticking by her.'

'Well, he must really love her.' Emily shrugged. 'It's almost funny when you think about it.'

'Funny? Are you crazy?' Gus asked.

'No, but look, the way you describe it makes it sound as if it's this hilarious comedy, with a cast that is completely mad. But it's you, and you are the cast and it's funny and crazy; and there are tears, laughter, kisses, love, everything. I mean, Leigh, did you really wear only pink?' Emily proved her point about it being funny by laughing. Lucy junior burped.

'It is *not* funny,' David said.

'I guess not. Must be my hormones.' She burst out laughing again. The others looked at her as if she was mad.

Eventually she recovered and put the now sleeping Lucy down in her cot. Then she returned to the sitting room, and to the dilemma.

'So, what I think we need to do . . . do you have drinks?' David went to refill the glasses. 'What we need to do is to look at this sensibly.'

'How on earth can we?' Leigh protested.

'That's what I am here for,' Emily replied. 'Firstly, you are all shocked and hurt and betrayed, so the issue here is Tanya.'

'I'm never forgiving her, I really won't,' Leigh said.

'That's fair enough and you've made a decision. Do you think . . .? No perhaps not.'

'What?' David asked, going to sit next to Emily.

'Do you think that they set us up?'

'What?' Gus asked.

'Oh my God. You mean Natasha, Eric's prizes, Tanya bumping into Emily; Howard,' Leigh shuddered. 'It was all a set-up?' Just as they began to make progress, they were again struck dumb. Emily realised that she hadn't been much help.

An hour of silence passed.

'Do you think we should find out for sure if it was a set-up?' Leigh asked.

'What good would it do us?' Gus replied.

'It's over now,' David mused.

'My God, that's it!' Leigh exclaimed.

'What?' Gus asked.

'It *is* over now, that's what we have to remember. Whatever happened to us in the past, it's over. I will never forgive Tanya for what she did, and I will never accept what she did, but it's over.' Leigh looked almost jubilant. 'But when things are over we lose things.' She looked sad again. Everyone stared at her, they were trying to keep up with her dialogue, but it wasn't proving easy. 'The house. I am talking about the house. It's gone. David lives here, and Tanya, not that I give a shit where she lives, I bet she'll live in Hollywood with her bastard friends. And Eric, he'll go with her. That leaves Gus and me. I know it wasn't that long, but you know, sometimes I think I'll look back at that time as the time that changed me so much.' Leigh's anger had turned to nostalgia. Still the others let her speak, they could sense that she was unleashing something inside her. 'I know I went ga ga over Gus and, no offence, Gus, I think that maybe it was just because I was confused and alone and feeling vulnerable. Not that you're not lovely and the loveliest man I know, but to go quite so far with an unrequited crush at my age, well it's a bit much. But you know I feel better now. I know we're just friends.' Gus nodded which confused Leigh further. In the film they'd watched, it looked as if they were going to get together. How could that be? She shook her head, that must have been all in her head.

Gus and David exchanged glances. David, who had known Leigh all her life, had never seen her like this. Part of him was pleased; Leigh was getting all the tension out; part of him was scared; it was the stuff nervous breakdowns were made of. Gus was worried. He knew how therapeutic getting thoughts out could be; he also knew how dangerous it could be. He'd seen it before. Leigh's thoughts were running all over the place; anger; sentiment; loss; gain. He hoped that they could bring her through it; he blamed Tanya.

'I mean it's farcical. They made a film of us. In a few months, I don't even know how many months it was; they filmed us and we didn't know and then there's a film and it's a whole film. Not that I can remember much of it; it was too much of a shock. And they seriously think we'll let them release it? Is that what they think? Because we won't. We'll never let them release it will we?' Her voice was shrill. Everyone shook their heads. It was not their turn to speak. 'No, of course we won't. I mean why would we? Because Tanya says so? We always do what Tanya says don't we? Do you remember when I was little and I first became her friend, well I didn't become her friend, I became her clone, didn't I? I dressed like her, I copied her, I did everything she suggested. She was always Batman; I never got to be Batman. She always made me be Robin and I never got to save anything. I was just her sidekick. That's all I've ever been, her sidekick. And now, I am her victim, because she used me. She used us all; she used us for her ambition, for her career. It makes me sick, it makes me want to kill her.' Leigh was angry again. She had come full circle. However, she still wasn't ready to stop. 'Bitch, she is the biggest bitch. When she told me to move from Bristol I did, when she said I had to stay with Jason on that mattress I did. When she wanted to go out, I went with her and when she wanted to stay in I did. Then, when we moved to the house in Fulham – Oh, I'm going to miss that house so very much – when we moved in it was like I got some freedom. I did what I wanted, I don't know why but I did. I felt free. That house gave me enough strength to be free, but it also made me crazy. I got free then got crazy, it was my prison and it was my key. Shit, I don't know, I don't know. How the hell am I ever going to know? I feel like I'm going mad, I don't know what to do, please help me, someone help me.'

'I will fucking well kill her,' David hissed.

'Tanya?' Emily asked.

'Look what's she's done, how could she?'

'I don't know. I don't know how anyone could do that to anyone.'

Gus put Leigh to bed. Emily cried. David held Lucy junior and prayed for a good future for her.

Gus sat on the bed, stroking Leigh's hair. She was such a delicate person, such a china doll, he felt his heart break for her; he loved her. He wasn't in love with her, but she had become one of the most important people in his life. She was a great friend, a valuable friend. She was a special person. He needed to be strong for her, to take care of her; he had to get her though this. He needed to get them all through this, because, even though the filming was over, he felt dirty, soiled, invaded. His privacy was all but nothing and he felt as if someone had burgled his life.

Later, when David, Gus and Emily retired, they felt that there had been no progress. They were all adamant that the film would never be released, but that still didn't help them deal with how they felt about being filmed. Gus had a shower and scrubbed himself almost raw. David wouldn't, or couldn't, let Emily touch him. They all went to bed without the first clue about what to do next.

Tanya and Eric returned to the empty house. Tanya paced, Eric fretted. She begged him to let her call them at the pub, but he wouldn't. Harvey and he had finally realised the full awfulness of the situation, and found no words adequate to describe it. He looked at Tanya, she was a mess. Tanya wasn't a cold calculating bitch. He was sure that although he believed this, the others wouldn't. He knew that Harvey had been pulling her strings all the way along.

He wanted to hate Harvey but couldn't. Harvey was too honest about what he'd done. He admitted to manipulation; he was dishonest but he was honest about it. Eric didn't understand him, but he had a sneaking suspicion that Harvey would find a way to get everyone to agree to release the film.

As he put Tanya to bed he lit a joint and wondered how they would ever come out of this intact.

John, James and Sally were having a drink. Sally's nerves were in shreds, so they took it on themselves to try to calm her. They knew that, effectively, their jobs were over; their work done. All that was left was to see if the film would be released. They all prayed that Harvey would achieve it.

Bob and Amanda spent the evening at her flat. He was experiencing a very intense worry attack. The film, going home to LA empty-handed, the friendships that had been broken; everything. Amanda found herself without the words to comfort him. She had no words to comfort herself.

Lucy invited Millie round to her flat, where she proceeded to get her drunk. Millie was worried mainly about Gus, but also about everything. After all she didn't want her acting debut never to be seen. Then she felt selfish and got more upset about that. Lucy, who by now thought she should be sainted, pacified, listened to her and hugged her. She wondered how it was that, by working on this film, she had become such a nice person. It worried her slightly.

Harvey and Cherry spent the evening in the apartment in Knightsbridge. Harvey outlined his seven-day plan once again, to Cherry. It gave them a badly needed focus.

Day one was over. The only plan Harvey had had for day one was to get them to watch the film. On day two, he would leave them alone and ensure that Tanya did the same. On day three he would go and see them. He would gauge how they were feeling and would act accordingly. It would be time to start implementing the final phase. If they talked about suing, or going to the police, he would then tell them about Tanya taking full responsibility. Although she wasn't their favourite person he would bet his life on them not going to the police. He would ask them to think about it, and he would arrange for Emily to see the film.

. Day four would depend on day three. He would send Eric round, because Eric was still liked. Then, when Eric reported back to him, he would decide if he would then go and see them again. If Harvey did go round on day four, he would try to talk them gently round. Day five would see him trying to get them to forgive Tanya. He would see them to discuss Tanya's unhappiness (and that, he was sure, was genuine), and he would try to make them believe that he cared more about their friendship than he did about the film. He would not mention the film; he would not let them mention the film. Day five would be a day of persuading them to release the film by not talking about it. Day six would be money day. He would just go in and offer the money. The arguments and objections would have all been raised by then, so it would be time to talk cash. Therefore, on day seven he was confident he would get full consent.

Cherry approved the plan, because she had no better idea, and although they tried to believe that they had everything under control, they went to bed, holding each other for comfort; because they needed it more than they ever would admit.

Chapter Sixty-Three

Leigh woke and wondered for a minute where she was. She turned over and saw Gus sleeping beside her. He looked beautiful. At first she thought she was on holiday again, although they'd had twin beds in Barbados. Then she realised that they were in David and Emily's spare room. Next she remembered why she wasn't in her room. Finally she remembered she didn't have a room. She felt a little bit shaky as she got out of bed and she was careful not to wake Gus. She walked into the sitting room, found the drinks cupboard and poured herself a brandy. She drank it and immediately felt sick. She poured another one and went to sit on the sofa.

Why couldn't she make sense of it? It wasn't just the film that she didn't understand; she didn't understand her behaviour in it. She felt scared and vulnerable. She felt sick and violated. She felt lost and empty. She felt everything at the same time and none of it made sense.

The sudden realisation of what had happened nearly knocked her off her feet. Tanya must have hated her so much to do what she did. Leigh believed that it had been done to *her*; the others were just victims because they happened to be there but Leigh was the true target. And in order to make Tanya hate her that much she must have done something very bad. That's what it came down to. It wasn't Tanya's fault, it was her fault. She had caused it by being so bad. Leigh was full of self-loathing. She hated herself. She hated herself more than she hated anyone. She had nothing going for her, she was a mess, a disgrace, and she deserved all the pain she felt. Chanting voices filled her head; *'Loathsome, hateful, disgusting, useless, ugly, boring, weak, pathetic, loathsome, hateful . . .'*

She couldn't shut them off, they got louder and louder until she felt as if they would burst out of her and she would see them. They would attack her; they would kill her.

She was mad. She had gone mad. She had lost her best friend; she would never have Tanya to look out for her again; no one would look out for her. She was alone. Her head hurt badly, she went in search of some painkillers.

She crept into the bathroom, thankful for the peace in the flat. It was in stark contrast to the war going on within her. She felt the cold tiles beneath her feet and wondered if she would ever feel anything but cold again. She walked over to the medicine cupboard and opened it. Inside, she could barely make out what was what. Creams and pills, creams and pills. She pulled a bottle out; it was full of pink tablets. Although she didn't know what they were, she thought they would get rid of the pain.

Without *seeing* the label she pulled the lid off and took two. She swallowed them and felt sick again.

The chanting started once more and Leigh put her hands over her ears and automatically closed her eyes. It wouldn't stop. She retched. The chanting got louder and louder as she backed herself against the wall. She was back in the playground again; in a circle, the children pulled at her blonde curls, they told her she had a boy's name; they chanted at her. And this time, Tanya didn't come and save her. No one came to save her.

She felt the tears numbing her cheeks. The pain was getting worse. She got another pill and put it in her mouth, gagging slightly as she swallowed it. Then she took another and another and another. She wasn't thinking; she had no idea what she was doing; she just wanted the pain to stop.

She had no idea how many tablets it took to ease the pain but they worked and she thanked God as she lay down among the remaining pink tablets that she'd somehow scattered on the floor and went to sleep.

It was David's turn to get up for Lucy junior. As he cradled her in his arms after changing her nappy, he realised that he was dehydrated from the amount of alcohol he had drunk earlier. He walked with Lucy to the kitchen, where he stopped at the sink and noticed the empty brandy glass. He wondered whose it was, because he knew for a fact that Emily had cleaned up everything, as she always did, before she went to bed. He panicked as he sensed something wrong.

Running to the bedroom he shared with Emily, he woke her up, and put Lucy into her arms. Lucy, sensing the panic in David's voice, started crying and Emily held her close and leapt out of bed at the same time. David ran out of the room, just as Gus, on hearing the commotion and noticing Leigh's absence, got out of bed. They ran into the bathroom instinctively.

She looked so sweet; she looked so peaceful as she lay among the pink pills. David wanted to hug her.

Gus, acting instinctively, pushed David out of the way and leaned down to check if she was still breathing. She was. Barely.

'Call an ambulance,' he shouted. David stood rooted to the spot, tears still streaming. Emily, who had put Lucy back in her cot, came up behind them.

'Shit,' she screamed.

'Call an ambulance,' Gus repeated. Emily ran straight to the phone. Gus rolled Leigh into the recovery position, she was heavy all of a sudden.

Emily tried to keep calm as she spoke to the emergency services. 'What's she taken?' she shouted to Gus from the doorway. She was panicking about Leigh and about Lucy, because Lucy was screaming and she had never left her before when she cried. Gus was now propping Leigh up in his arms and trying to bring her round. He kept hold of her as he reached over and picked up the empty bottle.

'Ibuprofen,' Gus shouted.

'Do we know how many?' Emily called back.

'No,' Gus answered. He was so frustrated, he couldn't believe what had happened but he wouldn't lose her. He wasn't going to let her go. He kept checking Leigh's airways were clear but she showed no signs of regaining consciousness. 'David, get me a spoon,' he commanded. David looked at him, blinked and ran to the kitchen. He came back with a dessert spoon and a teaspoon.

'I didn't know which one,' David stuttered, passing the spoons to Gus. David started praying, he prayed harder than he ever had in his life.

Gus opened Leigh's mouth and gently stuck the teaspoon down it. Nothing happened.

David knelt down and started talking to her. 'Don't leave me,' he pleaded. 'Please don't leave.' Emily came up behind him and hugged him.

'The ambulance is on its way. I need to go to Lucy.' She felt the tears on her cheeks as she went to the nursery.

Gus poked the spoon down Leigh's throat again, he was sweating; his face was shiny with sweat and tears. This time Leigh gagged. He wouldn't remove the spoon and David watched in horror, as Gus made her vomit.

'Thank God,' Gus said. David ran over to the loo and threw up as well.

Gus cradled Leigh in his arms once she had stopped being sick, and tried again to bring her round. She was still unconscious. Gus started praying. David sat down by the bath and tried to breathe slowly.

The doorbell rang, and Emily ran to get it, with Lucy in her arms. As she led the ambulance crew to the bathroom, she felt close to collapse. She saw David: he looked so frail; Leigh looked peaceful; Gus looked shattered. She wondered how on earth they would ever get over this.

The ambulancemen said that Gus had saved her life, as they

put Leigh on a ventilator to regulate her rapid breathing. David insisted on going with them, but Emily had to stay behind. As she sat down on the sofa, after they'd gone, cradling Lucy, she burst into tears. She was crying for everyone.

Gus's role changed when they got to the hospital. He was no longer the doctor, he was the worried friend and David's support. They waited outside the cubicle while Leigh was examined, they waited while she was taken to get her stomach pumped. Although she had been sick, they had no idea how many pills she'd taken and they were not taking any chances. It seemed like a million years later when they reported that Leigh was no longer in a critical condition. Gus and David sobbed together in quiet relief.

'Shouldn't we call some people?' Gus asked. He felt he was responsible.

'I've called Em,' David replied. 'Who else needs to know?'

'Her parents?' Gus asked.

'They don't speak much any more. I guess that might be one of the reasons she ended up in this mess.' David blamed himself.

'How come?'

'Well, she moved to London and they wanted her to stay near them in Bristol. They thought by moving to London she would be subjected to bad influences and they thought they wouldn't see her enough. Crazy isn't it? They don't see her at all now. Anyway, as she's going to pull through, it should really be Leigh's decision whether they find out.' David looked sad, he felt drained. But he was also relieved.

Neither of them mentioned Tanya or the film.

They stayed with Leigh all night, and were there when she woke up. Gus touched her cheek, David said he was sorry. Leigh apologised and they all cried together. It was as if that release solved a lot of things. It was a turning point. Leigh tried to explain to them, although they were tired, they needed to know, to try to understand. And as Leigh explained, they all understood a little. She promised them that she didn't want to die; she assured them she was relieved to be alive. She was. She was so thankful that she was still alive.

She knew she had a long way to go, and she explained to Gus and David that she would need help, and possibly a lot of it; she said that she knew that she had problems and she really had to try to like herself. That was what it all came down to. She told them that she would be fine, she was almost feeling fine now, but she would need their support to help her through. They told her that they would always be there for her.

Reluctantly Gus and David left Leigh so that they could get some sleep. So much had happened in the last twenty-four hours. It would take them a lot longer to recover.

The following day Emily visited the hospital. Emily seemed to have grasped Leigh quickly; she understood, somehow, how everything that had happened to her led to this event. She understood that no one could have noticed because the signs were subtle. Moving to London, the upheaval, the crush on Gus which happened overnight, the rows with Tanya, the piece of elastic that Tanya seemed to have Leigh on (Emily knew that Leigh would get some distance between them only to be catapulted back), and finally there was the film.

Leigh could have saved a lot of time if she had gone for counselling to Emily instead of to the hospital psychiatrist. Emily realised that Leigh's main problem came from the fact she was painfully insecure. It was as if everything she did was built on this insecurity, which is why the film triggered this reaction. She had just regained some confidence when she had to watch her behaviour on screen. The humiliation would have made her feel just as insecure as she had been to begin with. Emily was correct.

Leigh had asked Emily to call Sukie, who in true Sukie style dropped everything and came straight to the hospital.

'LeeLee,' she managed before she started crying.

'I'm going to be all right,' Leigh reassured her. She told her as much about what had happened as she could – but she was so tired. Finally she explained her reliance on Sukie.

'I feel so guilty,' Sukie said as she held her hand. 'It's an ego thing with me. You know how I love my team to adore me, to need me, to heed my advice. I shouldn't have tried to make you someone you weren't.'

'My whole life has been me being someone I'm not. It's not you. For my parents, for Tanya, for Gus. If I'd known who I was in the first place I wouldn't have leaned on you so much. But it's going to be different now. I'm going to be me.'

'And I'm going to stop interfering.' They hugged, cried and talked some more. Sukie felt the burden lift from her shoulders. Leigh had been the toughest protégée of them all. Now they were talking as friends for the first time. Sukie told Leigh to take as much time off work as she needed. Then she told her that the decision she had to make about the film was the first decision that the new Leigh would have to make.

The first Harvey knew of his plan having gone awry was when he turned up at the pub in Putney to see his cast. He walked through the pub and spoke to a girl behind the bar who phoned upstairs then led him to the flat. Emily didn't know Harvey; she had never met him before.

'I don't know who you are,' Emily said. She was tired and she was not in the mood for visitors.

'Harvey Cannon.' He stuck out his hand and Emily flinched, she was finally meeting the man behind the whole thing. His plan for day two was thrown when Emily, wearily, told Harvey that Leigh had tried to kill herself the night before. She had used up all her emotion, she told him straight. Harvey was struck dumb. He couldn't believe what he was hearing.

'Is this some sick way of getting back at us?' he asked.

'No, although that would be preferable to the fact that Leigh is at the moment lying in hospital after having her stomach pumped because she took an overdose.' Emily stared at him.

'Does Tanya know?' he asked.

'I doubt it. After all why do you think Leigh did it?' Emily was not too tired to be angry with the man in front of her. He looked upset, he sounded upset but that didn't generate any sympathy in her.

'I have to tell her. I know that she's seen as the enemy, but she needs to know. I can't even believe it myself, but there's one thing I've learnt now, and that is that it wasn't worth it. It wasn't the right thing to do. Nothing is worth this, Emily, believe me, I would rather destroy the movie than destroy people's lives.'

'Do what you want. After all, it won't change the fact that Leigh could have killed herself. But you're right about one thing, it wasn't worth it.'

'I know,' Harvey said, sadly, as he got up and left.

His mind was in turmoil as he took a cab to Fulham. As he got closer, he played the events back in his mind. First Tanya, getting her to agree, then making the film, there were the tantrums and the tears, and then laughter and finally the love. And now death, or near death. He had no idea why Leigh did what she did, but he knew that it was something to do with him. If not all. He couldn't believe that the pretty, sweet girl had tried to do something so ugly. He had tears in his eyes as the cab pulled up in front of the house. He had never felt so guilty in his entire life.

Tanya and Eric turned white as Harvey imparted the news. He was white himself.

'We have to go to her,' Tanya said.

'Wait, wait until tomorrow,' Harvey advised.

'Why?' Tanya snapped. The guilt was murdering her.

'Because she's off the danger list but she'll be exhausted. Let her rest, and go tomorrow morning. Don't mention the film. I'm pulling the plug.'

'What?' Tanya asked.

'It's not worth this,' Harvey replied. He had never been so sincere in his life.

'What about the studio, the money?' Tanya asked. She wasn't sure how she felt any more. She was responsible for Leigh trying to kill herself. But Harvey pulling the plug?

'Fuck them. This is about life, Tanya, real life. It's not a show. Honey, I am sorry for everything I have put you through and the job offer is still on, *if* anyone will hire me after this, but I cannot live with myself trying to persuade those kids to let me release this, not after what has happened.'

'You're right. Fuck the film. When I go tomorrow I'll tell them, I'll tell them that *they* are more important.' Tanya began to see a light. She looked at Eric. Harvey looked at Eric.

'Don't you think it's a bit late for that?' Eric said, quietly.

Chapter Sixty-Four

The following day Tanya got ready to visit Leigh in hospital. Eric was going with her. More than ever before, Tanya needed to talk to Leigh, the question was whether Leigh would talk to Tanya.

When they walked on to the ward, the first thing that Tanya noticed was that Leigh was flanked by Gus and David. Emily was also there, holding Lucy junior. She almost faltered; she hadn't seen them since the screening. She didn't know how they would react, especially after what had happened. Eric sensed this and he took her hand and led her to the bed. Tanya hung back a little as Eric greeted them.

They looked up and then at Leigh. She seemed composed.

'LeeLee, are you all right?' Eric asked, unable to keep emotion from his voice.

'I'm fine, Eric, thanks, or nearly anyway.' She smiled at him. She felt peaceful and she felt as if she was being put back together.

'Leigh?' Tanya said. She was Leigh again not LeeLee. Leigh looked at her for a long time. She made a decision.

'Can you all leave us?' she asked. Everyone looked at her.

'Are you sure?' Gus said.

'Wouldn't it be better if we stayed?' David asked. Leigh shook her head. As they walked from the ward they looked back.

'Close the curtain,' Leigh commanded, and Tanya obliged.

'I'm sorry,' Tanya said.

'So am I. It was a stupid thing to do.'

'Why did you?'

'I didn't know what I was doing. I thought that without you I'd never be safe.'

'What?' Tanya asked.

'Crazy isn't it? For over twenty years you saved me, or so I thought. I couldn't do anything without you, I needed you. You let me need you.' She paused, she felt amazingly calm.

'I know.' Tanya did know, she had lived most of her life, needing Leigh to need her.

'And then you betrayed me so much that I knew I could never forgive you, which scares me, because I always thought I needed you. I need you, yes, but I can't forgive you, that drove me mad. I thought that I wouldn't be able to survive, especially after the humiliation you subjected me to. I thought I would never recover. That's why something in me snapped.'

'I still don't understand why you did it.' Tanya looked at her pleadingly.

'It isn't about you, Tanya, it's about me. I felt low, humiliated, scared, alone, I don't know. There were voices in my head – do this, do that – it wasn't a decision I made, it was a decision that made me. I can't be any clearer than that. What you did was wrong, we all know that, I think you do too. But it wasn't just that. It was everything and more.'

'We're not releasing the film.'

'Really, after all you've done for it?'

'It wasn't worth it, Leigh. I know that now. Isn't it funny how you get clarity when things are over?' Tanya looked pensive.

'It's true. The film is over and you've learned things. Our friendship is over and I've learned a lot. I don't hate you Tanya, but I don't love you any more. I don't want you in my life. I don't want to fight but I don't want to need you. You need to leave my life, you understand that don't you?' Leigh had tears in her eyes; Tanya had them too.

'I understand. I just wish I didn't hate myself and you didn't hate me.'

'Don't you see, it was never you I hated, it was me. It was always me.' Leigh smiled, sadly, and she turned her head away so the tears could fall properly.

As she made her way out of the ward Tanya couldn't see; her eyes were so full of tears she was rendered almost blind. The others, minus Emily and Lucy junior, saw her and rushed forward. She collapsed into Eric's arms and kept saying she was sorry, over and over again.

Eric helped her to the nearest waiting area and sat her in a chair. He kissed her, and Gus and David looked at each other. Tanya looked up.

'It's going to be fine,' she said. 'I mean Leigh's OK, which is the important thing, right? Our friendship is over but we'll cope. Leigh is going to be better off without me. You all will.'

'Tanya,' David started. 'I don't know. I have no idea what to say. I don't blame you for Leigh, but you know, she is right, she will be better off without you.'

'I want to see her,' Eric said. 'I know you guys aren't each other's biggest fans but do you think you could keep an eye on her?' Gus and David nodded.

Leigh had stopped crying as Eric approached. He kissed her on her forehead and stroked her corkscrew curls.

'You idiot,' he said.

'You're the first one who's said that to me. Everyone else is pretending I didn't do anything wrong.'

'Well you did. You stupid moron of a girl. Do you know how special you are?'

'I'm beginning to.'

'Good. Now I know that this friendship you have with Tanya is over and I am not even going to try to question it. But, that being the case means that I guess we won't see so much of each other any more. I want you to know I love you and think you're the sweetest person in the world. I'll miss you, but I'll never forget you.' Eric had tears in his eyes.

'I'll miss you too.' Leigh pulled him close and hugged him. They held each other for a long time.

'I promise you that the film will not see the light of day publicly. It'll be destroyed,' Eric said, as they parted.

'I've been thinking,' Leigh started.

'What?' Eric asked.

'Why don't we let them have it?'

'Have what?'

'Have their film. It's done, it's over, if they want it let them have it.'

'Why?'

'Dunno. I guess I was thinking that it would be an appropriate goodbye gift.' They hugged again. Eric decided not to mention Leigh's views on the film to Tanya. Leigh knew that she needed to talk to Gus and David again.

Chapter Sixty-Five

After Eric had left, Leigh thought of little else than their conversation. She knew that somehow if she could see it released, it would be a show of her strength; strength she needed to see for herself. She believed it would also be an appropriate way to put the lid on her friendship with Tanya. A dramatic end to a dramatic friendship. She needed to move forward, she needed to close the door on the past.

Gus collected Leigh from the hospital and took her straight to Emily's flat, where David, Emily and Lucy junior were waiting as a welcoming committee. David and Emily felt apprehensive although she insisted that she was fully recovered, they were still incredibly worried about her. David felt more responsible for Leigh than ever and he had vowed that he would take better care of her.

Leigh hugged them both as she walked into the flat and she planted a kiss on the sleeping Lucy's head.

'I am so glad you are here, Gus has been fussing over me, it's quite tragic really.'

'Tough. We'll all fuss over you. Come and sit down,' David said. They all went into the sitting room.

'Can I get you a drink?' Emily asked.

'No thanks, but I would like to talk to you,' Leigh replied. They all looked at her and nodded. 'I don't want you to think I'm any madder than I was, but I've been thinking. I thought that we might let them release the film after all.'

Gus, David and Emily stared at Leigh. 'But . . .' Gus faltered. He had no idea how to respond.

'Why?' Emily asked.

'Well I guess it was the film that triggered all this stuff. But it wasn't the cause, was it? We've all been through the cause and I don't want to again, but it wasn't the film. Now I feel stronger than I've ever been and I think that releasing the film will help me to believe in my own strength.'

'I guess there's a certain logic in that,' David said. 'But isn't that giving in to Tanya yet again?'

'I know why you think that, but it isn't. It's my decision. Of course, finally it's your decision too, but Tanya isn't here, she isn't pulling my strings any more. I bet she'll be delighted if we do give them the go ahead, but I'm not doing it for her, I'm doing it for me.'

'I'm not sure LeeLee, have you thought about the implications? What happens if this film is a success?' Gus asked.

'Then we'll all be famous.'

'But do we want that?' Gus was nervous for himself now, the idea of being filmed and watched by the crew was bad enough, the idea of being watched by the public terrified him.

'We need to discuss it, sure, but think about it. We have to get paid for it surely? We could all use new starts; we could all use the money. I know that's not everything, but don't you see, we are in control. That is the whole point. We're in control of this film now. We spent months being spied on while they controlled us, now the roles are reversed. We could get them to destroy the film but is that the best option for us? We are the decision makers and if we think that the film will change our lives for the better then we'd be silly to let pride stand in the way.'

'What do you suggest?' Emily asked

'It's not just up to me, I want to make a decision we are all going to be comfortable with. If that means we destroy the film then fine, but if it means that we release it . . .'

'You really want this, don't you?' Gus asked. His terror had subsided slightly, but he was still unsure about how he felt.

'I do, I really do. I have never been in control of my friendship with Tanya, and I've barely been in control of my life until now. If I can make this decision, then I know I can make all decisions.'

'If it's what you really want, then I'll agree to it,' David said. He still felt guilty about what happened to Leigh, he would have done anything she wanted.

'No. I am telling you what I think, but I refuse to decide for you. You have to be sure that you want this too.'

'I can't be sure,' Gus said. 'I don't know what the implications are, and although I agree it would be a fitting end to the past year, I'm not sure that I want to be famous.'

'That's if we are going to be famous, it might flop,' David pointed out. 'But if we do get money, well I know I would love the opportunity to leave my job.'

'Gus?' Leigh asked.

'I feel a bit uncomfortable about everything still.'

'That's fair enough. I have an idea though. How about we interview Harvey?'

'What exactly do you mean?' Emily asked.

'We get Harvey over here, and we ask him what the film will do for us. We find out all the benefits, then we make our decision. But not until we make him sweat a little, after all, it's the least we can do.' Leigh laughed.

'I would like to see him squirm,' Gus concurred.

'So that's agreed then.' Leigh couldn't stop smiling. She could physically feel the presence of her strength, and it gave her a whole new lease of life.

Leigh asked David to call Harvey and arrange a meeting. They decided that the meeting would take place in two days time. David laid out the conditions of the meeting. Tanya was not to be there; Eric was. That was all Harvey was told.

This new development surprised Harvey. He hadn't yet destroyed the film; he hadn't told Poplar (even though he had sent them the final cut and they loved it, but that was another story). In his heart, his dream film was dead. David's call confused him. David hadn't given anything away on the phone. When Harvey asked questions, he refused to answer them, leaving Harvey completely in the dark.

He thought back to the blackest time of the film; the David and Emily saga, and he remembered how he had felt that the film was controlling them. Well now the cast were controlling him.

Harvey shut himself in his office with his computer games, he had no idea what else to do. He turned to his old friend, instinct, who told him that things would turn out all right. For once he couldn't trust it. This was his punishment. All he could do now was to play along and let his cast do what they wanted. It was all he deserved.

He went to tell Cherry about the meeting, putting on a façade of bravery. If he could convince everyone that they were still OK, that their careers weren't over, then maybe he could believe it. The full implications of what he had done finally dawned on him; he had put his whole future, and the future of Cherry, Bob and Tanya into the hands of three incredibly pissed off individuals. He had never felt so stupid in his life.

Leigh was still physically weak so she went to bed early that evening, Emily was working behind the bar, and Gus and David were babysitting.

'What do you really think?' Gus asked David, once they were alone.

'I don't know what to think. So much has happened to us. First finding out about the film, then Leigh. We didn't really have time to let anything sink in before we careered off into the next disaster. I still can't get my head round the fact that they actually filmed us,' David replied.

'Neither can I. I think that's the problem. The whole idea is bizarre, and I'm angry. Bloody angry. Leigh stopped me in my tracks a bit, but it's all here now. I can't believe Tanya did that to us, and even worse, I can't believe Eric knew before we did and didn't tell us.'

'It's all so fucking confusing. I'm so angry with Tanya, and I'm also sad because despite all her faults she was a friend, a good friend. I've known her most of my life. And Eric. Well, I'm upset with him. I kind of understand why he did what he did, but that doesn't excuse things. Oh shit, what are we going to do?'

'I don't know. I can forgive Eric, I have to because he was as much of a victim as us for most of the time. I just wish he'd told us all when he found out. At least we could have done something.'

'Yeah like foiled their plan and messed up their film.'

'Exactly. But we didn't. Look, David, how are we going to resolve this?'

'Give Leigh the decision.'

'Are you sure?'

'No, but look at us, we don't know what to do. Neither of us wants the film released, I'm sure, but at the same time, we wouldn't mind if they paid us. We're only human and we are just as capable of selling out as Tanya was. But then again, we will have to live with our decisions for the rest of our lives. And I'm not sure that I'm ready to be a film star, whether we're successful or not. My mind is in knots over this and to be honest I've got Emily and Lucy to think about, I don't want or need to think about this anymore.'

'So basically because of our complete inability to make a decision we go along with Leigh?'

'At least we'd be doing something good. She feels stronger but she's not fully recovered, and by letting her do what she wants we could help her recover.'

'I guess. I guess that's as good a reason as any to base our decision on.'

'Right, so we go along with her. We let Harvey come over and we grill him, then we turn to LeeLee, ask her what she thinks and we subsequently decide what we want to do. But we go along with her.' David knew what he meant but got confused in the explanation.

'You mean that we let Leigh decide but make her think it is

our decision too,' Gus translated for him. David nodded.
Harvey's future was now in the hands of just one person.

On the day of the meeting Harvey was nervous as he rang the
doorbell to the flat above the pub. He was nervous as they all
greeted him. Cherry had wanted to go with him, but he had
said no. It was he they had asked for and he was not going to
try to manipulate this meeting. It was their meeting. Everyone
else involved, including Tanya, sat in the flat in Knightsbridge
and waited. They were nervous and scared. Tanya also felt very
alone.

Harvey looked at his cast, minus Tanya, and sat down.

'How are you?' he asked Leigh.

'I'm going to be fine. No permanent damage.'

'Good.' Harvey sat still.

'Let's get to the point,' Leigh started. Harvey almost laughed
at the role reversal. He was the one who would normally say that.
'This has been a huge nightmare for us, I don't need to tell you
that. But the nightmare is over. All of it. I came through the
other end; as did we all. We might not be fully intact and we'll
never be the same again, but we are survivors. That said, it
doesn't excuse what you did. You spied on us; you lied to us; you
were like Big Brother, playing with our lives. That is unacceptable. It was like you were playing with us, with our lives. Our
real lives weren't real. Whatever your reasons, there can be no
justification for what you did to us. You made our lives *public*. But
that's enough recrimination, we all know what you did, you
know what you did. What I am saying now, is, that I want you to
give us one good reason to let you release this film.' Leigh had
never been more composed in her life.

Harvey was stunned by Leigh. He couldn't reconcile the
sweet, fluffy girl of his movie with the girl who stood before him
now. As he frantically searched for an answer to her questions, he
also looked for the 'old' Harvey. He had made billionaire studio
heads do his bidding, so how could he be rendered useless by

these people? He looked at them. They were all staring at him impassively apart from Eric who had bowed his head slightly. He took a deep breath; he had found his strength.

'Remember the story I told you about the big powerful studio in LA?'

'Yes, but that's not the issue. We need more than stories,' Leigh replied. Harvey felt the calm sweep over him. He knew what he was doing once more.

'This movie will make you famous.' It was his game now, not theirs.

'What if we don't want fame?' Leigh asked. Harvey smiled, slowly. He wanted to savour the moment; after all he had come back from disaster.

'I'm sure you're interested in what fame brings with it,' Harvey teased.

'Go on,' David prompted, he was feeling uneasy.

'Money.' He looked around the room once more. Everyone apart from Eric was now looking at him with rapt attention.

'You know you asked for one reason,' Harvey continued. They all nodded.

'I'll give you a million.'

'A million reasons?' Leigh asked.

'No, a million dollars. Each. You let me release this and you can all have one million dollars. Apart from Emily of course, but we'll discuss that as a separate issue.' Harvey smiled. He had regained control.

Everyone was dumbstruck. No one spoke. No one moved. It was as if Harvey had turned them to Stone.

Leigh looked at everyone. 'It's a lot of money,' she said. She forgot all about giving Harvey a grilling and thought about the future.

'It is,' Emily agreed.

'Shit loads,' Eric added.

'Enough to give Lucy a great life.' David looked at Emily. His objections had all disappeared.

'Enough for us to buy a flat, LeeLee.' Gus looked excited.

After all, money spoke to people; especially people who weren't rich. All Gus's doubts evaporated.

'It's enough full stop. Whatever we've been through, we did come out the other side. Harvey, you've got yourself a deal.' Leigh smiled, her sweetest smile and she stood up to shake Harvey by the hand to seal their fate.

'You mean you are really going to let me release this film?'

'Of course. Did you ever doubt it?' Leigh laughed.

'Actually I did.'

'Well you should always remember Harvey, everyone has their price.' Leigh kissed everyone. 'Now it really can be over,' she exclaimed. She was about to suggest a drink to celebrate, then she remembered something. 'Gus?'

'Yes?' Everybody including Harvey turned to look at Leigh.

'Millie. You should phone Millie.' Gus looked at Leigh. He had wanted to phone Millie, badly, but since Leigh's overdose he wondered if seeing Millie, or forgiving Millie, might be seen as a betrayal.

'Really? You think I should?'

'I know you should.' As Gus went to the phone, Leigh knew that, now, it was all over. Finished.

As Harvey made his way back to Cherry and the apartment in Knightsbridge he played Leigh's words over and over in his head. It was true he had made their lives public lives, and with that thought, he knew that not only did he have his film, but he also had his title.

Chapter Sixty-Six

Harvey got Cherry to draw up contracts before anyone could change their minds. No one could quite believe that they'd pulled it off, but no one dared question their good fortune. The cast couldn't believe they were going to be film stars, but they didn't even consider changing their minds.

The contracts that they all signed were simple. They got one million dollars and in return they had to agree to publicise the film in the UK. Eric and Tanya had already agreed to do any other publicity that was required. They had to *pretend* to still be a cohesive group while they publicised the film; they had to act like friends. Everyone agreed and the contracts were signed.

It was left to Tanya to tell Eric that he was supposed to release a statement saying he had given up smoking cannabis.

'No way,' Eric said.

'Why not? I'm not asking you to give up, just to say you have. Firstly darling, you're going to be seen smoking on screen soon, which might generate some police interest in your life. Also we're moving to LA, and Harvey is pulling every string possible to ensure that we don't get deported. Your drug connections, as innocent as we believe them, might not help.'

'So if I don't do it, I might not be allowed to stay with you?'

'No.'

'I don't have to say that I don't believe in the medicinal qualities of it?'

Tanya sighed. 'No.'

'I guess I've sacrificed more to be with you. So, just for my precious, demanding, high maintenance fiancée, I'll do it.'

'That's what I thought you'd say.'

As Harvey, Cherry and Bob took the contracts and the movie back to LA, they felt both sad and excited. As Amanda packed up her flat, she looked to the future. As John signed a new contract to work on his next film, he knew he would miss everyone and everything; as James took Sally to work with him, they both felt nostalgic. Lucy was particularly lost. She had spent all her time with Tanya. When it was time for Harvey, Cherry, Bob and Amanda to board their plane, there were tears flowing everywhere.

Lucy was going to follow them out to LA when Tanya and Eric did. She had taken up Harvey's offer to find her a screenplay to co-write, but she still felt sad as she waved them off.

In London, normal life continued for the cast of the film. David changed nappies; Leigh went back to work; Gus worked hard and in his spare time looked for a flat for himself and Leigh to buy (just as friends), for he was still dating Millie. Leigh and Gus had discussed where they would live, and although Leigh was healthier, she didn't feel strong enough to live alone. Gus didn't feel able to let her live alone and so it was he that suggested they buy together. They didn't see Tanya, they rarely saw Eric; but they carried on and waited for their fame. Emily had been given a generous contribution for her part, especially the childbirth soundtrack!

Tanya and Eric still lived in the house in Fulham for nostalgic reasons. They could easily afford the rent. Brian had been informed and was furious at first and then delighted. He planned to sell the house when the film was a big hit. He would make a fortune.

*   *   *

Poplar loved the film. Steve Delaney had declared Harvey a genius and set about hiring the best marketing people available. The release date was in six months.

Harvey Cannon had won again. But this had been the toughest battle of his life.

Chapter Sixty-Seven

It was months later that they made their first television appearance, on the *Patsy Maid* show on daytime TV.

Although they had been put through their paces by the press, this was their first live on-air interview. Harriet Brown, their publicity adviser, briefed them beforehand, but she couldn't combat all their nerves. Leigh was still worried about her appearance, Tanya was trying to be cool, while being largely ignored, Gus was panicking about what he should say and Eric had somehow (despite Tanya's best efforts), got stoned. David was almost frozen with fear.

'Just relax and be yourselves,' Harriet said looking at each of them and changing her mind. 'What I mean is, treat this like the press interviews, but appear confident, amusing, look at the cameras and smile. Above all, as the studio said, make sure you all come across as friends.' Harriet gave her best publicity smile and tried to feel relaxed. It was hard to be relaxed with her charges however, as it was clear that David and Leigh were refusing to talk to Tanya. Eric was trying to pacify everyone, and Gus was clearly torn between his friendship for Eric and his feelings towards Tanya. They had managed to get the press to fall in love with them, somehow, but the television audience would be a big test.

As they were given the cue to walk on to the set, smiles somehow found their way to their faces. They managed to stay there as they cheek-kissed Patsy and sat down. Then the questions started.

'Gus, is there any romance between you and LeeLee, now that you know her true feelings for you?'

'Well, LeeLee and I are the best of friends, and we've agreed that that is the best relationship we could possibly have.'

'And how do you feel about that LeeLee?'

'Oh I totally agree with Gus, we are so close as friends and that's what's important.'

'Right, but of course romance did blossom between Eric and Tanya. Tanya, was that just a stunt to publicise the film?'

'Patsy, you saw us get together on-screen, now could you call that a stunt?'

'Right.' (Sarcastic smile from Patsy). 'Eric, what are *your* feelings on the accusations of your relationship being a publicity stunt?'

'Well Patsy, to be honest, you saw how Tanya and I argued at the beginning, and you saw the film, so you know how difficult she could be. I am not the sort of man who would put myself through that unless I really wanted to, so it can't be a publicity stunt.' Leigh, David and Gus smiled, as did Patsy despite herself. Tanya shot Eric a dirty look.

'David, are you enjoying fatherhood?'

'Yes.'

'Even though you're not the father?'

'He is her father, he's the best father she would ever wish for,' Leigh cut in.

'What if the real father, on seeing all this fuss, decides to come forward?'

David's eyes darkened. 'We'll deal with that when and if it happens.' Patsy decided to move on. After all he had a knock-out fist.

'So, how do you all deal with accusations that the film is a huge con? That not only did you know you were being filmed, but that you had a script and you are actually actors, or have acted before?'

'That's absurd,' Tanya replied.

'Look we are who we are. I'm an imaginative pharmacist, Gus is a dishy doctor, LeeLee is a cute advertising executive, Tanya is a hot producer and David is an Internet nerd. That's who we were when we started out and that's who we are now. But you all know us now and you know the real us because you watched a part of our lives,' Eric finished.

'Well that's all we have time for. Thank you for coming . . . Ladies and Gentlemen . . . the cast of *Public Lives.*' Patsy hugged and kissed them all as if they were her friends, and threw a final cheesy grin to the camera.

As they left the television studio, they felt tired of all the publicity; as they thought of the money, they realised they had sold out. As Leigh said, it didn't matter that they'd sold out because it was their past that people would see, and one thing her stupid overdose had taught Leigh was that you had to look to the future.

They all kept that thought with them – their futures – as they pasted smiles on their faces and got ready for their next appearances.

Chapter Sixty-Eight

Première

The cinema was full of the usual celebrities who would go to any party where the press would be waiting for them, and people who weren't quite celebrities but nonetheless managed to get invitations. There were, perhaps, more people than expected due to the huge media interest surrounding the film. Everyone who was anyone (and quite a few people who weren't anyone) had turned out in all their finery. The guest of honour was a member of the royal family who had been roped in because the première was being held to support her 'favourite' charity. It was a glamorous, expensive affair.

The public turnout was huge. But then, with all the attention *Public Lives* had received, it wasn't surprising. The crowd were cheering as they waited for the stars to appear.

Harvey arrived with Cherry on his arm. He wore a tuxedo; she wore a silk dress with handmade silk shoes. They were the proud parents of the evening. As they stood in the entrance waiting for their children, they were elated.

The studio heads from Poplar, including Steve Delaney, had flown over. It was fitting that the world première should be in London; they all wanted to be there. They knew from the media coverage that the film was going to be a sure-fire hit, and, because this meant they were saved, they could afford to celebrate.

Bob and Amanda followed closely behind, with James and Sally, and John and his date. The first thing Bob said to Harvey was, 'It isn't raining.' They smiled. Now that they had resettled in LA, they almost missed the London climate.

Tanya and Eric were with Jason and Serena. But Tanya felt hurt that she was not with her ex-housemates. They were the stars; they had been friends. As she smiled at Eric sadly, she realised the true implication of the past tense.

The cameras flashed wildly, as they made their way through the crowds to the cinema entrance. Tanya looked lovely in her black dress and she portrayed an air of supreme confidence. Eric, in his tux, looked half-groomed. Because of his nerves, he had smoked a fair bit before leaving the flat, so he had no trouble smiling broadly for the cameras.

The flashbulbs turned away from them when Gus and Millie, followed by David, Emily and Leigh began to walk down the red carpet. Gus looked impossibly handsome and the women in the crowd screamed for him; he smiled shyly. Millie tightened her grip on his hand. She wore a cream trouser suit and high-heeled slingbacks – even Cherry would have approved. Emily looked different and definitely slimmer. She wore a long, black evening gown and linked her arm through David's. He felt uncomfortable in his black tie and he looked it. He was the least happy about the occasion. Leigh wore a low-cut pale lilac dress with jewelled high-heels. The dress was beautiful, the shoes sensational and Leigh's hair, which had grown back to an almost acceptable level, was stunning. Tanya gasped when she caught sight of her; she looked absolutely ravishing.

Tanya felt a stab of exclusion. When they reached the entrance where Eric and she were waiting, they all waved for the crowds before stepping inside. The cheer was louder than before.

'You look lovely,' Tanya said to Leigh.

'So do you,' she replied. There was no warmth left for Tanya. She knew there never would be. Everyone shook hands and muttered greetings, all caught up in the unreal atmosphere. They were getting used to being stared at, but were not yet able to enjoy it as they moved slowly though the foyer.

It still felt awkward, them being together. They only knew what to say when they were being interviewed. They could answer questions as professionals, but they couldn't interact personally.

Tanya was desperately trying to find the right words. Leigh refused to look at her. David stood as close to Emily as he could get, and Gus and Millie did the same. While Tanya was trying to think of something to say, Harvey and his entourage approached.

'This is it. Your big night. I bet you thought it would never come. Well, you all look wonderful,' Harvey said, as he kissed each girl on the cheek, and shook the men by the hands. Tanya felt hurt; he was to blame (wasn't he?) but they were greeting him so warmly.

They chatted some more as the cinema filled up.

'Where's Lucy?' Millie asked.

Harvey looked at her, he had a feeling someone was missing. Just as Cherry was about to phone her, Lucy walked in wearing leather trousers, an obscenely revealing top and a pair of cowboy boots.

'Those fuckers took my photo then had the cheek to ask who I was.' She kissed everyone, breathlessly. 'What are we waiting for?' she demanded, and everyone burst out laughing.

They went to take their seats. The moment had arrived.

The cast sat in one row, the crew in another and the studio executives behind them. Everyone was nervous. Leigh grabbed David's hand; David gripped Emily's; Gus pulled Millie's hand out of her lap and held it; Eric gently stroked Tanya's hand, their fingers entwined. The houselights dimmed.

A cartoon version of each of them had been designed and superimposed on the opening sequence. Complete with sub-titles:

Tanya Palmer spies on her friends; Tanya's caricature winked as the real Tanya left the house. *Eric Reed likes the odd joint;* Eric's figure blew a smoke ring. *David Monroe web wizard;* complete with laptop, a love-heart on its screen. *Gus Carter doctor;* he was wearing a white coat and a stethoscope which had a beating heart on the end of it. *LeeLee Monroe cute advertising exec.* She was all in pink with pink hearts and pink flowers in abundance.

As they watched, the cast smiled at each other. They couldn't help but feel a tiny bit proud.

They watched along with everybody else, but felt that they were alone. Although they were by now familiar with what they were seeing, in a way it felt as if they were seeing it for the first time.

Leigh could only think about the strangers watching her; even the celebrities who were there were strangers. She felt like crying, just as she did when she first saw the film. Gus felt a stab as he saw Natasha for the first time. He was glad that she had been excluded from the première, (one of his conditions on signing the contract), and he hoped he never met her again. When Howard appeared, it was Eric's turn to feel uncomfortable, (he had been excluded for the same reason as Natasha). Tanya was worried about audience reaction; after all she was being judged on all counts. Emily thought it was an adventure and David just watched it without betraying a flicker of emotion.

The audience were laughing at Eric. Then they were laughing at David's Website ideas. They laughed at Gus and Leigh's friendship. They laughed at Leigh's pink clothes. They especially laughed at the kebab scene. They laughed when Tanya flashed her fake boobs; they laughed when Howard ended up with curry on his head. They laughed at the ineptitude of the men when they were trying to put the barbecue together; they laughed and laughed.

They booed out loud when Tanya had one of her numerous rants at Leigh and Eric. Tanya had the grace to feel ashamed.

They cooed when David met Emily, they ohhed when Eric kissed Tanya. They clapped when Leigh said she was over her crush; and when Lucy junior was born, there wasn't a dry eye in the house.

The people who were in the film were bewildered by the reactions. They didn't expect people to get so involved; they didn't understand all the laughter. It was their lives, how had it become a comedy?

The film wasn't exactly as they remembered, although what happened, had happened. It wasn't as it had happened, (which is why the editing team had a job). The sequence of events had been changed and although the events were real, they didn't feel real.

The viewers saw five people building a relationship in a house. They saw the relationships grow and fall apart. They saw relationships develop outside and inside the house. Friendship and love, that was what they thought when the film ended. It was a film about friendship and love in a house in a tree-lined street in Fulham.

Millie's interview had been running throughout the film, but the end sequence, the last sequence, was one, just before Emily's labour began, where everyone was in the sitting room. They were all crowded on the sofa. Tanya was on Eric's lap, David sat on the arm next to them, Leigh sat on the sofa next to them and Gus sat on the arm next to Leigh.

'What's the best thing about living here?' Millie asked.

'Well there isn't really a best thing, because living here with these guys is the best thing. It's just the best thing ever.' And with that sentence, Leigh ended the film.

The audience laughed as the credits rolled, and then they burst into applause.

Leigh looked at Tanya. Tanya shrugged. Leigh shrugged back. It wasn't real. It hadn't happened that way; it was a film; a story. That's all it was.

Life isn't art; art isn't life. It is all distortion.

Post-Première

This story was written with vivid accuracy. Accuracy not only available because I was the main protagonist of the story, but also due to the storyteller's demands on the meticulous memories of everyone involved. It will come as no surprise to learn that Lucy wrote the book, after all, when the film was a huge success everywhere. Harvey thought that it was time to tell the whole story. It is characteristic of Harvey that, in this case, the book came after the film. So, I, Tanya, and Lucy worked together to tell you everything as honestly as we could.

I know that I don't come out looking that good. In fact that could be classed as the biggest understatement of the year. I know none of you will read this and say, 'I'd like to be *her* friend', but I can't blame you for that. I manipulated my friends; I lied to them; I lost them ultimately.

There are still some things that I can't tell you. To question why I was so quick to sacrifice Leigh's friendship would be to question why I had it in the first place. I cannot answer either question. And when she took that overdose, I thought that I had killed her. But I also realised – and try to understand this – that I had been killing her for years.

I can tell you what happened to us after The End. I suppose as the reader, that is what you want to know. Every end begs a beginning after all . . .

Once the première was over, and the hullabaloo had died down, Eric and I moved to LA. Cherry found us an apartment which is heaven. As is the sun. I am in the place of my dreams, I have the job of my dreams, I have the man of my dreams. If you were hoping that at some point I would receive retribution for my behaviour . . .? I still might. I don't know that, and hope you are not too disappointed. I did pay though. You might find that hard to believe. I paid by condemning myself to a life of guilt, a life of incomprehension; I will never understand what I did. If that is not enough for you, then I am sorry. But I have to tell you that I am happy. Even with my demons I am happier than I have ever been.

Cherry and Harvey got married; it was like a royal wedding, but then, as I discovered, Harvey *is* Hollywood royalty. I work with him; I produce on his ideas. I won't talk about my latest project because this book isn't about self-promotion.

Lucy spends most of her time in LA, she loves it here and has fallen in love. His name is Harry and he's a scriptwriter; they worked together on Lucy's first screenplay. I wish you could see Lucy smitten, she is something else. She still lives in London, but I don't think for much longer. She and I have grown close, especially working on this book; she is my best friend and I never bully her. Although I think she bullies me.

Amanda and Bob established themselves quickly as the best editing team in town. They work together, and live together; it's mad, but they are so in love.

We have our community here, and although we meet famous people all the time: actors, directors, producers; I know the community is our core. I've learned the importance of that; it might have taken me a long time, but at least I know now.

David has vowed never to forgive me and will never talk to me again. Emily has tried to talk him round, but he is adamant. I am not part of his life, therefore I will never be part of his family's life. He took his money, left his job and he and Emily run the pub together. He is building an Internet site, what else? I can smile at that now. Apparently it's something to do with parenting. I hope he achieves it, I genuinely do. He is happy, I know that, and although we haven't heard of any wedding plans, I am sure that David and Emily will be together for ever.

Eric is with me and he says I make him happy. When I wake beside him and he kisses me, I believe that I can make him happy.

We make each other feel right. He says that his only plan at the moment is to love me and get a suntan. You may question his sanity, after all, we all did at some stage, but I know that we are right together and we are for keeps. Please believe that I love him very much. He is still trying to build his ultimate joint.

Gus forgave me enough to continue his friendship with Eric and his relationship with Millie, who, annoyingly, didn't seem to get much blame for her somewhat hapless contributions, but that's another issue. Gus had an awful time at work; there were queues of women outside Casualty trying to see him. He had to change hospitals. Apparently everything is fine now. He and Eric talk every week and, because of Millie and her desire to become an actress, they have even spoken about visiting us.

Leigh will never forgive me, but I will never forgive myself. She terminated our friendship. She said that it was time to move on. She has definitely moved on. She lives with Gus, in a flat they co-own, she is seeing a male friend of Sukie's, and I think she is happy. She is enjoying her celebrity status, she loves the attention. She goes to parties, she mixes with the rich and famous, she *is* rich and famous. I laugh every time I realise that we are all rich and famous. She still works with Sukie, of course. I did write to her, but she didn't reply. I hope that this book might be a way of communicating with her; we'll have to see. It is the first time I can remember Leigh not being in my life. I can't help believing that it is a good thing for her.

Howard didn't follow us to LA, but landed a plum job in a TV soap opera. Ironically he plays a gay man. I don't keep in touch with Howard; it still makes Eric uncomfortable.

Oh, and I almost forgot Natasha. Well, she is publicly, very publicly, dating a rock star who happens to be the heir to one of the largest family fortunes in the UK. He would have been a wonderful catch, if it weren't for his penchant for drugs, snakes and wearing red dresses.

I like to think we got our happy ending after all.